EIRINI

Titles available in this series

Yannis
Anna
Giovanni
Joseph
Christabelle
Saffron
Manolis
Cathy
Nicola
Vasi
Alecos
John
Tassos
Ronnie
Maria
Sofia
Babbis
Stelios
Kyriakos
Monika
Emmanuel
Theo
Phaedra
Evgeniy
Ludmila
Pietro
Eirini

Greek Translations

Anna

published by Livanis 2011

EIRINI

Beryl Darby

ISBN 978-1-9997176-74

Printed and bound in the UK by
Print2Demand
1 Newlands Road, Westoning,
Bedfordshire MK45 5LD

First published in the UK in 2021 by

JACH Publishing
92 Upper North Street, Brighton, East Sussex, England BN1 3FJ

website: www.beryldarbybooks.com

Author's Note

My grateful thanks to Carla for agreeing to be on the cover and the invaluable information she gave me about cattle farming.

I hope my portrayal of Australian outback life has been reasonably accurate for the years I have covered.

August 2016

Ronnie was surprised when she was told there was a parcel waiting for her at the post office. When she collected it she knew it had to be copies of Luke's mother's memoirs, but she had expected him to e-mail it to her. She shifted the large parcel more comfortably in her arms and waited for a gap in the traffic so she could cross the road and be in the shade. She walked carefully down the uneven steps to the waterfront area and sat in the shaded snack bar that overlooked the sea.

Having ordered a frappe she looked across to Spinalonga that was shimmering in the heat and no doubt crowded with tourists by this time. She was tempted to open the parcel and begin to read whatever the old lady had written, but resisted the urge. It would make the parcel more difficult to carry once she had unpacked it as it was likely to be loose sheets that could blow away in the wind.

She thought about the visit she had received from the Australian couple who had asked her to paint some pictures of Spinalonga as it had looked almost a hundred years ago. She had used her imagination based on the scant information she had been given. Apparently she had done a good job as Luke had replied that his mother was delighted with them and said the area was exactly as she remembered. Ronnie did wonder how accurate the old lady's memory was.

She was grateful that John and Nicola had been able to

translate the diaries that she had found in her house in Kastelli so she knew that her great grandparents had lived on Spinalonga and her grandmother had been born there. She hoped that these memoirs would not have to be translated, although she knew John and Nicola would be interested and willing to do the task.

Finishing her frappe she picked up her parcel and walked along the waterfront to the centre of the town where she could take a taxi back to the self catering apartments she and Kyriakos rented from Giovanni. It was far more convenient for both of them to live there during the tourist season and return to Kastelli at the end of October. It meant she could go to Plaka and commence painting early each morning whilst Kyriakos slept in having only returned from his taverna in the early hours.

She would have no opportunity to open and start to read them that afternoon as she and Kyriakos always spent the afternoon together before he went to open the taverna. Once he had left she must complete some paintings ready to take to Saffron the following morning. Provided Kyriakos did not ask her to go up to the taverna to help she would have an opportunity that evening to start to read them. She would have to curb her impatience until then.

1922 - 1937
LIFE ONE
Fourni

Compared with the other village children I realised later that I was very privileged. I never went hungry and always had warm boots in the winter and two jumpers and a shawl for cold days. Some of the children had to wear the same clothes in the winter as they had during the summer with just a shawl to give them some extra warmth; often they had no shoes, let alone boots.

We were quite a close community, everyone knew their neighbour. My mother owned six cottages in the village and so did her sister. Each week my mother would visit all twelve occupants and collect the rent money that was due. My aunt and uncle lived in Mavrikiano at the time and once a month they would come to visit us and collect the rent money. My grandmother, who lived in Fourni, would walk to our house and we would spend the day together as a family. I am not sure how old I was when my uncle's mother died and I do not remember ever meeting her. She had left her house to her son, and my aunt and uncle announced that they would be moving to Elounda as it was nearer to my uncle's work and the house was large enough for my maternal grandmother to live there with them and be looked after when she became older. Her house would then be rented out and the income given to my aunt as recompense for looking after her mother

Most of the cottages consisted of one large room. On one wall would be the loom where the cloth was made for clothes

9

and bedding and if you passed by during the afternoon you could usually hear the creak of a loom being used. On the far wall would be the large bed where the parents slept. It was raised off the floor by sturdy legs and a small wooden step ladder was needed to climb up onto the mattress. For a modicum of privacy and also for warmth in the winter there were heavy curtains on both sides and at the foot. All manner of items were able to be stored in the space below. The children would sleep on pallets on the other side of the room.

A door led into a scullery or kitchen area where the food preparation was carried out before it was finally placed on the fire in the living room to cook. Herbs and spices to add to the dishes were also stored out there along with the cooking utensils. There was no sink or running water. The water was collected from the well each morning and heated over the fire. Dishes and pans were washed in a bowl outside so the water could be thrown away or tipped into the privy to keep it as clean and fresh as possible. The privy was usually shared by three or four neighbours and those who were waiting would knock on the wooden half door and request that the occupant made haste.

My father was the school teacher and four mornings each week he would walk up the hill to Kastelli where the school was situated. This meant we had a larger house than our neighbours. I had a small room of my own where I slept and we did not have to share our privy. I did not go to school, of course. It was not thought necessary for a girl to be able to read and write her letters or add numbers together. It was considered far more important that girls should learn to cook and weave and generally know how to look after a house when they were married.

The boys would attend school in the morning four days each week, and as soon as they left they would go up to the fields to help their fathers. The farmers grew a variety of different crops. Everyone had a few olive trees on their land and grape vines, some had orange, apple, plum or almond trees with vegetables like onions, courgettes, cabbage, beans and melons growing beneath them. Carob trees flourished wherever their roots could gain a hold in the dusty, arid soil. Depending upon the time of year and which crops were being harvested, the villagers often worked together to ensure that as much produce as possible was collected and taken to the weekly markets in the coastal towns before it became over ripe and spoil. This arrangement was accepted without question and no one was paid as they knew their neighbour would help them when it was necessary. When the farmers returned they would bring back slabs of salt and fresh fish or anything else that could not be obtained from the pedlar when he passed through.

We girls would join together and play, mostly we played tag, hide and seek or knuckle bones. Sometimes we would compete with each other seeing who could make the most intricate design with cat's cradle or drawing pictures in the dust on cart track and deciding who had drawn the best one. On occasions we danced together trying to replicate the steps we had seen our mothers perform. We were very much allowed to do as we pleased, but we were obedient. If my mother called me to go indoors to help her with the cooking or spend some time sitting at the loom under her instruction I obeyed.

As the village girls became older they were expected to help up in the fields. On a Friday the women would often go up as well to help gather the produce and load the carts ready to be taken to the market on the Saturday morning. I begged to be allowed to join them as I was lonely without my companions. My mother said that field work was beneath us, but my father said it would be good for me to realise how hard the villagers worked. Finally my mother relented and dressed in my oldest clothes and my hair tied up in a scarf like the other girls I walked up to the fields with my best friend, Anastasia.

She led me to the field where her father was cutting water melons and leaving them next to the stalks. She said we had to collect them and load up the cart. Anastasia told me to hold out my arms and she placed three large melons in them and managed to pick up another three to carry herself. We took it in turns to carry them this way, but I could not manage to pick up and balance more than two melons in my arms which made Anastasia giggle and she would place one on top that I held in place with my chin. The melons seemed unending. Just as I thought the cart was full there were more waiting for us. Anastasia scrambled up on the cart and began to move the melons forward and balance more on top so there was space for me to put up the ones I was carrying. I had never realised how heavy melons were. My arms and back began to ache, but I refused to say I was tired and going home. I did not enjoy the work but I was determined not to complain and assured Anastasia that I would be there again the following day.

The older boys would help their fathers with the cutting, but we girls were not allowed to use the sharp knives and were only expected to gather the produce and either place it in a box or directly onto the cart. When the beans, peas or courgettes were cut they were thrown directly into a box and we were expected to lay them out evenly until the box was full and a piece of cardboard could be tacked across it. It would take two of us to lift and carry it across the rough ground to the cart and then we would not have the strength to lift in up onto the flat bed and have to leave it for one of the boys or men to deal with.

Every so often one of the older boys would arrive and appear to lift the boxes with ease. I liked it when Elias came. He was so good looking and had a lovely smile. Anastasia teased me about liking him and she made me blush. My childish crush on him did not last long. As I bent to place a piece of cardboard over the beans he placed a large red slug on my bare arm. I screamed and he thought it was funny. I began to cry and Lucas came over thinking I was hurt. In between my tears I told him Elias had placed a large slug on my arm. Lucas patted my shoulder.

'Dry your eyes,' he said. 'I'll speak to Elias and tell him if he does such a nasty thing to any of the girls I'll knock him into a patch of stinging weeds or a thorny bush. A slug, worm or caterpillar will not hurt you at all, although no one wants one put on their arm.'

I smiled. grateful for his understanding and sympathy. He stayed beside me and loaded the boxes onto the cart.

'Why are you working up here anyway?' he asked. 'You're the school master's daughter.'

'I don't want the villagers to think me too grand to help in the fields, besides, when my friends began to work up here I missed them.'

'Doesn't your mother expect you to work on her loom in the afternoons?'

'She usually spends some time showing me in the morning but I am not accomplished enough yet to do more than weave a strip of cloth that can be used as a dish rag. She has taught me how to knit and sew, but I am not very good at those things either,' I sighed.

'I'm sure you will soon become as proficient as she is. I must leave you now and go up to help my brother with the bee hives or you'll not have any honey to sweeten your cooking.'

'Aren't you frightened that you will be stung?'

Lucas shrugged. 'It happens sometimes.' He raised his hand to me and walked away.

After that I always tried to work as closely as possible to Lucas as I was sure that Elias would not do anything nasty to me if he was around.

One day when Lucas came to the fields he had some nasty welts on his arms.

'What have you done to your arm?' I asked.

He smiled ruefully. 'Some bees were angry at being disturbed and consequently stung me.'

The next week when I saw him they looked no better.

I pointed to them. 'Your stings look no better this week. Maybe you should ask the doctor to look at them when he visits the village next.'

Lucas glanced at his arm. 'They're nothing, they don't hurt now and I wouldn't want to trouble the doctor with so trivial a matter.'

Not everyone was willing to be friendly with Lucas or work close to him as it was well known that his uncle had been declared an incurable and sent to a leper colony some years ago. No one else in the family had become infected but the villagers were still wary in his presence. although I found him kind and considerate. I was not able to work as fast as the girls and boys who had been up in the fields since they were five or six years old. When Lucas saw I was falling behind the others when filling boxes or picking the apples or oranges he would tell me to take a break. Whilst I took a welcome rest he would pick the fruit that was on the higher branches, finally giving me a wink and walking away.

When the men returned home from the market the women always had hot water ready for them to have a bath in the metal tub. Once the men had finished their ablutions his wife would have her turn followed by the children. This meant they were all clean and ready to go to Church on Sunday wearing the best clothes they possessed. My father, mother and I had a bath twice a week and would wear clean underwear each week.

After my father had finished teaching he would spend some time out in our garden in the afternoon. We did not have to depend upon the farmers for all our vegetables as we usually had sufficient. He would allow me to go with him to search for the eggs that he hoped our hens would have laid and also to feed them. I enjoyed throwing the grain and green weeds to them and watching them squabble between themselves for them. I was not allowed out there when he removed the used hay from our privy and replaced it with fresh. My mother would ensure that all the doors and windows were firmly closed but the unpleasant smell still seemed to penetrate the house.

Although I did not go to school my father taught me my letters and numbers at home during the evenings. Father made learning a game, asking me to count how many olives were on his plate or how many pips there were in an apple. Each day he would add another number, then he would say the number to me and I had to select the correct number of pips or olives. I soon became adept at this and he would write the numbers down on a piece of paper and I was asked to add them up or subtract them. At first I was allowed to use olive stones to help me, but then he took them away and said I should understand how to do the exercise without aids.

I found learning to write the letters of the alphabet easy, but when my father asked me to write my name I remember I shook my head and felt near to tears. Patiently he wrote it down for me and explained that it was most important that I should learn how to do that as it was something I could be asked to do when I was grown up. It took me three days before I could put the letters in their correct order.

Once I had mastered that he gave me other words to learn and the more I learned the easier they seemed to become. Finally he said the time had arrived when I should learn to read and he took down the Bible from the shelf. He asked me to read any words that I knew that were printed on the first line that he pointed to. I stammered and stuttered, doing the best I could.

My father was patient. He read the words to me and showed me how to build up the letters to make a word so I could recognise it in the future. When he had taught me for three years I was able to read anything that he put before me and used to look forward to being allowed the newspaper when he had finished reading it. He said I was an apt pupil, better than many of the boys in his class and if I continued to progress at my present rate I could eventually become a school teacher. That prospect excited me and I tried harder than ever to please him.

He told me stories of the ancient heroes and the Gods who lived on Mount Olympus and controlled everything that happened on the earth. For a long time I believed these stories were true and when we had a thunder storm with lightning over the hills I was sure it was Zeus throwing his thunderbolts and I would hide in a dark corner or pull my bed cover over my head hoping he would not find me.

My father explained that the mythology was just a way the ancient people had of understanding why events like storms, high winds and earthquakes happened. Now we knew better because science had progressed and when the people began to follow the Christian religion they stopped worshipping all the old Gods. I did not doubt the truth of anything he told me, but I wished I knew who caused the weather to change and how crops decided it was time for them to start to grow. Surely the deity we prayed to in Church each week could not be everywhere controlling the events that happened?

He began to tell me the history of our island, how we had been ruled by many different nations and finally the Turks had controlled us, levying heavy taxes and making strict rules that we had to abide by. This had led to the War of Independence where we had finally been victorious and regained our freedom, and finally became part of the Kingdom of Greece, although we still considered ourselves to be Cretans. Although I found the history of the previous two hundred years interesting, it did not fascinate me the way the mythology had.

I think my father realised that I was not very interested in what is now known as 'political history' as he brought back from the school a book he called an Atlas. There were coloured pictures inside that he told me were maps of different countries and asked me if I knew why it was called an Atlas. I thought for a moment and replied it was because Atlas had to hold up the world on his shoulders for ever as a punishment.

He had smiled, pleased I had remembered the story and told me that no one was holding up the world and earth was spinning around the sun in space. I felt quite frightened. If it fell down where would it go and what would happen to all of us? My father did not know the answer to those questions, but assured me that such a thing could not happen as we were controlled by gravity. I remember I nodded sagely, but I did not understand then and I still do not understand how we can be spinning round and round continually and I do not become dizzy.

I had to find where Crete was situated and it took me a long time to discover the island that was my home. I could not believe how tiny it was by comparison to some of the other vast stretches of land. My father said that the blue colour that surrounded everything was water and called the sea. I wanted to know why it did not wash over our land. Once again I was worried; if I did not fall off the small area of earth that my father told me was the island of Crete would I be washed off?

My mother had scoffed at my imaginings, but my father treated my fears seriously and explained that on rare occasions when there had been a particularly severe earthquake the sea had risen higher and engulfed some of the land. I wanted to know if we were safe living in Fourni or should we move to somewhere high in the mountains. He shook his head and told me to look at the high hills that surrounded us, saying that the sea would not be able to reach over them and flood our valley so we were perfectly safe.

Most days my afternoons were spent either in the garden with my father, up in the fields or at the weaving loom under my mother's watchful eye. I enjoyed my evening lessons, the time I spent in the fields with my friends and going to Church on a Sunday and accepted that this was how everyone lived. I would help my mother with the cooking, learning at the same time how I should add herbs and spices to make a dish more succulent. She also taught me how to knit, crochet and weave during the winter months when it was no pleasure to be outside with my friends and my skills did improve. Without realising it I was being educated to be a good wife to someone at a future date.

As Anastasia and I became older we would discuss the village boys, deciding which one we preferred and for what reason. If we traced the families who lived in the village they were all related in some way, cousins, second cousins, aunts, uncles, grandparents. Neither Anastasia nor I ever said anything derogatory about any boy as we were never sure who he was related to and if our comments would get back to him.

Some members of the families had moved out from Fourni into one of the outlying villages, like my aunt when she had married into a new family. Her husband could have moved to Fourni and lived in one of her cottages, but he said it would be more practical for them to go to his mother's house in Elounda as it was larger than ours. His mother was older than my grandmother and he said they would be able to accommodate her and look after her in her old age. Although they came on a fairly regular basis to collect the rent money they also came when it was my aunt's name day as this usually coincided with a Saint's Day and they knew they would be welcome to join in the local festivities. If there was a wedding it was a very grand affair with all the inhabitants of Fourni along with those who had left the area returning to wish the newly weds well and participate in the feasting and drinking.

Trestle tables were set out in the main square and the women folk had spent days preparing copious amounts of food and scouring their largest containers to present it in. My mother would join in with this activity. Although she would often spend a short while in the evenings sitting with a villager she did not really have any close friends in the village. The men would go to the kafenion or a bar where they could drink and play cards or backgammon. My father rarely joined them. He said he preferred to spend his time at home teaching me. He did not want to listen to their political opinions which often led to bad feeling, and occasionally blows being exchanged.

About once every month a doctor would ride into the village but there was rarely anyone who needed his attention. If an accident had occurred the unfortunate victim would be loaded into a cart and taken to the hospital which I understood was in the town of Aghios Nikolaos where his injuries would be attended to. It never occurred to me that I might be sick as I had never felt ill except when I ate too many plums and had to make numerous visits to the privy before my stomach ache passed.

The last time they visited us my uncle announced that they were taking my grandmother down to live with them in the village of Elounda. I did not understand all their conversation and it would have been considered bad manners to ask for an explanation. After they left my mother said they had decided to take my grandmother to Elounda due to my grandmother's health as she had not been well recently. They thought the fresh sea air could help her to recover. My uncle had assured my mother that he would arrange for one of the farmers to take back news of her mother to Fourni when he returned from the market each week.

I knew I had another aunt who lived in Plaka and I asked why my grandmother had not gone to live with her. My mother pursed her lips and informed me that we did not talk about her or have anything to do with her. I was curious but I knew better than to ask my mother for more information.

Spring arrived along with a message from a farmer. My father said that we would go to Elounda to visit them. He considered it too far for me to walk there and back in one day so he arranged for one of the farmers to take us in his cart. I was so excited. I had never ridden on one of the carts or been anywhere outside of my village. Walking in the local fields to gather wild flowers or herbs did not count as leaving the village; whichever way we went the village was always in sight

My mother spoke to me sternly that morning saying she would expect me to be very good and quiet when we visited as my grandmother was gravely ill, unable to make the journey to visit us and could not be left alone for the day as she could not walk. I nodded, but all the while we sat in the cart and the donkey plodded slowly onwards I wondered what had happened to her legs so that she was unable to walk. I could only imagine that she had broken a bone and it was refusing to mend.

The farmer stopped in a small square and we alighted. I looked around quite fascinated and tugged at my father's arm.

'Pappa, is that the sea?' I asked pointing to the water I could see stretching far out into the horizon.

My father nodded. 'I'll take you for a walk later so you can see it properly.'

I was excited at the prospect but did not know whether this was out of consideration for me or to leave my mother and aunt alone to talk privately with my grandmother.

I was shocked when I saw my grandmother. She was propped up by pillows on her bed and she grasped the sheets like a life line with hands that were thin and claw like. Her face was yellow and her cheeks sunken, making her eyes look enormous. I was not sure what was expected of me. Should I kiss her cheek as I had in the past or just say hello? My mother kissed her and then instructed me to do the same. Reluctantly I leaned forward and placed a kiss on her cheek. She smiled, or I think she tried to smile, but it turned into a grimace of pain. I felt tears coming into my eyes. Why had neither of my parents told me how ill my grandmother was?

I sat silently whilst my aunt brewed coffee for my parents and gave me a drink of water as I was considered too young to drink coffee. She held a cup of water to her mother's lips and urged her to drink just a few sips. I was relieved when my father finally stood up and said he would take me to see the boats. I waited until we were well away from the house before I asked my father what was wrong with my grandmother.

He shook his head sadly. 'She has an illness that has affected her liver.'

I had no idea about a human liver. Occasionally my mother would cook liver in a red wine sauce as a special treat. I stopped and looked at my father anxiously.

'If we eat liver will our skin turn yellow and will we become ill?'

He assured me it had nothing to do with eating animal liver. He promised to spend some time with me during our next lessons explaining how a human body worked.

I was silent for a while and then I dared to ask when my grandmother would recover, although I had an idea of the answer.

'She will not recover,' my father replied. 'There is no medicine to help her, but your aunt will look after her and attend to her every need so she is as comfortable as possible.'

I did not know what to say and I was grateful when my father pointed to the boats and took me closer to look at them.

They were brightly coloured and each had a name painted on the side. On some of them men were hanging nets over the side to dry and inspecting them for damage and others were on the shore with buckets in which fish flapped around desperately. I watched fascinated as the sun glinted on their shiny scales as they twisted and turned. Women appeared at regular intervals, inspected the buckets and then pointed out a fish they wanted. It was caught deftly, the head banged on the ground and it was then placed in a string bag whilst the woman handed over some coins.

Seeing the fish killed did not worry me as I had seen the lambs slaughtered for our Easter feast but as we stood there the smell of fish became more pungent and I found myself gagging. My father thought this was the result of seeing the fish killed and hurriedly suggested that we walked on. Further round the bay there were no boats and pebbles led down to where the sea lapped against them, the sunlight dancing on the ripples.

My father said I could remove my shoes and dabble my feet in the water and tell him if it was cold. I was hesitant to do this.

'Suppose a big wave comes and washes me away?'

'It is perfectly safe or I would not suggest it. I'll walk down with you and hold your hand.'

The water was cold on my bare toes and I retreated rapidly. I wiped my feet on my skirt and replaced my shoes. We returned to the track and continued to walk along looking at the beach until the bushes blocked the view and I was not tall enough to see over them.I was enjoying the novelty of being beside the sea and watching the waves wash in and out and when my father said we should return to the house my heart sank. Would my grandmother be dead when we returned?

My aunt and my mother had prepared a simple meal of bread, cheese, tomatoes and olives and I realised I was extremely hungry. My father had smiled at me as I helped myself to yet another slice of bread and commented that the sea air had stimulated my appetite. I cast surreptitious glances at my grandmother as we ate but she looked no different from the way she had earlier.

Having finished our meal I helped my mother take the used plates outside and rinse them whilst my father went to the village well and drew two buckets of water. He poured the contents into two large pots and returned for some more. My aunt placed both pots on the fire to heat ready for when she would wash my grandmother that evening.

I sat quietly whilst the adults talked in soft voices so as not to disturb my grandmother who appeared to be asleep. I wondered why my other aunt was not there also. I did not like to ask if I could return to the beach and it seemed a long and boring afternoon until my father announced that we should use the privy and go to meet the farmer for our ride back to Fourni. Dutifully I kissed my grandmother farewell and waited whilst my mother and father made ready to leave.

As we walked back to the square I turned and took a last look at the sea. In the distance I could see some more land and in my ignorance I asked my father the name of the country. At first he frowned and then he laughed and told me that it was not another country but an island and considered a part of Crete. As we waited for the cart to arrive he told me there were many islands off the coast of Crete and in the sea that stretched up to the Greek mainland, some of them were large enough for people to live on and others were no more than large rocks. I asked if the island I had seen had people living on it.

My father crossed himself as he explained that it was used exclusively to house those poor souls who suffered from leprosy to prevent them spreading infection amongst the villagers. I imagined he meant there was a hospital there and that was where Lucas's uncle would be living and receiving treatment.

I described my visit to Elounda to Anastasia and she listened to me wide eyed when I told her about the sea and that I had put my feet into the cold water. She thought that was very brave of me and I did not tell her how tightly I had gripped my father's hand. I also told her about the colourful boats and the fish, but I did not tell her how my grandmother had looked.

As my father had promised, he drew the figure of a human and placed inside the body the vital organs that we all had. He described how our hearts beat to push blood around our body, that our stomachs digested the food we ate and extracted the goodness from it before we expelled the waste when we visited the privy.

I could understand how you could break a bone by falling; I had seen Andreas with the bone sticking out of his arm when he fell out of a tree. He screamed in pain when it was pushed back into place and bandaged, but now it was as good as ever. I did not understand how diseases could attack these organs my father told me about. They were cushioned inside our bodies so should be protected from harm. My father was unable to tell me how you caught a disease or what could have caused it to attack you, but he assured me that it did not happen to young people like myself. It was only when you became old and the body was wearing out that it became susceptible.

Within days the memory of my grandmother being so ill had faded to the back of my mind. I was in love. When I went up to the fields Lucas smiled at me.

'I missed seeing you around. Is everything well with you and your family?'

'My grandmother is very ill and we went to Elounda to visit her. It is so different down there from our area. The people do not farm, they go out on the sea and catch fish.' I described how the sunlight had glinted on the sea and small white caps of the waves had lapped gently at the pebbly shore.

Lucas listened avidly and sighed. 'I wish I could go there with you and see it for myself.'

I surprised myself with my immediate reply. 'One day we will go there together.'

Lucas smiled. 'I'd like that.' He squeezed my hand and returned to plucking the tomatoes carefully from their stalks and placing them gently in the boxes. From then on Lucas occupied my thoughts during the day and my dreams at night.

Consequently I was surprised when a message came from Elounda announcing that my grandmother had died in the early hours that morning. My mother cried and my father did his best to comfort her, promising her that he would make arrangements immediately so they could attend the funeral. When I heard this I felt both apprehensive and excited at the same time. There had been four funerals where Fourni villagers had died previously but I was too young to remember any more than the processions of people all dressed in black, whilst they lamented loudly and the church bell tolled mournfully.

I was not sure if I felt resentful or relieved when my father said that I would not attend. He and my mother would arrange for a farmer to take them to Elounda and they would stay there overnight. My mother would stay with her sister for a week, but my father would walk back to Fourni the following afternoon.

They were unwilling to leave me alone in the house overnight and my mother spoke to Anastasia's mother and asked if I could spend the night there with her. I had never spent a night away from my own home and I was excited at the prospect. My father carried my pallet down to their house and placed it beside hers, moving the table closer to her parents' large bed, which left little floor space. Admonishing me to be good and help Anastasia's mother in any way I could, both my parents kissed me goodbye and I watched them ride away in the cart, my mother dressed all in black and my father wearing his good suit that he wore to church on a Sunday along with a black shirt and the addition of a black arm band.

That evening Anastasia's mother gave me a bowl of pasta with tomato sauce and a bowl of green leaves. I ate it hungrily and would have liked to ask for more as I saw her serve another bowl full to her husband. I was offered another slice of bread which I accepted and mopped my bowl clean of the remaining sauce.

Anastasia and I were told to go to bed and we climbed onto our pallets. We whispered and giggled together until her father extinguished the oil lamp and told us to be quiet and go to sleep. I felt quite disorientated when I was woken up in the morning by Anastasia scrambling over me to make her way to the privy.

Anastasia and I were given two rusks and a glass of warm goat's milk each after we had rinsed our face and hands. We sat and prepared the vegetables ready for their evening meal whilst her mother sat at the loom, her shuttle moving swiftly and rhythmically. As the morning wore on my stomach growled angrily as I was hungry again. I hoped I would at least be offered a piece of bread and not have to wait until the evening to put some food in my stomach. Finally I was given two more rusks and some olives.

My father arrived home just as it was growing dark and collected me and my pallet from Anastasia's house, thanking her profusely for caring for me. He sat beside the fire in our cottage and removed his boots. I was glad I had had the forethought to check that the fire was still alight during the day. I placed two pots of water on the fire and brought in the bowl I used to wash the dishes so he could soak his feet once it had heated up and said I would make a meal for us.

I had only helped my mother to prepare a meal and never cooked one myself. I looked on the shelves in the scullery and decided I would be able to repeat the meal I had eaten at

Anastasia's the previous evening. I took another bowl of water into the living room and placed it on the fire. Whilst waiting for it to boil I chopped up some onions and tomatoes and drizzled them with olive oil before adding some olives and a few cubes of feta cheese. When I removed some slices of bread from the barrel they felt hard, but I knew that once I had sprinkled them with water they would soften.

Once the water in the pot began to boil I tipped in some pasta and then asked my father how I would know when it was cooked. He told me he would test the pasta and tell me when it was soft and ready to eat. I prepared to the table and waited patiently until he declared the pasta was cooked. My father would not allow me to take the pot off the fire and into the scullery. I watched him whilst he strained the water out and tipped the pasta into a large bowl and I then stirred in the tomato paste.

To me the dish tasted just as good as the one I had eaten the night before and my father praised me, saying I had done very well to be able to prepare a meal with so little notice. I assured him it had not been difficult as I remembered the ingredients that Anastasia's mother had used and we had a plentiful supply of all of them.

I offered to make a meal for us each evening whilst my mother was away, but my father shook his head and said we would share the cooking. I could not be expected to lift heavy pots of boiling water off the fire or cut up meat with the sharp knives that my mother used. He suggested that he asked the butcher for a chicken or rabbit that could be jointed and cooked and that would make a meal for at least three or maybe four evenings.

I slept well that night, back in my own little private room without Anastasia breathing down my neck.

My father bought a rabbit from the butcher and had asked for it to be skinned and gutted. I was so pleased when he placed it on the table that it no longer had its head with sad, glazed eyes staring at me. He removed the back legs and put them aside, saying they would be for our meal that evening. He would place them on a wire grill and bake them on the fire whilst I prepared the greens that would be boiled to accompany them.

The following day he removed the front legs and some of the flesh that was with them and told me to put the carcass into a pot over the fire with an onion until all the flesh had fallen from the bones. He strained it carefully and removed as many of the tiny sharp bones as possible, warning me that if I felt one in my mouth I must spit it out and not swallow it or it could lodge in my throat. He instructed me to put the flesh away ready for our meal the following day. That evening we drank the liquor as a soup, thickened with a little barley, accompanied with bread and followed by some plums that I had picked from the tree that belonged to one of our neighbours. I had not been greedy, taking only six for each of us and I did not think they would miss those as the tree was well loaded.

The front legs and flesh that my father had taken from the rabbit he placed on the wire grill over the fire and we ate that with some bread and raw onions that I had pulled from our garden. I asked what I should do with the flesh that had been stripped from the carcass and he said that I should chop the larger pieces and it could then all be mixed with some rice and herbs to make our meal the following evening. I looked at the scullery shelf and could not see any rice and wondered if the dish could be made successfully using pasta.

I asked my father and he said that rice was definitely necessary to make a pilaf. He took some lepta coins from the little pot above the fireplace and told me to go to the local general store the next morning to buy a bag of rice and anything else that I considered necessary. I felt very grown up to be entrusted with the errand and checked the shelf carefully before I suggested to my father that I bought some more coffee at the same time.

From the hook behind the scullery door I took the cloth bag that my mother always used when she went shopping. With this over my arm and the coins safely in my apron pocket, I walked slowly down the village street hoping I would be noticed and thought important by our neighbours. The shop keeper knew me from the numerous times I had been there with my mother and he asked if she was quite well as I was doing the shopping. I assured him she was just spending a few days in Elounda with family.

If you wanted to know what was happening in the village the women would ask the shopkeeper and the men would ask at the kafenion.

The shop keeper regarded me keenly. 'I heard there had been a funeral and you had spent the night with Anastasia's family.'

'My grandmother had been very ill and it was her funeral that my parents attended. My mother has stayed down in Elounda so they can comfort each other.'

'Have they got this electric thing down there?' he asked.

I had no idea what he was talking about. 'What do you mean?'

'We've been told that we will have wires that bring lights into our houses so we won't have to use oil lamps any more.'

'When is that going to happen?'

'How do I know? They say they will gradually take it to all the villages.'

'I'll ask my father and see if he knows.' I would also ask him to explain what electricity was and how it went along a wire.

The shop keeper weighed up the rice and coffee for me and took the lepta coins I offered in payment. 'Let me know what your father says about it. Doesn't sound safe to me.'

I assured him that I would tell him whatever I could discover, placed the rice and coffee in my apron and began to walk back up the road. I heard a donkey coming behind me and moved to one side to let it pass. I did not want to be poked in the back with the owner's stick. To my surprise and delight the donkey was being led by Lucas.

'Good morning, Lucas. Why are you down here and not up in the fields?'

'I was about to ask you why you are in the village,' he replied.

'Are you on an errand for your mother?'

I explained that my mother was staying with my aunt in Elounda and I was looking after my father until she returned.

'You will make a fine wife for a lucky man when the time comes for you to be married.'

His words made me blush deeply and I managed to ask him where he was going with the donkey.

'The donkey needs to have her hooves trimmed and new shoes fitted. I'm taking her to Kastelli.'

I knew that Kastelli was the nearest village to us, situated at the top of the hill where my father's school was, but I had never been there.

'Is Kastelli as big as our village?'

'It is larger. I'll take you there one day and you can take me to Elounda.'

He squeezed my arm and I wished that I was able to accompany him that day. I decided from his gesture and suggestion that he must like me and hoped he would soon feel the same about me as I did about him

It appeared that he did as he began to seek me out when we were working in the fields and stop and talk with me. Finally he suggested that when I took a break I joined him in the next field where he would be picking apples. I worked as fast as possible and then excused myself saying I needed a break and hurried to where I could see Lucas working. He motioned me to sit down in the shade beneath the tree and sat down beside me, his shoulder resting against mine.

Lucas said he would not be able to stay long but he just wanted to tell me how much he liked me. I assured him that I liked him too. He seemed to hesitate and then asked if my parents had already arranged a betrothal for me. I looked at him in surprise and said nothing had been mentioned to me and my father wanted me to be a school teacher.

We sat there in silence for a few minutes and then Lucas said he must return to work. He rose and brushed his trousers down, telling me to brush my skirt also and he would see me next week. I obeyed, but stood there feeling very unsettled. Why had Lucas wanted to know if I was already betrothed?

As I was not one of the farmers' children I could take a break whenever I wanted and for as long as I liked. I worked as fast as possible so no one could accuse me of slacking and I did not feel guilty about the amount of time I spent with Lucas.

At first our courtship progressed slowly and we just held hands, then Lucas placed his arm around me and I leaned against him. He said he had found a secluded spot where we would not be seen and asked if I would be willing to go there with him. I would have gone to the moon with him had he asked. He gave me instructions and said we could go there the following Friday afternoon.

That day he came and checked how our work was progressing and then announced that he was going to see if the almonds were ready. This was my cue to excuse myself a few minutes later and hurry after him. He was waiting just past the bend in the road and helped me over the low wall. Grape vines had been trained to trail along wires and they were in full leaf. Bending double we ducked beneath them and into the cool green tunnel.

Once safely hidden from any casual passer by we sat down and Lucas pulled me towards him, kissing me full on my mouth. I closed my eyes, my heart jumped and I could feel it thumping in my chest. Lucas pulled away and said he had been wanting to kiss me for weeks. I pushed myself as close to him as possible and asked him to kiss me again and I reciprocated with an intense pleasure. I don't know how long we stayed there, pressing our lips together time and again, before Lucas said he must go back. I was to wait awhile before I also returned so no one would know we had been together.

I counted to a hundred and then a further hundred before I crept out of the vineyard. My lips felt bruised and I hoped they were not red and swollen so that my mother would remark on them when I returned home. No one commented on my absence and I continued to work until the last cart had been loaded. I walked back with Anastasia and she asked why I had taken such a long break. I blushed deeply and said my stomach was not good. She accepted my blushes as embarrassment and asked no more.

At each of our meetings amongst the grapevines Lucas and I became a little bolder with each other until he finally lifted my skirt and pulled down my drawers. The first time we made love is a memory I will never forget and after that it became a regular occurrence. Each time Lucas declared how much he loved me and would ask my father's permission to marry me when it was my Name Day. I asked why we should wait until then and Lucas asked how old I was, but I could not say with any certainty. He said he was sure that by my Name Day I would be fifteen and until I reached that age my father would not consider I was old enough to marry anyone. Although I was going to have to wait an unbearable amount of time I was deliriously happy.

Just a few weeks later Anastasia told me she was going to be married to Elias.

'Are you happy to marry him?' I asked.

Anastasia shrugged. 'I have to marry someone. My father thinks it's time as I have been a woman for almost a year now.'

'How old are you?'

'I think I will be nearly sixteen by the time I'm married.'

I longed to tell her that I was going to marry Lucas, but resisted and hugged the precious secret to myself.

Lucas and I continued to meet regularly until it was no longer possible to lie amongst the grapevines unseen. We used to sneak into a shepherd's hut and hope he would not return early from the hills as the weather deteriorated.

I took no notice when I did not bleed that month and it was not until I was due the next time that I realised how long I had been without the monthly inconvenience. I could hardly wait to see Lucas and tell him I was having a baby; our own little babe.

31

Would it be a boy or a girl? Would it look like him or like me? As I lay on my pallet I caressed my stomach gently and told the small life that was developing there how much Lucas and I would love him or her.

I hurried up to the shepherd's hut and waited eagerly for Lucas to appear, but he did not arrive. As I walked back I scanned the fields but there was no sign of him. A feeling of dread clutched at my heart. Suppose he had been injured whilst working or was too ill to leave his bed?

I hid the bags of pasta and rice from the scullery in my room and told my mother that we needed more. She looked puzzled and searched the shelves, convinced there should be plenty there. I offered to go to the shop for her and left the house rapidly when my mother had done a second search for the missing items. I took a detour on my way to the village shop and passed the house where Lucas lived.

I screwed up my courage and knocked timidly, waiting until his mother answered. She had obviously been doing the washing as her sleeves were rolled up and she wiped her wet hands on her skirt. She asked my business and I asked if Lucas was there. She shook her head and I could see tears gathering in her eyes. I felt faint. Surely Lucas was not dead? That news would have gone all around the village faster than a bird can fly.

'Lucas has gone away. He decided he no longer wished to work on a farm and has gone to Aghios Nikolaos to find work there.'

I could not believe my ears. Lucas would not have done such a thing without telling me of his intentions.

'When will he return?'

She shrugged. 'He has no plans to return.'

I did not thank her for the information. I turned away so she would not see the tears streaming down my face and walked down to the shop. I scrubbed at my face with my skirt before I entered and hoped it would not show that I had been crying.

I placed the bags of rice and pasta on the table and went to my room. I lay on my bed sobbing fit for my heart to break. I was heart broken. Lucas had sworn his love for me, said he wanted to marry me and had now gone away without telling me.

My mother opened my door. 'What's wrong? Why are you crying?'

I could hardly speak I was so distraught. 'Lucas has gone away. We love each other. Lucas said he wanted to marry me.'

'You'll get over him. It is always painful when a first love ends.'

I shook my head. 'How can I get over him? I'm carrying his child.'

My mother looked at me in horror. 'Are you sure? Are you speaking the truth?'

'I have missed two courses and my stomach already feels larger.'

'Does Lucas know you are pregnant?'

'I had planned to tell him this week now I'm certain.'

She pursed her lips. 'I'll speak to your father when he comes home from school.'

I thought she would ask my father to go to Aghios Nikolaos to look for Lucas, but how wrong I was.

My father regarded me sternly. 'I am very disappointed by your irresponsible behaviour.'

'Lucas and I love each other,' I protested.

My father shook his head. 'A man will say that to a woman so he can have his way. No doubt Lucas realised you were pregnant and that is why he has left the village so abruptly.'

'But we love each other,' I said again.

'Had I known of your interest in the young man I would have spoken to him and said that such a liaison was out of the question. If Lucas had wanted to marry you it would be for the property that belongs to your mother and aunt that you will eventually inherit. Once the first flush of romance was over you would have become bored with each other. It would be no life for you living with a poor, uneducated farmer and expected to work up in the fields all year round. You need a companion as well educated as yourself, someone of your own intellectual ability.'

I shook my head. 'Lucas is not uneducated. he attended your school.'

My father shrugged. 'He has a modicum of knowledge. Besides, his uncle was declared an incurable come years ago. I would not want to welcome Lucas into the family and there was no way I would have given you permission to marry him.'

I was inconsolable. I hardly left my room. I could eat only a few mouthfuls of food and I could not stop my tears from flowing continually. I could not believe that Lucas had schemed to inherit the cottages my mother owned and taken advantage of me as my father had said.

My mother whispered to her friend that I had been raped and the culprit had left the village. This gossip was spread around the village as I am sure my mother knew it would be. Anastasia visited me and said how very sorry she was that I had suffered such a terrible experience and all the villagers were shocked. The fact that Lucas had left the village proved that he was the guilty party. It was a good thing that he had left or he would have suffered a severe beating or worse, even his parents had disowned him due to his actions. This did not help me at all. I wanted to scream at her and say that Lucas had not raped me; I had given myself to him willingly time and time again. She said that Elias had tried to persuade her now they were officially betrothed but she had refused his overtures and said he must wait until they were married. I just cried all the more after she left.

My parents sat with me and told me that they had arranged for me to go and stay with my aunt and uncle in Elounda hoping that a change of scenery would help me to recover. My father added that Elounda was closer to Aghios Nikolaos and the hospital should I have any problem when my time came.I did not ask what problem I might have; I did not care. I felt a glimmer of hope.

Lucas's mother had said he was going to Aghios Nikolaos and the town must be reasonably close to Elounda. He had wanted to go to Elounda so maybe I would find him there. Then I was beset by fear; suppose Lucas returned to Fourni to look for me and I was not in the village?

My mother packed all my clothes in a clean sack, then sat on the edge of my bed and said she needed to talk to me seriously. She told me that although she was paying my aunt for my keep, I should help her as much as possible. She also told me what I could expect when the time came for my child to be born. I had not expected to experience any pain. I had seen animals give birth with no sign of distress and assumed I would do the same. I pushed the unpleasant thought to the back of my mind. Any amount of pain could be inflicted on me if I could find Lucas in Elounda and present him with a healthy child.

My life in Fourni ended and I was never to see the village again.

1937 - 1938
LIFE TWO
Elounda

My aunt and uncle were not unkind to me, but I had not realised how religious they were. After our meal on my first evening with them I was asked to clear the table and wash the dishes. This was no hardship and I did it uncomplainingly as I was not a guest to be looked after, but a member of their family now and would be expected to help.

When I returned to the living room there was a yellow light illuminating part of the room as if the sun was shining. This must be the electricity that had been talked about and not yet reached Fourni. I screwed up my eyes to look at it, but the glare hurt them and I looked away quickly. I would have liked to ask my uncle about it but he was reading from the Bible and my aunt was listening to him with her eyes closed and a rapt expression on her face. I sat quietly, waiting until my uncle finished reading. I had expected some conversation to take place then, but to my surprise I was told to go to bed and not to forget to kneel and say my prayers.

I had been allocated the room that had served as my grandmother's bedroom. I had removed my clothes from the sack and placed them in the chest earlier. There was a small window high up in the wall that let in the light during the day and I was shown the switch that I had to put down to make the electricity work when it was dark.

'Make sure you switch that light off before you get into bed,' my aunt commanded, 'And don't forget to say your prayers,' she reminded me again.

I knelt beside the bed to say my prayers as instructed. It would be the first time I had slept in a proper bed and not on a pallet on the floor and I hoped I would not fall out during the night. I left the door open so the light from the living room would penetrate once I had switched off the artificial light.

It was only a short time later that my aunt switched off the light and closed my door. I was in complete darkness. A feeling of panic overwhelmed me as I rose to my feet. I was not sure if I could find the switch for the light and did not want to incur the wrath of my aunt by daring to put the light on again. Even if I did find the switch I would have to turn the light off and find my way back to my bed in darkness. I waited until my eyes had adjusted to the lack of light and then climbed onto the mattress, pulling the bed cover up to my chin.

The sun woke me in the morning and I looked around the unfamiliar room. I opened the door timidly and peered out. There was no sign of either my aunt or uncle and the curtains were still drawn around their bed. I crept as quietly as possible into the scullery and opened the door to the yard to visit the privy.

I did not dare make myself a cup of coffee as that would have meant using the fire in the living room. Even if it was still alight it would need to be raked and the wood replenished. I looked around for a cup and the remains of a bucket of water from the previous day so I could quench my morning thirst. I was hungry, but again I could not find where my aunt kept the rusks and help myself. I would have to talk to my aunt and some arrangements were going to be necessary if I was to stay living with them.

I returned to my bedroom, leaving the door open to indicate that I was awake and lay back on my bed. I think I fell asleep again as the next thing I knew was my aunt calling to me from the doorway.

'Why are you not up? Are you unwell?'

I sat up abruptly and apologised. 'I was awake earlier and I had no wish to disturb you or my uncle so I returned to my bed.'

'Have you said your prayers?'

I hesitated. It had not occurred to me that I should say prayers when I awoke.

'At home I only said them before going to bed.'

'This is your home now,' she said firmly. 'You should say a prayer when you awake in the morning, thankful that you have survived the night. There is never any need to sit idle; the time can be used to say a prayer.'

I bowed my head and replied meekly that I would remember her instruction.

'Get yourself up, then girl. There's work to be done.'

I joined my aunt in the living room and asked to be shown where the plates, cups and utensils were stored. I dared to ask if I could make up the fire if I woke before her in the morning and make myself a cup of coffee and eat a rusk.

'You can certainly make up the fire and when you have done so you can put a pot of water on it ready for your uncle to wash and shave. If you need something to eat first thing you can help yourself to a rusk.'

I softened a rusk in a little warm water and ate it gratefully before helping my aunt to prepare the vegetables ready for our evening meal. She would cross herself before picking up a sharp knife to ensure that she did not cut her hand and again before she dealt with the fire so she would not be burned. Before we ate a lunch of rusks dipped in olive oil, accompanied by a slice of feta, a prayer was said again. I decided that this ritual was something to which I must become accustomed.

I had expected my aunt to work on her loom during the afternoon and I would be left to amuse myself but she told me to get my shawl as we were going out. I did not ask where we were going but she handed me a small jug and led me to where the shops were located.

I was taken into each one and introduced as her niece whom she was looking after. The shop keepers looked at me curiously and I was sure that when my aunt visited the shops alone she would spread the lie that I had left my home village having been raped. She showed me where I could go to buy vegetables and fruit, and the general store that sold rice, flour and coffee, along with the spices she used in her cooking. It seemed strange to me to have to go to a shop to buy produce that grew in abundance at Fourni and I asked why the villagers did not grow their own vegetables. She told me that the soil here was poor and not good for growing anything except carob and olives. Now I knew why the farmers loaded up their carts and made such regular trips each week.

We walked past an area where chickens were pecking at the ground and she told me I would be expected to go there to purchase an egg as it was cheaper than buying one from the village shop. Further along there were some goats tethered and I was told I should knock at the door of the cottage and hand my jug to the lady who lived there. She would either pour some milk from a churn that stood inside the door or go and milk a goat. I waited until the jug was handed back to me, expecting to carry it back home.

'Drink it,' my aunt ordered. 'A jug of milk each day will be good for you and the child. I will give you a lepta each day so you can pay her.'

She stood and watched whilst I drained the jug to the last drop. 'Waste not, want nor,' she announced self righteously.

Having reached the end of the row of cottages we turned down towards the sea. I caught my breath. There was something awe inspiring and fascinating about the way the small waves lapped at the shore. I stopped and stared until my aunt took my elbow and gave me a little push to make me walk on. She showed me the area where the women congregated to do their washing. Large flat rocks had been placed to make a shallow pool that was fed by the sea gently moving in and out. I hoped my aunt would not ask me to go down there to do the household washing until I was more familiar with the expanse of water that seemed to stretch across to some land opposite.

I could see men working down by the shore, but there were no fishing boats visible and I asked what they were doing. My aunt explained that they were working on the salt flats, shovelling the salt that accumulated there into large mounds. This was then shovelled into sacks to be stored ready for transportation into the town and around the villages.

'That is where my uncle works, then?'

She looked at me scornfully. 'Don't be silly; he is not a manual labourer. He is the supervisor. He works for the Ministry of Industry recording the amount produced, keeping a record of the weight and number of sacks that are sent to other areas of Crete and over to the mainland of Greece. He is also responsible for ensuring that the other employees carry out their tasks efficiently.'

'I would be interested to go and see the work being carried out. I have never seen salt being harvested before.'

We walked a little nearer but I could not really see what the men were doing and there appeared to be women and children working there also. I determined that I would return anther day and go closer. It was possible that Lucas was working there. In the distance I could see two windmills and a woman trudging back leading a loaded donkey.

'Is the lady with the donkey carrying salt?' I asked.

'No, she will have been to the mill to have her barley or wheat ground into flour.'

'I didn't realise that the grain had to be taken to a mill to be processed. My mother always bought hers from the village shop.'

'There are a lot of things that you do not know and need to learn,' my aunt remarked as we turned to go back to the village.

'Is salt collected further along the bay?'

'The Plaka area is not suitable and they concentrate on growing carob or fishing.'

I was tempted to ask after my other aunt who I had heard lived there, but thought better of it.

'May I stay down here a short while, please?'

'I see no reason why not. Do not go near the sea as you are unfamiliar with it and don't be too long as there is work to be done.'

'I would just like to sit and watch the sea. I certainly won't go near it,' I assured her. 'I know my way back to the house and I won't stay very long and give you cause to worry.'

I sat on a rock and stroked my swollen stomach gently. I felt calmer and more at peace than I had for some months.I was no longer crying continually, but my heart felt like a stone inside me.

Reluctantly I returned to the house after a short while and thanked my aunt.

'I would like to go out each day. I'm sure a walk and the fresh sea air will be beneficial to both me and my baby.'

I received no answer and hoped I was not going to be confined to the house unless sent on an errand by my aunt.

The next day my aunt presented me with some fine cloth that she had woven, some knitting needles, a crochet hook and some wool, informing me that it was more important to make some clothes for my baby than wasting my time wandering around outside. I had to admit that I had not given any thought to how my baby would be wrapped and kept warm.

I fingered the fine cloth admiringly. 'If I go for a short walk would you be kind enough to show me how to cut it and make a nightdress when I return?'

I had no idea how large it should be and I certainly did not want to waste the precious cloth. I think she was pleased that I had asked for her help as when I returned I found the material was spread out on the table with some newspaper pinned to it.

'I have made you a very simple pattern, just a back and a front that can be stitched together to form a nightdress.'

'It looks so small,' I exclaimed.

41

My aunt laughed. 'It will probably be far too large for the baby for a number of weeks. Sew the sides together and down the side of the sleeves. When you have done that I will show you how to finish it.'

I sat and stitched carefully until my fingers felt quite sore. I handed the unfinished garment back to my aunt and watched as she laid it flat and cut a half circle.

'That will be for the head to go through. Make sure you turn the edges under and stitch them firmly. No loose cottons must be allowed to get into the baby's mouth.'

Once completed I held the nightdress up for her inspection.

She nodded. 'Now turn it inside out and make another row of stitching inside the seams to make it smaller.Once you have done that do the same again. As the child grows the stitches can be undone.'

Later I was to realise how practical this advice had been and I took advantage of it on a number of future occasions.

Each evening my uncle read from the Bible and when he decided he had read sufficient he would replace the book on the shelf and cover it in a cloth to keep it dust free. I would have liked to read some of the Bible for myself but I did not dare to ask. Once the reading was finished it was a signal that it was time to go to bed. There was no conversation. When I went out to the privy at night I would often stand in the yard for a few minutes, pleased to be away from the claustrophobic atmosphere inside.

I was not allowed to knit during the evening when my uncle was reading from the Bible as the click of my needles were an annoyance and distraction to him. Instead I would sit and sew the nightdresses, although I was hardly able to see by the feeble light that the electric bulb shed around the room. My uncle sat directly beneath it to illuminate the page he was reading. I wished it was my father reading to me from one of his books and I would have been invited to lean over his shoulder and probably read a passage aloud.

Each day, once I had finished helping my aunt to prepare the evening meal, I was allowed to go out for a walk or visit the village shop on her behalf. My walks always took me down to the shore and I would look at the fishing boats, scanning the faces of each occupant in the hope of seeing Lucas. I walked along to the salt pans at Elounda and watched the men working for a short while, hoping I might see Lucas amongst them. I would have liked to cross the wooden bridge that led over a canal to the windmills, but it looked narrow and I was concerned I might lose my balance now I was becoming larger and more unwieldy. I began to get to know the villagers by sight and be greeted by them. I wished I could meet a girl about my own age and become friendly with her. I missed the company of Anastasia, but although the local girls smiled back at me none of them tried to strike up a conversation and I noticed they often crossed themselves as they passed me by. Maybe they had been told I should be avoided.

I tried my best to be useful to my aunt, but she would look at anything I had prepared, purse her lips and give it further attention. It was the same with my stitching of the little nightdresses and knitting of a shawl and blankets. She would comment that my stitches were not straight or I had dropped a stitch in my knitting and she would insist that I unpicked the work and started again. I felt frustrated and useless. A baby was not going to know if the stitching on a nightgown was straight. Had I been able to sit beneath the oil lamp in the evening I am sure my handiwork would have been better.

When I went for my walk I would take my knitting with me in my apron pocket and sit on a flat stone by the shore where I was able to watch the fishermen unloading their catch and knit at the same time. I seemed to make fewer mistakes when I was away from the watchful eye of my aunt.

The day came when I woke with a gripping pain in my stomach. I had never experienced such agony before. As I struggled off the bed thinking I needed the privy, there was a rush of water and the

43

pain came again. Horrified that I had made a mess on the floor I went out to the scullery to find a rag to mop up the water. My aunt heard me and followed me out.

'I'm so sorry. I woke up with a bad pain and I was unable to get to the privy in time,' I explained tearfully.

'Go back and lay on your bed whilst I mop up the floor. This is the start of the baby arriving. Tell me when the pains begin to come regularly. That will be the time to send for the local woman who is a midwife. I'll get you prepared.'

Once my aunt had cleaned up the floor she placed me on two cushioned chairs with a pile of old towels beneath them, gave me frequent sips of water and sponged my hot forehead with a damp cloth. I felt frightened. My mother had told me I would experience pain, but I had never had such a pain before as those that began to rack my body at regular intervals, each one seeming worse than the last.

The village midwife arrived and examined me. She assured me that all was well and the pains were natural. I was to relax as much as possible and she would tell me when I had to start to push my baby out. My aunt retired to the living room and began to heat water on the fire ready to wash me and my offspring. By mid-day I felt exhausted and would like to have slept if only the incessant pains would stop to give me some relief.

I do not know how long it was before the midwife ordered me to start to push. I felt as if I was being torn apart and gasped and panted, gripping the sides of the chair with my hands. Just as I felt I could not accept any more pain I heard the midwife say I was nearly there and only one more push would have the baby born.

It was like music to my ears when I heard the first mewling cries and the midwife said I had a boy. Now maybe I could rest. I closed my eyes, but the midwife began to pummel my stomach and I begged her to stop. She refused, saying that she had to expel the after birth or I would be seriously ill. I felt something slip between my legs and then she left my bruised body in peace.

Whilst this had been taking place my aunt had washed my baby and placed one of the tiny nightgowns over his head, wrapped him in a knitted blanket with a small cross pinned to it. After she had smeared his forehead with charcoal as an additional precaution against evil spirits she placed him in my arms and as I looked at him the tears streamed down my face. If only Lucas was there to share this wonderful moment with me. The midwife placed my nipple in the baby's mouth, explaining that it would give him comfort although I would have no milk for him yet. She then washed me, removed the soiled towels, placed a thick clout between my legs and I was allowed to lie back on my mattress with some more clean towels beneath me.

Her work completed satisfactorily the midwife took her leave and said she would call the following day to check that all was well. To my surprise my aunt brought a wooden cradle into my bedroom, placed old towels and strips of sheets inside and then took my baby from me and laid him down. She said my father had sent the cradle from Fourni that I had used as a baby. Knowing how displeased my parents were with me I was touched by their thoughtfulness. That evening my uncle wrote a short letter that he asked a farmer to deliver to my family the following day, simply telling them that I had given birth to a boy and all was well.

I felt desperately tired. I had not realised how much effort it took to give birth. I felt clumsy and inept at washing and dressing my baby but provided I fed him as necessary he did not complain. He seemed content to lie in my arms and I would look at his tiny fingers and toes, little nose and small pink mouth and wonder at him. He was so perfect.

Father Phillipos came to the house and christened my baby three days after he was born. I insisted that his name was to be Lucas. My aunt had sniffed in displeasure and said that my father would be disappointed that the child had not been named after him. My uncle agreed to be his godfather but there was no celebration of my son's birth as there would have been if I was in Fourni and married to Lucas.

It was forty days before I was allowed to leave the house as I needed to protect myself from any danger. Father Phillipos then visited again and gave me his blessing which allowed me to visit church on the Sunday. I was quite surprised that as I walked to church a number of people came up to greet me and I was delighted when I saw my parents were there waiting for me. I hoped this meant they would be taking me back to Fourni with them, but my father said that it would be far better to stay in Elounda as I was now accepted by the villagers here. If I returned to Fourni I would forever be shunned as I had no husband and the child would be stigmatized also.

Although I was disheartened by this, baby Lucas was my first concern. He must not suffer in any way, particularly when the fault was not his. Each morning my aunt insisted that I joined her in prayer and asked forgiveness for my sin of conceiving a child out of wedlock. I recited the words she said without any feeling. Baby Lucas could not be considered a sin, he was conceived in love.

Although my aunt considered that I was a sinful young woman she doted on my baby. At the first whimper she would be lifting him from his cradle, crooning to him and kissing his little head. I'm sure if I had said she could have him and bring him up as her own son she would have been overjoyed. There was no way I would ever let my little boy be taken away from me.

I began to accept my responsibilities as a mother. Whenever the weather was neither too hot nor too cold or wet I would carry Lucas on my hip down to the village shops to make any necessary purchases for my aunt. I knew the fresh air would be good for him and I enjoyed having him admired by the villagers that I met. The villagers appeared to accept me now and were willing to talk to me, even the girls of about my age who had shunned me in the past were now friendly. If only Lucas had been with me my happiness would have been complete. I looked for him wherever I went.

I asked one of the girls why she had not spoken to me before my son's birth and she crossed herself before answering.

'We heard you had been raped and we did not know what to say to you. It was a terrible thing to happen and we were not sure if you would have a heathy child. Rumours went around that you might have tried to get rid of it and caused it some damage. We are all prepared to be friendly with you now.'

I shook my head in disbelief. I wanted to say that I was not raped, but I chose my words carefully. 'I would never have tried to get rid of my child whatever the circumstances of his conception,' I assured her.

During my afternoon walks I would take Luke with me down to the harbour to watch the fishing boats returning and unloading their catch. I was used to the sea now and its changing moods. The soft rhythm of the waves caressing the shore was soothing and when it was windy and the waves tumbled upon the rocks with a noise like thunder it was exhilarating. I still kept well away from the water but I was no longer so frightened that it would reach out and sweep me away.

One such afternoon I was a little later than usual. I had missed seeing the fish unloaded but there was one small boat making its way to the shore. I waited and was most surprised when I saw Despina jump ashore.

I waved to her and she walked over to where I was sitting. I asked her if she had been fishing and she laughed and said she had been to Spinalonga. For a moment I was puzzled; I had forgotten that my father had told me the hospital for the leprosy sufferers was situated there. I asked her if she was a nurse and she shook her head and replied that she just went over to help them.

Despina sat down beside me. 'I earn money to go over there and help them. Many of them have difficulty in doing the most simple jobs due to their hands having become crippled or their sight has been affected. I usually help by preparing the vegetables for a meal up at the hospital or collect a jug of water; little things that help them. If I pass a house and someone calls me I will always ask if they need something.'

47

'I thought they would be cared for in the hospital over there.'

'Only the most sick men and women are in the hospital. The others live in their own homes and look after themselves as best they can. The fittest men are gradually repairing and rebuilding the houses and some of the men from the mainland go over to help. There are some small shops over there and goods can be ordered from the mainland and one of the boatmen deals with the orders and payments.'

'Aren't you afraid that you will become sick?' I asked.

'I never touch them, not even their hands. They are allowed to have visits from relatives and friends. I have to be disinfected when I arrive and again before I am allowed to leave so I'm not likely to catch leprosy. The money I earn is useful as my mother is a widow and I have three younger brothers. They can only run errands or do odd jobs until they are older and stronger. Alexandros hopes he will be allowed to work with the men at the salt pans next year.'

After she left I thought about her words. The island did not seem so frightening, but much like the village of Elounda. Little Luke, as I called him, was growing rapidly and although I was able to knit and make his basic clothes at the moment he would need some boots when he began to walk. I would not want my son to go barefoot like the peasant children. I could not expect my parents to pay for boots; already they paid my aunt for our food. When they visited about every six weeks my father would press a few lepta into my hand and I would accept them gratefully, placing them in a small pot in my chest amongst my clothes. I doubted there would be sufficient money there to buy a pair of boots for my son and certainly not enough to purchase a pair for me when my current boots developed holes.

I had asked at the village school if I could have a position as a teacher there. He shook his head and said that it might be possible when Luke was old enough to attend school. That day was a long way off. There was very little work available for a woman in the village of Elounda. You were expected to live at home and help your mother, learning how to cook, weave and sew until such time as you married. You would then be fully occupied looking after your own house and caring for your husband's needs. This was not going to happen to me. I was unlikely ever to get married and have a home of my own to care for. Eventually I would probably return to live with my parents in Fourni and care for them in their old age.

I turned the problem over in my mind. If my aunt was willing to care for Luke some days I could go over to the island and earn some money. I would be very careful not to go near the inhabitants of the hospital as I would not want to bring back any disease with me. I decided to watch for Despina returning from the island and ask her for some more details. As I thought about the proposition I recalled that Lucas's uncle had been sent to the hospital there. It was just possible that he might know of some relatives in Aghios Nikolaos and I could ask them where I could find Lucas.

When I saw Despina next I questioned her closely.

'What are the people on the island like?'

Despina shrugged. 'No different from any other villagers, except those who have facial disfigurations. Often you would not know they were sick unless you looked at their hands and saw they were clawed.'

'Would I see the disfigured people?' I asked tentatively.

'Probably. They do not hide themselves away. Everyone is accepted however the disease has affected them. Some of them have a metal chair with wheels that they sit in and are pushed around.'

'Are you expected to do that?' I asked warily.

'Goodness, no. They would be far too heavy for me to manage.'

'How much do you earn for working on the island?'

'Ten drachmas each time I visit.'

Ten drachmas sounded like untold riches to me.

'Do you have to pay the boatmen to take you over?'

'Fifty lepta to go out and fifty to come back.'

'What happens in the winter if it is raining or the sea is rough?'

'The people still need help whatever the weather. The boatmen would not contemplate the journey if the sea was rough or the currents too strong. Their boats are their most valuable possession and they would not risk losing them for the sake of a few drachmas.'

'If I wanted to work there who would I ask?'

'I spoke to Father Phillipos. He sent a message to the priest in Aghios Nikolaos who spoke to Doctor Stavros about me working there. The Doctor must have agreed as Father Phillipos told me I could go over and to arrange my days with the boatmen.'

'Does this doctor live on Spinalonga?'

Despina shook her head. 'Doctor Stavros lives in Aghios Nikolaos and visits the island once a week unless he is called to one of the villages in an emergency. If you really want to work on the island I suggest you speak to Father Phillipos.'

'I'll have to ask my aunt if she is willing to look after Luke for me.'

'I expect she will be grateful for the extra money you earn.'

'It is not for her,' I said firmly. 'She is paid by my parents for our keep. This will be to buy Luke some boots when he starts to walk and new clothes when he needs them. I do not want to ask my parents for more.'

I approached my aunt cautiously. I said I had been looking for work in Elounda as I would need money to buy boots and clothes for Little Luke as he grew and I could not expect my parents to pay for them. Of course, my aunt took the opportunity of reminding me that if I was a respectable woman with a husband I would not have to concern myself with finding work.

When she had finished berating me I told her I wanted to ask Father Phillipos if I could go to Spinalonga and work there.

She looked at me in horror. 'Go to the leper island. Out of the question. You'll bring the filthy disease back here to all of us.'

'They are allowed to have visitors. I have been talking to Despina, she works over there, and she assured me that I was unlikely to catch leprosy provided I only helped them in the same way as she has done for the past year. Before she leaves each day she has to go through a disinfection room so she does not carry any germs back to the mainland with her.' I then had a moment of inspiration. 'It would be a way of atoning for my sins.' I bowed my head as if in penitence.

Immediately her attitude changed. 'So what do you propose to do with Little Luke if you go over to Spinalonga?'

'Would you be willing to look after him, just for three days each week? I would be able to pay you a little. I need to be able to earn some money so that I can clothe him properly as he grows.'

I could see her resolve weakening as she realised she would have my little boy all to herself for three whole days at a time.

'I'll speak to your uncle this evening and ask for his opinion.'

'Provided uncle agrees I will have to speak to Father Phillipos and ask him to gain the approval of the priest in Aghios Nikolaos and also Doctor Stavros. It could be some time before I have a reply.'

Now I was desperate to go to Spinalonga; sure I would find Lucas's uncle there and he would be able to tell me where Lucas was in Aghios Nikolaos. I busied myself with Little Luke in my bedroom whilst my aunt and uncle discussed my proposal. Once Little Luke was asleep I ventured out into the living room and waited with trepidation. If my uncle refused to sanction the idea I could not disobey him.

He regarded me seriously. 'I understand that you want to go to Spinalonga and help the sufferers there as atonement for your previous sins.'

'Yes, uncle.'

'So what would you do? You are not trained as a nurse.'

'I would not work in the hospital. I would do the same as Despina has been doing for the previous year, preparing their food for a meal, collecting a jug of water. Much the same as I do here each day.

'I need to ask Father Phillipos to speak to the priest in Aghios Nikolaos who in turn will speak with Doctor Stavros. I'm sure the Doctor would not allow anyone from the mainland to work over there if he thought there was any chance of them contracting the illness.' I did not mention that Despina had said the leprosy sufferers were allowed to have visitors.

Finally my uncle nodded. 'Provided you have the blessing of the priest and permission from the Doctor there should be no reason why you should not work there. Just remember that if you should show the slightest sign of the disease you would not be welcome to live in this house and have to stay on the island permanently.'

I had no choice, but to agree to that condition.

'I understand uncle. I promise I will be very careful and make sure I disinfect myself thoroughly each time before I return.'

I would pray each night that I would stay healthy. If I had to stay on Spinalonga for the remainder of my life I would never see Little Luke again. I counted out the lepta that I had hidden in my little pot. I had one drachma and thirty lepta. I could afford to go out to the island once and then I would have to pay my fare from the money I earned.

The next time I saw Despina I told her that I had asked to be allowed to work on Spinalonga and whilst I was there my aunt had agreed to look after my son.

'You could take him over there with you.'

I looked at Despina in surprise. 'What do you mean?'

'There are some young children living there. They have been born to parents who have leprosy, but they appear to be fit and well. Provided they stay that way they will leave the island when they are about two years old and go to relatives to be brought up.'

'Suppose the relatives will not have them or they have become ill in the meantime?'

'They would go to the orphanage if no one in their family would accept them, but if they are infected they will stay on the island.'

I shuddered at the thought of my son being sent to an orphanage. At least I knew my aunt or my parents would take good care of him if any awful event overtook me.

Spinalonga

The day I arranged to go over with Despina. I hugged Little Luke to me, unwilling to be apart from him for so long in a day. I told him that he was to be good for my aunt and that I would be home in time to put him to bed for the night. He was probably far too young to understand my words, but he smiled at me and waved to me as usual as I went out of the door. I thought the lump that came into my throat would choke me and I nearly turned back and said I had changed my mind.

I had never been on a boat before and as I climbed aboard it rocked alarmingly. Despina laughed at me and said I had nothing to be worried about as it was a calm day. There were four men already sitting on the boat and Despina nodded to them. Whilst the captain started the engine the mate threw the rope that had been used to keep us tethered to a buoy on the quay side into the water. The motion of the boat as it made headway towards the island made me feel sick and I clung tightly to the wooden seat until the mate came along and asked for the money for our trip. Nervously I released my grip and handed him fifty lepta.

'Aren't you coming back?' he asked, eyeing me suspiciously.

'Of course I am,' I answered.

'Then you pay for the return trip on your way out.'

'I'm sorry, I didn't realise.' I felt embarrassed and withdrew another fifty lepta from the pocket in my apron and handed it to him.

'We're nearly there,' announced Despina and I dared to lift my eyes.

The stone walls of the fortress seemed to tower above us. From looking at them from the shore I had never realised their height. There were a number of small boats tied up to a jetty unloading items and men were collecting them. Our boat nosed its way amongst them as the captain cut the engine and the mate caught a rope that was thrown to him. Once safely tied up the mate helped both Despina and I ashore and the men began to unload the boxes and sacks that the boat had been carrying onto the jetty. My legs felt like jelly.

'Come on.' urged Despina. 'Pick up a box that is not too heavy and follow me to the disinfection room.'

I lifted a box that was reminiscent of the ones we had used at Fourni to pack beans or courgettes and followed her up a ramp. Halfway up there was an opening to a dark, cavernous area and Despina stopped.

'Put the box down anywhere and we'll go in and disinfect ourselves.'

I placed it on the ground and followed Despina nervously into the dark area. As my eyes grew accustomed to the darkness I could see a shallow container on the ground.

'Hold your skirt up and walk through carefully. It's only the disinfectant, but you don't want to make your skirt wet.'

I obeyed her instructions and then followed her back out into the daylight. The men were carrying the boxes up the ramp and the boat was making its way back out to sea.

'Where are they going?' I asked, alarmed that we were being left on the island.

'They'll go fishing until they return to collect us. We'll take the boxes up to the top of the ramp and they can be collected from there.'

'What's in them?'

'Probably some fruit or vegetables. Could be other things that the villagers have ordered from the mainland. The men will have carried up the heavy items.'

54

As we reached the top of the ramp there were a large group of women, chattering and laughing together.

'What are they doing?' I asked.

'Their washing. The doctor arranged for large concrete troughs to be made and water piped to them. They actually have hot water as fires can be lit in the niches and the pipes pass above them. They also use the hot water in their bath tubs. I wish we had that at home. If we want hot water we have to boil it up on the fire.'

I agreed. It would be the height of luxury to have hot water that could be used to wash clothes and fill the tin bath once a week for our use.

I could see there was a dirt road going in both directions and there were a number of houses. The men with the boxes and sacks had disappeared.

'Where have the men gone who were on the boat with us?'

'They would have taken any building materials up to where the men are working and left the lighter boxes containing food for others to collect. They help with some of the heavy or difficult construction work and also clear up any rubbish that cannot be burnt and used as fuel. They'll take it back to Elounda for disposal. One of them is responsible for checking that all is in order with the generator. I can show you where that is another time. We'll walk up to the hospital and I can introduce you to Spiro. I expect he will want some water. When we've collected the jugs we'll come back down and I can show you where the fountain is,' Despina announced.

I followed her dutifully, trying not to look at the people we passed on the way. Many of them she greeted by name.

'Do you know everyone over here?' I asked.

'Goodness, no. There are far too many people living here for me to know them all. I've got to know the names of those I meet every time I come over. They are the fitter members of the community. Some are unable to stir from their houses without help. As I walk past a house where I know there is a crippled person I call out and ask if there is anything they want. Usually it is a jug of water or some bread.'

'So who looks after them if you are not here?' I asked curiously.

'They have a system where a crippled person has to live in a house where the other occupants are able to look after them. They make sure they have all they need before they go off to work and a meal later in the day.'

'Where do they work?' I had not envisaged anyone on the island being capable of working.

'Spiro runs the hospital and some of the other men and women help him with the patients. I always visit him first in case he needs more water. Other people run the shops, some grow the vegetables that are sold in them or provide the eggs or honey. The shops are down the other way, I'll show you later. Then there is all the building that is going on.'

'Building?' I was feeling totally confused. It did not sound as if these people needed help.

'No sooner does everyone have somewhere to live than a new patient arrives who needs a house.'

As we climbed up the steps to the hospital I could hear the bleating of a goat and stopped. There, tethered beside a house, were four goats.

'Do goats live here?'

'Two belonged originally to one of the patients. A gift from a farmer. They've been allowed to multiply and Babbis takes care of them since Panayiotis died. The milk the nannies give goes to Spiro at the hospital. Have you ever milked a goat?'

I shook my head. 'Never.'

'Don't worry; you'll not be asked to deal with them. I understand you have to know how to do it or the milk squirts everywhere but in the bucket. What about chickens?'

'My father used to keep some and I would help him look for eggs.'

'There are quite a lot further round. They're kept on some scrub land higher up that isn't really suitable for planting vegetables. The owner collects the eggs and sells them in a shop. If he runs out he asks the customer to go up with him and they'll search around until they find one or two.'

'What other shops are there?'

'The baker, a dressmaker, barbers, grocers, greengrocer, and tavernas; the same as in any village. Here we are.' Despina knocked on the wooden door, although it was open, and called loudly for Spiro.

A man shuffled forwards a broad smile on his face. 'Good morning, Despina. I see you have a friend with you. I trust she is only visiting and not joining us permanently.'

'This is Eirini. She has come to help the same as I do.'

'We do appreciate any help we are given. Doctor Stavros should be here soon and if you could collect a container of fresh water so he can wash his hands it would save one of my helpers having to go down.'

'Of course. Is one enough? We could bring back two.'

'That would be even better. Could you call in at the shop on your way? I could do with some more barley so the women can thicken the vegetable soup for the patients' meals.'

Despina picked up two large metal containers and handed one to me. 'If there's some barley there we'll bring it back along with the water. Come on, Eirini.'

Despina began to trip lightly back down the steps and I followed her more cautiously.

'It looked terribly dark in the hospital.' I commented.

'They have the electric light now, but Spiro uses it sparingly. Most of the patients spend their day asleep apparently so they do not need light. It was probably far darker when they only had oil lamps. The people used to save up their oil so Spiro could have it.'

'Do the patients always have vegetable soup?' I asked as I hurried to catch her up having reached the road.

Despina shrugged. 'It depends what has been sent over. If

there's a chicken or some fish Spiro is always asked first if he wants it for the hospital and then the women will make a soup from that. It's practical to make soup as the patients need to be spoon fed and most of them cannot chew anything solid.'

Once back on the main pathway we walked past the ramp and continued on down the dirt road. Despina stopped at one of the shops and stood a short distance away from the other customers.

'Good morning everyone. This is Eirini who has agreed to come over and help as I do. We've just been up to Spiro and he wanted to know if there is any barley available.'

The people moved to one side as the shop keeper came forward and held up a bag.

'You'll need to take it carefully. There's a hole in the bag.'

'I'll put it in my apron pocket. It should be safe enough there. Is there any chicken or fish?'

'Ask Thranassis. He may have some. I know they sent over some figs. Stop by Theo's and you can take some back for Spiro. He loves figs. and his are not ripe yet.'

I followed Despina down the path and she pointed out the different shops to me. Before each one there were people examining the produce that was on show and haggling with the shop keeper. A man sat on a chair in the barber's shop whilst his hair was trimmed and another sat waiting his turn. It was a scene that was repeated daily in any village.

She called to a man called Thranassis and asked if he had any fresh meat or fish.

'Nothing fresh today. There are a few sausages that came yesterday.'

'The patients would have a job to eat sausages, but I'm sure some of the others will enjoy them.'

Despina moved just a few steps to where people were gathered outside of a shop displaying fruit and vegetables.

'I hear you have some figs,' called Despina.

'Came this morning.'

'Can I have some for Spiro, please.'

The man, whom I understood to be Theo, picked some up in his hands and came outside to us.

'Put them in your apron pocket, Eirini,' ordered Despina. 'If they are soft we don't want the juice running on to the barley.'

The man placed them in my apron pocket and I had to control my horror as I saw his disfigured face and clawed hands. Two large lumps were on his forehead and another on the side of his face making one eye almost closed; his face resembled a grotesque mask.

'Thank you,' I managed to stammer and took a step backwards.

Feeling totally unnerved by the man's appearance I continued to follow Despina down the path.

'Don't you have to pay the shopkeepers?' I asked.

'No, they keep account and Spiro will pay them from the money the patients pay him to stay in the hospital.'

'Where do they get their money from?'

'The government gives them a pension. Most of the vegetables will have been grown here. The customers pay the shopkeeper and he pays the farmer. That way the money circulates and stays on the island.'

'What about the items that come from the mainland? Who pays for those?'

'Manolis deals with all that. He keeps ledgers and everyone's pension is entered into it. He then deducts the amount from your account and pays the supplier on the mainland.'

A queue of men and women were standing in an area that formed a small square and Despina explained that they were all waiting to have access to the water fountain.

'Water is brought over in barrels from Plaka each morning and that's fine for washing yourself or your clothes, but the water from the fountain is fresh and pure so everyone wants that to drink and prefer it for their cooking.'

I stood patiently in the queue until we were able to fill the containers that Spiro had given us. I tried not to look at the people curiously as some hurried away and others lingered to talk to a friend. I did not feel threatened as they kept away from us, only sympathy for their plight.

Once the containers were full of water they were heavy and we climbed the steps to the hospital slowly. I removed the figs from my apron pocket, relieved that none of them had split and left their sticky juice behind. Despina called to Spiro and placed the bag of barley and the figs at the door along with the two full jugs of water. Spiro's face lit up with a smile when he saw the figs.

'I'll ask Phaedra to bring the vegetables out for you and a couple of pots. Call her when you've finished and then she can start cooking.'

We sat outside of the hospital and chopped courgettes, carrots and onions as Spiro had requested. My fingers were quite sore by the time we had finished. The Doctor arrived and I realised that he was the same doctor as visited both Elounda and Fourni. I wondered if on a future occasion I would dare to ask him if he knew Lucas's uncle then I realised that I did not know the man's name nor the village where he had lived. I would have to remember the names of the other villages in the area and then ask if he knew of a man who had come from one of them.

Doctor Stavros hardly glanced at me. He nodded to Despina and she asked him for a moment of his time.

'I just want to introduce you to Eirini. She has agreed to come over and be a helper on the island.'

The doctor nodded. 'I was told there was going to be a new helper. Speak to Manolis and he'll arrange your name to be added.' He turned away and entered the hospital.

'Why do I have to speak to this man, Manolis, and what will my name be added to?'

'Manolis keeps a record of all the helpers. When I go to collect my money we'll speak to him and make sure your name is added to the list so that you can get paid. You won't get any money this week, but when you come next week you'll be paid for the days you have come over previously.'

'I haven't enough money to come over again,' I admitted. 'I had expected to be paid this time.'

'Wouldn't your aunt or uncle lend it to you?'

'Maybe,' I replied dubiously.

'I could pay for you to come over on the next two days and once the following week. You'll have to promise to pay me back three drachmas as soon as Manolis has paid you.'

'Of course I will, but how will he know if I have been here?' I asked.

'Always go and speak to him so that you receive your money promptly. That way there's no argument. If you forget it will be no good trying to argue as it's doubtful that anyone will remember seeing you on a particular day so you won't get paid.'

'Where will I find him? There seem to be so many people around.'

'I'll show you, but he's always up at Flora's house. Anyone would be able to direct you.'

'I'm a bit nervous about speaking to anyone,' I admitted.

Despina smiled at my concerns. 'You don't have to worry. They're decent enough people. Just because they've been sent here doesn't mean they're criminals. They'll not try to molest you or steal your money from you as you go back to the boat.'

'I'm more concerned that I won't know what they are saying to me. When we were waiting for the water I heard some of them talking together and I couldn't understand them. It could be embarrassing.'

'They know if they have a speech problem and would be most unlikely to try to engage you in conversation. They will call out a greeting to you and will be quite happy if you just respond to that. I've finished my pot of vegetables, have you?'

'Just about.'

Despina scrambled to her feet. 'I'll call and tell Phaedra we've finished the vegetables.'

'What do we do then?'

'Phaedra will probably ask us to go for some more water for her cooking. We can go down a different way and you can see where the chickens are kept. When we come back I'll take you up to meet Manolis.'

I followed Despina closely as she began to make her way up the steep path. I thought we were going to reach the summit of the island, but then she began to go down again and there, penned behind some low wire were about twenty chickens. I stopped and looked at them, memories of my home and collecting eggs with my father brought tears to my eyes. If only Lucas had not gone away I could still be living in the village, happy with my husband and child.

'If you go further up,' Despina added, 'you see the bee hives. I keep away from those. One of the men here knows the flowers they like and is hoping they will multiply. He knows how to deal with them and extract the honey. When he has enough he takes the pots down to the grocer, where we got the barley, and he sells it in his shop. Sometimes Spiro asks for honey as it is soothing for open wounds.'

I nodded as if I was knowledgeable about such things. I had sometimes given Little Luke some honey on the end of my finger when he was fretful with the pain in his gums as his first teeth began to push through.

When we regained the path we were only a little further down from the steps to the hospital.

'We walked in a loop,' explained Despina. 'I wouldn't normally use that route, but I wanted to show you where the chickens were kept. When we've collected the water we'll return the quick way and then go up to Manolis.'

There were fewer people queueing for water and this time I dared to lift my eyes and look at my surroundings. There was a small road leading off to the right with a flight of steps leading to a higher level.

'What's up there?' I asked.

'Some houses have been built up there and they're also building some more. The ground is flat so it is easier to dig down for the footings. There's a magnificent view across the bay to Elounda. I'll take you up there the next time we come over and you can see for yourself. There's no time now or we'll lose our place in the queue and I expect Phaedra is waiting for the water.'

I was not that interested in looking at the view. 'What about that tunnel? Where does that lead?'

'There's a small beach where the generator is situated. A path leads up the hill to the graveyard and church.'

'I thought I saw a church by the steps where we climbed up to the hospital,' I frowned.

'You did, that's where Father Minos holds services on Sundays and Saints' Days. The other church is only used for a funeral service. The carpenter who makes wooden coffins or crosses lives in a house by the graveyard. He also makes beds, tables and chairs for the new arrivals who don't have anything except a sack of clothes with them.'

My clothes were the only possessions I had when I was taken to live with my aunt and uncle, but at least I had a roof over my head and a bed to sleep in. These people arrived with nothing and were totally dependent upon the good nature of the other inhabitants to provide them with somewhere to live and a chair to sit on.

Despina gave me a little nudge. 'Go on, you're next at the fountain. If you hang around someone else will push in front of you.'

I moved forward obediently and filled my container then stood to one side whilst Despina filled another. 'Right, we'll take these up and then go to see Manolis.'

We placed the containers just inside of the hospital door so they were in the shade and Despina called out to Phaedra that they were there for her. There was no answer, but as we turned to leave someone could be heard shuffling along to the doorway.

'Who collects the water when you are not here?' I asked Despina.

'I don't know. Spiro probably has an arrangement with one of the men to bring it up.'

We returned to the main path and Despina led the way further up before stopping behind a queue of people.

'Either Manolis arrived late this morning or everyone wants to give him an order. He's not usually this busy when I come up. If he has a bill for someone Flora goes to find them and they have to sign their name in the ledger to agree to the amount being deducted from their account.' Despina sat down on the grass. 'We might as well sit down whilst we wait.'

'Won't we lose our place in the queue?'

'At the moment we are last. When someone else arrives we'll tell them they are after us.'

The queue to Manolis moved slowly but we finally reached the table where he had a large ledger and a spike that held the bills that had been paid.

'Hello, Despina. I have your money here. You came three times last week as usual. Right?'

'Of course you're right, Manolis. This is Eirini. Doctor Stavros has agreed that she can be added to your ledger as a helper and paid accordingly.'

Deftly Manolis turned the ledger upside down and opened up the last page where there was a list of names. He added my name and then smiled at me.

'Another helper is always welcome. How often do you plan to come over?' he asked.

'I thought I could come three times a week, the same as Despina.'

'Fine. Make sure you come to me each time you come over so that I know you have been here when you come for your money.'

'I'll remember.'

'Can you sign your name?'

'Of course,' I answered indignantly.

'I have to ask as many cannot. Sign there to show that you are now an official helper.'

I signed my name with a flourish and I could see he was quite surprised with my penmanship.He turned over the page and then wrote my name at the top, inserted the date on the line below and placed a tick beside it.

'Provided you come again twice more this week I'll have thirty drachmas waiting for you next week.'

I nodded. It seemed a very easy way to earn money.

'Here you are, Despina.' From a bag he took thirty drachmas and handed it to her.

'Thank you, Manolis,' she said as she placed the money inside the pocket of her bodice.

'Aren't you worried that the money could be contaminated?' I asked as we walked away.

She shook her head. 'I told you, no money is allowed to leave the island if the lepers have handled it. Manolis collects money from the bank to pay the helpers so we know it is clean. If people on the island ask for some money he will deduct it from their account and bring it from the bank. They can only use it over here once he has given it to them.'

A young girl with only one arm arrived and went straight to Manolis's side. 'I've spoken to Yannis and he said he couldn't leave what he was doing at the moment. If you are still here in about an hour he'll sign for the cement delivery then. He also wants some more.'

'How much more?'

'He thought three sacks would be sufficient.'

'Remind him that he still needs to sign for the spade and trowel that I brought over last week and check exactly how many sacks of cement he wants at the same time. Tell him I'm packing up in about another half an hour and if he hasn't paid me by then I expect him to be my first customer tomorrow.'

'Do people often owe money for the goods they've had?' I asked quietly.

'Manolis has no problem with the money from Yannis. He's allowed a certain amount from the government for rebuilding expenses, but Yannis still needs to sign for the items so the money can be taken from the account. If he overspends one week he will have less money to buy materials the next week and if that continued for any length of time the allocation would be used up and the building work would have to stop. Manolis keeps a strict eye on the account and tries to stop Yannis from overspending. Manolis knows no one is going to run away so he can use his discretion and allow some of the residents to run up small debts. Come with me and we'll see if the boat is returning yet. If they've found a good fishing ground they could be quite late coming back, but if their catch has been poor they'll be happy to return to the shore early. They won't want to hang around waiting for us.'

'Suppose they arrive and you haven't seen them?'

'They'll sound their hooter when they tie up. If you hear that you make your way down to the jetty as quickly as possible. Don't forget you have to disinfect before you leave so you can't just run down and jump aboard.'

'I didn't see the men disinfect when we arrived.'

Despina wrinkled her nose. 'They say there is no need as they are dealing with building materials and the rubbish. Make sure you sit well away from them when we return as they will have placed the sacks on the boat and they can be pretty smelly. Once they've transferred them to the rubbish cart they'll go back to the boat and be hosed down. That's considered necessary to stop them from bringing any germs back with them. The Captain then hoses the boat down to ensure it is clean ready for the next day.'

I immediately made sure I would sit nowhere near the men or the rubbish and I would certainly not tell my aunt and uncle or they might forbid me to go to the island again. Although I was sitting well away from the rubbish sacks there were buckets of fish stored beneath the wooden seats and the water slopped over the sides due to the movement of the boat. I kept lifting my feet so that the sea water did not run onto my boots. I would not want to smell of fish when I returned home.

As soon as I entered the house my aunt accosted me. 'Did you get paid?' she asked.

I shook my head. 'I get paid one week in arrears. I'll not have any money until I have visited twice more this week. I'll be paid when I go over next week. I'll have a wash and then I must see Little Luke. Where is he? He probably wonders where his Mamma has been all day.'

'He's asleep at the moment. I put him on your bed. That cradle really is getting too small for him now.'

'I will buy him his own bed as soon as I have earned sufficient money,' I assured her. A bed would take priority over a pair of boots or he would end up with deformed legs where he had to curl them up to fit the cradle.

'You should make him a pallet. A child doesn't need a bed.'

I considered my aunt's words. It was true. None of the village children had ever slept in a bed any more than I had until I came to Elounda. The only reason I had a bed now was because it had belonged to my grandmother.

'I can certainly make him a pallet. Would you help thread up the loom for me so I can weave some cloth, please?'

'You should know how to do that for yourself by now,' she replied acidly. 'You should have sat and paid attention instead of wandering out each day for a walk by the sea. What is it like - over there?'

I considered my answer. 'It's really no different from here or Fourni. There is a village where most of the people live and they have shops along the main road.'

'Shops? What kind of shops?'

'I didn't look in every one, but Despina says they have a barber, a seamstress and also some tavernas over there.'

'Where do they get their goods from?'

'Apparently many of the people grow vegetables and they are sold in the shops.'

'What about the people? What did they look like?'

I remembered the man who had given me the figs. I was certainly not going to describe his features to her.

'I saw very few of them. Despina and I collected some water and then sat outside the hospital and prepared vegetables. She introduced me to Doctor Stavros when he arrived and I realised that he is the same doctor as visits this village.'

My aunt looked at me in horror. 'You mean he visits the lepers and then comes into our clean houses, bringing their germs with him?'

'I'm sure he is very careful not to take anything contagious away from the island. He would not want to become infected. When we arrive we have to go through a disinfection room before we are allowed to go up to the village and we have to do the same again before we get on the boat to come back. I expect he has to do the same.' I did not mention the men who dealt with the rubbish. 'Later Despina took me to meet Manolis so my name could be added to the list of workers and that will mean I can get paid.'

The next day I carried Luke down to the local shops with me and bought some suitable cotton to weave into the cover of a pallet for him. Despite her grumbling, my aunt showed me how to set up the warp and the weft and ensure that the tension was correct.

'You'll not get that finished today,' she observed. 'If you're off to that island again tomorrow I'll do a bit for you, provided Luke doesn't need attention all the time.'

'I'd be very grateful,' I replied honestly. I was slow and clumsy compared with my aunt when she worked on the loom. 'There is one thing that is worrying me.'

She raised her eyebrows and I continued. 'If Luke is sleeping on a pallet on the floor there is nothing to stop him from rolling off.'

'You'll have to make some side pads. Get the pallet made first and we can tackle those later.'

I did not enjoy sitting at the loom weaving and insisted that I took a break in the afternoon so that I could take Luke out for some fresh air. I was quite pleased to know that I would be going over to Spinalonga the following day and could leave the work to my aunt. Whilst we were out I walked to the end of the village and looked at the grass that was growing there. It would take a considerable amount to stuff the pallet so that it was soft and comfortable and I knew that it would have to be renewed on a regular basis. I had never considered before how time consuming it was to look after a small child properly.

I met Despina and she paid my fare to the island as she had promised. I was not so nervous this time as we drew away from the shore. The men disembarked first and we made our way to the disinfection room before walking up to the main road.

'We'll go up to the hospital first,' she announced. 'Spiro is bound to need something or we can sit and make a start on the vegetables. When Manolis arrives we'll go up and let him see we are here again and we could walk back round the island and return through the tunnel to the square if there is sufficient time.'

I was not sure if I wanted to walk around the island and back through the tunnel that looked grim and forbidding, but I also felt I must do whatever Despina suggested. As we reached the steps leading up to the hospital a priest emerged from the church.

'Good morning, ladies. I know you, Despina, but who is your companion?'

'This is Eirini. She has joined me as a helper over here.'

'I am happy to welcome you,' the priest beamed. 'I am Father Minos. You are welcome to enter the church at any time if you wish to say a private prayer.'

'Thank you, Father,' I managed to say, but I had no intention of entering the establishment. There were more than enough prayers said by my aunt and uncle.

'Are you on your way up to the hospital?' he asked and Despina nodded. 'Then I will accompany you. Spiro sent a message to me a little earlier to say my presence there would be appreciated.'

'No doubt you will have a sad duty to perform,' said Despina and crossed herself. I followed suit.

Father Minos sighed. 'It is sad that people have to suffer so much before they pass on and reach Heaven. Once I have confessed them and given them the last rites so they can pass on peacefully I can only feel a degree of happiness that their suffering on earth has ended.'

As we climbed the steps I thought about his words. I had been sad to hear about the death of my grandmother, but I had not thought that dying would be a blessing for her and a release from her illness.

Father Minos entered the hospital immediately and there was no sign of Spiro. Outside were two empty containers and Despina handed one to me. 'We'll collect the water. We may have to go back again for more as the deceased will need to be washed.'

I gave a shudder. I would not want to have the task of washing a dead body.

'What happens after that?' I asked as we retraced our steps down the hill.

'The funeral will be held tomorrow in the church on the other side of the island. If the person had sufficient money to pay for a coffin that will be placed in the graveyard with a wooden cross at the head. If they died penniless they will be placed in the tower.'

'The tower?'

'I prefer to call it that rather than the charnel house. There are many bodies in there of the people who died earlier on the island, before the doctor or Father Minos arrived.'

'Do they stay there for ever?'

'There is nowhere else for them. When the Turks were here they used the land a short distance away for their burials as there was sufficient earth to dig a grave. There is very little suitable land available and none of them would want to be placed in the Turkish graveyard.'

I thought of the churchyard in Elounda where I had gone to pay my respects to my grandmother. There were large, ornate sarcophagi around with the names engraved on the top or sides of those who were interred.

'Why don't they have a sarcophagus?' I asked. 'Then they would not need to dig into the ground.'

'Who is going to pay for that? They have no family. Besides, a sarcophagus would take up more space than a grave. It is more important to have houses for the living than grand memorials to those who are dead.'

As we passed the baker I sniffed the air hungrily. 'That smells good,' I commented.

'Freshly baked. Would you like some?'

I hesitated. Was it wise to eat any food that was prepared over here?

Despina had already stopped and signalled to the baker that we would each like a roll. She took four lepta from inside her bodice and placed it on the counter. The baker pulled two freshly baked rolls from the oven and offered them to us on his metal skillet. Still I hesitated.

'It's quite safe,' Despina assured me. 'They have come straight out of the oven so any germs will have been killed by the heat.'

My reluctance left me and I took the fresh roll, holding it in my apron so I would not burn my fingers.

We stood in the queue for the water fountain, munching happily on our rolls. Mine was as good as any roll I had ever tasted.

'Where does he get his flour from?'

'It's brought over by one of the other boats from Elounda or Plaka. They don't use the one we come and go in as it is used mainly to bring over cement and tools and then take back the rubbish.'

'And the fish,' I added.

'The fish are no problem as the scales are always scraped off before it is cooked so it is clean enough. Do you want to go up the steps and see where the men have built the new houses? They're just finishing off the remaining three. I'll keep your place in the queue and you can leave your container with me.'

I admit I was curious and I hurried up the steps, hoping no one would ask my business, and looked at the hive of activity that was taking place. In one area there were men working; some mixing cement ready for those who were rendering the walls, whilst doors and windows were being fitted in place. One man appeared to be directing the operations and checking on the work as it was being done.

It resembled a small private area, a collection of houses was arranged just inside the walls of the old Venetian fortress. There was a small grassed area and I thought it would be a very attractive place to live rather than being crammed together in the old Turkish houses that had been repaired. Not wanting to be noticed I began to descend the steps carefully as they were uneven in height. I had not noticed this on the way up and wondered how many unwary people had fallen when going down to the main square.

There was only one woman in front of us when I returned to the queue and Despina was chatting happily with her. The woman moved forward to fill her jug and Despina turned to me.

'How is the work progressing?' she asked.

'I don't know, but everyone seemed to be very busy.'

'When someone new arrives they are given shelter in a house along with others. They are told that if they want a house to call their own they have to join the work force and help to build it.'

'Suppose they refuse?'

'Then they will have to remain in a shared house. Once the original occupants begin to object they are moved on somewhere else. Sooner or later they agree to help with building. If they are physically unable to help then a house is made ready for them.'

'So everyone has a house and lives alone.'

'Some of them arrive as a married couple and others live together from choice after a while. These people are no different from anyone else and some have formed bonds as strong and binding as wedding vows. Where do you think the children come from?'

'I didn't think you were allowed to get married if you were a leper.'

'Officially you're not, but how do you keep the men and women apart over here? There's no reason why they shouldn't live together and Father Minos is always willing to give them his blessing.'

'What does the government say about that?'

Despina shrugged. 'Who is going to tell them? The doctor does not approve, of course, but he cannot prevent the people from living together and children being born.'

I thought this information over. I could not envisage any woman wanting to be married to one of the badly disfigured, sick men and having his child.

Having been requested to take three more containers of water up to the hospital, prepared some of the vegetables and visited Manolis, Despina declared that there was insufficient time to walk around the other side of the island that day. I was not sorry. The containers were heavy once they were filled with water and I found climbing back up to the hospital carrying them was exhausting. I was not sure I wanted to see a graveyard and the charnel house that she called the tower anyway.

Even with my aunt's help it took me some time to complete the pallet for Luke. I collected fresh grass every day and would lay it out to dry in the sun. I was about to start to stuff the pallet when my aunt stopped me.

'It will be more sensible if you make the side pads first. If you stuff the pallet now by the time you begin to use it the grass will need to be renewed.'

She re-threaded the loom and instructed me to make three pieces of cloth as large as the one I had woven originally. She did not tell me how these were to be used, but I worked assiduously until all three were completed. One piece she cut in half and told me to sew the side seam firmly. Having completed this to her satisfaction she then folded the cloth in half and told me I must now make a seam down the centre.

Still uncomprehending I followed her instructions. It was then that she explained.

'One side will be left flat and tucked beneath the head of the pallet. The other side will be stuffed with grass and that will protect his head should he wriggle up. When you have done the same with the other piece it can be stuffed with rags to stop him from rolling off the bottom.'

I understood now and went about the task willingly. I then had to repeat the process on the long lengths of cloth so they could be placed at the sides of the pallet and the flat pieces tucked firmly underneath. I had to admit that I would not have thought of this ingenious idea myself. I hoped that when he was strong enough to crawl he would not discover a way to climb over the sides, although I would make sure my door was closed at night so he would be unable to go very far.

Meeting

I continued to go over to Spinalonga three days each week and began to become familiar with the island and the occupants. It was no longer a place to be feared. I would hold a conversation with someone, without stammering my excuses and hurrying away. I no longer felt so dependent upon Despina. She had walked with me around the island and shown me the Turkish graveyard, the church where the funerals were held and the current graveyard. I had no wish to go over to the tower where some of the deceased were placed.

She explained that the large piece of machinery down by a small beach was the electric generator. It sent off a humming noise that sounded like a bee continually hovering nearby. There were two men working down by it and she said they checked regularly to see that all was in working order.

'What would happen if it broke down?' I asked.

'No one would have any electricity,' she replied.

That was obvious and not the answer I wanted to my question. Would the contraption explode or start a fire? I would have to ask my father the next time he and my mother came to Elounda to see me.

I had no hesitation now about visiting the shops and I would stand alone in the queue for the water whilst Despina called on housebound villagers and tended to their requests.

It was whilst I was waiting my turn at the water fountain that I met Fotini. She had a happy smile on her face that made me smile back at her.

'Are you living here?' she asked.

I shook my head. 'I come over as a helper three days a week. Are you a helper?'

She looked at me as if I had said something incredulous and threw back her head and laughed. 'I have leprosy, the same as everyone else over here.'

There was not a blemish on her face and her hands were slim with each finger straight.

She saw me looking at her and continued. 'I'm fortunate. So far I have not developed any nodules on my face, but I expect they will come eventually. My poor husband has lost his looks. One side of his face is as handsome as ever and the other is disfigured.'

'How sad.'

Fotini shrugged. 'It doesn't matter how he looks. He is the kindest and best husband in the world. and he dotes on our little girl.'

'You have a little girl? How old is she?'

'Near enough two years,' she smiled.

'I have a little boy, he's not even one year yet.'

'Have you brought him with you?'

'No, my aunt looks after him on the days when I come here.'

'Where does your husband work?'

My face flamed. 'I don't have a husband.'

'Oh, I'm sorry.' Fotini was immediately contrite. 'I didn't realise you were a widow.'

'I'm not. The man I loved deserted me when I was pregnant.' This was the first time I had admitted this to anyone, even myself. Tears came into my eyes and I rubbed them away with my hand.

'I didn't mean to upset you.'

'I know it was unintentional,' I sniffed

'Come up to my house until you feel more composed. You can sit outside if you prefer.'

I hesitated. This was the first time someone had shown me any sympathy and I wanted to sit and cry and blurt out the whole sad story.

'I'm supposed to be getting some water for Spiro.'

'If he needs it urgently someone else will collect it. I bought some peaches from the shop on my way here. Come and have one.'

'I shouldn't eat your food.'

'I bought three. That will be one each. Vivi can have a little from each of us. A whole one would not be good for her.'

My resistance left me. 'Where do you live?'

'Up there.' She pointed to the steps that led up by the fortress wall. 'When I arrived there was a small house nearly finished and I moved into that. The neighbours were kind and welcoming and Aristo was living only three houses away. When we were married I was able to move my possessions into his house as it was larger than mine.' Fotini mounted the steps easily and I followed more cautiously.

'So your original house is empty now?'

'Goodness, no. Christos was only too pleased to move in immediately. He and Aristo have become good friends. I'm glad we live up here rather than down amongst the other villagers. We are all younger and fitter than they are. We mix with everyone, of course, but we tend to gather together in the evenings for a drink and a chat.'

'My aunt and uncle don't mix with their neighbours except on very special occasions.'

'No, my parents didn't. My father was a tax collector so he was not popular. Here we are.'

Fotini stopped outside of a small house that had a blue painted door and a blue curtain at the window. Compared with many of the other houses on the island it looked remarkably well cared for.

'Would you like to look inside? Aristo painted the walls and then painted a blue frieze around them.' Fotini opened the door where a man was sitting with a small girl on his lap. 'Has she been good?' asked Fotini.

'Of course. I told her you had gone down to the village and if she was good you would bring her back a treat.'

'That's bribery,' smiled Fotini. 'I've brought Eirini back with me. She's a helper and I thought she would like to see how beautiful you have made our house. I've also brought some peaches and we can sit outside and eat them. I'll just get a knife and a plate. Vivi will need to have some small pieces cut up for her.'

I stood and watched the happy scene. This was how I envisaged Lucas and I would have lived, except we had a little boy.

'Your little girl is quite beautiful.' I said honestly.

'I am told that she looks like me when I was small,' smiled Fotini. 'My sister and her husband visit me occasionally. Yiorgo has a camera and he takes a photo of Vivi every time he comes so he can show my mother.'

77

'What about your father? He must be proud of her.'

Fotini shook her head sadly. 'My father will have nothing to do with us. Why do you live with your aunt and uncle? Do you not have parents?'

'My parents sent me to live with my aunt and uncle when I became pregnant. They thought it would be better for me to live where I had no memories.' The tears came into my eyes again.

'Do you see them?'

'They visit regularly and they love Little Luke.'

'Where do they live?'

'In Fourni.'

'Fourni,' exclaimed Fotini. 'That is close to Kastelli where I lived.'

'I've never been there. Lucas said he would take me there and I said I would bring him to Elounda as he had never seen the sea.'

'How sad. Have you no idea where he is now?'

I shook my head. 'He told his family he was going to Aghios Nikolaos for work. They may have heard from him by now but I certainly have not.'

Fotini raised her eyebrows and looked at her husband. He shook his head.

'Maybe later.'

I felt I had outstayed my welcome.

'I ought to go. I hope Spiro has not been waiting for the water. I'll fill the container and take it up to him and then I must let Manolis know that I'm here.'

'When will you be here again?' asked Aristo.

'Next week,' I answered, wishing I could come over again before then. I felt these people were my friends.

'You must come and join us again. It is refreshing to meet someone from the mainland.'

'I would like that,' I replied sincerely. 'I only meet people in Elounda when I go shopping or when I take Luke for a walk. They always seem far too busy to stop and chat.'

'You must bring your little boy over at some time.'

I shook my head. 'I'm sure my aunt and uncle would not allow me to do that. It was only because Father Phillipos spoke to my aunt and uncle that they finally agreed that I could come over here.'

'We are allowed to have visitors,' Fotini reminded me. 'My sister and her husband come.'

'I'll see.' I did not want to refuse outright and possibly offend them, but I could not see my aunt allowing me to bring Luke over here with me. I rose to my feet. 'Thank you for my peach. I really enjoyed it and by the look of Vivi she did also,' I smiled.

'Oh, what a mess you have made of yourself,' exclaimed Fotini. 'I'll take you inside for a wash and clean dress before the wasps get the scent and come to bother us.' She scooped Vivi up in her arms and headed towards the house as I made my way cautiously back down the steps to the water fountain.

I returned to the hospital with the container of water and Despina looked at me curiously. 'Where have you been?'

'I met Fotini and she asked me to go up to her house and meet her husband and daughter. I sat there chatting with them for a while,' I added, feeling guilty.

'Nice people,' commented Despina.

'They've asked me to visit them again the next time I come over.'

'The people living over here love to sit and chat with someone new. That can be as helpful to them as fetching their water. They feel they are accepted and it often means they have some snippet of information that can be passed on to their neighbours later.'

'I'll have to listen out for any local news or events that I can tell them about, although nothing seems to happen in Elounda.'

After my departure Fotini and Aristo sat and discussed me and my situation, although I did not know this at the time. When I arrived the following week I went up to the hospital with Despina as usual, collected water and sat and prepared vegetables. I realised I would far rather be spending my time talking to Fotini and Aristo, but I was not on the island for pleasure.

I walked up to where Manolis was sitting outside Flora's house so he could record that I had been to Spinalonga that day. I knew I would not be paid until the end of the week and had taken twenty lepta from my savings. It should be more than enough for a bunch of grapes, but they could cost more on Spinalonga than those on sale in Elounda. As I walked back past the village shops I bought a bunch. I hope that this would show Fotini and Aristo that I had appreciated sharing the peaches with them the previous week.

As I mounted the steps I felt apprehensive. Maybe they were only being polite asking me to visit again and would not be pleased to see me a second time. If they did not answer when I knocked their door I would return to the hospital and ask Spiro if there was anything more I could help with that day.

As I reached the top step I could see Aristo sitting outside the house and I took that as a sign that I was expected. I approached along the dirt path that led to the houses, but Aristo did not look up to greet me. I felt a cold fear grip my heart. Had something terrible happened to Fotini or little Vivi?

'Aristo,' I said when I was nearly upon him, 'Is everything alright?'

He looked up and then I could see that he was not Aristo.

'Lucas!' I could hardly breathe his name and my legs would no longer hold me. I sat down on the path and looked at him again to make certain that I was not mistaken.

'Lucas, is it really you?'

He nodded. 'Come and sit closer to me so we can talk.'

Somehow I regained the use of my legs and walked to where he was sitting. I sat a short distance away, although I would have liked to throw myself into his arms and cover him with kisses.

'I am so sorry, Eirini. Once I knew I was sick I also knew that marriage between us was impossible. I thought it better to leave immediately so you could find another suitor.'

His words did not penetrate my numb brain. 'What are you doing here? Are you a helper?'

'I live here,' he answered quietly.

'You live here? You mean you - you're a...' my voice tailed off.

Lucas gave a deep sigh. 'I have leprosy.'

'Why didn't you tell me? I would have come here with you.'

Lucas shook his head. 'That would not have been possible unless you had contracted the disease also. I prayed that I had not infected you. You're not sick are you, Eirini?'

I shook my head. Tears were running down my face - I was not sure if they were tears of joy or sorrow.

'I asked to become a helper. I hoped I would be able to find your uncle and he could tell me of any relatives that you had in Aghios Nikolaos. I would then go there and ask if any of them had any news of you.'

'I have no relatives in Aghios. When my sickness was confirmed I told no one, not even my mother. My uncle had been sent here years ago and it had taken a long time for the family to be accepted again by the villagers. I did not want to bring more shame on my family. To have had a second member with the same disease would have meant they were shunned again by the community and probably had to move elsewhere.'

'How is your uncle?'

'His days are numbered. He is in the hospital being cared for by Spiro. I spend some time each day up there with him, but I do not think he is always aware of my presence.'

I did not know what to say. Poor Lucas being diagnosed as an incurable and having no one to turn to for help or support; and now watching his uncle die from the disease knowing the same fate awaited him. I dried my eyes on my apron, completely forgetting that I had some grapes in there. They tumbled out onto the grass.

'I bought these for Fotini and Aristo. I ate their peaches last week.'

'I know. When I came home later from the hospital they

asked me if I knew a girl called Eirini who had lived in Fourni. I could not believe it and bombarded them with questions, but they declared they did not know the answers. Tell me, Eirini, why are you living in Elounda with your aunt and uncle now?'

I sat and told Lucas how distraught I had been when he had left Fourni and that my mother put it about the village that I had been raped.

'Because you had left so abruptly and no one knew where you were it was assumed that you were the culprit. I tried to tell my parents that you were no more guilty than I was and that we had wanted to get married. I hardly ate or slept, I spent all my time crying, until finally my parents decided that I needed a change of scenery where I had no memories of you. That is why I am in Elounda. There is no work available there, but Despina told me I could earn ten drachmas each time I came here as a helper.'

'If you are living with your aunt and uncle why do you need money? Surely they feed you and your parents should provide you with a small amount to cover any new clothes that you need.'

'My parents pay my aunt and uncle for my keep, but I cannot expect them to buy boots and clothes for Little Luke.'

Lucas stared at me. 'Little Luke?'

I nodded. 'Your little boy, Lucas.'

'I have a son?' Lucas spoke disbelievingly. 'Had I known I was ill I would never have risked making you pregnant.'

'I'm pleased you did. He's a beautiful, delightful little boy, nearly a year old now.'

'So where is he?' Lucas looked around.

'My aunt looks after him three days each week so I can come here. She adores him and I know he is in safe hands with her.'

'And your parents?'

'They visit me every few weeks. The next time they come I will ask after your parents and I can give you any news of them.'

Lucas frowned. 'I would not want them to know I was over here and tell my parents.'

'Don't worry. I will ask after my friend Anastasia and ask if you have returned from Aghios Nikolaos. I can then ask after your brother and your parents. I will not tell anyone that you are living here.'

'Tell me more about my little boy. Is he healthy?'

'Completely.'

Lucas let out a sigh of relief. 'I feel guilty that I made you pregnant and caused you so much suffering. It would be even worse if I had given you a tainted or maimed child.'

'Little Luke is an absolute joy. Every day I have wished that you were there to see the pleasure he gives to me. When I saw Fotini and Aristo with their little girl I felt quite resentful. We should have been a family like them. When I first came to Elounda I looked everywhere I could think of for you, hoping that when you saw me again you would still want to marry me and Little Luke would get to know his father.' I reached over and placed my hand on Lucas's.

He looked at me and then withdrew his hand. 'I don't think you should touch me, Eirini.'

'I want to touch you. I love you, Lucas. I want to be held in your arms again and feel safe and happy.'

Lucas shook his head and an awful doubt entered my mind.

'Have you found someone over here that you have decided you prefer?' I dreaded the answer.

'No, I have not looked at any other woman. I just feel we should be very careful as I would not want to infect you.'

I considered his words. 'If I did become infected I would be able to come over here and live with you.'

'Much as I would love to have you here I would not want to watch you being ravaged by the disease. You have seen the men and women who live on the island; many of them are not a pretty sight due to their facial growths. That is nothing, we accept each other, but when it affects your limbs so you are unable to do anything except sit all day and wait to die, in pain, miserable and often lonely. That is a living death and I would not want to condemn you to that fate.'

I touched Lucas's hand again and this time he did not withdraw it. 'I would willingly take my chance if it meant I could be with you. Not everyone is disfigured. I often do not know if a person is sick or if they are on the island as a helper. '

'It affects different people in different ways. Some succumb to the physical disabilities quickly, but remain facially unscathed.'

'You are as handsome as ever,' I assured him.

Lucas shrugged. 'Maybe now, but who knows how I will look in a year or even five years time? Only my arm is infected at present, but it could spread at any time.'

'Have you asked the doctor?'

'He cannot give an answer. He brings us medicine that is said to help alleviate the disease. Not everyone takes the capsules as they make you nauseous. Why add that to your problems?'

I do not know how long we sat there. I tried to convince Lucas that I would willingly become diseased if it would allow me to live there with him. It was not until I heard the boat sound the hooter that I realised that I must leave.

'I'll be back in two days,' I promised. 'I'll look for you again up here a soon as I have completed some tasks for Spiro.'

Lucas nodded and squeezed my hand before he released it. 'I love you, Eirini,' he declared.

'Where have you been?' asked Despina when I rushed back to the jetty and boarded the boat. 'We were almost ready to go without you.'

'I was talking to one of the people who live here and the time passed more quickly than I realised.'

I sat in the boat as if in a dream. A surge of hope rose in me. If I missed the boat taking me back to the mainland I would have to stay on the island with Lucas; then I thought of Little Luke. I could not desert him.

Once home I hugged Little Luke to me. 'I've found your Pappa,' I whispered and he smiled at me as if he understood.

That night I could not sleep. I kept trying to think of a way I could take Little Luke over to meet his father and also how we would be able to join Lucas on Spinalonga permanently. Father Minos was allowed to live there and he was free of disease, Manolis was on the island every day and I knew he had a relationship with Flora. Doctor Stavros visited regularly and examined the patients without suffering any ill effects and Despina and many others had been visiting and mixing with the inhabitants for over a year. There should be no reason why I could not live over there.

I could not wait to visit Spinalonga again and the time seemed to drag interminably whilst I tended to Luke, helped my aunt and visited the shop for her. When I was there I realised I should have asked Lucas if there was anything he wanted me to take over from the village for him. I made a mental note to ask him the following day. I was beginning to have so many questions for him and I turned the problem of living on the island permanently over and over in my mind. I could not claim to be sick as the doctor would take tests. He might also think I was being neurotic about visiting the island, scared that I would become infected, and he might withdraw permission for me to go over there.

I was the first person waiting for the boat the next morning, arriving before Despina or the men, and waited impatiently for them to arrive.

'You're early,' commented Despina.

Usually I was the last to arrive, rushing to the boat at the last minute having spent as long as possible with Luke and settling him with my aunt.

'I was up early and there was no reason to hang around at my aunt's.'

'You look tired,' remarked Despina. 'Did your little boy give you a disturbed night?'

I was about to say that Luke always slept throughout the night, but then thought that could be an excuse for looking tired, having spent half the night awake considering schemes to enable me to live on Spinalonga.

'He may be cutting another tooth.' It was not an outright lie as he still had a number that needed to come through.

'That always makes them miserable. I remember when my little brothers were teething. My mother would walk the floor with them but still they cried and grizzled until the tooth had broken the gum.'

I nodded in agreement and Despina continued. 'It must be difficult trying to keep him quiet so he doesn't disturb your aunt and uncle in the night.'

'We do have our own little room and I can shut the door. If he is really fretful I take him into bed with me. That seems to comfort him.'

I kept my eyes riveted on Spinalonga, willing us to arrive quickly. I hurried through the disinfection process and then waited in a frenzy of impatience as Despina stopped to talk to a woman who had called out to her as we passed.

'She would like some water,' explained Despina. 'She knocked her jug over. Do you want to fetch it or go on up to the hospital?'

'I'll go up to Spiro,' I replied. I wanted to fulfil any requests Spiro might have, prepare the vegetables as quickly as possible and let Manolis know I was on the island. I could then meet Lucas with a clear conscience.

Lucas was waiting for me and I sat down beside him, placing my hand on his.

'Tell me how you spend your time over here. Aren't you bored and lonely?'

Lucas smiled. 'There is always more than enough to do. Before my uncle became so sick I worked with the other able bodied men helping to repair a house or aid in the construction of a new one. When my uncle had to enter the hospital I decided I would be more use helping Spiro. Many of the patients have to be lifted from their mattresses. The women cannot manage that, they do not have the strength.'

'How is your uncle?'

Lucas shrugged. 'He seems no worse. I told Spiro that I wanted to have some time to myself at my house this afternoon, but if he was concerned he should send for me immediately.'

'Will you continue to work up at the hospital after - after - your uncle.....' My voice tailed off. I was embarrassed that I had asked such a question.

'If Spiro has need of me I will go to help, but I also help with the bees and I am learning to read and write properly.'

I looked at him in surprise. It had never occurred to me that Lucas had received little effective schooling.

'But you attended my father's school in Kastelli.'

Lucas smiled. 'As it suited me. I would turn up in the winter months when it was warm and dry inside but in the summer I preferred to be outside working in the fields. Whatever I had learned in the winter I forgot in the summer.'

'So is there a school over here?'

'Yannis holds classes for anyone who is interested. Once the people began to receive their pensions they had to sign for it in Manolis's ledger. Many of them could only put a cross beside their name. He taught his wife how to write her name and she suggested that he showed some of the others. When the weather is bad we sit inside one of the tavernas and a glass of wine certainly helps my concentration.'

I looked at him in surprise. 'You have some tavernas with wine available?'

'We are no different from any village on the mainland. When the people first received their pensions they had to decide how to spend the money. We are allowed to order goods from the mainland shops and two men decided they would open tavernas. We pay them for a glass of wine and they spend the money in the shops that some of the others have opened or buy more wine to keep us happy. Sometimes I will spend an evening down there playing backgammon, dominoes or cards.'

'So you are not lonely?'

Lucas shook his head. 'I am not lonely for companions, but I am heart sick. I should be in Fourni, married to you and enjoying our little boy.'

'So let me come here to live with you,' I pleaded. 'You must have been infected when we spent time together in Fourni. You do not become sick overnight. I did not become ill and we have a healthy child.'

'Lepers are not allowed to marry.'

'I thought Yannis was married to Phaedra, and Fotini and Aristo are married.'

'They are fellow sufferers, but even then it is against the law. Doctor Stavros does not approve, but Father Minos will give a couple a blessing. Everyone is allowed visitors now, but no one is permitted to stay on the island overnight. The only way you could live here would be if you were declared an incurable by Doctor Stavros. I cannot wish such a fate on you.'

'If you can have visitors why do you not send a message to your parents so they could visit you here? I'm sure they would be overjoyed to see you again.'

'And how long would it be before the village knew I was here? It is better to leave things as they are and not risk my parents being ostracized.'

'If you can now write why don't you send them a letter? You do not have to say you are here.'

'I would soon be traced. I would have to ask Manolis or one of the boatmen to take the letter to the mainland and then ask one of the farmers to take it to Fourni. Whoever delivered it would say how they had come by it. I am not prepared to take the chance.'

Nothing I could say would make Lucas change his mind and

he made me swear that I would not disclose his whereabouts to my parents or anyone else.

With each of my visits we became a little bolder with each other. We now held hands, rather than just touching them together. As the afternoon wore on we would move over to the perimeter wall of the Venetian fortress so we could see when the boat that would take me back to the mainland was approaching. I no longer had to rush down the perilous steps and through the disinfectant when they sounded their hooter.

One afternoon as we walked across the grass to the Venetian fortress wall I stumbled and Lucas placed his arm around me. My whole body tingled at his touch. I looked up at him and he bent his head as if to kiss me, then pulled away abruptly.

'You must not miss the boat, Eirini.'

'I'll be back next week,' I promised. 'My parents are visiting this weekend and I will ask if there is any news of your whereabouts and how your parents are keeping.'

'Be discreet,' Lucas warned me.

My parents greeted me and as usual they admired Little Luke. My father pressed a few lepta into my hand and I accepted gratefully, although I now had the money I earned on the island safely hidden away. That was for Luke, the few lepta my father gave me were for me to spend on myself if there was anything I wanted.

I asked after Anastasia and my mother said she and Elias were expecting their first child and how happy both sets of prospective grandparents were. It hurt me to hear this. Lucas and I should have married and then my parents and his would have been happy and welcoming when Little Luke was born. She told me more of the village events, but I was hardly listening.

Finally I asked, trying to sound casual, if Lucas had returned to Fourni.

My mother shook her head. 'Not as far as I am aware. No one has heard anything from him since he left.'

'Not even his parents or brother?'

'No,' answered my mother shortly.

'How sad for them. Are they all keeping well?'

'I believe so. I see them occasionally when I go shopping.'

I did not pursue my questions further. I could at least tell Lucas that his family were all well.

Whilst I tended to Little Luke I could hear my father and uncle talking quietly together.

I heard my uncle say 'I'll think about it, but I don't think it's a practical idea for people of our ages. It's something for the young and adventurous. The journey would take weeks. It could be hazardous and what about the cost? Have you considered that?'

'I would find out all the details before I made a decision. I read about it in the newspaper and it sounded attractive. At the moment it is only an idea.'

I would have loved to ask my father for details of his idea and the journey that would take time and could be dangerous. As I entered the room they stopped speaking and I joined my aunt and my mother in the scullery and began to help them with the meal they were preparing.

I thought of Lucas constantly and desperately wanted to take Little Luke over to Spinalonga to meet his father. I would have to tell my aunt where I was taking him and I was certain that she would forbid me to do any such thing. I began to chatter to her after my visits to the island about Fotini and Aristo.

'I have made a very good friend on the island,' I said.

'A friend? How can you have a friend who is a leper?' she asked.

'You would not know that she and her husband were afflicted.' I did not mention that Aristo had growths and nodules on one side of his face. 'Fotini used to live in Kastelli and we talk about our villages.'

'You are not allowed to marry if you are leprous,' declared my aunt.

'I believe they were married before they went to the island.' I lied blatantly to my aunt.

'That just proves how infectious the disease is. One of them probably infected the other.'

I ignored her remark and continued. 'They have the most beautiful little girl. Whilst we talk I sit and play with her.'

'You play with her?'

I nodded. 'The doctor has declared that she is free of infection.'

My aunt pursed her lips and shook her head doubtfully. 'I don't think it wise that you should touch her.'

'I don't, although I am sure there would be no problem. I make daisy chains for her and she wears them as a necklace whilst I am there. Her aunt and uncle visit regularly. Her uncle has a camera and he takes photographs of her to take back to show her grandparents. I am waiting to hear when they are visiting next and then I plan to take Luke over with me so he can have a photograph taken. I would like one to remind me of how he was as a baby.'

I had said it, I had sown the seed and although I was not sure how I would explain the non-existence of a photograph, I felt it was a plausible reason for taking Luke over there with me. I did not mention my plan to Lucas. I wanted the visit from his son to be a surprise for him and I also did not want him to forbid me to take him over. I did not know when I would get another opportunity.

My aunt shook her head. 'I don't approve. Apart from the risk of him picking up an infection you will have to take him over there in the boat. Suppose he fell overboard?'

'I will make sure it is a calm day and hold him tightly all the time.'

I told Despina that I planned to take my little boy over to visit Fotini and Aristo and their daughter. 'Of course, I will be unable to do any work that day as I will be looking after him so I will not expect to be paid.'

'Just don't ask Manolis to record your visit. You may have to pay the boatmen extra for taking your boy over.'

'I hope not, but I will make sure I have some extra money with me.'

I could hardly wait. I dressed Little Luke carefully, packed a clean blouse for him and some extra cloths so I could change those that he soiled before I took him to meet Lucas. I did not want to introduce him to a wet and smelly baby.

The boatman took my sack from me and looked surprised. 'Are you staying over on Spinalonga?'

'Oh, no,' I replied. 'I have to take my little boy with me today as there is no one available to look after him. I have some clean clothes in there for him. We will be coming back with you as usual.'

Luke looked around as we left the shore, but he was certainly not frightened by the motion of the boat and sat quietly on my lap. I hurried through the infection room and carried him carefully up the steps to where I met Lucas. There was no sign of him. I was overcome by a feeling of dread. Was he ill? In the hospital maybe?

I went over to Fotini's house and knocked her door. She looked surprised to see me.

'You're early today. We were not expecting to see you until you had completed your work.'

'Do you know where Lucas is?' I asked.

'I believe he said he was going up to help Papylos collect some honey.'

I had no idea how long Lucas would be up there and I did not want to make the stiff climb carrying Luke.

Fotini saw my despondent look. 'Why don't you stay here and I'll ask Aristo to go up and tell Lucas that you have arrived and want to see him now. I'm sure Papylos can manage on his own.'

I sank down gratefully on the grass. Little Luke was becoming heavy to carry around and I would be pleased when he could walk for a short distance just holding my hand.

'If it's no trouble. I don't want to disturb Aristo.'

'No trouble at all. I imagine you have come early so you can introduce Lucas to his little boy.'

I nodded. 'I want it to be a surprise for him. Please ask Aristo not to tell him.'

Fotini smiled and called out to Aristo who appeared in the doorway, telling him rapidly that he must go and ask Lucas to come home immediately, but not to tell him the reason.

I gave Luke a drink of water and one of the rusks I had brought with me. He was not interested in the rusk and sat plucking at the grass with his little hands. I checked that he was not too damp and that his blouse was still clean and sat and waited as patiently as I could. Every so often he would pull himself to his feet whilst holding onto my arm and then sit back down heavily. He seemed to realise that the ground was too uneven for him to take any faltering steps and began to crawl away from me. After a few yards he turned and smiled at me and then set off again at a faster pace. I rose and followed him, scooped him up in my arms and took him back to where I had left my belongings. He gurgled with laughter and thought it a great game.

I was so busy playing with him that I did not realise that I was being watched. A shadow fell across the grass and I looked up to see Lucas standing there. His eyes were on Little Luke and I stood him up against me.

'Say hello to your Pappa,' I said.

'This is my son?' asked Lucas with a catch in his voice.

'Of course. Sit down and he can get to know you.'

Lucas sat down beside me and I moved Little Luke between us. He immediately put his hands on Lucas's legs and tried to crawl over him.

'I'm not sure if he should touch me.' Lucas sat completely still.

'He has no cuts or broken skin for the germs to get in. There should be no problem provided he does come into contact with the area that is infected on you. I'll change his cloths and when he's dry you can hold him.'

93

Lucas watched as I deftly removed the soiled cloth from Luke and replaced it with a clean dry one. 'There you are,' I announced. 'Now you can say hello properly to your Pappa.'

Lucas took Luke in his arms gently. 'He is beautiful. A perfect little boy. He would be the joy of my life, after his mother, of course.'

I sighed deeply. 'I would ask for nothing more than for us to be together as a family. If I spoke to Father Minos do you think he would agree to us coming here to live with you?'

Lucas shook his head. 'You know you can only come to Spinalonga if you are leprous. I thank God that you are not infected. I have to forgo the pleasure that a life with you and Luke would give me. Until a cure for the disease is found we have to accept that we have to live our lives apart.'

'Do you think a cure will be found?'

Lucas shrugged. 'Who knows. I understand from the doctor that a remedy is being searched for, but it could take years before one is found and proved to be effective. Come on, little man, let Pappa give you a ride on his back.'

Lucas knelt and I placed Luke on his back. His legs were not long enough to go around Lucas's girth and I steadied him with my hands. Slowly Lucas crawled around on all fours and Little Luke crowed with joy. From time to time the other residents either left their houses or returned home and looked at the scene curiously before smiling and continuing on their way as they saw Lucas playing with Little Luke. Finally Lucas declared he needed a rest as his knees were becoming sore. I lifted Little Luke down and he tried his best to climb back onto Lucas. Eventually he gave up and began to crawl away across the grass.

The game continued until Little Luke began to grizzle and I took a bottle of water from my bag and the rusk he had rejected earlier. He seized both and for a short while he sat between us quietly.

'I should show him to Fotini and Aristo. Maybe he and Vivi could play together. I'll go now whilst he's occupied.'

Fotini opened the door to me immediately.'I didn't want to intrude but I was hoping you would ask us to join you. Vivi rarely has another child to play with, only adults. I'll ask Aristo to bring her toys out.'

Aristo brought out a box containing a cloth ball and rag doll along with some coloured wooden bricks. I felt guilty. I had never thought to make a rag doll or cloth ball for Luke. Fotini then brought out bread, cheese and fruit which she placed on a cloth on the grass and instructed us to help ourselves. I did not hesitate; I peeled some fruit for Luke and helped myself to a slice of bread and a wedge of cheese.

'Will you bring Luke over with you the next time you come?' asked Fotini. 'I could look after him whilst you worked in the morning.'

I shook my head. 'I cannot bring him regularly. I have to make an excuse to my aunt for having him here.'

'Where does she think you are today?' asked Lucas.

'She knows I am here, but I said that Fotini's sister and her husband were coming today to take a photo of Vivi and I was going to ask them to take one of Luke.'

Lucas raised his eyebrows. 'So how are you going to explain not having a photograph when you get home?'

'They have to go to be developed apparently and that takes time. Isn't that right, Aristo?'

'Perfectly correct. Even so, they do not always come out well.' He smiled and winked conspiratorially at me. 'If he turned his head at just the wrong moment the photo would be of the back of his head and quite useless. You would need to bring him again.'

I looked at him, quite speechless for a moment. 'That is an excellent idea, Aristo,' I said finally, wondering how many times I could use that excuse.

Most of the afternoon was spent sitting happily on the grass watching the children play together and eating a little more as we fancied. Finally Lucas rose to his feet and walked over to the fortress wall.

'I can see the boat coming,' he said sadly. 'You will have to go, Eirini but I cannot thank you enough for bringing my little boy to visit me.'

'I will bring him again,' I vowed.

'I'll carry him down to the jetty for you,' offered Lucas, but I shook my head.

'You must say goodbye to him here. I would not want Despina or one of the boatmen to see you and word get back to my aunt.'

I placed a clean cloth between Little Luke's legs and hoisted him onto my hip. Lucas stood behind me, placed his hands on my shoulders and kissed the back of Little Luke's head and then mine. I drew in my breath sharply. Had I not been holding Little Luke I would have thrown myself into Lucas's arms.

'Go now,' ordered Lucas, his voice hoarse and I knew he had the same longing surging through him as I had.

Desolately I walked back to the steps, negotiated them carefully and looked back when I reached the bottom. There was no sign of Lucas.

I felt close to tears as the boat drew away and began the return journey to Elounda. I looked up as we passed the fortress walls and saw Lucas waving to me. It brought a lump to my throat. Why was life so cruel?

'Did you get the photo?' my aunt asked as soon as I reached the house.

I tried to smile. 'Oh, no, not yet. It has to go to be developed in a dark room. If the light gets in it is spoiled. They will take it over the next time they visit Fotini.'

With that my aunt had to be content as I took Luke into my bedroom and changed his soiled clothing. As the tears streamed down my face he looked up at me and frowned, his own face crumpling up ready to cry tears of sympathy.

Consequences

I returned from Spinalonga and shook my head sadly at my aunt.

'The photo of Luke was useless because the negative was spoilt. I will have to take him over another time.'

'Each time you take him over you expose him to infection. Better to go without the photograph.'

'I am terribly careful with him,' I assured her. 'He was quite happy to sit on the grass and try to build Vivi's bricks up into a tower.'

My aunt looked at me in horror. 'You allowed him to touch a leper's belongings?'

'Vivi has been declared free of leprosy by the doctor. Before I allow Luke to touch her bricks I make sure they are disinfected.' I had never told so many lies in all my life. I had been brought up to always tell the truth.

'So when are you taking him over again?'

I shrugged as if it was of no great importance. 'When Fotini tells me her sister and brother in law are visiting again.'

'It will soon become too cold and windy for you to take him over.'

'Then I will have to hope that they plan to visit within the next two or three weeks. I wouldn't dream of taking him in the boat if the sea was rough.'

'I should hope not. You'll have to stop going over in the winter months. They've managed well enough over there without you before now so they can manage again.'

I tilted my chin defiantly. 'I will go over provided the boatmen say it is safe. The people tend to rely upon the help we are able to give them.'

I knew there would be days when it would be impossible for the boat to make the short journey to Spinalonga, but I did not want to dwell on the concept of Lucas being cold and wet. At the same time I knew I was being ridiculous. Lucas had his pension along with everyone else. He could afford to buy a new pair of boots and a cape to keep him warm. Fotini had knitted shawls for the women and scarves for the men, selling them to the villagers to make some extra money. I would ask her to knit a scarf for Lucas and pay her so that it was a present from me.

'I am going to make a rag ball for Luke,' I announced. 'I saw Vivi playing with one and I'm sure he would like one. She also has a rag doll and I thought I might try to make one for him.'

'You're far too friendly with that family,' muttered my aunt. 'No good will come of it, mark my words.'

I took Luke over to Spinalonga again and Lucas was delighted. He said he was sure that Luke had grown in the intervening weeks and we spent much of the time walking backwards and forwards on the grass holding Luke's hands as he revelled in being able to walk, although he was still unable to do so unaided. Lucas gave him some more rides on his back and this time Vivi joined him. Both children squealed with terrified delight as Lucas pretended to throw them off and I made sure they did not fall.

'Well?'asked my aunt. 'Was the photograph successful?'

I was quite startled as I had forgotten that was my excuse for taking Luke over to Spinalonga with me.

'I hope so,' I replied, 'But I will have to wait until it is developed before I will know.' How many more times could I make the photograph an excuse for taking Luke to the island with me?

Whereas there had been days during the summer months when it had been almost unbearably hot on the island it was now being swept by a cold wind. The little fishing boat had rocked alarmingly as we crossed the stretch of water from Elounda to Spinalonga, although the fishermen and Despina appeared quite unconcerned.

I pulled my shawl over my head and around my shoulders as I

walked up the steps to the hospital. I hoped we would be able to find a sheltered corner to sit and prepare the vegetables. I gave an involuntary shiver as I placed the water container just inside the door. I had felt hot as I climbed back up the steps with the heavy metal container, but now the heat had drained from me.

'What's wrong?' asked Despina.

'It's colder over here than I realised. I should have worn my cloak.'

'We can sit inside whilst we prepare the vegetables. Spiro won't mind and we'll be out of the wind.'

I was not sure if it was safe to sit inside the doorway of the hospital but I really was feeling too cold to care and nodded agreement. Having finished them and called to Phaedra that they were ready we returned down to the water fountain for two more containers of water and struggled back up to the hospital with them. I was feeling thoroughly miserable. It would be so cold sitting outside on the grass with Lucas and I hoped he would know of a sheltered spot where we could get out of the wind.

There were few people around as I made my way down the village street, past the shops and then up the steps. Lucas was not sitting there waiting for me as he had been previously. Maybe his uncle had taken a turn for the worse and he was up at the hospital with him or maybe he was ill. My heart lurched inside me. What would I do if Lucas was not in his house? I approached tentatively and before I could knock the door opened and Lucas stood there smiling at me.

'I wasn't sure if you would come,' he said. 'You must be cold.'

I nodded, my teeth were chattering, but I was uncertain if that was entirely due to the cold wind. I stepped inside Lucas's house for the first time and looked around. It was small, but clean and tidy; his dishes and cooking pots were stacked neatly on a shelf and the cover on his bed was smooth. On the table stood a jug of water and a bowl of apples whilst a small fire burned in the hearth.

'I'm afraid it is not as well decorated as Fotini's house, but I am not artistic like Aristo.'

99

'It is warm and I ask for nothing more at the moment. I had not realised how cold it would be on the boat and then on the island. I should have worn my cloak rather than just my shawl.'

Lucas took a step towards me. 'I can make you warm, Eirini.'

I looked at him and he spread his arms out. In a flash I had dropped my shawl to the floor and was being held by him. My heart was beating so quickly I thought it would burst through my bodice. We stood there in a close embrace and I wanted to shout with joy.

Lucas finally released me, but I knew exactly how I wanted to spend the rest of the afternoon now. I began to shiver again.

'You are still cold? Shall I build the fire higher?' asked Lucas solicitously.

I shook my head. 'There is only one way in which I will become warm.' I slipped my hands up beneath his shirt.

'Eirini,' he protested.

'Yes, Lucas. Yes. There is only one way you can make me warm.' I pressed my body against his and felt his immediate response.

'Eirini,' he said again. 'This should not be.'

'Lucas, it has to be. I cannot keep my distance from you any longer.'

I pressed myself even more tightly to him and heard his swift intake of breath. He hesitated and then his arms were round me and he buried his face in my hair before kissing my neck. Reluctantly I struggled out of his arms and began to remove my clothes. He took hold of my hands.

'You're quite sure, Eirini? You know the risk you may be running.'

'I love you, Lucas. It is worth any risk to be with you.'

Lucas resisted no longer and finally we stood naked before each other. Lucas lifted me onto his bed. 'There is still time for you to change your mind,' he said.

By way of an answer I linked my fingers behind his neck and pulled his mouth down onto mine.

As the weather deteriorated I was only able to go to Spinalonga occasionally and certainly could not take Luke with me again. The boat would lurch and rock alarmingly whilst I clutched at the sides and hoped we would not capsize. Each time Lucas would be waiting in his house for me and we would spend the afternoon in each other's arms. I was blissfully happy, despite having to return to Elounda after each visit, although as soon as I saw Little Luke I was happy again.

I did feel guilty that I still accepted ten drachmas each time I visited although I only worked in the morning. No one seemed to notice or remark on the fact that I was nowhere to be seen in the afternoon.

How long our clandestine meetings would have continued I have no idea. The day came when I realised that I was pregnant. It was only to be expected as we had thrown caution to the winds, revelling at being alone together for some hours before I had to dress and hurry down to catch the boat. I hoped the boatmen did not realise that I had only left Lucas's bed a short while earlier.

I turned the dilemma over in my mind. I would have to tell Lucas, but I had now accepted that there was no way I would be allowed to live on the island as his wife. That would mean I had to tell my aunt and uncle and also my parents. I dreaded their reaction to my news.

I managed to keep my condition hidden until I was more than three months. When I told Lucas he was at first horrified and then contrite.

'I should have been more strong minded and refused you.'

'You must not blame yourself,' I assured him. 'I did not make it easy for you.'

'So what will you do?'

'I have to tell my parents and hope that my aunt and uncle will allow me to continue living with them. That way I will still be able to visit you.'

Lucas looked at me doubtfully. 'I cannot see them being willing to give you a home and also permission to come over here whenever you please.'

'Then I will have to find somewhere else to live.' I spoke confidently, but I had no idea where else I would find a lodging with a small child and another on the way.

'Maybe the doctor could help?'

'If he can find me somewhere to live I would accept his help, but if you are suggesting anything else I would not contemplate it. I love Little Luke and I will love this next one just as much. They are a part of you, the man I love. Had you not become ill we would have married and be living happily together.'

Lucas shook his head sadly. 'It is my fault.'

'I place no blame on you. I do not know how you contracted leprosy but I do know that it was not deliberate on your part. I just wish that you had not visited the doctor and had the disease confirmed. You have no outward signs, apart from your arm, and no one would have known.'

'There is no guarantee that in a few months or years I will not be as disfigured facially as many of the others. Think of the stigma that would be attached to you and the children if that happened. I could not have agreed to marry you knowing I was an untouchable.'

We held each other close, both of us wrapped in our own miserable thoughts.

'Whatever happens,' I said finally, 'I promise I will come over and tell you.'

My parents visited that weekend and I waited until after they had accepted the refreshment my aunt offered. My mouth felt dry and my stomach was churning uncomfortably.

'I have something to tell you,' I said finally and all eyes turned on me. 'I am expecting a baby.'

I thought my mother was going to faint. She went white and swayed on her stool.

'Have you been seeing someone behind my back?' asked my aunt.

I ignored her and continued. 'I found where Lucas was living.'

My father clapped his hand to his head. 'You have done this deliberately so I have to let you marry him now.'

'That's not possible,' I answered.

'Why not? Is he already married?'

I shook my head. 'He's on Spinalonga.'

There was a hush as this news was registered by my parents and then my aunt spoke in a shrill voice.

'So that's why you have been going to Spinalonga, you deceitful girl. You were not atoning for your sins but committing more. You'll not stay in my house, you harlot.'

'If you are able to find me board and lodge somewhere else I will be happy to leave.'

My father held up his hand. 'Now, listen, this situation needs to be thought about. You cannot return to Fourni but nor can you be thrown out on the street, particularly as you already have one child.'

'I will keep Luke and look after him,' my aunt said immediately, but my uncle frowned at the idea.

'You will not,' I answered just as quickly. 'Little Luke is my child and wherever I go he goes with me.'

My mother covered her face with her hands and groaned. 'What are we going to do?'

'Mamma, I wish I knew. Lucas and I love each other. I did not know he was on Spinalonga until I had been working there for some weeks. When we did finally meet we tried to keep ourselves apart, but it was impossible. I would be happy to go over there and live with him, taking Little Luke with me, of course, but it is not allowed. All I can ask is that I am allowed to live somewhere locally so I can visit him and take his children over to visit him occasionally.'

Despite my brave words to my aunt about going elsewhere

and taking Luke with me I did not know where I could go. I had the money I had saved up from working on Spinalonga but that would not last for ever. I considered Despina. Would her mother allow me to stay with them if I paid for my lodging? I would be able to take Luke to Spinalonga with me and whilst I worked Lucas could look after him. The complication was the child I was expecting at present.

'Go to your room, Eirini,' ordered my father. 'I need to speak to your aunt and uncle.'

Reluctantly I obeyed him. This was my future they were discussing. I had a right to know what they planned for me.

Finally my father called me out to rejoin them.

'Some months ago I read in the newspaper that Greek people were being welcomed in Australia and there were plenty of opportunities for work there. I have found out more information and I had planned to make this suggestion to you when Luke was older. Now I believe this is the only answer.I will make arrangements for us to travel to Australia as soon as possible. When we arrive you will declare yourself a widow.'

I gasped in horror. 'Australia! I cannot go to Australia. I would never see Lucas again.'

'You really do not have a choice, Eirini. Your aunt has agreed that you may stay here until such time as we travel to Piraeus and sail to Australia. I hope it will be soon so I only have to pay for one child rather than two.'

I shook my head. 'I do not want to go. I would rather be a beggar on the streets.'

'Don't be so stupid,' declared my father. 'If I allowed you to stay here and continue to see Lucas how many more children would you end up having? It would become common knowledge that their father was on Spinalonga and you and your children would become outcasts. That way you could well end up being a beggar. I am offering you a new start to your life. Your mother will look after the children and you will be able to find some suitable work.'

'I want to stay here with Lucas,' I replied mutinously.

'It is out of the question. We are prepared to make considerable sacrifices for you and you will have to be obedient to our wishes. Your aunt and uncle have agreed to purchase the cottages that your mother owns and it will take the remainder of our savings to pay for our travel and somewhere to stay upon our arrival.'

I shook my head. 'I do not want to go.'

'It has been decided,' my father said firmly. 'There will be no more visits to Spinalonga so you cannot think you will be able to hide away over there.'

'I have to see Lucas. He has a right to know what is happening to his son.'

My mother spoke for the first time. 'He does have that right. I suggest that you go over with Eirini. That way you can speak to Lucas and also ensure that Eirini returns with you.'

I felt helpless and breathless, my stomach churning painfully and I hoped I was not losing my baby.

'Very well. I will return next week and hope the weather is clement enough for us to make the boat trip. This will give you time to get used to the idea. In the meantime you will not leave the house unaccompanied for any reason.'

'You mean I am a prisoner,' I spoke bitterly.

'It is for your own good,' my mother spoke sadly.

I went to my room, closed the door, took Little Luke into my arms and sobbed.

Carrying Little Luke in my arms I accompanied my father mutinously to the boat. I had refused his offer to carry Luke for me and I was now regretting that. Despina looked at me curiously.

'You have not been over for a few days. Have you been unwell?'

I shook my head. 'I will talk to you later.' I could not explain my situation to her on the boat where my father would be listening to everything I said.

I was helped off the boat and onto the jetty whilst my father held Luke. He was still holding him when he stepped ashore and when I went to take him he refused.

'He is too heavy for you to carry in your condition.'

I flushed and ignored the remark. 'We have to go through the disinfection room,' I said and led the way.

I walked up the main road to the square accompanied by my father, waving to some of the shop keepers as I passed by. I mounted the steps and walked across the grass to Lucas's house. When he saw me standing on his doorstep a smile of pleasure spread across his face.

'Eirini, I was so worried. Have you been ill?'

'No, may we come in?'

'Of course.'

My father entered hesitantly and wiped the seat he was offered with his rag of a handkerchief before he sat down with Luke on his knee.

'What is the problem?' asked Lucas, seeing my white, tear stained face and puffy eyes.

'I will tell you what the problem is.' My father spoke angrily. 'You made my daughter pregnant when she was hardly more than a child and then disappeared without a word to anyone. By pure chance and misfortune she came to Spinalonga as a helper and discovered you were here. Once again you have made her pregnant, but I can assure you it will be the last time you have the opportunity.'

Lucas hung his head. 'I am so sorry. I did not intend such a thing to happen the first time and certainly not again now. I am sure Eirini has told you why I left Fourni so abruptly. Had I not been sick I would have asked if we could be married. I love Eirini. I could not believe it when I found she was coming over here. We both tried to be very circumspect and keep a distance between us, but eventually our feelings for each other took over. It is my fault, I should have had more self control.'

'Both of you should have exercised more self control. You knew the risks you ran. Who knows if you have infected Eirini and the child she is carrying?'

'I pray that she and both our children remain healthy. I would not want to wish my fate on anyone, least of all those that I love dearly and Eirini knows this.'

'You should have thought of that before you rekindled your association.'

Luke struggled down from my father's knee and clutched at Lucas's leg. 'Pappa,' he said, looking up with a smile on his face.

Lucas lifted him and sat him in the crook of his arm. 'Please,' said Lucas, 'Even if I am denied the sight of Eirini please let my children visit me.'

'That will not be possible. I am taking Eirini and the children to Australia. They will start a new life there. Provided they stay healthy they will never need to know their father was an untouchable.'

I could not bear the stricken look on Lucas's face.

'I will tell them who their father was,' I declared. 'I am not ashamed of a good man who unfortunately contracted a disease. I will make sure they only ever think of you with love and respect. I am not going to be allowed to come over here again, but before I depart I want to speak with Father Minos. Lucas, please look after our little boy whilst I am gone and allow my father to stay here in your house as it is cold outside.'

Before either Lucas or my father could reply I had opened the door and was running across the grass to the steps. I hoped I would find Father Minos at the church and not administering the last rites to some poor soul in the hospital. I entered quietly and was relieved to see him on his knees before the altar. I did not like to interrupt him and sank down on a chair, wishing my heart would stop beating so fast. I should not have run across the grass, but I was determined that my father would not stop me from leaving Lucas's house.

107

Father Minos rose from his knees and looked at me curiously. 'I heard someone open the door and I was expecting to see one of my parishioners waiting for me. You are one of the ladies who comes over to help, yes?'

I nodded acknowledgement. 'Please may I speak with you, Father?'

'Of course, unless you feel the priest in your home town would be more suitable.' He took the seat next to mine.

'I don't think he would understand.'

'And you think I might?'

'I am sure of it. I understand that you gave Phaedra and Yannis a blessing on their union and Fotini and Aristo had a proper wedding in your church.'

Father Minos smiled. 'I cannot forbid men and women to live together so the least I can do is give them a blessing so they will not feel guilty.'

'Suppose one of them was not suffering from leprosy but wished to be with the person they loved and live on Spinalonga?'

Father Minos shook his head. 'That is not possible. The law does not allow it. Only infected people are allowed to live here.'

'You are not infected but you live here,' I said accusingly.

'I had to receive a special dispensation to allow me to live here and I am not allowed to return to the mainland.'

'What about Manolis?' I persisted.

'Manolis is employed to keep the accounts for the islanders. As the book keeper he is allowed free access to the island, but he is not allowed to stay overnight. The laws set out by the government have to be obeyed.'

I was becoming more dejected and despondent as he spoke. I had hoped he would be able to solve my dilemma for me.

'You obviously have something troubling you. Do you wish to confide in me?'

I sighed deeply. There was no reason why I should not tell the priest about Lucas and I. He listened carefully, not interrupting or making a comment until I finished and turned my tearful gaze on his face.

'This is a most unfortunate liaison that you have formed. Lucas has been confirmed as having leprosy. If you have caught the disease from him you will be sent over here. You would not be allowed to have your son with you and your unborn child would only be allowed to stay here for a few years if he or she was healthy. You were obviously prepared to take that risk.'

I lowered my eyes. 'Lucas and I love each other. We tried to keep apart but it was not possible. Our first child was conceived in love, likewise this one that I am now carrying. I know Little Luke is fit and well at the moment, but there is no guarantee he will stay that way. he may have already inherited the disease and it will show as he becomes older. If I am in Australia and either of us become sick there is no way we can return to Spinalonga. Would you be willing to speak to my father and ask him to let us stay locally?'

'I understand your reasoning and I can ask him, but I feel I will have little success in changing his mind. Believe me when I say you are young and in time your heartbreak will ease. You will be in a new country and build a new life for yourself and for that you should be grateful to your father.'

I sat there quietly. I knew Father Minos was giving me as much help as possible without condemning me for my actions or my father for his decision.

'There is one other thing,' I approached the idea that had just come into my mind timidly. 'I know I cannot marry Lucas, but would you give us a blessing and also bless our son? Would it be possible for me to be known as Mrs Tsantakis and for my children to have that surname also?'

'A person may call themselves by whatever name they wish. I will accompany you back to Lucas's house and speak with your father, but I can promise nothing. Provided Lucas is willing I can give you and your son a blessing in the name of Tsantakis, but that is all. Do you wish to say a short prayer with me before we depart from here?'

I nodded. Although I despised my aunt for her continual crossing of herself and the hours she and her husband spent with the Bible there was no reason why I should not say a prayer with Father Minos.

I joined him, kneeling on the cold, hard floor and listened.

'Please help this young woman to accept the separation from her loved one that is about to be forced on her. Help her and her family to stay safe and well, during their voyage to Australia. If it is your will please enable her to build a new and happy life for herself and her children in a new country and put the sadness of the past behind her. Amen.'

Father Minos rose. 'Shall we go?' he asked.

Lucas and my father looked up in surprise when I re-entered the house accompanied by Father Minos.

'Eirini has confided in me and also asked me to speak with you. I cannot change the sad situation that has arisen but she has made a request that I am happy to comply with if you are in agreement.'

My father frowned. 'My daughter cannot stay in Crete. I have made arrangements for us to travel to Australia where she can start a new life.'

Father Minos nodded. 'I understand that you feel that is for her own good. Eirini has requested that I give her and Lucas a blessing as if they were able to be a legally married couple. Are you compliant with that idea, Lucas?'

Lucas nodded. 'I know that now I am an untouchable we can never be legally married but a blessing from you, knowing that we are not condemned for our past sins would be welcome.'

'Eirini has also asked that your son be blessed in the name of Tsantakis and that in future she will also be known by that name.'

'Is that legal?' asked my father.

'Perfectly. You cannot change your baptismal name but you may be known by any name that you choose.'

Lucas reached for my hand. 'Are you sure, Eirini?'

'Quite sure. I will be proud to bear your name and have our children also known by the same name.'

Father Minos turned to my father. 'Please accept your daughter's decision and give me your word that you will not try to dissuade her later.'

I looked at my father beseechingly and finally he nodded. 'Very well.'

I knew that having made such a promise to the priest he would keep it.

Lucas and I stood together whilst Father Minos gave us his blessing whilst the tears ran down my face. Lucas wiped them away with his finger and kissed me gently.

'We can ask for nothing more, Eirini.' I could tell he was keeping his own emotions in check.

'I will find work and save all my money. When I have enough for our passage back to Crete I will return, I promise.' I made the promise in good faith, not knowing then that events would conspire against me.

Lucas spoke to my father and I realised he had made the requests whilst Father Minos was still with us.

'Please allow Eirini to write to me so I have news of our children. I am allowed to receive letters and also to send them provided they are disinfected. I know I was not a good pupil, but I am improving my education with the help of a man who lives here.'

My father made no reply, but if he attempted to stop me from communicating with Lucas I will remind him that the request was made in front of the priest.

'The other thing that I ask is that you do not tell my parents I am on Spinalonga.'

'I have no intention of having anything to do with your family,' replied my father stiffly. 'We should leave now, Eirini. We have kept the boatman waiting long enough.'

'He will sound his hooter when he is ready to return. There would be no point in us waiting for him down on the jetty.'

'That is true,' agreed Father Minos. 'I think Lucas and Eirini should be allowed a short while alone together to enable them to say goodbye. When Lucas has bade his son farewell we could walk back to the church together and wait there for Eirini to join us.'

'I also wish to say goodbye to Fotini and Aristo.' I knew that would take me only a few minutes, but it could prolong the amount of time I was allowed to spend with Lucas.

My father removed his time piece from his pocket. 'I will expect you to join us at the church in fifteen minutes.'

I sobbed in Lucas's arms and nothing he said could console me. Finally he released me. 'If you wish to see Fotini we must leave now. I will accompany you to the church and stay with you until the boat arrives.'

'I will always love you, Lucas,' I declared vehemently as he kissed me one last time.

Impulsively I threw my arms around Fotini's neck and kissed her goodbye. 'I will not be coming back,' I said in a voice choked with tears. 'Lucas will explain. Please look after him for me.'

My father and I sat in silence during the journey back to the mainland. Despina looked at me curiously and once we had landed I walked over to her.

'I am sorry, Despina, but I will not be visiting Spinalonga again. My father has decided that we are emigrating to Australia.'

Her eyes opened wide. 'To Australia? How exciting. I would love an opportunity like that.'

'I would prefer to stay on Crete,' I answered. 'In case I do not have another opportunity I will say goodbye now, Despina.'

Arriving at my aunt's I took Little Luke into my room. I left my door open a crack whilst I dealt with him and I heard my father talking to my aunt.

'I actually felt sorry for them,' he said. 'Lucas is not a bad man and he adores his son.'

'You mean you condone their behaviour?'

'Not at all, but had Lucas not fallen ill and had they showed restraint originally I would eventually have agreed to their union. I spoke with the priest who lives on the island. Eirini had already spoken to him and made some requests. Father Minos gave them a blessing, along with Little Luke.'

'That does not change the situation,' answered my aunt sharply.

'Eirini also asked that in future she and the children will be known by the name Tsantakis.'

'And you agreed?'

'Reluctantly, but there is nothing I can do to prevent her using that name. In retrospect it will add credence to the fact that she is declared to be a widow when we reach Australia.'

When I went out, accompanied by my aunt, I would look across at Spinalonga and strain my eyes in the hope that I would catch a glimpse of Lucas, but the distance was too great.

Doctor Stavros had taken blood tests from all of us. My father explained that it was necessary for all of us to be certified free from all disease before we would be allowed to enter Australia. I certainly did not want to find out that Little Luke was infected unless I was also and we would be able to go to Spinalonga to live, despite the inevitable consequences of the disease.

Within a few weeks my life in Elounda ended and I was given no choice but to accompany my parents on the voyage to Australia.

1939 - 1949
LIFE THREE
Australia

I was so consumed with misery that I remember little of the
remainder of my time in Elounda. We travelled from my aunt
and uncle's by donkey cart to Aghios Nikolaos and then we
transferred to a large motor vehicle that was called a bus. Luke
had been good whilst we were on the cart, looking around at the
countryside and the herd of goats that we passed, but once on the
bus he was restless. Now he was trying to walk whilst holding
on to something. He wanted to be on his feet the whole time and
continually wriggled off my lap and tried to reach the seats in
front or behind us.

I was so relieved when we reached Heraklion. My father led the
way to the port, and loaded down with our belongings we followed
him. Waiting there was the biggest boat I had ever seen. My father
showed our tickets and we were led on board to the cabin where
we could spend the night. Before we left the harbour my mother
and I walked up and down the deck with Luke, hoping he would
be tired and sleep throughout the night. I was not sure if I would
be able to sleep, but when I finally curled up on the hard pallet
with Luke in my arms I must have gone to sleep immediately as
the next thing I knew was someone banging on the door. I sat up
in a panic. Were we sinking?

My father opened the cabin door and a man called to him that
we had arrived and should make ready to go ashore. I had sufficient

time to place clean dry cloths on Luke before I followed my parents and the other passengers up to the deck and disembarked.

'Are we in Australia?' I asked my father and he shook his head at my ignorance.

'Don't you remember looking at the Atlas with me and seeing how far away the different countries were from Crete?'

'That was a long time ago,' I answered.

'We have just travelled from Crete to mainland Greece. From here we will catch a far larger vessel to take us to Australia and it will take us considerably longer than one night. I have paid for two adjoining cabins so you and Luke can have your own beds. You are getting too large now to share a pallet comfortably with him.'

That was true. In the last few weeks it had become very obvious that I was expecting a child.

For the remainder of the morning and part of the afternoon we sat outside a taverna close by the harbour. I ate an indifferent meal of moussaka, feeding some of it to Luke. My parents had chicken kebabs but said the meat was tough. There was salad and bread available, followed by grapes and coffee. I peeled some of the grapes for Luke and made sure there were no pips.

Eventually my father said it was time for us to go and once again we gathered up our bundles and took our place in a queue waiting to board a boat that was at least three times larger than the one we had travelled on earlier. The man who showed us to our cabins took my sack and also my mother's whilst my father struggled with the two he was carrying so I could carry Luke down the narrow stairways.

When we reached our cabins we were each given a key so we could lock our doors and directed to an area where we would be able to have some food each day. Next to our cabins were two rooms that the man called the toilets. In each there was a ceramic bowl for our toilet needs and a sink with a tap above it that let out a stream of warm water when turned which then ran into a pipe beneath and out into the sea. At the time it seemed

115

like the height of luxury to me; no need to go out in all weathers to the privy.

I looked around the cabin curiously. Set in the ceiling was a light that could be switched on and off from my bed and shed sufficient light so that I would be able to see to attend to Luke easily when it was dark. I would be able to lay Luke on the table between our beds when I washed and changed him. In the wall there was a round window, that opened only a few inches but after I had struggled to open it I found it let in only the smell of the harbour and closed it again.

My father knocked my door and said we should make our way to the eating area and also make ourselves familiar with the layout of the vessel. We walked down a narrow passage way following an arrow that said 'Restaurant' and another sign next to it that said 'Taverna' in Greek lettering, to where a door stood open and inside we could see long tables and chairs. My mother and I sat down whilst my father went up to a counter where two men were standing. He returned swiftly.

'There appears to be little choice. Baked fish or keftedes served with salad and grapes to follow. Apparently we each have to go up and select our meal and bring it back to the table. I'll look after Luke whilst you and your mother go up.'

I looked at the two plates that were on display and they did not look appetising. I chose fish, thinking that would be easy for Luke to eat, and was given a fresh piece from a covered container. I helped myself to salad and two slices of bread, then dared to ask if there was any milk available and pointed to where Little Luke was sitting on my father's lap. Without answering me the man took a metal can from beneath the counter, punched two holes in it and poured some into a jug. He added some water and handed it to me. I looked at it doubtfully and dipped my finger in and placed a little on my tongue. It did not taste like goat milk but it was not unpleasant. I smiled and thanked the man. My mother carried her plates to the table and then returned to carry the jug of milk for me.

I took Luke from my father and fed him some small pieces of fish and held the jug for him whilst he drank gratefully. He seemed quite happy with the taste. I hoped I would be able to get more milk each day. Although Lucas had some teeth now he needed soft food supplemented by milk.

As we ate our meal more people arrived in the dining area and sat at the table waiting for a waiter to come and take their order. My father took pity on those nearest to us and explained they had to go to the counter. Hesitant conversations were begun and I listened to the other travellers. Most of them were young men and discussed the various employment options they believed would be open to them once we arrived. I listened avidly, but the only work they seemed to know about was in the construction business, mining or farming.

Having finished our meal my father insisted that we explored the ship so we would know our way up onto the deck for some fresh air and be able to find our way back to our cabins. He carried Luke up the narrow stairs that led from one deck to another and finally we reached the open air. Luke wanted to stand and my father and I held his hands.

There were many people around and I did not want to lose sight of him. When the hooter sounded signalling that we were about to leave the harbour many of the people drifted over to the railing at the side of the ship for a last look at Greece and to wave to anyone who had come to see them off. We stood amongst them, my father holding Luke firmly. as we watched the ship nose its way carefully out of the harbour. An announcement was made over a loud speaker telling us that in the event of an emergency a siren would sound. If that happened we should make our way up to the deck where the lifeboats were stationed. The boats looked very small, no larger than the fishing boats I was used to seeing in Elounda. There was no reason to stay up on deck any longer and we began to make our way back down to our cabins. I was not sure if I would have found my way had I been alone, although there were lights and signs to help.

'When you have settled Luke your mother and I will come to your cabin. There's work to be done.'

I looked at him in surprise. Were we expected to return to the restaurant and wash the dirty dishes? If so I would certainly ask for some more milk for Luke.

When my father knocked quietly on my door I saw he had some books beneath his arm. He sat down on my bunk and placed them on the table.

'We have to take advantage of the time we spend on board to learn the language that is spoken in Australia.' He spoke quietly so as not to disturb Luke.

'Don't they speak Greek?' I asked.

'Some may, but we need to be able to ask for whatever we want and understand the answer. We cannot rely upon a Greek speaker to be available all the time. I have a dictionary here so we can look up a word in Greek and see what it is in English.'

'Why are we learning English rather than Australian?' I asked.

'That is the language they speak there. The country belongs to Great Britain and it is easier for them if the English language is spoken.' He opened up a book and placed a sheet of paper before my mother and myself. 'First you need to familiarise yourself with the different letters they use. Write each letter down in Greek and then the English one beside it. Before you go to bed try to memorise at least half of the alphabet. Once you know your letters we can progress to simple words.'

My mother looked doubtful about the task ahead of her and my father assured her he would help her. I was pleased to have something to occupy my time and my mind when I was not dealing with Luke. It would be like returning to my childhood when my father first taught me how to read and write.

I did not sleep well that night although I had locked my door as my father had instructed and prayed fervently that the siren would not sound during the night. I was concerned that should there be an emergency during the night I would not be able to unlock my door or find my way up to the deck where we had been shown the lifeboats. There was a constant hum in the background and the letters my father had tried to teach me were going round and round in my head.

As soon as I was dressed I carried Little Luke along to the eating area with me and asked if it would be possible to have some milk for him. The man who served me spoke Greek and said I could go there at any time I wished during their opening hours for milk or food for Luke. He was so much nicer than the man I had seen the previous night. I asked him what kind of animal the milk came from as it did not taste like goat's milk.

He seemed to think my question amusing. 'We cannot keep goats on the boat. It is tinned milk that comes from a cow and will not sour until it has been opened. It may taste a little different but it will be just as good for your child.'

I sat at the table and crumbled bread up in the milk and fed it to Luke. I would have appreciated something to eat and drink myself, but I did not like to ask.

I was just wiping Luke's mouth when my mother appeared. 'We've been looking for you everywhere. We went to your cabin and there was no answer and when we went inside you were not there. Why didn't you knock our door and tell us you were coming down here?'

'I didn't want to disturb you and Luke was hungry.'

'Stay here,' ordered my mother. 'I'll find your father and then we can have something to eat and drink. I suppose you have already satisfied yourself.'

I shook my head. 'I only asked for milk and bread for Luke.'

I waited as instructed until both my parents arrived.

'Please do not worry us again like that, Eirini,' said my father. 'When you were not in your cabin we thought you may have gone up on the deck and become lost.'

'I would not try to go up to the deck alone and carrying Luke. I would have expected you to look here for me first,' I replied.

'We should have realised,' my father sighed. 'This is a new experience for all of us. Please do not wander off anywhere on your own. Knock on our door and we will accompany you to ensure your safety.'

I was about to say that I was no longer a child to be looked after when two young men entered the restaurant. They grinned at each other and then looked at me and winked. I ignored them, but I now knew why my father was concerned for my safety. Most of the passengers were young men and no doubt they would be searching for any woman who was willing to accept their attentions.

Our days became monotonously routine. We would visit the dining room and make our meals last as long as possible before returning to our cabins and I was instructed to keep my door locked at all times. My father said he would knock and announce himself before I was to turn the key.

We would take Luke up on deck each morning and the first time I saw the vast expanse of the sea I could not believe it. Whichever way I turned there was no sight of land. It made me feel sick and frightened to know I was in the middle of nowhere and if the ship should sink we would all drown. One night it was very rough the ship pitching and rolling and the waves slapping at the side noisily. I waited in trepidation for the siren to sound, not daring to remove my clothes or try to sleep.

Each morning we walked up and down on the deck with Luke so that when he had eaten some lunch he was willing to have a sleep during the afternoon. This was when my father produced the exercise books again.

Every day we sat in my cabin like children in my father's class. I mastered the letters swiftly, but my mother struggled. My father was sympathetic.

'It is not necessary for you to be able to write the language. You will gradually recognise the written words. It is more important that I help you to speak so you can make your needs known.'

I did not realise at that time that my father had no more

knowledge of the language than I had. He would read a sentence from the book and ask us to repeat it and tell him what it meant. After two weeks I asked him if I could borrow the book each night and do some further studying of my own. I wished I could ask someone who spoke the language if I was saying the words correctly.

The six weeks we spent at sea seemed never ending and when we finally docked at the port of Darwin I let out a sigh of relief. At least we were not all going to drown at sea. My father led us to a lodging house and said we would spend the night there before continuing our journey.

'I thought we had arrived, Pappa.'

'We have arrived in Australia, but we are going to board another boat tomorrow to take us to a town called Derby. There is quite a large Greek community living there along with pearl diving, a port and an airport. I believe I will be able to find some work there.'

My heart sank. 'How long will we be on the boat?' I asked.

'No more than two or three days. We are only sailing down the coast.'

I was relieved that we were not crossing a vast expanse of sea again, but I was nearing the end of my pregnancy and I did not want to have my child born on a boat. I was thankful that Luke was such a good and docile little boy and hoped the next child would be the same.

My father had spoken optimistically when he said two to three days. It was over four days before we reached the town and were able to disembark along with the other passengers.

We went to a lodging house at the edge of the town and rented two rooms. We had to share the bathroom and kitchen with the people in the next room and provide our own food. This meant going to the local market and general store for our provisions. I had a reasonable vocabulary now although I found it difficult to say a complete sentence I decided this was when I would use the language that I had been taking such pains to learn. I would not point to an article that I wanted but say the name. If I was not understood then was the time to point and ask to be corrected.

The town of Derby was much larger than Elounda and very different. In every street there was a light that was switched on when it grew dark by a man riding on a bicycle. He had a long pole and would reach up and pull down a metal projection and the bulb would light up. They were never alight in the morning so I could only assume that as dawn broke he rode around again and pushed the projection back into place. On some street corners there was a small kiosk and sometimes someone was inside holding a black implement up to their ear and talking at the same time. I was told this was a public telephone.

At first I was totally bewildered, but I gradually found my way around and it was not as daunting as I had first thought. Everywhere I looked there was someone with a black skin. I was told these were Aboriginal people and they had lived in this area for centuries. There were people from other countries, from what I could judge by the languages I heard them speaking, but they all appeared friendly enough and would smile as we passed each other in the streets. There were no donkeys, but men rode around on large horses that they then tethered to the railing outside a building and mounted the steps to go to wherever they wanted.

Many of the shops sold the same items, leather bridles, saddles, saddlebags that hung each side of a horse the same as our woven panniers did on a donkey. There were some strange looking trousers. They would not reach up to a man's waist and they were held up by long straps that went over the shoulders. I saw some of the men wearing them over their trousers. There were shops that sold boots, they looked very big and heavy after the soft leather ones most of the men wore at home, but there were also shoes designed for ladies to wear. One clothes shop seemed full of shirts for men, but there were other shops that sold a variety of both men and women's wear. There were general stores and two pharmacies and supplies were brought to them in a motorised vehicle that my father said was a lorry.

Wherever I looked there was a building that called itself a tavern. Some of them advertised food, others rooms to rent or gambling facilities. The taverns were well lit and all had a bar where men would be seen drinking at all times of the day. One had a notice saying entertainment was available and I thought it meant there was singing and dancing as happened sometimes in the Greek tavernas. I asked my father if it would be possible to go one evening and my father told me to avoid the premises as it was the local brothel.

At one end of the street there were some large wooden buildings where men unloaded sacks of animal feed from a lorry. This happened every day except Sunday. Men would arrive and load up their own vehicle or horse drawn cart with the goods they needed. There were two churches, one at each end of the town. Had it not been for the crosses that hung above the door I would not have known that either were a place of worship; they looked no different from the other buildings except for the pitch of their roofs. Beside one was the school house. It was a one storey building with a fence around it. Children could be seen exercising in the fenced off area and I looked at it with interest. This would be where my children would go to school.

On the opposite side of the road was a far larger building with a big red cross painted on the side. My father told me the building was the hospital and he escorted us there as he said we needed to know where to go if one of us was sick or had an accident. A woman sat behind a desk and spoke to us when we arrived. She soon realised that we did not understand her and indicated that we should sit on one of the chairs. She disappeared though a door and eventually returned accompanied by a young woman. She spoke with my father in Greek whilst he presented the papers he had saying we were all free from any disease, explained that we were newly arrived and needed to be assured that we could use the hospital facilities if necessary and also the cost.

She took me behind a curtain and felt my stomach carefully. I was pleased to see that her hands and apron were clean. Finally she informed me that the baby was in the right place with the head well down. She said that when my pains started or my waters broke I should go immediately to the hospital where I would be cared for until I could return home. I looked at her in horror and shook my head.

'I cannot stay here for forty days.'

'I understand that you are abiding by your religious beliefs, but you cannot stay in the hospital unless you are sick. Other people need a bed and our attention. I will speak to the priest on your behalf and ask him to come to bless you and the child.'

'I could have the baby at home. This is my second child so I know what to expect.'

She shook her head. 'It is far better that you enter the hospital. Here we have all the equipment that is needed. Do you have a waterproof to cover your mattress?'

'I will sit on the chairs as before so the mattress will not be soiled.'

'That is not satisfactory. If a chair slipped you and the baby could be badly injured. Should you have a problem that needed the attention of a doctor he would not be able to treat you if you were lying on a chair. Trust me, you will find the birth easier and be more comfortable if you are on a bed.'

Still I argued. 'Could I not buy a waterproof sheet of my own for the mattress?'

'There is no reason why you should not have waterproof sheets for yourself and also for your children's beds. but no nurse or doctor would be willing to attend you at your home.'

Finally I had to give in. I could not expect my mother to act as a midwife.

We returned to where my parents were waiting and I told

them I had to go to the hospital to have my child when the time came. They wanted to know if there was something wrong and the nurse reassured them that all was well with me and repeated the arguments she had used to persuade me.

'The best thing you can do now is go home and get as much rest as possible. You will need your strength; giving birth can be an arduous event.'

This sounded very contrary to the way the women on Crete gave birth. They would often work up in the fields until their labour started and on many occasions a child had been born behind a stone wall with no adverse effects and the woman had continued with her work. I did recall how exhausted I had felt after giving birth to Little Luke.

My father asked where he could find the priest as he wished to speak with him and be reassured that the blessing that we would be given would protect me from evil when I left the hospital to continue with my confinement at home.

When the time came I had Dimitris very easily. I had obeyed the lady at the hospital and had spent ten days there. I was examined and declared to be whole, I had not been torn inside. Although the birth this time had been relatively quick and easy I still felt very tired and grateful that I only had to tend to Dimitris's needs. My father had brought Luke to visit me and he appeared to accept his younger brother. The priest arrived the day before I was due to return home and blessed us, congratulating me on having such a healthy child.

I spoke to my father that evening and he reassured me. 'You have been blessed so no evil will befall you. We will abide by our religious customs and wait until Dimitris is forty days old before you go out.'

My mother cared for Luke whilst I gave most of my attention to Dimitris. My father had been pleased when I said I was calling my second son after him. Although still confined to the house I asked for the language books so I could continue to study English and look up unknown words in the dictionary. I found out that the lady who had attended me was called a midwife and I tried hard to increase my vocabulary further and also understand the grammar. I did not want to be considered rude when I tried to communicate with people.

Once I was able to leave the house my mother and I would go shopping together, Luke walking between us whilst I carried Dimitris. We found it difficult to buy the food we were used to having in Crete. We had become accustomed to the milk being in tins and that olives and olive oil were prohibitively expensive as they had to be imported from the New South Wales area of Australia. We were offered slabs of white fat for cooking and a greasy yellow spread they called butter for on our bread. Most of the meat appeared to be beef which was cheap and occasionally there was lamb available, but that was expensive. There were Warrigal Greens in the shops and they were very similar to our horta. We bought those to eat as a green vegetable and also to make ourselves a salad of sorts with onions and tomatoes, but no lemons or the fresh herbs that we would have used at home were available, only bunches of dried ones. We became used to eating very different food.

Each day my father went in search of work and eventually returned to say he had been offered work restocking the shelves in one of the larger Greek owned general stores. He would be responsible for bringing the boxes from the stockroom into the shop for the assistants to re-stock the shelves. I felt sad. This was not work for an educated man. He explained that he did not speak the language well enough to be a teacher, we were not in the mining area, he could not dive for pearls, and being unable to ride a horse he was unsuitable for work on a cattle ranch. Although there was plenty of construction work taking place as new homes were being built to house the families that were coming into the area he had been told he would be too old for such strenuous work and the same applied to the work available down at the docks or at the airport. He would earn sufficient to pay the rent each week and he was sure that something more rewarding would eventually become available.

The first time I had heard an aeroplane arriving I thought we were having an earthquake and ran outside. When I saw what looked like an enormous bird in the sky I thought it must be a sea plane like the one that landed regularly in the bay at Elounda but it did not go into the sea. I waited for a crash that did not happen and after a while I became used to the occurrence.

When Dimitris was three months old I also began to look for work. My father managed to persuade the shop keeper to employ me in the afternoons to also replenish the stock on the shelves whilst my mother looked after Luke and Dimitris.

The work was not arduous and I became friendly with the two other ladies who worked there in the same capacity. Poppi had not long been married and her husband worked in the dockyard. She said they were saving hard so they could purchase their own house as at present they were living with his parents. Katarina was older and needed some extra income to help finance her parents who were both too old to work. The money I earned was sufficient to cover the cost of our food. We were managing.

As I worked in the shop I became more familiar with the language and tried to read the various notices in the shop and remember the names of the goods. One notice said 'Best Value'. What was value? I had never heard of a food called 'value' before. I would have to look the word up in the dictionary when I returned home rather than confess my ignorance to Poppi or Katarina. I was becoming accustomed to seeing the price in dollars rather than drachma, but found it impossible to calculate whether certain items were costing more or less in Australia. Although we spoke Greek together at home I was also teaching Luke the English names for items as he would need to speak the language when he started school.

In the mornings I would take Luke out for a walk whilst I

carried Dimitris. As he became heavier my mother would offer to look after the boys whilst I did the necessary shopping. In this way I was able to explore more of the town and began to recognise people and greet them. It was during one such walk that I was horrified to find there was a leprosarium in the town.

I had heard Bungarun mentioned, but I thought it was an area not an institution where those suffering from leprosy were sent to live. There were high walls and a barred gate with a notice declaring its purpose and forbidding anyone to enter without permission. As I looked through I could see people moving around and I was rooted to the spot. This looked more like a prison than a hospital. I thought back to Spinalonga and how everyone there was free to move around on the island and live a normal life, even having visits from their relatives and friends. My heart ached for Lucas. I had written to him, telling him about my life in Australia and that he now had a second son, but I had not received a reply.

There were three imposing buildings, one was the Town Hall, another the bank and a third was a court house. At the back of the court house was the prison. Depending upon their offence, usually being drunk or involved in a brawl, the convict would serve their time there, usually no more than a few days until a fine was paid on their behalf and they were released. If they had committed a serious crime, whereby they had killed a man whilst fighting, stolen a horse or some cattle they were sent up to Darwin for sentencing. Newspapers were delivered each week and they usually had accounts of the crimes the people had committed.

There were two blacksmiths and most days there were horses tethered outside waiting their turn to be re-shod and strange metal objects hanging up inside. Further along and almost out of sight were two large wooden buildings and on one side there were a number of fenced enclosures that always seemed to be full of cattle.

It was only later that I found out this was the slaughter house for the cattle. They would be driven from their ranch and along a trail behind the town to be corralled in an enclosure. Some of those slaughtered were kept here for our food and also for their leather hides, whilst other carcasses were collected by a motorised vehicle and taken down to the port to be shipped to other areas. Sometimes the cattle were moved away whilst still alive. They were herded into the back of an open lorry and packed closely together, their heads above the slats of wood that kept them confined. They were obviously frightened and I would cover my ears when I heard their calls of distress.

At the other end of the town were more cattle pens and these were the animals that were being taken out to the ranches. The first time we saw them being moved we stood and watched in fascination as the men on horseback kept them on the track that led behind the town and stopped them from straying. Once those at the front were moving the others followed them.

It was during one such walk that I saw a notice pinned to the door of one of the taverns asking for staff. I decided I would ask what kind of work they expected. The interior was hot and smoky, men were sitting at the tables smoking their pipes. They took frequent drinks straight from the bottles of beer that were with them. Conversation stopped as I walked in and I was tempted to flee. Instead I held my head high and approached the counter.

The man behind the counter looked at me curiously. 'Are you looking for work?' he asked.

I nodded. 'What work are you offering?'

'General work. Looking after the customers. Encouraging them to buy more drinks.'

'How do I do that?'

'Chat to them, make them think you are interested in their conversation, laugh at their crude jokes. Come up for more beer when you see the bottles are half empty and get a drink for yourself.'

'I don't drink.'

'You can have a glass of water for all I care. They'll be paying for it.'

I nodded. 'Good pay?'

'Depends how hard you work. Come this evening.'

I told my father I had been offered a job in the tavern. He frowned at me.

'I'm not sure you should work there. Some of the customers appear very rough.'

'I've agreed to go in this evening provided Mamma will look after the boys. If I'm not happy I don't have to stay.' Depending upon the amount of money I received I might be forced to stay working there however much I disliked it.

I was in for a rude awakening. I was not expected to serve the customers, but to sit with them and encourage them to buy more alcohol, remembering to go to the bar and bring back more bottles of beer before the current ones were empty. As the group of men I was sitting with decided they had drunk sufficient they rose and one of them tapped me on the shoulder.

'Upstairs,' he said.

I was not sure what he meant.

'You. Me. Upstairs.'

The truth dawned on me and I shook my head. I was certainly not going up to the man's room as I knew now what he was suggesting.

I shook my head. 'Home,' I replied. 'Children.'

He looked at me in disgust and walked over to where another woman was sitting and spoke in her ear. She rose and gave me a broad wink as she linked her arm through his and they walked off to the stairway.

I went up to the bar. 'Go home now,' I said. 'Children.' I held out my hand. 'Money.'

'Tomorrow. I'm busy now.'

I stood there and he waved his hand at me. 'Go. Come tomorrow.'

My father was waiting for me when I returned home. 'Were you busy?' he asked.

I shook my head. 'Not really. I have to go back tomorrow for my money, but I don't think I want to work there.'

I had no intention of returning to work there until I saw the amount of money that was pressed into my hand the following day. If I could earn that amount every evening my father would be able to give up filling shelves at the general store.

I plucked up my courage. The worst the man could do was tell me to go away as I was not wanted.

'Work,' I said. 'Same as last night. No upstairs.'

He shrugged. 'Up to you. If you go upstairs you earn three times as much.'

I shook my head. 'No upstairs,' I repeated.

I kept to my resolve and refused invitations to accompany any of the men up to the upstairs rooms. Somehow my mother got to hear of the work that was expected of me and rounded on me angrily.

'You are working in a brothel. That is disgusting and degrading.'

I shook my head. 'I only sit and drink with the customers. I never go upstairs with any of them.'

'So you say.'

'I am speaking the truth. Why doesn't Pappa come to the tavern one evening? He would see that I am speaking the truth. Be grateful that I am able to earn sufficient to enable you to put food on the table. I would never do anything that made you or my children ashamed of me.'

'You should have thought of that years ago. You have two children who have no father.'

I tilted my head defiantly. 'They do have a father and had you and Pappa not insisted that we came to Australia they would have been able to get to know him. I am not ashamed of loving Lucas.'

'Well you should be. And working in that tavern you'll end up with a bad reputation in the town.'

This was only the first of many such conversations with my mother. Nothing I could say could make her understand that I was just a 'draw' to get the men to spend their money more freely on alcohol, encouraging them to move from beer to whisky as the evening progressed. The other girls who worked there thought I was stupid to turn down the extra money the men were willing to pay if I went upstairs with them and offered to show me ways to avoid becoming pregnant. I replied that if that was a service they required they should go to the brothel.

With the money I earned we were able to purchase some very necessary new clothes. My mother had patched and darned the ones we had brought with us, but they looked extremely worn and shabby. The next thing we would need would be new boots or shoes for when the rainy season arrived. When it rained the roads became a river of mud and I was unable to take Luke out for a walk. When I went out I lifted my skirt as high as possible hoping it would not get too splashed and dirty and I found the cyclones frightening as the winds howled and blew anything around that was not firmly fixed to the ground.

Afterwards I was grateful for the heavy rain. Whilst unloading his goods at the general store the owner slipped and fell, breaking his arm in the process. I was asked to work some extra hours, but I made the excuse that I was needed at home with my children and my father would be able to work for longer each day. The arrangement worked well and by the time the shop keeper had his arm removed from the plaster cast he had become quite appreciative of my father who had kept the accounts meticulously and suggested that he applied for re-training as a book-keeper.

I encouraged my father to go ahead and promised to work extra hours in the shop to make up for his absence each morning. I found it tiring as I arrived home late from the tavern on the evenings when I worked there and then had to be up early to go to the shop. I devoted as much free time as I could to my boys and despite my mother's continual complaints about working in a tavern even she realised that we would not be able to live decently without the money that I brought home each week.

It took my father no more than eight months to obtain his certificate saying he was a qualified book-keeper. He was allowed to place an advertisement in the window of the general store and had written it in Greek and English. His customers were mostly Greek immigrants who patronised him because he was able to explain to them in their own language how much tax they had to pay and the reason the government was demanding the sum. He very quickly worked out a system, quite legally, whereby he was able to increase their expenditure claim and reduce their profit margin. For this they were grateful and they were prepared to pay him more than his usual hourly rate as no one liked paying their taxes. I worked less hours in the shop, but I did not give up my evening job in the tavern.

We had been able to leave the original lodging house and move into one that had two bedrooms. a living room and our own kitchen and bathroom. Both my mother and I had had a problem for some time getting used to cooking on a machine that ran by electricity, having an oven beneath and some electric plates on the top. It cooked everything far more quickly than the open fire that we had been used to in Crete. We both burnt our hands and also the food on occasions until we had become used to it.

To my mother's (and my) amazement there was a cupboard where we could store meat or fish as it was constantly cold inside and this was called a refrigerator. Instead of having to rely upon an open fire for all our hot water there was a large container over the bath and a smaller one over the kitchen sink. When the electricity was switched on the water inside these was heated.

It was in a better area of the town so of course the rent was twice as high, but with the money we now had coming in we could afford the luxury.

Fred

I had come to terms with my mundane life now. I had heard nothing back from Lucas, and although my heart ached for him I found my boys were a comfort. I could fill up the shelves with the stock automatically and even answer a question from a customer when they were searching for a particular item, although I still avoided answering the telephone. Poppi and I became friends and would spend our break time together; she would talk about her husband and I would talk about my boys. I even began to find that spending an evening in the tavern was quite interesting now I spoke the language well enough to follow the men's conversation.

It was in the tavern that I heard the men discussing the war in Europe and saying that Australia had joined with England to prevent the further advance of the German army. I did not know what this would mean and when the opportunity arose I asked them. They were of varying opinions; it would make no difference to us as we were too far away and others were saying they felt it was their duty to enlist to show solidarity and support for Australia.

The next morning I asked my father if I had understood correctly that Australia had allied itself with England and we were now at war.

He smiled at me. 'You don't need to worry about that. We are safe enough over here and the war will soon be over now we are sending more troops to fight.'

I was reassured and at the same time I was pleased that my father would not be expected to fight due to his age and that both my boys were far too young. I thought of Lucas. He would not be expected to go and fight and would be safe enough on Spinalonga.

Our life continued as before, except that gradually there were fewer customers in the tavern each night as more men were needed to work long hours at the both the port and the airport. Derby was being used as a refuelling station and many of the men who had previously worked on the ranches took the opportunity to move into the town and earn better wages at the docks, airport or in the iron industry whilst some of them had travelled to Darwin to enlist.

My father invested in a wireless so we could keep abreast of the official news rather than listening to rumours, but much of the time it was depressing. The war had not ended swiftly as my father and others had predicted. Whatever resistance the German armies encountered they seemed to sweep out of their way until the country capitulated and agreed to be annexed.

The news became more worrying when we heard that Japan had also entered the war. They were systematically working their way through Malaysia and getting closer to us. Even more distressing was the invasion of Crete in May 1941 by the Germans and they were using their control of the country to assist their entry to Africa. I bought an Atlas and would sit with my father tracking the progress of the armies of both countries.

The bombing of Pearl Harbour in America in December of 1941 gave us cause for hope. The Americans had declared war on Japan and were optimistic that they would succeed in stopping Japan from advancing further along the Pacific coast.

Although the radio reports praised the progress that had been made during the various battles that had been fought they continually mentioned the number of casualties Australia had suffered. When the newspapers arrived the townspeople would seize upon them eagerly and scan the names of those killed in action or listed as missing hoping they would not see their loved one included.

Living in Australia we still felt relatively safe from both the Germans and the Japanese until Sydney harbour and Darwin were bombed, but they were many miles away. Our feeling of security was short lived as Broome was bombed followed by Derby. We should have realised this was inevitable as Broome had an airport. Aeroplanes and sea planes were destroyed and much loss of life ensued. Derby was attacked in an attempt to cripple the port and destroy the airport which was being used as a refuelling station. The bombs destroyed two large oil storage containers on Stokes Hill, the resulting fires causing even more destruction.

After the initial onslaught Derby was bombed regularly and when we heard planes arriving we would take shelter wherever we could and pray that we would be spared unlike the many poor souls who lost their lives. Poppi's husband was killed when a bomb hit the airport and she was inconsolable. We began to live in constant fear of the Japanese invading the town.

Some food stuffs were in short supply, but we were certainly not starving. We heard later that as many had died from malnutrition in the European towns as had been killed when their buildings were bombed and collapsed around them.

Like so many others we survived and when Japan surrendered in August 1945 and Peace was finally declared in Europe we all breathed a sigh of relief and celebrated, dancing in the streets, hugging and kissing our neighbours.

At last I could go to work knowing that my boys would be safe either at home or at school. By now Luke was fluent in both English and Greek. He complained about the English language saying so many words were written using the same letters but meant different things and asked why they could not have a separate word for everything as they did in Greek. I could not answer him, but I sympathised as I still had problems ensuring my sentences were constructed correctly when I was speaking.

Dimitris was almost equally as fluent and I knew he would have no problem with making himself understood. Now the boys were older they became curious about their history; why were they living in Australia if they were Greek? I considered my answers carefully and told them that Crete was a very poor country, most people were either fishermen or farmers, and their grandfather had seen better opportunities for both of them if we moved here.

Dimitris looked at me mutinously. 'I would like to be a fisherman.'

'If that is what you want to do then I'll not stop you. It is an honourable way to earn your living, but think carefully; you are out in all weathers, the sea can be rough and your boat wrecked and you then have no catch to sell.'

'I still want to be a fisherman,' he said. 'Can we go down to the harbour this afternoon? I like to look at the boats and ships.'

Almost every day he asked to go down to the port area where repairs to the buildings were taking place and trade was beginning to increase. I would ask Luke where he would like to go and he would say he did not mind so on most of our walks we either visited the harbour or the river where Dimitris would try to catch a fish and both boys learnt to swim in a safe area. I still did not venture into the water.

Inevitably the question of their father was raised and again I was cautious. I considered them too young to understand fully and I told them that he was too sick to travel with us. They could see that I was upset and did not pursue the subject. I heard Luke whisper to his brother that their father must have died and that was why I was sad when I spoke about him. I did not enlighten them and they never asked about him again.

Gradually the men began to return to Derby, some with horror stories to tell about their experiences, many of them too traumatised to speak about the events they had seen and taken part in and still mourning for lost comrades. I found it difficult to sit and listen to them without shedding a tear.

This was when I met Fred Anstruther. He was sitting alone one evening and appeared deep in thought. The bar man told me to take him another bottle of beer and my drink and join him. I placed the beer on the table and slid into the chair opposite him.

He looked up and frowned. 'I didn't order that.'

I smiled. 'I'm sorry, maybe I misunderstood the bar tender. May I join you?'

'Free country.'

'Thanks to brave men like you.'

He shrugged. 'We did what was necessary. Over and done with now.'

'Where did you fight?'

'What's it to you?'

'The men who sit together recount their personal experiences. I find them harrowing to listen to. I would like to know more about the countries they visited.'

'We didn't exactly have much time to go sightseeing unfortunately.'

'Where were you?'

Fred sighed. 'Started off on the Greek mainland, evacuated to Crete and then shipped over to North Africa when Crete fell.'

'Crete!' I drew in my breath sharply. 'Where were you on Crete?'

'At Chania, then we had to beat a hasty retreat down to Preveli.'

'Did you go anywhere near Fourni or Elounda?'

Fred shook his head. 'Not that I recall. We passed through many villages. Why?'

'I come from Crete. My family came here in 1938. We miss our home. Please tell me as much as you remember of your time there.'

'I'm not sure you'd be interested in my experiences.' Fred picked up the second bottle of beer.

'I would be interested in anything that you can tell me.'

Fred shrugged. 'After the battle of Maleme we were ordered to make our way across Crete to the coast opposite Africa where we would be taken off by ship. When you compare the size of Crete to Australia it looks like a quick journey. We had a map but all the signposts and names of the villages and towns had been taken down to confuse the Germans and we would not have been able to read the words anyway. I doubt we would have made it without the help of an Englishman we happened to meet up with. He led us part of the way and then handed us over to some resistance fighters. They were brave men. Mind you, all the Cretans were brave. The women fought alongside the men in many cases, just using a farming implement as a weapon. They certainly suffered from the Germans if they were captured.'

I shuddered at the thought.

'Are you sure you want me to continue?' Fred noticed my reaction and looked at me in concern.

'I need to know. I have some family still over there.'

'I hope you have. They will be able to tell you how the Germans raided their farms and took their crops and livestock leaving them with nothing. Everyone was on the brink of starvation. If a resistance worker had taken refuge in a village and the Germans discovered this the whole village suffered. Men, women and children were slaughtered, villages burnt to the ground. This only made the resistance more determined in their efforts.'

I could not help the tears that were running down my face.

'I'm sorry I have upset you so much, but you did ask. Let me get you another drink.'

'Just some water, please,' I managed to stammer.

Fred went up to the bar, returning with a glass of water for me and another bottle of beer. 'Are you sure you wouldn't like a beer? Costs the same as a glass of water.'

I shook my head and took a sip of my water.

'Have you heard anything from your relatives?'

'Nothing. We have written to them but had nothing back. We have to assume they are dead.'

Fred reached across the table and squeezed my hand. 'Don't despair. I understand that it was pretty chaotic over there. Your letters could have been lost or sitting somewhere waiting to be delivered.'

'It is three years since the war ended.'

'Write again, and you could try writing to the Greek Embassy and see if they have any information.' Fred drained his bottle of beer. 'I'm bushed. I'm off to bed. How about you?'

'I don't go upstairs,' I replied firmly.

'That wasn't what I meant. I was asking if you were staying here or going home.'

139

'I'll go home. Nice to have met you.'

'Likewise. Be here tomorrow and we can talk some more.'

I knew his eyes were following me as I waved to the bar tender, walked across the room and out of the door.

I was not sure if I should meet the man the following evening, but I needed the money and he had been pleasant enough and not expected me to go upstairs with him.

When I entered the tavern I saw Fred playing pool. I collected a bottle of beer and some water and went and sat at an empty table. As soon as he saw me he handed his cue to another and joined me.

'I don't want to interrupt your game.'

'I was only passing the time. I wasn't sure if you would come after the way I upset you yesterday. Now you are here we ought to introduce ourselves. I'm Fred Anstruther. Who are you?'

'Eirini Tsantakis,' I replied holding out my hand.

'I'm pleased to meet you Reen.'

'My name is Eirini.'

'And my name is Frederick, but I'm known as Fred.'

I could only smile at his reasoning. 'So what did you do when you returned from the war?'

'My parents owned a ranch. My father had run it profitably for years and taught me all I needed to know. The problem was that the ranch hands had enlisted and it was impossible for him to manage it just with Hank. My mother had died whilst I was away and I think he just gave up. He sold the stock and did not buy more. When I arrived home he rode out with me on a few occasions, then just seemed to fade away. I think he had only been waiting for me to return. Fortunately there was plenty of money available as I had to get the hands accommodation re-roofed where a cyclone had taken a fancy to it. The perimeter fencing had to be checked and that took time, then I had to supervise the repairs to the water pipes leading to the troughs and also find some reliable and experienced ranch hands.'

'So why are you in Derby now?'

'My men are staying at the hostel until my new herds arrive. They've been serviced by a bull and checked over by the vet so I need to make the final payments. My men will brand them before taking them back to the ranch and getting them settled in. I admit I'll be pleased to get back to the peace and quiet, able to ride around on my horse without being mown down by a car or lorry.'

'So you keep cattle and then kill them.'

Fred shook his head. 'People have to eat. At least my cattle are free to roam around, they're not kept penned up like some. Do you like cows?'

'I'm not sure. I had never come across them until we came here and I avoid the area where they slaughter them.'

'Very wise. I accept that it happens to them but I don't want to witness it.'

'So why don't you do some different work?' I asked curiously.

'I was brought up on the ranch and cattle are all I know. What about you? Why are you working in a rather dubious tavern?'

'I work in a shop some days but it doesn't pay enough to keep us.'

'Who is 'us'?'

'My parents and my two boys.'

'So your husband didn't come back from the war?'

I swallowed hard and did not answer as tears pricked at the back of my eyes.

'I've upset you again. I'm sorry. That was not my intention. Tell me about your boys. How old are they?'

'Luke is twelve and Dimitris is ten.'

'Do they speak English?'

'Of course. Luke was born in Crete, but Dimitris was born here and I have brought them up speaking both languages.'

'I wish I had some boys.'

'You have only girls?'

Fred shook his head. 'I have no children. I'm not married. I had

141

a girl I met in Darwin but when I returned and told her that if we married I would expect her to live on a cattle ranch she left me.'

'What's so difficult about living on a cattle ranch?'

'Well, for a start, she was a town girl, used to the bright lights and entertainment that could be found there. On the ranch you're miles from anywhere; just the grazing land as far as the eye can see and your transport is a horse. That life doesn't suit some women. Good place to grow up as a kid. You can run around as you please, ride a horse, learn respect for the surroundings.'

I nodded. It sounded more like the life of freedom that I had experienced in Crete. I was very aware of the dangers that surrounded my boys in the town.

'It sounds like village life on Crete. I had never been out of Fourni until I went to Elounda to live with my relatives. The farmers have donkeys that they ride but I had never seen a horse until I came here. I found them quite frightening.'

Fred grinned at me. 'I'll introduce you to my horse. She's gentle enough.'

'I expected you to have a motor vehicle.'

'I have, but that costs money for petrol. A horse costs nothing to ride and has to be fed and exercised anyway. More practical to ride into town on her than drive and it takes about the same amount of time.'

'What about your schooling if you lived on a ranch in the middle of nowhere?'

'My parents taught me the basics and when I was ten I went to a boarding school in Broome.'

'A boarding school? What is that?'

'Where you stay and sleep over. All of us kids lived too far away to go home every day.'

'So you stayed there all the time? I would hate to have to send my boys away.'

'No, on a Friday morning my mother or father would ride over bringing my horse with them. I would go back home for the weekend and on a Monday morning we'd make an early start and do the journey in reverse. Allowances were made for travelling so we had a Friday afternoon and a Monday morning off from school.'

'How long did it take you to ride back and forth?'

'About an hour to an hour and a half.'

'And you did that every week?'

'Unless it was holiday time; then I was at home for weeks. How about you?'

'The girls were not expected to go to school. My father was the local school teacher and he educated me at home. I probably learnt far more than I would have done had I gone to school. He had hoped I would become a school teacher.'

'So why didn't you?'

'I had Luke. I asked if I could be a teacher in Elounda but they said not until Luke was older.'

'Couldn't your father have spoken up for you?'

'He was the teacher in Kastelli.'

Fred frowned. 'I thought you said you had moved to Elounda.'

'I went there to live with my aunt and uncle. My parents stayed in Fourni.'

Fred held up his hand. 'Now, hold on a minute, I'm getting confused. Wasn't your husband in Elounda? Why didn't you live with him?'

I looked down at my hands and toyed with my glass of water. 'There were reasons,' I said at last.

'I'll not pry into your private affairs although I admit I'm curious. Do you enjoy working here?'

I was surprised and relieved at the sudden change of subject. 'No, but it's a job.'

'If I hadn't met you to talk with I would be bored to tears.'

'You could spend your time with your ranch hands who are in town.'

'I'll see more than enough of them when I get back home

143

and they don't want their boss breathing down their necks and watching every move they make. Up to them if they are stupid enough to drink too much.'

'I ought to get us another drink or I'll be asked to move to another table.'

'Why don't we go for a walk rather than sit here talking? You could come and meet my horse.'

I hesitated. 'If I leave now I'll have some pay docked. I have to make sure I sell a number of drinks each evening.'

'Leave that problem with me. I'll go up to the bar.'

Before I could protest Fred left the table and I could see him talking earnestly to the man at the bar.

'That's settled,' said Fred. 'I've paid for a couple of extra beers that I told him I had before you arrived as you were late meeting me. Asked him to take that into account on your behalf.'

I looked over at the bar man and he nodded. I was not sure if I wanted to go to see Fred's horse but I had a feeling that I would have no option.

'We'll stroll down to the stables and you can meet Blaze. I'll walk you home afterwards.'

'Blaze? Is that her name?'

'She has a white mark on her forehead and when necessary she can gallop like the blazes. You can give her a sugar lump as a good night treat.'

'She likes sugar?'

'All horses do, but they should not have too much. Better to give them an apple to crunch on, but I don't think we'll find a greengrocer open now.'

Fred held open the tavern door for me and then took my arm as we walked along. 'Don't want you catching your foot in one of the ruts and twisting an ankle,' he said.

As we passed the shop where the strange looking leather trousers were sold I pointed them out. 'Why do some of the men wear those over their trousers?'

'They're called Chaps and they wear them for a variety of reasons. If you're on a horse all day cloth trousers are soon rubbed thin by the horse's flanks. If you're out in the bush cloth trousers get snagged and if you should come across a snake your legs are protected.'

'So why do they wear them around the town sometimes? It's very rare that we see a snake here.'

'They're probably going to drive some cattle. The poor beasts get very stressed when they are cooped up in a lorry and they can end up pretty dirty, if you get my meaning. You don't want that on your cloth trousers, leather ones can be wiped clean.'

I could see the logic behind the clothing now. I would not want my clothes to be soiled and smell of cow manure.

'Here we are.' Fred walked over to a stable block and opened the top half of the door. The horse inside pricked up her ears and stretched her neck out. Fred stroked her gently. 'See the blaze on her forehead?'

I nodded. She was enormous. I only reached as far as her shoulder. 'How did you ride a horse this big when you were only ten years old?'

'I had a smaller one, more of a pony than a horse. They're not all as large as Blaze. Few women are capable of riding and controlling a horse this size so there are plenty of smaller breeds that we use.'

'Why do you have one that is so big?'

'I took a fancy to her. It also means that when I am out on the ranch supervising I am higher up and can see what is going on. Do you want to give her a sugar lump?'

'I'm not sure. Will she bite me?'

'No, you do it like this.' Fred placed a sugar lump on the palm of his hand and held it beneath the horse's mouth. 'Just keep your hand flat and she'll take it from you.'

I watched as her lips curled back and I could see her enormous teeth. She passed her lips over Fred's palm and the sugar was gone. Fred took another lump from his pocket and placed it on my hand. 'Just remember to keep your hand flat when you feel her lips tickle you.'

Nervously I placed my hand below her mouth and it took all my resolve not to clench my fist and move away as her lips touched me.

'See? Nothing to it. That's all you're getting tonight, girl. I'll bring you an apple tomorrow.' He patted the horse again and then closed up the stable door. 'Now, I'll walk you home. Not good for an unescorted lady to be round by the animals quarters at night. Some of the hands would think she was looking for action.'

I was not sure of the route back to my house from the stables so we returned to the main road, Fred still holding my arm, until I reached the side road that led to my house.

'I live down there.'

Fred nodded. 'When you take a lady home you mean you will take her to her front door and ensure she is safely inside so lead on.'

I was not sure if I wanted Fred to take me to the door of my house as my father was probably waiting up for me and would want to know why he was bringing me home.

'I've had a thought,' said Fred as we walked along. 'Would your boys like to see my horse?'

'Maybe. I'll ask them and let you know tomorrow. This is where I live.' I stopped outside and I could see my father sitting in the window area. 'Goodnight, Fred.'

I opened the door and my father looked up. 'Who is your friend?'

'He's a rancher in town buying some cattle.'

'Why was he walking you home?'

'Just being polite. We'd been talking about the time he spent in Crete during the war.'

'Really?' As I had expected this diverted my father's attention away from me. 'Where was he stationed?'

'I don't think he was in any one place for very long. He said he and his men had to walk across Crete to a place called Preveli where many of them were taken over to North Africa by ship.'

'I'd be interested to hear more.'

'I'm sure he would be willing to talk to you. I'm off to bed, Pappa.' I escaped thankfully to my room.

As I readied my boys for school that morning I asked them if they would like to meet a horse that belonged to a friend and feed it an apple. Luke was immediately enthusiastic, but Dimitris was more hesitant.

'Do horses bite?' he asked.

'I fed it a sugar lump on my hand and it didn't bite me,' I answered. I wanted them to meet Fred's horse as I thought he might be offended if they refused. I would not have taken them near her on my own but I felt it was quite safe if Fred was with me. 'I'll see if I can arrange for you to see the horse on Saturday when you're not at school.'

I told Fred that my father would like to talk with him about Crete and that the boys would like to meet his horse. Fred smiled with pleasure. 'I'll get some apples so they can feed her, much better for her than sugar. I'm not sure I can tell your father any more than I told you, but I'm happy to meet him. Where's the best place to eat here?'

I looked at Fred bemused. 'I don't know. My mother always cooks our meals. I could ask my father if you could join us.'

'I don't want to be a trouble to them.'

'That would be no trouble. In fact I think my mother would be offended if you were asked to join us and then refused.'

Luke was ecstatic when Fred cut a piece of apple and placed it in his hand so he could feed Blaze. 'She tickles when she takes it. Can I give her some more?'

'One more piece and then it's your brother's turn.'

I looked at the height of the horse and the height of Dimitris. He would never be able to reach high enough to give Blaze a piece of apple.

Fred lifted Dimitris up and sat him on his hip. 'I want you to put your hand on mine and I'll put the apple on your palm. You need to keep your hand flat so I'll hold your fingers so you don't curl them up.'

'She won't bite me?' he asked nervously.

'Not if you do as I say. Now, are you ready?'

Dimitris obeyed Fred and when Blaze rook the piece of apple he turned to me with a smile. 'I did it, even though I was frightened.'

'You're a brave boy,' commented Fred. 'Do you want to give her another piece?'

'Will you hold my fingers again?'

'Of course. Your hands need to grow a bit bigger before you can do it easily.'

'Can I go for a ride on her?' asked Luke and Fred shook his head.

'She's far too big for you to ride. You can sit on her and see what the world looks like from up there.'

Fred placed Dimitris back on the ground, undid the lower door to the stable and led Blaze out. She seemed even larger once she was outside the stable. He held her bridle with one hand and pulled a bale of straw over.

'Stand up on that and I'll give you a lift up.'

I had to laugh. Luke sat on the horse's back, his legs sticking out at the side as they were not long enough to go round the girth of the horse.

'It's a long way up,' he said, as he curled his hands into her mane. 'It must be fun to ride a horse so you can see what's going on around you.'

At first Dimitris shook his head when Fred offered to place him on the horse's back, then decided he must keep up with his older brother.

'Will you hold me? I don't want to fall off.'

'Provided you sit still you'll not fall. I'll make sure you're safe.'

'I wish I could ride her,' said Luke. 'How big do I have to grow before I can sit properly on a horse?'

'They're not all as big as Blaze. I had a pony when I was your brother's age and she was easy enough for me to ride.'

'Can I get down now?' asked Dimitris and Fred lifted him back to the safety of the ground.

'Are you going to ride her?' asked Luke and Fred shook his head.

'Later today I'll take her out for some exercise. I'm sure you've spent enough time admiring my horse. How would you boys like an ice cream?'

Whilst Fred had a beer and the boys and I had an ice cream Luke plied him with questions about his horse and also his cattle. Fred was patient and took pains to answer Luke and draw Dimitris into the conversation. Finally I said I must take the boys home for a mid-day meal and that Fred needed to attend to his horse. Reluctantly they rose and thanked Fred, Luke asking if he could see the horse again.

All the way home they talked of nothing else except the horse and as soon as they entered the house they began recounting their experience of feeding and then sitting on the animal to their grandparents. When they finally quietened and were eating their meal I decided this was the time to speak to my father about a visit from Fred.

'He said he is quite willing to talk to you about his experiences in Crete, but he wanted to take you out for a meal in town. I said I thought Mamma would prefer to cook for us at home as usual as we're not used to eating out.'

'I'm sure your mother would cook a far better meal than we could expect at one of the taverns. They all appear to sell steak and chips.'

I gave a little shudder. If Fred ate steak he could be eating some meat from one of his own cows.

'I expect he'll be in the tavern this evening and I'll ask when it will be convenient for him.'

I was disappointed when I spoke to Fred as he said he was leaving town the following day.

'I need to check that all is well at the ranch and look the stock over. I don't want to find I have a sickly one in the herd.'

'What do you do if one is sick?'

'Take them well away from the others. They could just be suffering a bit of stress from the travelling in which case they'll recover in a couple of days. If they get worse I have to dispose of them.'

'How do you do that?'

'I shoot them, of course.'

'Shoot them!' I gasped in horror.

'Most humane way of killing them. No point in leaving them to suffer for days until I am able to arrange a visit from a vet and then pay him to shoot them.'

'You have a gun?'

'Of course. Only practical when you are in the outback. Never know what you may encounter. Provided I find no problems I'll be back in town in a few days and we can arrange for me to meet your family then.'

'Will you ride out on your horse?'

'Well I'm not planning to walk. Why?'

'If you're not leaving too early could I bring the boys to see you ride out? They haven't stopped talking about you and your horse.'

'Why don't I ride past your house when I'm kitted out and ready to go?'

'I'm sure they would love that. I won't tell them. It can be a surprise.'

Fred grinned at me. 'They're two nice boys. A credit to you.'

I blushed with pleasure.

Fred had ridden to the house as he had promised and shown the boys how he mounted his horse and controlled her with the use of the reins and also using pressure from his legs.

'If you use your legs you can get her to turn left or right without pulling on her mouth,' he said and demonstrated. 'Her mouth is soft and sensitive. If you damage it she'll resist being harnessed and you end up with an uncontrollable animal.'

'Like having toothache,' said Dimitris.

'Similar sort of thing,' smiled Fred. 'Be good for your Mum whilst I'm away. If she gives me a bad report about you there'll be no more ice cream.'

'I like Fred,' observed Luke as Fred rode away. 'I hope he does come back.'

I did not realise until after Fred left town how much I had enjoyed his company each evening and I looked anxiously for him to appear at the tavern. The conversation I had to listen to was boring and I had to pretend to be interested. I would linger longer than necessary up at the bar when ordering more beer for the men, ignoring the crude remarks they made about me as I walked back and forcing a smile on my face.

I was relieved when Fred did finally appear. I excused myself from the table I was sitting at and ordered a beer and my usual glass of water and walked to his table.

'Service with a smile,' I said, and my smile was genuine.

'Thanks. I didn't like to interrupt you.'

'You thought I was enjoying myself?'

Fred shrugged. 'You were working.'

'That doesn't mean I was having any pleasure from sitting there listening to them bragging about how much money they had earned this week and all they planned to do with it. I'd rather talk about cows. Did your herd arrive safely and all of them healthy?'

Fred threw back his head and laughed. 'I've never known my cow talk to be of interest to a woman before.'

'I'm interested in anything that I know nothing about. I consider it part of educating myself,' I answered primly.

'Then you'll be pleased to know that they all made it safely to the ranch and they all appear to be well.'

'So now you just have to fatten them up ready to be slaughtered.'

Fred shook his head. 'No these are heifers. I'm hoping that most of them will be in calf. It will depend upon the quality of their offspring whether I keep them to calve again or get rid of them. I'm hoping there may be some bullocks as I can sell those for breeding at a good price. I'd keep the best one for myself to serve my herd and that would save me from having to pay for a bull to be brought to them.'

'It sounds very clinical and controlled.'

'It is. The cows do not fall in love with the bull; likewise the bull has no affection for a particular cow. It's just the mating instinct the same as in all animals. From the bull's point of view the more the merrier.'

'And the cows have to tolerate his attention.'

'They don't usually object. Anyway, enough about me. How are your boys?'

'Still talking about your horse. We have to arrange an evening when you can come for a meal and talk with my father.'

'Any evening will suit me. I'm here for a week.'

'Are you buying more cows?'

'No, I have other business I want to attend to.'

The evening passed swiftly, although I have no recollection of what Fred and I talked about. We suddenly realised we were the only people left at the tavern and the bar tender was leaning on his elbows yawning.

'I'll walk you home,' said Fred. 'It's too late for you to be wandering about on your own.'

I did not resist when he took my arm as we walked along the road.

Two evenings later he came to the house, bringing a bottle of wine, for a meal that my mother and I had prepared. We tried to make the food as Greek as possible, having made taromasalata and falafel to start and keftedes, dolmades or moussaka to follow. If he did not like those dishes there was fried chicken and kebabs. Fred ate everything that was offered to him and declared that all of it was delicious.

'I didn't get the opportunity to eat this kind of food when I was in Greece. We had standard army rations and when I was in Crete we ate whatever we could get our hands on, same as the locals.'

I sent the boys off to bed and left my father and Fred to talk about Crete whilst I helped my mother in the kitchen. We took our time as I had a suspicion that some of the information Fred would have for my father was not suitable for a lady's ears.

When Fred left he shook hands with my parents and thanked them for their hospitality; they in turn said he was welcome to return at any time.

Decisions

I was taken by surprise at the end of the week when Fred asked me to marry him. I hesitated.

'I am not sure if my parents would permit me to marry you.'

'You are an adult. You do not need their permission.'

'It's a bit complicated.' If I agreed to become his wife I would have to tell him about Lucas and the reason my parents brought me to Australia.

'Tell me the problem and I hope I can sort it out for you.'

'I have to consider my boys.'

'Of course. I wouldn't expect you to leave them here. Is that your only concern?'

I shook my head miserably. 'I can't talk about it here.'

'Then we'll go back to my hotel. There's a lounge there that guests can use and it's often empty in the evenings. I'll sort out the bar tender and we can go there.'

I allowed Fred to lead me to his hotel and into the lounge area. It was crowded with men who were listening to a football match on the wireless. They were commenting so loudly on the match that although the volume was turned up high the words of the commentator could hardly be heard.

'This is impossible,' said Fred as he closed the door. 'We'll go up to my room. You'll be quite safe, I promise. I've never forced a woman.'

I followed Fred up to his room and he indicated the bed and a chair. 'You can sit on my bed. It's more comfortable than the chair.' Fred sat down on the chair and I sat on the end of his bed.

'So what do you need to talk to me about? I realise it would be a big move for you, but you wouldn't be expected to herd the cows. All I would ask is a meal at the end of the day, my laundry done and the ranch kept reasonably clean and tidy.'

I shook my head. I was not afraid of hard work. 'I'm not married, Fred.'

'What do you mean? You're not married? You led me to believe that you were a widow.'

I gave a deep sigh. 'I'll have to tell you what happened. When you've heard you probably won't want to marry me.'

Fred leaned forward and took my hand. 'Whatever happened in the past is over and done with. I love you, Reen. Nothing will change the way I feel about you.'

'It might.'

I proceeded to tell Fred about meeting Lucas and falling desperately in love with him. How my parents had taken me to Elounda when I was pregnant and told the villagers that Lucas had raped me and run away.

'Scoundrel,' growled Fred, and I held up my hand and shook my head.

I sounded very naive and childish when I said I had gone to work on Spinalonga, hoping to find his uncle and ask if there were any relatives in a nearby town where Lucas might be living. Looking back I was only sixteen and had no experience of life outside of Fourni and Elounda.

I explained that, by chance, I had found that Lucas was living on Spinalonga having been diagnosed with leprosy.

'That was why he had disappeared from the village. He had no idea he had left me pregnant and had a son.'

'Why didn't he tell you why he was leaving?'

'The stigma. You know how the people here who live in Bungarun are treated. Their relatives do not go near them or admit they are in the leprosarium. Lucas did not want word of his illness to get back to the village so he did not even tell his parents he was sick.' I wiped a tear from my eye. 'I still loved him, and although we tried to control out emotions it was impossible. I found I was expecting his child again.'

'So why didn't you marry him?'

'Lepers are not allowed to marry in the eyes of the law and I would not have been given permission to live on the island unless I was sick. Eventually I had to tell my parents I was expecting another child and Lucas was the father. I was forbidden to ever go to Spinalonga again or to see Lucas. My father had already looked into the possibility of leaving Crete and making a new life in Australia and my news made him hesitate no longer. I insisted that before I left I had to go to Spinalonga and tell Lucas.

'My father went with me and whilst we were there I spoke to the priest and asked if he would give Lucas and I a blessing the same as he would for any other couple on the island who wished to consider themselves married. He agreed. I also insisted that in future I would be known by the name Tsantakis and so would my children.'

I was really crying now and Fred handed me his handkerchief.

'Your father didn't object to this?'

'He didn't like it, but the priest had said I could have my way. and my father would not disobey the priest. When my father thought about it later he realised it was an advantage. He could declare me a widow.'

'So poor Lucas never got to see his children?'

'I managed to take Luke over twice and then again when we had our last meeting. My father gave us fifteen minutes alone to say goodbye.' I spoke bitterly and dropped my head in my hands and sobbed.

Fred moved from the chair and sat beside me on the bed, placing his arm around me. 'You poor girl. Such trauma and you were hardly more than a child yourself. Do the boys know about their father?'

I managed to compose myself sufficiently to answer. 'No, they have never asked and I know they think he died. I may tell them when they are older and can understand.'

Fred sat there silently, his arm still around me. I did not expect him to want to marry me now he knew my history. I made to get up.

'I should go home now. You don't need to walk with me.'

Fred tightened his arm around me. 'You are not going anywhere yet. You don't have to tell me any more as it distresses you so much, but you cannot leave here until you have recovered. What would people think if they saw you walking along the road with tears streaming down your face?'

I cried some more and Fred held me until I finally quietened. He placed his finger beneath my chin and turned my face towards him.

'I still want to marry you, Reen. I'll not pressurize you. I'll come back to Derby in a week and you can let me know your answer then.' He kissed me lightly on my forehead. 'We'll have a quick drink. I think you need something stronger than your usual water, then I'll walk you home when you're ready.'

From his drawer Fred took a small bottle and poured a little into a glass adding water to it for me. He poured a more generous measure for himself. I took a sip and shuddered.

'What is it?'

'Just a very small whisky.'

'I don't like it.'

'It won't hurt you and will help you to recover. You were very courageous telling me about Lucas and the boys and I know how much it upset you.'

'I had to tell you the truth. I'll understand if you decide you no longer want to marry me when you've thought about it.' I took another cautious sip of the whisky.

'Don't be silly, Reen. I'll not change my mind.'

I slept remarkably well that night, maybe it was the whisky, but when I awoke a number of questions were in my mind. What would happen to my boys if I married Fred and went out to his ranch to live? Where would they go to school? Would Fred no longer be interested in my boys if I gave him a son of his own? Would it even be safe to have a child miles away from any medical help? If I was expected to cook where would I buy the ingredients? Would I be expected to cook a meal for the ranch hands? I would have to ask Fred a lot of questions before I could give him an answer.

I knew in my heart that I would never see Lucas again. However hard I tried to save I would never have sufficient money for the fare for myself and the boys to return to Crete. Lucas had not replied to any of my letters, although I had no guarantee that he had ever received them. I had to face the fact that he could have met someone else and did not want to keep in contact with me or that he had succumbed to the ravages of leprosy and died. Both thoughts tore at my heart strings. Although Fred seemed to be a nice, kind, man, he was not Lucas.

Fred was waiting for me at the tavern when I arrived and immediately said we would go back to his hotel where we could talk quietly without any interruptions. He led me up to his room without even glancing into the lounge to see if it was occupied. I sat on the edge of his bed and twisted my fingers together nervously.

'Please don't refuse me, Reen,' he begged.

I took a deep breath. 'We haven't known each other very long and before I make a decision either way I need answers to some questions that have been bothering me. If I married you what would happen to my boys?'

'Happen to them?' Fred seemed puzzled by my question. 'They would come to the ranch with us, of course.'

'What about their schooling?'

'They could go to Broome, same as I did.'

I shook my head. 'I would not want them to be away from me. They would feel they were unwanted.'

'You say your father educated you and wanted you to become a teacher. There's no reason why you shouldn't teach them at home. Later, when they decide what they want to do with their lives they may well need to go away for more education. I promise I will never force you to separate from them.'

'What about my parents?'

Fred frowned. 'They'd be welcome to visit, but I'm not sure it would be a good idea to offer them a home with us. I've heard from others that this can cause friction. You'll still be able to visit them. Once a month we will drive into town, bringing the boys with us and collect the supplies we need.'

'I was going to ask you how I would buy food,' I smiled.

'Well that's your answer. You make a list of everything we would need to keep us going. I'll help you until you are familiar with the quantities that would be necessary. We don't want waste and nor do we want to run out of something essential. That would mean me riding into town.'

'Suppose one of us fell ill? We are miles away from a doctor.'

'We do have a telephone but if that should happen it would be quicker to use my truck to drive here or to Broome. Both towns have a hospital. I'll teach you how to drive and in a real emergency you would be able to get help. I'll teach you how to ride a horse as well. That way you'll always have some transport available.'

I was still hesitant. 'Suppose I hate living with you on a ranch in the middle of nowhere?'

'It may take you a while to get used to a different way of life, but there's no reason why you should be unhappy. I'll treat you right. I would expect you to give it a fair trial, say a year, and if you do hate living there with me I'll bring you back to Derby to live with your parents again.'

'What about the boys? Would you bring us all back to Derby if they were unhappy?'

'If that was what you wanted.'

I believed Fred and I also knew that if we were unhappy I would simply refuse to return with him after a visit to the town for supplies and seeing my parents.

'Can I have some more time to think about it? It's a life changing decision that I have to make.'

'I can stay here until tomorrow afternoon, then I must get back. My hands are relatively new and I don't want to find they are taking advantage of my absence to shirk their duties. Most of my money is invested in the ranch and I can't afford to return and find the cattle have any infection caused by neglect. I could lose the whole herd if that was the case.'

'I promise I will come tomorrow morning with my decision.'

I turned Fred's proposition over in my head all night. I was tempted to accept, but a part of me said I was being foolish. Having seen my boys off to school I turned to my mother.

'Fred Anstruther has asked me to marry him,' I blurted out.

My mother turned on me immediately. 'Don't be stupid. You cannot marry him. You hardly know the man. You have no idea what the conditions are like in the middle of nowhere and you would be at his mercy with no one to turn to for help.'

'Fred has promised that if I am unhappy he'll bring me back to Derby to live.'

'Men make promises that they find easy to forget. All he wants is a housekeeper.'

I felt both hurt and furious and my mother's reaction decided me. I said no more and helped her with the morning chores before leaving at my usual time to go to work at the shop. I called in and told them that I had some urgent business in town and would be in for work as soon as I had completed that.

I entered the hotel nervously, unsure whether I should ask at the reception desk for Fred or make my way up to his room. I decided I would go to his room and only ask for him if I was unable to locate him. Fred opened the door and looked at me anxiously, trying to gauge my answer. He looked as exhausted as I felt. He held out his hand to me and I took it.

'I will marry you, Fred, if your offer is still available.'

A broad smile spread across his face and he pulled me into his arms. 'I couldn't sleep. I didn't know what I would do if you refused me.'

Fred was reluctant to release me and I was acutely reminded of the emotions I had felt when Lucas had held me. Finally he led me over to the bed and I sat down whilst he went to his wardrobe and brought out a bottle. It was not whisky this time, but wine.

'I've borrowed some decent glasses from the bar. This is for a celebration.' The cork popped out and he poured clear, sparkling liquid into the glasses and handed one to me.

He held his glass up. 'To my future wife. May we live happily ever after.'

I gave a little giggle and did not really know what to reply. I took a sip of the wine and found it delightful, much nicer than the occasional cheap bottle that we treated ourselves to at home. Before I realised I had emptied the glass and held it out to Fred for a refill. He shook his head.

'I don't want you to claim that I made you drunk and then took advantage of you. Now we are officially engaged I think we should cement the relationship.'

He pushed me gently down on to the bed and began to kiss me whilst he also occupied himself in undoing my blouse. Afterwards I was not sure why I had not resisted him, as I had not drunk too much wine. The remainder of the morning was spent confirming our engagement in between having more wine until we had consumed the whole bottle between us. My head was reeling, but it was not the wine that had affected me. Fred had been gentle and patient until I was no longer able to resist his overtures.

I dreaded returning home to the recriminations I would receive if I mentioned marrying Fred again. I decided that if I was asked I would say I was still considering the proposal and listen to my parents' objections without commenting.

It was only later that night when I lay in bed that night that doubts began to enter my mind. Maybe Fred had no intention of marrying me and it had just been an empty promise on his part to get me into his bed. Would my boys be happy to have Fred as a step father and would he be good to them? They had never been beaten and if Fred raised his hand to them I would leave him immediately. I could not broach the subject with them until I was certain that Fred would return the following week as he had promised.

I spent the remainder of the week worrying. Each evening that I spent at the taverna I looked for Fred to enter and when he finally appeared I was so relieved. I ordered more drinks for the men whom I was sitting with and excused myself shortly afterwards to go to sit with Fred. I did remember my mother's warning and asked him to tell me more about the ranch.

'What do you want to know?'

'Well,' I wasn't sure what I did want to know. 'Does it have running water or do you need to collect it from a well?'

'We have an Artesian well on the property. The water comes up naturally from the ground below and it is piped to the house and the cattle troughs. There's a generator that provides electricity for the water pumps and also for the house. It's good clean water.'

'What about cooking? Would I have to cook for the ranch hands?'

'There's a large electric range that you can cook on. It has ovens at the side and the top gets hot so you can boil food on that.

EIRINI

You'll be able to use the ovens to bake our bread Every other day a man rides to Derby or Broome and brings back bread along with any other items the ranch hands decide they need. I only expect you to cook sufficient food for us. They cater for themselves.'

'Where do they cook?' I dreaded hearing that I would have twelve men invading the kitchen area.

'At their quarters. Most of the time they use an open fire and cook outside. When I'm there I usually join them. Steak cooked over a camp fire tastes good.'

'It seems that steak is all the people here eat.'

Fred shrugged. 'It's plentiful and cheap. Anything else worrying you?'

'Is there a bathroom?'

'Yes, but I'm having a decent one installed. I'm not sure if I'll be able to get that completed before you arrive.'

'What kind of improvement does it need?'

'Well, at the moment it's outside and you stand under a bucket with holes in it and the cold water runs through. That's fine for me when I've been working outside but I can't expect you to cope with that. You need a bathroom inside. There's a suitable room and I've employed a plumber to fix a proper shower and feed the warm water to it. You may have to be patient for a while and use the outside one until it's completed.'

Until I had boarded the boat for Piraeus I had never had the luxury of a toilet inside the house or warm water from a tap. I did not really want to go back to the old days of having a privy at the end of the garden. I had never used a shower, but I made sure the boys had a bath each day and I had one three times each week.

'I hope that won't take too long to organise. The boys have been used to having a bathroom inside.'

Fred grinned. 'They'll probably find roughing it for a week or two quite a novelty.'

'You did mean it when you said that if I was truly unhappy you would bring me back to Derby, didn't you?'

Fred nodded. 'I certainly would not make you stay with me provided you had given it a fair trial. I wouldn't expect you to say you wanted to return the first time we had a cross word.'

'What about the boys if they were unhappy?'

'I can't think why they should be. They'll have their own horses to ride and far more freedom than here in the town. I'll make sure they're watched over and kept safe until they become used to the life. They must be obedient. If I say they cannot go to an area I will have good reason and they must accept that without question.'

Fred was certainly allaying all the fears that my mother had planted in my mind.

I left the tavern early and went back with Fred to his hotel. I could not stay too late or I would be questioned by my parents and I asked Fred to leave me at the bottom of the road.

'It's better that they do not see you walk me home or my mother will keep me up half the night telling me how foolish I am and how unsuitable it is for me to marry you.'

'You'll have to tell them at some time.'

'I know,' I sighed. 'Couldn't we just have a very quiet wedding at the Magistrate's office?'

'I expected you to want to get married in the church.'

I shook my head. 'That could take months to organise. Now I've made my decision I want to be married as soon as possible.'

Fred bent and kissed me. 'That suits me. I'll find out how we go about organising a ceremony. You'll probably need to produce your immigration papers or proof of citizenship.'

I had not thought about that. 'My father keeps them.'

'Then you will have to ask him to give yours to you. We don't want to have to wait whilst there is a search done and you are provided with duplicates.'

I thought it very unlikely that my father would allow me to have the legal papers, but I knew where he kept them. If I could take them without his knowledge it would save a tremendous amount of trouble and I would face the consequences later. I could not be accused of stealing as by law they belonged to me.

'What about the boys? Will there be any problem about them coming to live with us?'

'Shouldn't be. Luke will be listed on your immigration form as he was only a baby at the time and Dimitris was born here.'

That was a relief to me. I did not want to tell Fred that I planned to take the papers without my father's knowledge or permission.

'I'll find out exactly what is needed and if you have them by next weekend we can see about registering a marriage ceremony.'

I knew it could be difficult for me to take the necessary papers without either of my parents knowing. My mother went shopping for vegetables most days, but sometimes she would ask me to bring something back from the general store so she stayed at home. My father brought the shop keepers' account books back to the house to work on them in peace and only went to the shops if he had a query or was returning their books. I knew the papers I needed were in a drawer in the living room.

Once I had them I would need somewhere safe to keep them. I could not walk around with them tucked into my bodice as they could become creased and stained. There was nowhere I could safely hide them in my room. If my father discovered they were missing it would be the first place he would look.

Whilst I was working in the general store an idea came to me. I would purchase a large, strong envelope and place them in there. I would then take them to the bank and ask them to look after them, giving them instructions that they were not to be handed to anyone but me.

My opportunity came two days later when my father declared that he was taking a set of books back to the shop keeper along with his bill for the work and my mother said she would walk with him and do her shopping. The boys were at school and I would be alone in the house for a short while.

'I expect I will have gone to work by the time you return,' I said. 'I'll make sure the door is locked securely.'

I had done this on previous occasions so I was not questioned. As soon as they left I went to the drawer and searched through the papers. The rent book was there, along with receipts for our electricity payments and beneath those were our immigration papers. I removed mine, along with my Citizenship certificate and Dimitris's birth certificate. I checked the name on each one carefully to ensure I had those that belonged to me and not taken any official papers that my parents might need.

I replaced the receipts and the rent book in the drawer and took my papers up to my room where I wrote my name "EIRINI TSANTAKIS" in block capitals on the envelope before placing my documents inside and sealing the flap.

Making a visit to the bank would make me late in arriving at the shop and I hoped I would not meet either my mother or father on the way or they would want to know why I was not working. I hurried along the road and entered the imposing building nervously. I approached a counter where a man sat with an iron grill protecting him from customers.

He smiled at me and asked how he could help.

'I have some important documents that need to be kept safe for a few days. May I leave them here at the bank?'

He frowned. 'Do you have a bank account here?'

I shook my head.

'We cannot accept documents for storage unless the customer has a bank account with us.'

'So what can I do? I only need them to be kept until the end of the week.'

'You can open a bank account, then we would be able to accommodate your request.'

'How do I do that?'

'You will have to fill in a form with your details, have proof of your identity and deposit some money.'

'How much money?' I had visions of being asked for some hundreds of dollars.

'Five dollars is sufficient to open the account once you have completed the formalities.'

'Can I do that now?' I asked eagerly.

'I will ask someone to attend to you.'

I was led across to a table and given a form to complete. I read it through carefully and then began to insert my answers to the questions. I had to stop when it asked for my date of birth. I had only a vague idea of when I had been born and no birth certificate.

'I don't know my date of birth,' I confessed.

The man frowned. 'You said you had proof of your identity with you.'

I nodded. 'I have my immigration certificate and my Citizenship certificate.'

'Your date of birth should be on both of those.'

'Of course.' I sighed with relief. My father had completed our immigration and Citizenship forms and since then I had never looked at them in detail. I ran my finger beneath the seal of the envelope carefully and took the papers out. There was the date; 17th August 1922.

The man read through my form carefully, whilst my heart was pounding. Finally he looked at the forms I produced, declared himself satisfied and asked me to sign. He then placed his signature next to mine.

I placed the forms safely back in the envelope and licked the flap, hoping there would be sufficient glue left to stick it down safely. Some areas stuck down and others were loose. I signed my name again and again all along the flap of the envelope, hoping that would keep my precious documents safe until I collected it and gave them to Fred.

'No one else will be able to claim my envelope, will they?' I asked anxiously.

'Why should they want it? These papers are of no use to them.'

I hesitated, then wrote across the front of the envelope beneath my name "Only to be handed to Eirini Tsantakis". The man gave me a curious look, obviously wondering at my action.

I took five dollars from my purse and handed it to him. He wrote out a receipt and then to my horror said that an account book would delivered to my home.

'Can't I collect it?'

'It isn't usual, but there's no law against it. I'll mark it for collection.'

I gave a sigh of relief. 'I'll collect it at the same time as I come for my envelope. Thank you for helping me.'

I could not wait to escape and hurry to the shop, trying hard to think of an excuse for arriving late.

I realised I would have to tell Luke and Dimitris that I was going to marry Fred and we would live out on his ranch but I did not want to do so until I knew we had a date set for our marriage. I could then tell them that it was to be a surprise for their grandparents and they must keep it a secret. I did not want to encourage them to be deceitful, but I did want to avoid interminable rows and recriminations from my parents.

When the time came it was easier than I had anticipated. I sat on the beach with them and began by asking if they liked Fred. Both boys agreed that they had found him nice and friendly and Luke added that he also liked his horse. I asked tentatively how they would feel about living on a ranch without their grandparents and not going to school.

Luke frowned. 'We'll still see Grandma and Grandpa, won't we?'

'Of course. Every few weeks we will come into town for shopping and we can visit them at the same time.'

'Will we ride in on horses?' asked Luke eagerly.

I shook my head. 'That would not be very practical. Fred has a truck and we would load it up with all the supplies we needed.

We couldn't expect horses to carry that amount back with them.'

'What kind of truck?' asked Dimitris and I had to admit I did not know.

'How will we get to school?' was his next question.

'You won't be able to go to school for a while. I am going to get some school books and I will teach you at home until you are old enough to go away for schooling.'

Luke shook his head. 'I wouldn't want to go away from home.'

'No one will make you. You have to decide eventually what work you want to do when you are grown up and that may mean that you have to go to school in Broome as Fred did. He used to ride there on his horse and so did all the other pupils. They would stay there each night and then ride back home for the weekend.'

'They slept there? At the school?'

'Only for a few days at a time. Once you were used to it I'm sure you would enjoy being there.'

'I'm not going,' said Luke determinedly.

'You may change your mind later on. You have plenty of time before you need to think about that.'

'Is there a harbour close by?' asked Dimitris. 'I'd like to be able to see the ships and swim the same as we do here.'

'I believe it's quite a long way to the coast, but there may be a river fairly near. You'll have to ask Fred. He will know.'

A troubled look came into Luke's eyes. 'Does this mean you and Fred will get married and we will have a stepfather?'

'I'm thinking about it, but I want you to keep it a secret and not tell anyone.'

'Not even Grandma and Grandpa?' piped up Dimitris.

'No, not even them or your friends at school.'

'I'm not sure I want a stepfather,' said Luke. 'I want my proper father.'

I felt tears coming into my eyes. 'That isn't possible. If it was I would certainly not consider marrying Fred.'

'Is he dead?' asked Dimitris suddenly.

I took a deep breath. 'I believe so. He was on Crete during the war and many people over there died.'

'Have you tried to find out?' demanded Luke.

'Yes, I have sent letters and never had a reply.'

'Suppose he comes here looking for us and finds that you are married?'

I shook my head. 'I am certain he will never come here.'

Luke shrugged. 'I suppose Fred is as good as anyone else to be my stepfather. Will I have to do as he says?' His jaw jutted out pugnaciously.

'Yes, the same as you do for me and your grandparents.'

'Will he beat us if we disobey?'

'I hope you will never do anything naughty enough to deserve a beating. I'm sure another punishment would suffice. Just remember it is a secret at the moment,' I repeated, trying to keep the urgency from my voice and hoping I had not made a mistake by confiding in my sons.

The Ranch

Fred was surprised when I told him I had placed my documents in the bank for safe keeping.

'So your father gave them to you without a problem.'

'No, I took them without his knowledge. I was frightened he would refuse. Having taken them I thought I might spoil them or lose them if I carried them around with me,' I explained.

'I have to go to the bank to collect the men's wages so we can collect them together and then go to the Magistrate's Court and apply to be married. You'll have about three weeks in which you can change your mind about getting married.'

I shook my head. 'I'll not change my mind.' I had a suspicion that I might be pregnant and I did not want to be an unmarried mother for a third time. I felt I should tell Fred and hope that he

169

would still want to marry me. If he refused I would just have to face the consequences.

'You may decide that you no longer wish to marry me.' I took a deep breath. 'I think I could be expecting.'

'Expecting? You mean you're pregnant?'

I nodded and waited for his answer with trepidation.

'Really?'

'I'm not absolutely certain yet. I could just be late this month.'

Fred took me in his arms. 'I hope you're right. I thought I was too old now to expect to have any children.'

'You're not old, Fred.'

'I am fifteen years older than you. Time is not on my side. Are you happy about having another?'

'I know what to expect. My only concern is being miles away from the hospital when the time comes.'

'I'll bring you back to Derby in good time provided all goes to plan. Remember we have a telephone that can be used and in an emergency I can drive you here within two hours.'

With that I had to be content.

I tried to continue with my usual routine whilst Fred returned to the ranch and we waited to hear a date when our marriage could be solemnized and legally registered. I had mixed emotions. Was I making a big mistake that once made could not be rectified or would I be happy living with Fred in the middle of nowhere? I had to admit that I did not feel the passion for Fred that I had for Lucas.

I had not mentioned Fred again to my mother and I think she assumed I had refused his offer of marriage. After our short ceremony Fred went to load the truck up with supplies to take to the ranch with us and I returned home and began to pack my belongings and those of the boys.

'What are you doing?' asked my mother and my father looked up from the accounts he was working on.

'Packing our possessions. I'm going to live on the ranch with Fred and the boys are coming with me.'

'You must be out of your mind going off into the outback miles away from anywhere with a man you hardly know. Your father will not allow it.'

'You cannot stop me.'

For a moment my mother was speechless. 'You cannot marry him. He's not a Cretan, not even a Greek,' she declared.

'Had you not forced me to come to Australia I could have stayed in Elounda and been with Lucas as much as possible.'

'It was for your own good; to preserve your reputation and good name.'

'You spread a rumour that Lucas had raped me and run away to escape the consequences. You had no consideration for his reputation or for the feelings of his family. It was your own reputation that concerned you.'

'And what of your reputation now? What will the people we know in Derby think?'

'The people can think whatever they like. Fred and I are legally married so you won't have to worry about your reputation or mine.'

My mother began to cry. 'So what is going to happen to your father and myself when we get old? Who is going to look after us?'

'You should have thought of that before. Whoever looks after you, it will not be me.'

My mother stood by silently as I completed our packing, Luke and Dimitris watching me, and we were ready and waiting when Fred arrived with the truck. My father took me to one side as Fred placed our sacks in the back amongst all the other paraphernalia that was there.

'You are quite sure, Eirini?'

'Yes, Pappa. Fred has promised that if I am truly unhappy he will bring me back to Derby to live.'

My father sighed. 'I hope he is a man of his word.'

The boys and I kissed my parents goodbye and Fred settled us into the front of the truck with him.

We seemed to be driving for hours before we reached a fenced enclosure and Fred stopped in front of a gate. A collection of buildings could be seen further down the hillside.

'Hop out, Luke, and undo the gate. Wait until I've driven through then close it behind me and get back in the truck.'

We progressed slowly down the dirt road until Fred finally stopped before the buildings.

'Right, we're home. You boys help your Mum to take things inside whilst I get the truck unloaded.' Fred placed our sacks on the ground, then placed two fingers in his mouth and gave a shrill whistle. By the time he had unlocked the door to the house men could be seen running towards us.

'Just put your belongings inside and wait for me,' ordered Fred as the men began to unload the truck and take various items to the outbuildings.

I walked in and looked around. The room was almost as large as the tavern where I had worked. There was no sign of any beds, just a large table with chairs around it and more chairs and some small tables in other parts of the room along with a two large cupboards.

Fred brought in more sacks and boxes from the truck and dumped them at the side of the room. Taking a sack in each hand he went through the doorway and returned moments later with a jug of water and mugs for all of us. He poured and passed a mug to each of us and we drank thankfully as he indicated that we should sit down at the table.

'We'll have a talk first and I'll explain the ground rules to you, then show you your rooms and you can make yourselves at home. If there's anything you don't understand ask me.'

The boys nodded dutifully and Fred continued. 'You are not allowed anywhere near the cattle. If you spook them they could stampede and you would be caught up amongst them. They would trample you into the ground before anyone could rescue you. The other thing is the water pipes; you do not play on them. They must not be damaged. We check for leaks every day as we can't afford to waste water.'

'Where does it come from?' asked Dimitris. 'Is there a river here where we can swim?'

'It rises up from the ground naturally and makes a small lake. You do not swim in it as you would make the water dirty and no one wants to drink dirty water. You do not go into any of the barns or store rooms. Keep away from the ranch hands quarters and do not go near the stables.'

'I hoped I could feed Blaze,' protested Luke.

'Not yet. She's not had any proper exercise for some days so she'll be pretty twitchy and excitable. When she's calmed down you can visit her again.'

'Who looks after Blaze when you're not here?' asked Luke.

'Hank. He's my right hand man. He's taken her for a canter each day. Now, the gate you opened and closed, Luke, has to be closed at all times. Most of the time the cows are allowed to wander freely and they don't often come this close to the ranch. They are curious creatures. If they saw the gate open they would investigate without meaning to cause any harm but they'd leave a mess everywhere. If that happens whoever has left the gate open clears up the cow pats. When you get up tomorrow you stay in the ranch house once you've used the bathroom.'

'You've kidnapped us and we're prisoners,' said Luke dolefully.

I was about to tell Luke not to be so silly when Fred laughed.

'I haven't kidnapped you and you are certainly not prisoners. I don't want you to go wandering off outside and getting lost or hurt. You have to be aware that should you fall and break a leg or knock yourself unconscious you might not be found for hours. You are not in the town where people will be passing by. I'll show you round and explain where you cannot go. I expect you

173

to obey me and I'm a hard taskmaster, used to dealing with men not boys. Understood?'

'If we disobey will you beat us?' asked Dimitris.

I looked at Fred anxiously. I hoped I would not have to continually get my boys out of trouble with him. They were not naughty boys and had never been in trouble at school but these were different rules they had to abide by.

'There are other punishments I can think of that you would dislike far more than a beating,' said Fred grimly.

Fred sounded so severe and I wanted to ask him what punishments he had in mind if the boys disobeyed him.

'Just do as I say and there'll be no problem. The same rules apply to you, Reen. I don't expect you to play on the water pipes, but you have to realise that you are not in the town where you can ask for immediate help.'

'How do the men who drive the cattle avoid being trampled?' asked Luke.

'They ride at the side and behind, never in amongst them when they are moving them around. You'll be able to see how they work from a safe distance when you are with me. I don't want you going near them alone.'

Fred stood up and picked up my two sacks of belongings. 'Bring your sacks, boys.' He led the way through a door and down a hallway with rooms leading off from it.

'This is our room,' he announced and placed my sacks inside. 'You boys have a room next door.' Fred opened the door to the room opposite ours and the boys walked inside and deposited their sacks.

'We have a bed each,' said Luke. 'I've only shared one with Dimitris before and slept in the same room as Mum.'

'Later you can have a room each but until you're familiar with living here I guess you'd prefer to be together for company. Decide which bed you will have and then unpack. I'll get some food ready for you and afterwards we will go for a walk. I have something to show you, Reen.'

I followed Fred down the hallway and he opened the door at the far end. I gasped. 'The bathroom! It's finished.'

'Not quite. The plumber is returning on Monday. I wanted it to be a surprise for you, Reen.'

'So why did you tell me we could be using a bucket shower for a few weeks?'

'I couldn't be certain that it would be ready and I didn't want to raise your hopes.'

'Are there any other surprises for me behind the other doors?' I asked.

Fred grinned. 'Some are empty, others are used for storage. We'll go through the rubbish that's in there at some time and get rid of it. I'll keep them locked so the boys won't be able to go in.'

'There are a lot of rules for them to remember.'

'All common sense precautions until they are familiar with outback life. They'll soon settle. Do you want to see the kitchen?'

I followed Fred back to the main living room and through the door at the side. The kitchen was as large as the living room, with a range at the far end taking up most of the wall, there were shelves and cupboards lining the walls holding pots, pans and dishes. Beneath the window were two sinks and a long drainer.

I looked around in amazement. 'There's even a washing machine and a fridge!'

'We need somewhere to store the food that would go off in the heat. Didn't you have one?'

'There was a pantry and it was always cool in there.'

'You have one of those here.' He opened a door that I had thought was a cupboard and showed me the marble shelves. 'Not everything should go in a fridge. You'll soon know the best place to store the food. I'll bring in the supplies that we brought from Derby and later you can begin to decide where to put them. Now, unpack our belongings and then we'll eat. I expect the boys are hungry.'

We had a late lunch of bread, cheese, tomatoes and olives. The olives were a treat and I took my time removing the flesh from the stone. The boys were told to clear the table of the dirty dishes and I was expecting to wash them. Instead Fred announced we would now go out for a walk in the vicinity. From a hook behind the door Fred took down four water canteens.

'You make sure these are full and you carry them with you whenever you leave the ranch, particularly if we are driving into town. If you do find yourself stranded somewhere you need to have water with you.'

'Why didn't we have them today?' asked Dimitris.

'I had a large container of water in the back for emergencies. Had we broken down I could have kept you all hydrated and also used some of it to cool the engine if necessary.'

We left from a door in the kitchen area and Fred took us to a stand pipe outside. 'You fill your canteens here as this water is always cold. Don't leave the tap running, but any overspill will go into the bucket beneath.'

He supervised the filling of the canteens and looped an adjustable strap over our heads so the canteen hung down by our waists. We followed him over to the wooden fence. 'This is as far as you go unless one of the ranch hands or I am with you. Down there are their quarters and they are busy men. They don't want to have to deal with curious children. The stables are also down there along with the birthing pens. Right at the far end there is another fenced off area that is strictly out of bounds It's where all the cattle and horse waste is dumped when the stables and pens are cleaned out.'

'Who does that job?' asked Dimitris wrinkling his nose.

'Dave, the stable hand most of the time, but when the pens are in use everyone helps.' Fred pointed further over. 'Those are the store rooms. As I've said, you are not to go in them. The feed for the horses is stored there, spare equipment and horse tack. There is nothing of interest in there for you.'

Looking around me I could see no other sign of habitation

anywhere. Wire fencing could be seen delineating path ways in the open area and a line of water pipes on stilts led down to the ranch hands quarters and then further on into the distance. At intervals stacks of metal hurdles could be seen.

'Why are the pipes on stilts?' asked Luke.

'Two reasons. Firstly they cannot be trodden on by the cows and damaged and secondly if one of them has sprung a leak you will see a puddle on the ground beneath. If they were not raised up the water would run into the ground and you wouldn't know there was a problem.'

Luke nodded. 'That makes sense,' he said and Fred nodded approvingly at him.

'Why does that area have wire fencing instead of wood?' asked Dimitris.

'The cattle are allowed to roam freely. The wire fences are to stop them going beyond the boundaries of my land, but we don't want them wandering around the living quarters or the store rooms.'

Fred led us round to the side of the ranch house. 'These are the store rooms for the house. No need for you to go into them unless your Mum asks you to fetch something. Down there is where I keep the truck and the building next door has the petrol cans. Strictly off limits until you know how to drive.'

We walked past the buildings and down the hill to where there was a large pond and wind turbine that pumped the water up to a metal tower nearby. Pipes ran down from it and snaked across the land in various directions.

'This is where we get all our water. As I said, Dimitris, no swimming or even paddling.'

'Doesn't it ever dry up?' asked Dimitris.

'If that happened we would be in real trouble. The cows need about twenty gallons of water a day. Without that they would stop making milk to feed their calves. Within no time the whole herd would be dead.'

'Can I put my hand in?' asked Dimitris.

'Why do you think here is a fence around it?' asked Fred.

'To stop anyone going near it,' mumbled Dimitris.

'Exactly, and that includes you. It looks harmless enough, but I have no idea how deep it is and the sides could be steep so if you fell in you might not be able to get out.'

'Have you never been in it?' asked Luke.

Fred shook his head. 'If I had dared and my father had found out I would have received such a tanning on my behind that I wouldn't have been able to sit down for a week or more. Now, we'll go back to the ranch. I think your Mum should have a rest for a while. She's had a busy day. I need to take Blaze out to run off some of her energy. I'll be back in a couple of hours.'

I smiled gratefully. I was feeling tired and I still had to wash the dishes and prepare a meal for us for the evening. I had no idea what I should cook and I needed to unpack the various boxes that Fred had placed in there as the kitchen was bare of all ingredients except some remnants from our lunch.

'Shouldn't I start a meal ready for when you return?' I asked.

'No need to worry about that at the moment. We'll sort it later when I get back.'

I washed the dishes in a small amount of warm water and left them to drain. The boys helped me to open the boxes and placed the contents on the shelves or in the cupboards as I requested. I hoped I would remember where everything was when I needed it. Once finished I sank gratefully down in a chair and opened the box of school books I had brought with me. I gave the boys a book each and said they should sit quietly and read whilst I began to sort through the other books. I would need to decide how to construct lessons for the boys and get them into a learning routine as soon as possible. I would also need to understand how the range worked so I did not burn our food or serve it under cooked. That concerned me more than anything else at the moment.

It seemed a long time before Fred returned and carried in some flat boxes that he placed on the table. 'Get some plates and knives, Luke, and we'll have some supper before bed.'

Fred opened up the boxes. 'Pizza!' shrieked Dimitris in delight. This was something they had only ever had as a special treat.

'Where did you get that?' I asked.

'Rode into Broome.'

'You rode to Broome to get us a pizza?'

'Thought the boys would like that tonight and it would save you from having to cook. Blaze needed a good gallop. She was raring to go. I had to give her a good rub down when I got back. I should have showered,' Fred sniffed at his shirt.' 'I hope I don't smell too horsey and sweaty. I'll shower when we've eaten.'

Whilst Fred showered I washed the dishes and supervised the boys as they had a wash and cleaned their teeth at the sink.

'Once the bathroom is properly finished you'll use that. Until then we have to make do as best we can.' I hoped Fred would not expect me to go out and use the cold water bucket shower that night.

When I woke Fred was already up and dressed. He kissed me and asked if I had slept well.

'You don't need to get up yet. I'm up early every morning and I'll try not to disturb you.'

'I must get up. The boys will be expecting breakfast and I need to know how to use the electric cooker.'

'I'll show you later. We have plenty of food around for today.'

Once Fred had left I ran a bowl of warm water at the sink, took it into my bedroom and washed my body. I could still not face the thought of a cold water bucket shower. I could hear the boys moving around and insisted that they also had a wash at the sink, hoping that the promised plumber would return that day to complete the plumbing in the bathroom.

Having fed the boys and reminded them that they had to stay

in the ranch house they had mooched around disconsolately for a while, continually looking out of the windows to see if Fred was on his way and then retired to their bedrooms. I did not know what to do with myself either and began to examine the ingredients in my cupboards more carefully and plan for our evening meal.

When Fred returned he asked the boys if they had slept well and then told them that they would now go outside with him and be shown their daily jobs. I had no idea what he would ask of them and followed, ready to protest if he was going to ask them to do something way beyond their capabilities. He had said he was used to dealing with men, not boys.

'First, you fill your canteens. You'll not be going far but it has to be a routine that you get used to. Once back at the ranch take them inside and the water can be emptied into a jug and used for cooking. Don't leave it sitting in the canteen until the next day and keep topping it up or you could have microbes forming in there and end up with an upset stomach.'

'What's a microbe?' asked Dimitris.

'A germ that is too small for you to see and you don't want it inside you. Ready?'

The boys nodded and Fred waved his arm around. 'The fence runs all the way around the ranch house. Each morning you walk around and check that there is no damage anywhere. A kangaroo could have bumped into it in the night and broken the wood. They're heavy animals. Look for any holes, however small in the fence and in the ground beneath as a snake could slither through. This is why the store rooms are out of bounds. Just occasionally, if one has managed to get in, they could be curled up behind an outbuilding and you might not see it until you stepped on it.'

I shuddered at the thought. I had not considered that there might be snakes around.

'What should we do if we do see a snake?' asked Luke.

'Move away as fast as you can and let me or one of the ranch hands know. We'll deal with it. Don't poke at it with a stick or you're asking for trouble. In the unlikely event that one slithers across your path jump over it.'

'Are snakes often around?' Dimitris's face had paled at the thought.

'It's very rare that we find them down here so you should have nothing to worry about. Now, your next job will be to inspect all the water pipes to ensure there are no leaks. You only do that in the fenced area around the ranch. I don't expect you to follow them up to the cattle areas, the men will check those. Have a stick of chalk in your pocket and if you see a leak put a large cross on the pipe. That will save us from having to search for it. Understood?'

Both boys nodded and Fred handed them a stick of chalk each. 'Off you go then. Come back to the ranch house when you've finished checking.'

Fred walked back into the house with me. 'Is it safe for them to be out there if there are snakes around?' I asked immediately.

'They have to become familiar with the wildlife and how to deal with it. I've already checked around this morning and I saw no sign of any snakes. Provided you don't disturb them they won't attack you. I've given the morning checking job to the boys so they can develop a sense of responsibility. I'll continue to do a fence check each morning to ensure there are no problems. It should give you some time to get on with the laundry or cooking without having to worry about them for an hour or two. When the plumber arrives we'll leave him to get on and go down to the stables this afternoon.'

'What about the boy's schooling?'

'It won't hurt them to miss a few days. I'll show you how the cooker works whilst the boys are occupied.'

Using the cooker was not going to be as difficult as I had first envisaged. The electricity was kept switched on so the water in the house remained heated and the top plates were sufficiently hot to place saucepans on for the contents to simmer gently. There was a separate temperature control for the oven but I had no idea how long it would take a loaf to cook. I remembered the way the village women had cooked in Fourni, making a large quantity of dough, and once cooked and cooled would slice it and store it in barrels. When fresh bread was needed they would sprinkle the slices with water and it would taste as good as if it had come directly from the oven. I hoped I would be able to persuade Fred that it would be an ideal way of catering for the bread we needed each day.

Luke and Dimitris rushed through the kitchen door.

'We've found a hole in the ground by the fence,' shouted Dimitris.

'We haven't touched it. We've come straight in to tell you,' added Luke.

'Well done, boys. I'll come with you and you can show me where it is.' Fred winked at me and whispered in my ear 'I dug the hole to see if they would find it.'

I busied myself in the kitchen, removing a pack of meat from the fridge and placing it in a skillet on the hot plate. I would use that as the basis of our meal this evening. I placed a pan of water beside it and hoped it would not take too long to boil as I desperately wanted a cup of coffee.

Before I had a chance to make my coffee I heard a vehicle sounding its horn and saw Fred waving for the driver to undo the gate and enter. I hoped it was the plumber who had arrived. Luke ran up to the gate and ensured it was safely closed behind him and then both boys came back to the house.

'We've mended the hole,' announced Dimitris proudly. 'Fred put a stick in there and nothing came out so we packed it up with stones and mud.'

'Well done,' I said with a smile. They were obviously pleased at having completed such a simple job.

'And I checked the gate was properly closed,' added Luke. 'That's the plumber who has arrived and he's talking to Fred.'

'Then go and ask them if they would like a coffee. The water is about ready.' Suddenly life seemed very normal.

As we left to walk down to the stables that afternoon I saw Fred slip four apples into his pocket and guessed they were for his horse. The boys walked along with us, obeying Fred's instructions not to run off on their own. We had left the enclosure that ran around the ranch behind and we were in an open area until we reached the ranch hands' quarters. Once again there was a fence around the buildings that extended for quite a large area and incorporated the ranch hands living quarters, their wash houses, store rooms and stables. Further down there was a large open building with a corrugated tin roof. There were more fences, but this time only made from wire stretched between metal uprights and small areas of grassland were also fenced in the same way.

'That area is where we bring the cows when we know they are close to giving birth. Some like to stay out in the open and others prefer to be in a shed. Having them close means we can watch over them for any problems.'

He opened the gate and looked at Luke who immediately swung it back into position and fixed it securely with the hasp.

'Good lad,' said Fred. 'We're going to see Blaze and you can give her some apple.'

'What about the other horses?' asked Luke.

'The men will be out on their horses. That's why I thought it would be a good time to visit.'

I was relieved that the other horses were not there. I still felt very nervous of Blaze.

'Are they all out?' asked Dimitris and pointed to where a horse's head could be seen above the stable door.

'We'll have a look at that one when we've seen Blaze.' Fred cut an apple into quarters and both boys held a piece on their hand for the horse to take. Fred offered a piece to me and I shook my head.

'Let the boys give it to her,' I answered and wondered why Fred raised his eyebrows.

'Who checks the fences and pipes down here?' asked Luke.

'The ranch hands do that each day and I rely upon them to be conscientious. When I come down to the stables I give them a quick look over, but I don't examine them closely. Shall we visit the other horses now?'

'Are they as big as Blaze?' asked Dimitris warily.

'Nowhere near. You'll see.'

Fred opened the stable door at the bottom and inside was a pony, not even half the size of Blaze. She was loosely tethered and came forward for Fred to stroke her neck.

'Let's see who's next door, and Fred opened the next stable door. A larger pony was in there, but still very much smaller than Blaze.

'Can we give them some apple?' asked Luke.

'Yes, they need to get to know you. This one is for you to ride and the smaller one is for Dimitris.'

An indescribable look of joy came over Luke's face. 'Do you mean that, Fred? Can I really ride her?'

'You'll learn to ride her and how to care for her properly. If you neglect her I'll take her back and give you a good beating into the bargain.'

'I promise I'll be good to her.' Luke held out the apple and whilst the pony ate it he stroked her nose. 'What's her name?'

'Bessie. Now, Dimitris, do you want to give your pony some apple?'

Dimitris nodded, not as sure as Luke, but not willing to be outdone by his older brother.

Reluctantly Luke left the stable where Bessie was tethered and I heard him tell her that he would be back. He could hardly contain himself and I could see he was bursting to ask Fred questions. He managed to control himself until Dimitris had been introduced to Socks and fed him with an apple.

'Why is he called Socks?' asked Dimitris.

'Look at his front legs? They are white at the bottom, looks as though he is wearing a pair of socks.'

Dimitris giggled. 'I like that. Will he grow big like Blaze?'

Fred shook his head. 'He's a pony, bred to be small. He'll get a little larger but not much. He'll last you for a few years until you're big enough for a horse.'

'Can we ride them now?' asked Luke and his face fell when Fred shook his head.

'Riding and care lessons start tomorrow after you've done your fence and pipe jobs. Two of the hands will be down here and show you how to saddle up. They'll attach a leading rein and walk you round until they feel sure you won't fall off. Now we ought to meet the lady who's in the other stable.'

The horse that looked over the stable door was far larger than the ponies but certainly not the size of Blaze. 'This one is for you, Reen.'

'Me! I can't ride a horse.'

'You'll learn. I'll teach you.'

'I'm not sure that's a good idea at the moment, Fred.' I wondered what harm would come to the baby I thought I was expecting if I was jolted up and down on a horse.

'You'll come to no harm. I'll make sure of that. You only have to become confident sitting on her whilst she walks around. I don't expect you to gallop. Give her the last apple, then I'll introduce you to the men who are going to teach the boys.'

I held out the pieces of apple and felt her snuffling in my hand. 'What's her name?'

'Amber. Her coat is a lovely golden colour, like a piece of amber.'

Luke had looked at my horse in admiration and then returned to where Bessie stood patiently in her stable. He was stroking her neck and talking to her quietly and she continually twitched her ears in response.

'The boy's a natural,' smiled Fred and squeezed my arm. 'By the time he's grown he'll be riding a horse like Blaze without any trouble. I'll call the hands.'

Fred put his fingers in his mouth and let out a piercing whistle.

'Can you teach me how to do that?' asked Dimitris enviously.

'There's nothing to it. I'll show you where to put your fingers and after that it's just practice. Here they come.'

Two men hurried from their quarters to the stable block and Fred introduced them to both the boys and also to me. They touched their foreheads deferentially to me and called me Madam, making me feel quite embarrassed. We left both the boys down there with Hank and Jim, with the assurance that they would bring them back to the ranch later.

'We need to get back and see if the plumber has finished,' said Fred and I was relieved that I was not expected to have my first riding lesson that afternoon.

1950
LIFE FOUR
Ranch Life

Our life settled into a routine. Once the boys had inspected the fences and water pipes I settled them at the table with a lesson. I made the boys write essays about living on the ranch, correcting their spelling and grammar. I was not so proficient with Maths and often asked Fred if I had laid out an exercise correctly or to check the answers the boys had made.

Whilst they worked I would make a batch of bread. I had found a large preserving pan and this was ideal for mixing the dough. I had experimented with making a batch of bread that could be stored and moistened by sprinkling it with water. Fred and the boys were happy to eat it. Using this method I could cook more loaves than necessary at any one time and store them.

Each afternoon Fred would take us down to the stables and whilst Hank and Jim supervised the boys on their ponies Fred introduced me gently to Amber. Fred had produced a pair of trousers that fitted me reasonably well and promised that when we went to Derby next I would get a better pair. I had felt hesitant about wearing a pair of trousers like a man but Fred pointed out that a skirt was impractical as I would not be able to sit astride a horse in a skirt and preserve my modesty.

I was happy to sit on Amber's back and amble around the fenced enclosure, but I had to hand her over to Hank or Jim to give her the exercise she needed. The boys laughed at my temerity as both of them were now happy to trot without the control of a leading rein. I thought I might be braver after the baby was born.

Finally Fred said that the boys were proficient enough to ride up to where the herds were grazing provided they obeyed instructions and stayed close to Hank and Jim. Fred insisted that I accompanied them promising me that we would go slowly and I would have nothing to fear. He rode beside me whilst the boys rode ahead if us.

I had not paid a great deal of attention to the cows when they were in the pens at Derby and had not realised just how many there were. Whatever direction you looked you could see them grazing or lying beneath a tree whilst they digested the grass. The other ranch hands were riding around slowly, looking for any signs that a cow might be sick or lame, checking that the troughs were receiving sufficient water to satisfy the needs of the herd and putting out food supplements in rows of metal containers

I have to admit that having seen them I was then quite ready to turn for home and I think Dimitris felt the same. Luke was asking questions of Hank, listening carefully to the answers and then asking him yet more questions.

'How do you know if a cow is sick?' asked Luke.

'There are various ways to tell. She may be very excitable, could be breathing heavily and not moving easily, her appetite may have dropped off and you also look at her turds. If they are any different from normal you know there is something not quite right.'

'If she's in the middle of the herd how do you get her out?'

'We use a rope that is called a lasso.'

'How?' asked Luke.

'I'll ask Cliff to show you.' Hank placed his fingers in his mouth and whistled the same way as Fred did when wanting attention. He pointed to a particular ranch hand who rode over to us.

'This young man would like to see you rope a cow, Cliff,' said Hank with a grin.

Cliff raised his eyebrows. 'Which one?'

'Any one. It's just a demo.'

Cliff nodded and rode off so he was closer to where the cows were grazing. He took the lasso that was tied beneath his saddle, made an adjustment to the knot and swung it around his head until it finally dropped neatly over the cow's head. The cow looked up in surprise and as she leapt away the rope came loose and she was released.

'That's not much good,' said Luke scathingly. 'It came undone.'

'That was deliberate. If we really needed to catch her it would have stayed around her neck however hard she struggled to get away. Cliff would have gradually reeled her in and we would have a box waiting for her. Once she was inside a horse would drag the box back to an isolation pen down by the ranch and she would be released.'

'Can I come and watch the next time you have to really catch a cow?' asked Luke.

'I don't see why not, but you'll need to have Fred with you and stand well clear. We can't look after you if the cows decide to run in all directions.'

'Will you show me how to make and use a lasso?'

Hank grinned at the eager boy. 'It takes some practice to use a lasso.'

'Then I ought to start practising as soon as possible.'

Fred smiled. 'I think that boy has the makings of a good rancher.'

'Provided that is what he wants to do,' I answered quickly.

'I'll not force him, but he seems to enjoy the life. I'm not sure about Dimitris.'

'On the whole I think he is happy enough, but he misses the sea and the ships. He may well want to work in the dockyard.'

'And what about you? Are you happy living out here?'

I considered my answer. 'Yes, but I do have some problems.'

'Tell me.' Fred bent down closer to me.

189

'At the moment all is fine, but I am worried how I will cope when the baby is born. I know how demanding a small baby can be and when I had the boys I had either my aunt or my mother to help me. The only work I had to do was to attend to the baby. It's different now.'

'I'm glad you told me. You have to remember I've not been a father before so I have no idea what it involves to have a baby around. I'm sure we can find a solution. You're working hard every day with cooking, cleaning and laundry. Are you sure it isn't all too much for you already?'

I shook my head. 'I can manage at present and should be able to do so for at least the next five or even six months.'

'Would you like to ask your mother to come to stay?'

'No, I couldn't expect that of her and who would look after my father? I'm sure I'll be able to work out a routine so I can manage.' Fred looked at me speculatively but said no more.

As we rode back to the ranch the boys were allowed to trot ahead of us and Fred picked up the pace on his horse until Amber was forced to trot to keep up with him. I did not realise at first then I called to Fred.

'We're going too fast.'

Fred slowed and reined in beside me. 'That was only a gentle trot. You need to progress until you can jump on a horse and ride off as if the devil himself was chasing you.'

'Why should I need to do that?' I asked laughing up at him.

I then realised that Fred was serious. 'Suppose you are at the ranch on your own as I have had to take the truck into Derby for repairs. One of the hands brings you a message to say that one of your boys has met with an accident. You would want to get to him as fast as possible. How are you going to manage?'

My face paled at the thought. 'I hope the situation never arises.'

'So do I, but I also want to be confident that you would be able to ride there safely and as quickly as possible. You can take it slowly and I'll be patient with you, but by this time next year

I expect you to be able to gallop and keep up with the men. Now we'll trot again and next week we'll try a canter.'

I did not argue as I could understand the sense behind Fred's words. I just hoped I would soon feel less frightened when Amber moved faster over the ground.

I felt nervous the first time we returned to Derby for supplies and to visit my parents.

'I said some very hurtful things to my mother when I left,' I confessed. 'I may not be made very welcome.'

'Now is the time for you to make amends. I hope that when they see you and the boys are happy they will forgive me for dragging you away from civilisation. Do you have any friends you would like to visit whilst we're there?'

'Only Poppi. If she is still working in the general store I would like to see her. She helped me when I was feeling miserable or depressed and I tried to help her to come to terms with the death of her husband.'

'What happened to him?'

'He was killed in the war. I had no opportunity to say goodbye to her and she must have wondered what had happened to me.'

I had made a long list of food items that I felt we should buy, including fresh fruit and vegetables along with sacks of rice, flour and coffee. I agreed to go to the Greek general store where I had worked and asked them to have the items boxed and ready for us to collect later in the day.

Dimitris was excited and kept asking if we could visit the harbour whilst we were there. Fred promised that he would take the boys for a quick visit to the beach whilst I was at the general store. I was pleased that I would be able to have a short while alone with Poppi and explain my abrupt departure from the town.

I spent longer with Poppi than I had intended. She told me that she was still living with her dead husband's parents and was not earning sufficient money to rent a room on her own. She admitted that she was not particularly happy as they were not Greek and did not understand why she would want to mix with the Greek community rather than their Australian friends. She felt she was unwanted by them.

'Could you not move back and live with your parents?' I asked.

'There's no space. My sister and her husband are living there. Andreas was badly injured during the war and is unable to work. It would have been different if Bill had not been killed. We would have had enough money for a home of our own and I'd probably have a family by now.'

'You've not met anyone else?' I asked and she shook her head.

'I'm not looking for anyone. My parents have urged me to marry again and tried to introduce me to various Greek men whom they thought would be suitable, but they're not Bill.'

I knew how she felt. I had never looked for anyone to take Lucas's place. Fred had entered my life by an accident of fate

'Anyway,' said Poppi, 'That's enough about me, I want to know all about your life on the ranch.'

I told her how large the ranch was and how I had to work hard to complete my essential daily jobs along with teaching the boys.

'Don't you have any time to yourself when you can relax?' she asked.

'I usually manage to have about an hour to myself in the afternoon when I've had my riding lesson.'

'You're learning to ride a horse?' Her eyes opened wide.

'Fred gave me a beautiful horse. She's called Amber. He also gave the boys a pony each so we have riding lessons together. The boys are far more proficient than me.'

'The young have no fear,' she remarked. 'Do you have to clean the stable?' she asked, wrinkling her nose.

'No, there's a stable boy who does that. He's not very bright, but terribly conscientious and loves the horses. The boys have to take their turn during the week. It's called 'mucking out'. Later

Fred says he'll teach me how to drive the truck. I don't think that will be as frightening as riding a horse.'

'I'm pleased you're happy. Fred sounds like a really nice man. Now, I ought to get your order made up or he'll be back and want to know why we have spent so long chattering.'

'There's no rush. We'll call for it before we drive home. As soon as he comes back with the boys we'll visit my parents whilst he sorts out the feed he wants for the horses and cattle. I'll come in and see you the next time we come up to town.'

My mother looked surprised and then delighted when she opened the door and saw us standing there.

'You've come home. I said you had made a big mistake. You can all stay here with us now.'

I was about to say I had no intention of staying when Luke answered.

'I don't want to stay here, I want to go back to the ranch house. You won't make me stay, will you, Mamma?'

'Of course not. When Fred arrives we'll all go home together.'

My mother looked at me. 'So why have you come?'

'I wanted to see you and also to say I was sorry for the hurtful words I spoke when I left. You can see for yourself that the boys are happy and so am I.'

My mother gave a deep sigh. 'I suppose we should be thankful that you are no longer working at that tavern.'

'It brought some much needed money in. I would not have chosen to work there if I had been able to find lucrative work elsewhere, but I'm so pleased I was there when Fred came to town. It's unlikely we would have met otherwise. He's wonderful with the boys.'

'I have my own pony,' said Luke proudly.

'So do I,' added Dimitris, 'His name is Socks.'

My mother sniffed. 'That sounds like bribery to me. His way to get the boys to accept him.'

'Not at all,' I answered. 'The ranch is vast and the only way to get around is on horseback. It's practical for the boys to learn to ride. I'm also learning and later Fred is going to teach me to drive the truck.'

My father raised his eyebrows. 'Are you sure you are happy, Eirini? You know you can come home.'

I nodded. 'Yes, I am. I know it is all rather a novelty to me, but Fred is very patient with my mistakes. Like the time I forgot to ask one of the hands to buy some eggs when they were in Broome. Fred just shrugged and said we would just have bacon for our breakfast. I then realised I had forgotten to ask for bacon as well.'

'We had bread and jam that morning,' piped up Dimitris. 'I'd like to have that every day.'

Both boys had been used to having only a rusk with some milk each morning.

'You need more than that when you are out in the fresh air all day,' I replied firmly. 'If you had nothing substantial until the evening you wouldn't have the energy to go riding in the afternoon.'

'We only do our jobs and our lessons in the morning,' objected Dimitris. 'I'd still have enough energy to ride.'

'You wouldn't have enough strength to throw a lasso,' said Luke. 'Hank has shown me how to tie one correctly and I'm practising throwing it at a tree stump. I can hit it each time, but I can't get the noose to go over yet.'

The boys continued to chatter about the various new events they were experiencing in their lives to their grandparents until there was a knock at the door and Fred announced his arrival. He entered hesitantly.

'I hope I'm not intruding. I'm a little earlier than I had intended, but I have something I would like Reen to try on for size.' He opened the bag he was carrying and took out a pair of jodhpurs and held them up against me. He shook his head. 'They're not big enough.'

'They'd fit me,' said Dimitris immediately.

'I think they might. Better go and try them on.' Fred winked at me. 'How about you, Luke? Do you think these will fit you?' He took another pair from the bag.

Luke took them eagerly and both boys disappeared into the bathroom to try them on.

'You need to try yours, Reen.' He handed me the bag. 'If they're too big or too small I can take them back and change them before we leave.'

I waited until the boys came back and then went and removed my skirt and put on the jodhpurs. I saw they had buttons on the waistband along with a gusset at the front so they could be made larger and I smiled. That was thoughtful of Fred. We stood there as Fred and my parents looked us up and down, my mother clicked her tongue and shook her head, whilst my father smiled in amusement.

'I never thought I would see you wearing a pair of trousers, Eirini,' he said.

'Can I have some Chaps?' asked Luke and I frowned at him. It was not good manners to ask for something else when you had just been given a present.

Fred shook his head. 'They only make them in men's sizes. You certainly don't need Chaps yet awhile. Go and put your other trousers back on, boys. We must leave soon.'

'Can we go riding when we get back?' asked Luke.

'No,' said Fred firmly. 'When we get home the truck needs to be unloaded. I'll do the heavy stuff and you boys can help your mother.'

I replaced my skirt whilst the boys chattered excitedly, both convinced that jodhpurs would make them better riders.

I heard Fred talking to my parents. 'When we are more organised you will have to come and visit us. We have plenty of rooms, but we need to get them decorated and furnished properly before we have guests.'

'Will I have to ride a horse?' asked my mother and I heard my father laughing.

'Only if you want to. It's not compulsory.'

This was the first I had heard about getting the spare rooms decorated. They still needed to be turned out and rubbish thrown away.

On this occasion I parted amicably from my parents goodbye and promised we would visit again the next time we came to town.

As we drove home Fred asked how I had found Poppi. I explained to him that she was not happy living with her in-laws, but had no choice. He was sympathetic, but said no more and I began to ask him about turning out the rooms. Although my parents had welcomed me I still felt uncertain that they approved of my marriage and moving to a cattle ranch; maybe a visit from them so they could see that I was living comfortably would help.

'The rooms do need to be turned out. I know there is old furniture in there, some of it may be broken and goodness knows what other rubbish I might find. I won't expect you to help me. Sam can do that. I only had time to get the few rooms we use decorated before you arrived. The boys should have a room each as they get older, and we'll need another ready soon along with one for your parents.' I smiled to myself. Fred obviously did not realise that for some months the baby would be sleeping in our bedroom so I could attend to feeding during the night.

Our routine continued unhindered. Sam helped Fred and the boys remove all the items from the rooms where they had been stored. Broken chairs and old newspapers were taken by Sam down to the ranch hands quarters where they would be burnt on their fire whilst they cooked their steaks. There was a surprising amount of serviceable furniture that only needed to be cleaned and polished and this was moved into the furthest room and I would spend as much time as possible in there making each piece look respectable.

Sam, Bert and Pete then began to slap white paint on all the walls in the empty rooms. It worried me that they were working up at the house rather than being out with the cattle. Fred assured me that they were not needed up with the herd at present.

'If the other hands see a problem or need help they'll soon let me know. We need to get this work finished before the herd start to calve. When that happens they'll have to be brought down and kept close to the covered pens. The men will take it in turns to watch them overnight. Provided there are no problems they should be able to go back to their familiar grazing grounds about ten days later.'

'Why don't they calve where they are now?' I asked.

'Too risky. They could drop a calf anywhere and we wouldn't know if it was healthy. Again, if the mother is having a struggle to get the calf out we need to be on hand to pull.'

'Pull?'

Fred grinned at me. 'Are you sure you want to know the details?'

I nodded. I was a rancher's wife; I needed to know all that rearing cows involved.

'Well if we can't help by moving the calf around inside with our hands we try pulling on its legs as the mother presses down. If we are not successful as a last resort we have to tie a rope to the calf's legs. The cow is tied to a rail so she can't run away and a horse is used to pull the rope that is attached to the calf.'

I shuddered. 'That's sounds brutal.'

'It would be far worse if we left it. The mother would either die from exhaustion or the calf would die inside her and she would end up infected as it decayed. That would be the end of both of them. If the cow has to suffer the trauma it can often make her milk dry up or the calf can be too traumatised to feed from her.'

'What do you do then?'

'If she is producing milk we milk her and hand feed it to the calf until the calf learns how to suck and the cow accepts it. If she has no milk we use some from one of the other cows.'

'Does it happen often?'

Fred shrugged. 'We have a hundred heifers. Most of them will have no problem at all, but I expect we'll have to deal with six or seven. We just have to hope they don't all have problems at the same time.'

'When are they due to give birth?'

'Depending upon when they were serviced the calves could start arriving in six months. The hands will be able to tell by looking at them if they should be brought down to the birthing area. You don't want to rush them as this can distress them and they could start a premature labour.'

'Six months!'

Fred nodded. 'Were you expecting them to take longer? They're not elephants, you know.'

'It means they'll be calving at just about the same time as I am giving birth.'

Fred let out a roar of laughter. 'I'll make sure you are safely at the hospital by then in your own birthing pen.' He put his arms around me. 'I promise we won't call the poor child 'calf' or 'bull'.'

'I should hope not,' I answered indignantly. 'They need a proper name.'

'Are you thinking of a Greek name?' he asked.

I shook my head. 'This child will be part Australian and brought up here so it is far more fitting that he or she has a conventional Australian name.'

I could tell that Fred was relieved by my answer. The only Australian names I knew were those of the ranch hands. I needed to know some others and also bear in mind that this could be a girl child. I was even more ignorant of female names, but thought my mother would probably be pleased if a girl child was named Maria after her.

'I'll have to tell my parents that I am expecting when we visit next.'

'Is that a problem?'

I shook my head. 'Not really, I'm sure they'll be pleased to have another grandchild although they will realise that the baby will be arriving a bit earlier than it should be.'

'Too late to do anything about that now. We ought to go to the hospital whilst we are there and make a provisional appointment for your admittance. Once we are certain enough of your date we can ask your parents if you can stay with them the previous week. That way you'll be close enough to the hospital.'

'What about you and the boys?'

'I'm sure we can manage without you for a couple of weeks. The boys will probably love being allowed to eat steak cooked over a camp fire each night.'

'Maybe they could stay up with my parents?'

'Don't you trust me with them?'

'Of course I do. I'm just trying to make it easier for you if they are away. You won't have to be worrying about them all the time whilst the cows are giving birth.'

I still had the nightdresses I had made for Luke and they had also been worn by Dimitris. They had been washed so many times that they were almost paper thin. The next time we went up to Derby I must visit the haberdasher and buy some material to make some more. Needlework would keep me occupied during the time that I rested after my horse riding session each afternoon. I also needed to finish restoring the furniture so that the newly decorated rooms could be furnished and any necessary equipment could be bought. If my parents were going to come for a visit I could not expect them to have only a bed and a chair in their room.

I had found some old curtains and a bed cover and put them to one side. They would be ideal for making a pallet for the baby. Fred looked at me in horror when I told him.

'You cannot use those to make bedding for a baby. He'll have a crib at first and then a proper cot with a mattress.'

I tried to explain that even when the child was big enough to use a cot some padding would be needed to prevent him from banging his head and he understood my reasoning. When I went to look for them next they had disappeared.

'You seem to know what is necessary.' he said, 'But I'll not have you using old materials that could be holding all sorts of germs even after washing. I've noticed that the boys are growing out of their clothes. The fresh air and exercise is doing them a world of good. It's not fair that Dimitris should always have his brother's hand me downs. I think on our next visit to town we need to kit them out.'

I felt guilty that Fred should have to pay to clothe my boys. 'I'm sure Dimitris won't mind wearing Luke's old clothes.'

'That's fine for when he's helping to muck out, but he needs to feel respectably dressed when we go to town and visit your parents.'

'But, Fred,' I remonstrated, 'You have already spent so much money on us, making the bathroom, giving the boys the ponies and giving me Amber.'

'The bathroom was needed. I'd just been too lazy to get round to organizing it. I've done a deal with another rancher and when the calves are born he'll receive his money for the ponies and Amber in livestock. There's still money in the bank that can be used to buy whatever is needed.'

Each morning Fred rose early and checked the fences and water pipes cursorily. He had found that Luke and Dimitris were reliable and conscientious. He would then meet up with the ranch hands and ride up to inspect the herd with them. The boys would be set their daily lesson by me and I would go into the kitchen to bake the bread, do the washing or prepare our evening meal.

Once we had eaten some lunch Fred would then accompany us to the stables where the boys would be allowed to ride their ponies whilst I tried to become more confident sitting on a horse. We would leave the boys down there under the watchful eye of Hank or Jim and whilst I sat in an easy chair reading a book and

Fred sat at the table with his account books. I have to admit that I often dozed off for a short while.

Usually I heard Fred tell the boys to be quiet when they returned as I was asleep. With my eyes still closed I would protest that I was not asleep, I was just resting my eyes.

'What's the difference between having your eyes closed and being asleep?' asked Dimitris.

'If I was asleep I would not know what you were saying. With my eyes closed I can still hear you perfectly. Hank allowed you to canter around the field today and he says he will show you how to jump safely over low barriers.'

'You were listening, weren't you, Mamma,' remarked Luke. 'You never used to sit down in the afternoon and rest. Are you not feeling well?'

'I'm feeling very well, thank you, Luke.' The time had come to tell them that they were going to have a brother or sister. 'I have some exciting news.'

'Are Grandma and Grandpa coming to stay?' asked Dimitris.

'Not yet.'

'Are we going to have our own rooms?'

'When the smell of paint has gone. It would not be healthy to sleep in there breathing in the paint fumes each night.'

'So what is your exciting news?' asked Luke.

'I am expecting a baby. You'll have a brother or sister in a few months time.'

'Why don't we have it now?' asked Dimitris. 'Why do we have to wait.?'

'The baby has to grow inside me until it is big and strong enough to be born. I'll give you a proper biology lesson tomorrow.'

Luke looked at me with concern. 'Is that why you are having a rest in the afternoons and are so reluctant to ride Amber?'

'It is natural to feel tired when you are expecting a baby. I'm happy to sit up on Amber's back and have her walk around with me, even to trot for a short while, but I would not like to jolt the baby around too much.'

'Would it cry?' asked Dimitris.

I smiled at his innocence. 'No, I don't think so, but I'm sure he or she would not feel very comfortable.'

'What are you going to call it?' asked Dimitris.

'We haven't decided on any name yet; we need to see if it's a boy or a girl.'

'You could call it Hank or Jim if it's a boy,' suggested Luke.

I shook my head. 'I don't think so. We would not know if we were talking about the baby or the ranch hands, and the others might be offended because it hadn't been called after them.'

'If you had lots of babies you could call them all after the ranch hands.' Dimitris made a large circle with his hands.

'I'm not sure I want to have that many babies,' I smiled.

'If it's a girl you could call her Bessie.' persisted Luke.

'Definitely not,' I replied. 'Besides if I did have another one later on Dimitris would want me to call it Socks.'

He grinned cheekily at me and I realised that he had an impish sense of humour and had been teasing me.

Poppi

By the time we visited my parents next there was no way I could disguise the fact that I was expecting. My mother looked me up and down in disapproval.

'So that's why you married him. You were fortunate not to have been caught out before working in that disreputable tavern.'

'I behaved impeccably whilst I worked in the tavern. Anyone would tell you that, although no doubt you'd prefer not to believe them. I had already agreed to marry Fred and once that was decided we saw no need to wait for formalities.'

'You're lucky he didn't leave you in the lurch or didn't he find out until it was too late for him to back out?'

'I told Fred as soon as I was suspicious and he was delighted.'

My mother sniffed. 'Have you told your boys? What do they think about you having a child? '

'They're excited and being very good and considerate towards me. I wanted to ask if I could come and stay here for a few days before it's actually due. I've been to the hospital and they have given me a provisional date. Fred is worried that I might not get to the hospital in time as it takes about two hours to drive here from the ranch.'

'Why doesn't he come up to town and stay with you. You could both sleep at the hotel.'

I shook my head. 'Fred needs to be on hand at the ranch. It's calving season.'

'Just shows, his cows are more important to him than you.'

I felt the anger towards my mother rising within me. 'I understand that I'm not wanted. I'll stay at the hotel.'

'I didn't say you were unwanted. You can come here and bring the boys.'

'The boys are going to stay on the ranch with Fred. He'll look after them.'

'It's not healthy,' my mother mumbled. 'All those men cooped up together. Who knows what that will lead to?'

I could stay there no longer listening to her. 'I'm going to the haberdashers as I need to buy material to make some nightdresses. I'll come back later when Pappa is home. I expect you will have told him by the time I return.'

As I walked to the haberdashers I saw the boys sitting on a seat eating ice cream. 'Where's Fred?' I asked, wondering why he had left the boys alone in the town.

'In the grocers. He said he would not be long and we were to stay here until he came back.'

I could see that Fred was talking to Poppi, but standing so

that he could see the boys through the shop window at the same time. I wondered if he was ordering some surprise treat for me. I often found that what I really wanted to eat was not available and unlike when I was pregnant before I could not go to a shop and buy it. I decided not to spoil whatever he was planning, waved my hand and walked on to the haberdashers.

I selected the light cotton that I wanted to make the nightdresses and stood chatting to Enid. She wanted to know when the baby was due and was I going to be organised with everything I needed.

'I smiled. 'I'm hoping I won't find I need something urgently and have to ask Fred to come into town.'

'Have you made a list? What about nappies, rubber pants and a rubber sheet? Have you got a bottle just in case you have to give a supplement feed? If your milk suddenly dried up you could have a problem. I'm sure the chemist would be able to sell you one along with some milk powder.'

I had to admit that I had not considered that I might not make sufficient milk to satisfy a hungry baby. A rubber sheet for a crib could be bought at a later date along with some rubber pants. They had been a boon whilst we were travelling with Luke and when Dimitris was a baby.

'I'll buy some towelling to make into nappies next time we come up to town.' I picked up my parcel of material and then realised that I also needed a reel of white cotton.

'Will one reel be enough?' asked Enid.

'I expect so. I can always buy some more when I come for the towelling. I can't make nightdresses and nappies at the same time.'

Fred had given me some dollars to spend on whatever I needed, but I was not sure how much a baby's feeding bottle would cost. I did not want to be embarrassed by not having sufficient money with me.I would make out a list, as Enid had suggested, and buy something necessary each time I came up to town.

I walked back to the grocers, the boys were no longer sitting there and Fred was not inside the shop.

Poppi seemed a little flustered. She kept looking at me as if she wanted to ask me something and then changing her mind. I wondered if she thought she should tell me why Fred had been in there earlier. If Fred had arranged something as a surprise for me I would not spoil that for him by asking her.

She asked me many questions about my life on the ranch and how I was getting on with riding my horse. I began to wonder if she was interested in one of the ranch hands, although she had insisted earlier that she was not looking for anyone to take Bill's place. Despite being curious I was too well mannered to ask her outright. I would speak to Fred; he may have been taking a message to her and that was why he was in the grocer's shop. Finally I left the list of our requirements with her and arranged to collect everything later. I could not put off returning to my parents any longer and hoped that my father would be more understanding than my mother.

My father eyed me up and down and asked when the child was due. With a flush to my cheeks I told him the date the hospital had worked out. He nodded and made no comment except to say that I must come to stay with them in good time just in case they were out in their timing.

I waited anxiously for Fred to return with the boys. It was becoming late in the afternoon and we still had to take the boys to get them some new trousers and shirts.

Fred apologised when he returned. He had taken the boys to the beach and Dimitris had been busy searching in the pools that were left when the sea receded.

'I found three crabs, some sea anemones and snails and there was a little fish that Fred said I was not to touch.'

'What kind of fish was it?' I asked.

Dimitris shrugged. 'I don't know, but it had a spine sticking up.'

'Then it probably was poisonous and Fred was quite right to tell you not to touch it.'

'Would it have killed me?' he asked.

'Very unlikely, but it could have given you a very painful hand and arm. Any fish with a spine sticking up is best avoided.'

'Do you know what it was, Grandpa?'

My father shook his head. 'I'm afraid not, but I'll get a book from the library and see if I can find out by the next time you visit.'

'Can I join the library?' asked Luke. 'I've read all the books that we have at the ranch.'

'We'll call in and ask when we've been to buy your new clothes.'

'We ought to do that first,' protested Luke. 'The library closes earlier than the shops.'

'In that case we should go now.' I saw how disappointed my mother looked. 'When the boys have their new clothes they can come back and show them to you.'

The library was still open and whilst Fred went to the clothing shops to ensure they stocked items suitable for the boys I filled in the application forms for both boys to join the library and we were directed to the children's section. Luke looked along the shelves and shook his head in disgust.

'These are books for children. I want books that give me information, like the one that Grandpa said he could find the fish in.'

'There may be a section. I'll go back and ask the librarian.'

My question seemed to puzzle her. 'There is a section for history and biology that is suitable for children.'

'I think they want something a little more advanced. Would they be able to borrow books from the adult section?'

'Only adults can borrow books from the adult library,' she said smugly. 'Not all the literature is suitable for younger readers.'

'Then can I join the adult library please.'

She looked at me suspiciously and pushed a form across the desk to me. 'You'll have to fill that in.'

I completed it and handed it back as quickly as possible and returned to the children's library section. I saw Dimitris had already selected three books from the biology shelf and I trusted that they were suitable for a boy of his age.

'Come on, boys. We'll go to the grown up area and see if you can find what you want there, Luke.'

I stood and watched whilst Luke picked out 'Raising a Calf', 'A Healthy Herd' and 'Animal Husbandry'.

'Surely Fred can tell you all you need to know?' I said.

Luke nodded. 'He can, but I don't always remember to ask him. If I read it in a book I could make a note of anything that I thought was important and ask him later.'

The librarian raised her eyebrows when she saw the titles of the books the boys had selected, although I had to say that Luke's choice was for me.

Fred waved to us from outside a shop where he was waiting. 'I think they have everything we need here. I've picked out some items so the boys only have to go and try them on for size.'

The assistant offered me a chair to sit on outside the changing room and I accepted gratefully. I had not had my usual afternoon rest. The boys emerged together and stood before me.

'You look just like Hank and Jim,' I exclaimed. They both had check shirts and jeans tucked into some leather boots.

'Yes!' Both boys punched the air and Fred stood here grinning at their exuberance.

'I thought they were going to get the same sort of cloth trousers and shirts as they have now.' I was not sure if I liked my boys to resemble ranch hands.

'Not practical,' said Fred. 'It will be turning colder soon and they'll need a bit more protection than a cotton shirt when they're out.'

'Can we go and show Grandma and Grandpa?' asked Dimitris.

I looked at Fred and he nodded. 'It will have to be a quick visit. Time's getting on.'

Despite Fred saying we would only call briefly on my parents we stayed longer than we had intended. I know I went to sleep as Fred drove back and I think Dimitris may have done so also. Fred would not hear of me helping with any of the unloading and insisted that I went in and made myself a drink whilst he and the boys dealt with it. I was concerned that I still had to cook a meal for them, but once again Fred produced pizza that only had to be heated up for a short while in the oven. Having eaten and rested I felt my energy return and I insisted that I washed the dishes whilst the boys prepared themselves for bed.

Fred went down to the stables and checked with the ranch hands that all was well and I waited impatiently for him to return. I wanted to ask him about his conversation with Poppi. An awful thought occurred to me; was Fred regretting marrying me now I was pregnant and was he interested in Poppi?

He sat on the arm of the easy chair beside me and placed his arm around my shoulders. 'I thought you'd be in bed by now. It's been a long day for you.'

'I'm sorry,' I said.

'What are you sorry about?'

'That you felt that you had to marry me when I said I was pregnant.'

Fred pulled me closer to him and dropped a kiss on my hair. 'Don't be daft, Reen. I love you. What's put that thought into your head?'

'You left the boys outside and seemed to be talking very confidentially with Poppi. I thought you might have decided that you preferred her. She asked me an awful lot of questions about living on a ranch.'

'Do having babies always put strange and silly ideas into a woman's head? I wanted to talk to Poppi without having two little earwigs listening to every word. I've asked Poppi to come and stay here to help you. You're doing a grand job, but you're going to have a baby to look after. You said yourself that you didn't know how you would manage. I wanted to ask Poppi how she felt about living here as your helper. She's going to think the proposition over and said I would have to discuss it with you and I'll ride up to town in two weeks time. If you don't want her I'll tell her before she tells her in-laws and the shop keeper that she is leaving.'

I felt tears pricking behind my eyes. 'I am sorry, Fred.'

'What are you sorry about this time?'

'That I misinterpreted your motives.'

Fred knelt down on the floor so that his face was on a level with mine. 'If I suddenly had a stupid idea about exchanging you for someone else I would tell you. I'd not go behind your back. I'm not interested in her and if you aren't happy to have Poppi living here I'll have to find someone else.'

It took me only moments to make my decision. 'I'm sure it will work out well. I know I will need some help and she is my friend, probably the only real friend I have in town.' I knew I would be happy to have a woman around for company.

'So you want me to tell her she's welcome?'

I nodded. 'I can at least give it a trial. Suppose she doesn't like living here? What happens then?'

'We'll face that problem if it arises. Once she becomes used to a different way of life I'm sure she won't have a problem. You haven't, have you?'

I shook my head. 'I have you and the boys. She has no one she can turn to if she is unhappy.'

'I don't think she will be more unhappy than she is at present. She can live here rent free and I'll pay her a small wage for helping you. She can come up to town with us each month and visit her parents the same as you do. She may even feel more at home here as you and the boys can talk with her in Greek.'

'There's no room for her in the truck,' I remonstrated.

'Of course there is. The boys can sit in the back and she can be next to you in the front until you become too large to be squashed. She'll have to go in the back with them when that happens. You don't have to make a final decision tonight, Reen. You're tired. See how you feel tomorrow.'

I turned the question of Poppi coming to live with us over and over in my mind. Yes, I knew I would appreciate help with all the chores as I became larger and more tired, but did I want Poppi taking over my kitchen and installing her own routine for running the ranch? I knew I would have to change my routine to cope with a baby who would demand attention every few hours throughout the day and night.

I had a feeling that if I said I did not want Poppi to come and live here Fred would then ask my parents to come for an extended stay. I certainly did not want that and it would be difficult for my father to manage his book keeping work without continually travelling backwards and forwards to Derby. I knew Fred was doing this out of consideration for me, but for the first time since coming to the ranch I wished I was back in the town.

Fred rode up to Derby and returned to say that Poppi had agreed to come to the ranch on the proviso that if she was truly unhappy she would return to Derby and take her chance on getting a job and somewhere to live. She had assured him that she would not just walk out and leave us, but discuss the problem with us and give us adequate time to find someone to take her place. I smiled at the thought of Poppi 'just walking out;' she had no idea how far we were from the town.

Before we allocated a room for her Fred asked the boys which rooms they would like as their bedrooms. I was not surprised when Luke said he would like to stay in the room where he was at present and Dimitris said he would like the room next door. That meant that the room opposite our bedroom could be for the baby when it became old enough for a room of its own and Poppi could have the one lower down and opposite Dimitris. This still left four rooms unoccupied.

'Why did your father build such a large ranch house?' I asked Fred.

'The hands lived here at one time until their accommodation was built. My mother hated having them around all the time and when I began to swear and cuss the way they did my mother insisted they went elsewhere. I think she had also hoped to have some more children to fill up the empty rooms.'

'Do the ranch hands use bad language in front of the boys?' I asked.

'I have asked Hank and Jim not to, but I can't expect all of them to be watching their language when they are out herding. I'm sure as the boys become older they will pick up a few choice words.'

'Not in front of me, I hope, or their grandparents.'

'I'm sure they'll realise that they only use certain expressions when they are with the ranch hands. As they get older the hands would laugh at them if they said 'that is a silly cow' rather than using a string of expletives to describe her.'

I couldn't help smiling, but I did hope the boys would only use bad language when they were out of my hearing.

The room for Dimitris organised, his bed moved in and all his belongings, I turned my attention to the room for Poppi. I rummaged amongst the old furniture and found a chair, table and a mirror that would be suitable for her to use as a dressing table along with an old chest of drawers. One of the drawer handles was missing and I asked Fred to replace it. He removed all the handles from a chest of drawers that only had three legs and after I had cleaned and polished all of them I felt satisfied that they looked good enough. Beneath the window Fred fixed two shelves where she could place items that she might prefer to have on show. I was not sure if she would want to spend her evenings with us or prefer to stay in her own room so we moved one of the easy chairs in there so she had the choice.

I felt quite nervous when we drove up to Derby to collect Poppi. She was waiting at her in-law's house with her bags packed. Fred placed them in the back of the truck and suggested that she spent the remainder of the day with her parents whilst he ordered the necessary supplies for the ranch and I handed in the list at the grocers.

I took the boys to the library and both of them searched for books in the adult section. Luke was easy to please; anything to do with cows seemed to make him happy. Dimitris was more difficult to satisfy, having chosen two books on sea life he then wanted a book that described the construction of the Titanic and her subsequent sinking. I was not convinced that he was old enough to read about such a sad and traumatic event and spent time talking him into a book that had illustrations of ship construction from the earliest times to the present day.

By the time I had finished convincing Dimitris that he would find that book more interesting. Luke had read part of one of his books and decided that the information was much the same as he had read previously and he selected another that dealt with birthing problems in cows. Once again I was not sure if it was suitable reading matter for him but I had no energy left to argue.

The librarian raised her eyebrows in surprise when I signed them out. 'You have very divergent tastes,' she remarked.

I could not say the books were for the boys, so I just smiled and nodded. Before continuing to visit my parents we called in at the haberdasher and I bought the terry towelling that I needed to make nappies for the baby along with two more reels of cotton and a pack of needles. I had completed three nightdresses, but I still needed a further three. I could keep the old thin ones to use in an emergency.

I told my mother that Poppi was going to come to live with us to help me with the work, particularly when the baby arrived.

She gave her habitual sniff. 'So he needs two women to look after him now.'

'Not at all. Poppi is coming to help me. At present I have to do the cooking, laundry, cleaning and schooling the boys. I told Fred that I was not sure how well I would cope once I had the baby to care for as well. Unfortunately the birth of the baby coincides with the calving season so I cannot expect Fred to stay at the ranch and help me. He suggested that Poppi should be asked to come and work for us.'

'You want to watch her. Men very often get funny ideas when their wives are pregnant.'

I remembered my own stupid idea that Fred might be interested in Poppi. Maybe women also had funny ideas when they were pregnant.

'If there is a problem of any sort I can ask her to leave and Fred will bring her back to Derby.'

'So who would help you then?'

'I would just have to manage.' If my mother thought I was going to ask her to come and stay she was mistaken.

'Are you still riding?'

'I just sit on Amber's back and she walks around the field with me, nothing strenuous. One of the hands takes her out for some proper exercise each day.'

At the mention of Amber the boys began to chatter to their grandmother about their ponies and then Dimitris announced that he now had his own bedroom.

'I was allowed to choose which room I wanted. I'll be next to Luke and Poppi will be opposite me. Mamma says the baby will be in the room next to Poppi and opposite her and Fred when it is old enough.'

'You boys are just spoilt. When I was young we all slept in the same room. My sister and I had a pallet on the floor that we shared.'

'Dimitris and I shared a bed until we went to the ranch,' Luke reminded her. 'We then shared the room, but had separate beds. I like having a room to myself. I can put things wherever I want and know that Dimitris won't move them.'

When Fred arrived he said that Poppi was already sitting in the truck and hoped this did not mean we had to curtail our visit.

'You remember what I said,' my mother said as I kissed her goodbye.

My father smiled and tapped his head, nodding towards my mother. 'I'm pleased you are going to have some help and I'm sure everything will work out well.'

I was grateful for his support. Our only serious disagreement had been over my relationship with Lucas.

As we drove along Poppi looked about her. 'I've never been this far out of the town before. There are no houses anywhere.'

'Nor had I. It was quite a surprise at first but now I'm used to it.'

'Do you have neighbours?'

'Only cows.' commented Fred.

'We have the ranch hands that live close by.' I did not want Poppi to have second thoughts about staying with us before she had even arrived. 'There is always someone around.'

'Suppose your baby arrives early? You might not get to the hospital in time.'

'Hope you know how to deliver a baby, Poppi. I only know how to help a cow in labour.' Fred grinned and I banged his arm.

'Don't tease, Fred. That was a serious question.' I turned to Poppi. 'I'm pretty certain of my date and the hospital agree with me. A week before I'm due Fred is going to take me up to stay with my parents so I will be close by when the time comes.'

'Suppose it was really, really early?'

'Then I would have to rely upon you and Fred. Don't worry about it; I'm not. It's due at about the same time as the cows are due to give birth so I want to be well out of the way so Fred can concentrate on them and not have to think about me. I have had two boys already so I know what to expect.'

'That was quite a while ago,' remarked Poppi. 'Your body may have changed by now.'

I shrugged. 'Possibly, but I can do nothing about that.'

'What exactly do you want me to do at the ranch? Fred

mentioned some cooking, washing and a bit of cleaning. It doesn't sound much.'

I smiled. 'You'll be surprised. I have to start the washing first. It needs to be done every day, working clothes and decent clothes and underwear are done separately. Then there are the towels and the bedding that need to be washed.'

Poppi was looking more and more worried. 'Do you have to wash everything by hand?'

'No, thank goodness. I have a washing machine. If I have something like a blouse to wash I usually do that by hand and I'll do the baby's washing by hand.'

'A washing machine? I've never used one.'

'It's incredibly simple. You just put the water in and turn it on. There is a paddle inside that moves back and forwards to get the dirt out. It runs off the generator. Whilst it does the washing you can get on and do something else. When the weather is good it can be hung outside and when it rains there is a spare room where it can be hung up to dry.'

'If it is so easy to do the washing why do you need my help with that?'

'The jeans and working shirts can be quite heavy when they are wet. It is hanging them out that is tiring. I know I will find that more difficult as time goes on. Then I prepare whatever I decide we will have to eat in the evening and bake some bread if the barrel is getting low. When I've done that I sit down with the boys for a while and give them some lessons until we all have a snack lunch.'

'Don't the boys go to school?'

'They would have to go to a boarding school in Broome. Depending upon their career choice when they are older they may want to go to one of the towns for further education but at the moment I can teach them quite satisfactorily. My father helps me to plan lessons as he was a school teacher. I usually go down and visit my horse in the afternoon and at the moment I am making clothes ready for the baby so I sit down for an hour, sometimes more.'

'So if you are busy cooking, washing, teaching the boys, sewing and visiting your horse when do you ever get time to do anything else?'

'It's just a question of getting a routine going,' I explained. 'It was difficult at first. I kept going from chore to chore and never really completing any job. The boys are expected to keep their bedrooms tidy and sweep them out each day. I deal with our room, the kitchen and the living room. When you shower you are expected to leave the bathroom clean for the next person. I usually shower in the morning and it will probably be best if you do the same as the boys shower when they have been riding and Fred always showers before our evening meal. You can always have another shower if you want. When it was very hot I often had three a day just to cool down.'

'Now that will be a luxury. I was allowed a bath twice a week. They always claimed that we had to save water. Do you have a pipe from the town that brings it to you?'

'We have our own well and a pump that sends the water along the pipes. It will be easier to show you than try to explain. Water is still precious and we try not to waste any.'

Poppi looked out of the truck window again. 'There's still no sign of anyone. How much further do we have to go?'

I looked at Fred who winked at me. 'Well, if we're lost and there's no one to ask we could be driving for quite a long while, spending the night in the truck even.'

Poppi gasped in horror. 'You don't mean it?'

'No, we should be no more than half an hour. We'll unload and Reen can show you your room and you can unpack whilst she puts the finishing touches to our meal. The boys can tell you the rules whilst we eat.'

'Rules?' Poppi looked puzzled.

'There are certain important things that you have to know

but they are mainly common sense and I'm sure you'll have no problem.'

'I'm going to have an awful lot to tell my parents when I am able to visit them. They weren't sure I was doing the right thing by agreeing to come here.'

'If you really are unhappy Fred will take you back to town. I agreed to give ranch life a trial for a year. Of course I didn't know about the baby then or how happy the boys would be living here.'

'They're probably happy because they can do as they please and not have to go to school,' remarked Poppi.

'They certainly cannot do as they please. They have jobs that need to be completed each day along with the lessons I give them. They probably had more free time when they were in Derby. You realise there are no shops or taverns that you can visit so you are reliant upon us for your company. You'll be welcome to spend the evenings with us in the living room, we have a wireless and listen to the news and some of the other programmes. On a Sunday I usually listen to the church service that is broadcast. If you prefer to stay in your room reading no one will think you are being unsociable. I have joined the library in Derby. It is really so the boys can have some more advanced books than they have in the children's section. If you enjoy reading you could join the library as well.'

Poppi nodded. 'That's a good idea. I enjoy reading and knitting and I thought you might like me to knit a blanket for the baby or maybe a little jacket.'

'I'd really appreciate that. I am happy sewing, but knitting has never appealed to me. When I was in Crete we had a weaving loom and I was used to making clothes and anything else we wanted. Here you seem to be able to buy everything ready made.'

Poppi looked out of the cab window. 'Where are the cows?'

'They're up on the land at the back. They're not around the house area.'

'I'm quite pleased about that. I'm not sure if I like cows. I have found it quite frightening when I've seen them being driven from the pens at the back of the town.'

I smiled at Poppi. I knew exactly how she felt. 'There's the house.' I pointed through the windscreen to where the ranch house could be seen.

'It's enormous!'

'Not really, many of the buildings that you can see from here are the ranch hands quarters, stables and store houses. As we get closer you'll see they are not all clustered together as it appears from a distance.'

Fred drew up at the gate and Luke jumped off the back of the truck, opened and closed the gate. He did not climb back onto the truck but jogged along beside it as Fred drove down the track.

'Here we are. Fred and the boys will unload and I'll show you your room. We'll then have coffee or you can have a beer if you prefer and have what we call the town supper.'

'What's that?' asked Poppi.

'Pizza. It's a treat for the boys that we bring back and it saves me from having to think about a meal for them.'

Fred let out his usual piercing whistle and the men could be seen running up from their accommodation. Dimitris tried to emulate him but he only made quite a feeble squeak and gave an embarrassed smile.

I led Poppi through to her room and the boys carried her belongings in and placed them on the floor.

'Is this really my room?' she asked incredulously. 'It's so large and I have a proper dressing table. Before I had a small table and a square of mirror that I had to prop up with a book.'

'I'm afraid the furniture is not new, but it has all been cleaned and polished. It belonged to Fred's parents and had just been stored in the spare rooms waiting to be thrown away.'

'Thrown away? This is all far too good to be thrown out.'

'As long as you think you will be comfortable here. I'll leave you to unpack whilst I sort out the supplies in the kitchen and put the water on for coffee. Come back to the living room when you're ready and I'll show you the other rooms. Tomorrow you can see the rest of the ranch and be introduced to the hands.'

I hoped that Poppi would not be daunted by the daily tasks that I would ask her to complete and not ask Fred to take her back to Derby.

1951 - 1958
Babies

Poppi settled in well. She did not try to take over my routine, but worked along with me, doing the most tiring tasks. I did most of the cooking as Poppi confessed that she was not a good cook and had not been allowed to do any when living in her mother-in-law's house.

'She refused to eat anything that she was unfamiliar with so most of our meals consisted of steak and chips. I loved visiting my parents when I could enjoy something different.'

The boys accepted Poppi as a friend rather than as a servant. They were polite and courteous and did not mock her if she asked them the same questions time and again. She was very nervous of the horses and nothing Fred or I could say would persuade her to give Amber an apple or sit on her back. I had to admit I did not want her to become familiar with Amber; she was my horse.

Fred no longer checked the fences and pipes around the house, leaving the task entirely up to the boys as he knew they were conscientious and could be trusted. Once each week they were allowed to ride with him to inspect the herd and he would ask their opinion as regards the state of their health. Dimitris would nod and say they all looked good, but Luke wanted to go closer to inspect them.

'I can't see from here if one has a runny nose or left an unusual deposit on the ground. I could say that was from the wrong cow. What about that one that Matt is with?'

'He's penning her in so she is away from the others so he's obviously concerned.'

Fred whistled and pointed to the cow. Matt looked up and waved back at Fred. He drew a square shape in the air and then pointed back to the ranch. Fred raised his hand in acknowledgement and turned his horse around.

'Well spotted, Luke. Matt has indicated that we need to collect the box and take her down to the pens so she can be looked at properly. Provided you two keep well away from the herd you may stay here until I return.'

'Is she having her calf?' asked Luke.

'It's possible, but I hope not. It's too early. Stay where you are and keep an eye on the hands. If one of them tells you to move do as he says.'

'I'd rather go back to the ranch,' said Dimitris. 'I could read some more of my book.'

'Then you can ride back with me. How about you, Luke?'

'I'd rather stay here and see what you have to do.'

'Come on then, Dimitris.' Fred knew he could trust Luke to do exactly as he had instructed. 'I'll not be long.'

Luke watched as Fred and Dimitris cantered back to the ranch. He saw Dimitris take his pony into the stables and hoped he would not forget to give her a rub down and place a blanket over her back before he left her. Although it was warm once the horse's sweat dried it chilled them and they could become seriously ill. He saw Fred remove a box like contraption on wheels from a shed and attach it to his horse so that she dragged it behind her. As they progressed up the grassy track Luke returned his attention to the cow. She did look miserable and he wished he could go over and stroke her to give her some reassurance that all would be well.

When Fred arrived back with the box he called to Luke. 'You can come and join me and watch what we do.'

Luke was about to ride over when he remembered Fred's instructions. "Always look before you move. Make sure the cows are not coming your way." He checked that the herd was well away from him and cantered over to Fred's side.

He watched Fred detach the box from his horse and lift the metal hurdle at the end. Matt slipped a noose around the cow's neck and the two men tried to encourage her to walk into the box. She dug her heels in and refused to move. Fred gave her a hefty smack on her rump and she started forward; Matt immediately pulled on the noose and reluctantly she placed her front hooves on the ramp. Another slap on her rump moved her still further forwards and Fred closed the hurdle behind her

'Simple when there are two of you,' announced Fred.

'Did it hurt her when you slapped her?' asked Luke.

'Not a bit. It just surprised her so she moved forwards. I'll hitch the box up to Blaze again and take her down to the pens.'

Luke followed as Fred rode slowly back to where the birthing pens were situated. 'You can give me a hand now. Tie Bessie to the post and take hold of the rope and give her a bit of slack. I'll remove the gate and you pull her forwards.'

Try as he might Luke could not get the cow to move. Fred gave her a further slap on her rump and she leapt forwards taking Luke with her so that he landed on the ground of the pen. At the same time the cow released a stream of evil smelling faeces that splattered all over Luke's jeans. He stood up, still holding the rope and cursed the animal in the language he had heard the ranch hands use.

Fred roared with laughter. 'Don't you let your mother hear you say words like that,' he warned.

Luke glowered at him. 'Did you know that was going to happen?'

'You could call it a baptism of fire. I thought you might be pulled over but I didn't know you were going to be covered in cow sh -dung.'

'What did I do wrong?'

'Nothing. I just over estimated your strength, forgetting you are still a boy and not a man yet. Get back to the ranch and take those clothes off. Have a shower and hose down those clothes or they'll attract the flies. Leave them in a separate sack ready for your Mum or Poppi to wash.'

Feeling humiliated, Luke led Bessie back to her stable. Dave held his nose as he approached and grinned, making Luke aware that he had witnessed the incident. He hoped his ignominious fall had not been noticed by all the ranch hands.

Leaving Bessie with Dave Luke then made his way to the bucket shower.

Once washed and wearing clean clothes Luke returned to the pen where Matt and Fred were examining and discussing the cow. Luke waited until they stood away and then asked if the men knew what was wrong with her.

'We'll have to wait and see what develops. She may just be giving birth early. In the meantime we'll be scrupulous in examining all the other animals. If she has something infectious they could all have it and we'll lose the whole herd.'

'How will you know if it is infectious?' asked Luke.

'If it is Parainfluenza she'll recover in a few days. If she has bronchopneumonia she will probably have infected the others and they'll all start to show the same symptoms and start dropping dead.'

Luke looked at Fred in horror. 'That's awful. Is there no way to stop them from becoming ill?'

'Once a virus takes hold amongst them we're powerless to stop it. What did you do with your dirty clothes?'

'Hosed them off as you told me and put them in the sack ready for washing.'

'You need to go back and tell your Mum and Poppi not to touch that sack until it has been disinfected. Can't be too careful; occasionally these viral infections can be transmitted to humans.'

Without a word Luke turned Bessie and cantered back to the ranch house where he tied her to the fence. He ran around to the back and was relieved to see the sack of dirty washing sitting just where he had left it. He stood and looked at it; he should have asked Fred where he should put it for safety.

Luke entered the kitchen of the ranch and walked through to the living room where Poppi and I were sitting; I was sewing and she was knitting. We both looked up in surprise as Luke entered.

'What's wrong?' I asked immediately. Dimitris had told us that Luke was staying up with Fred to help with a sick cow.

'Nothing terrible. I was a bit too close to the cow that isn't well and I had to come back and shower and change. I rinsed off my clothes and put them in the sack but when I told Fred he said he would prefer that my clothes were disinfected, just to make sure any bugs were killed off.'

Poppi placed her knitting on the chair beside her. 'Show me which one it is and I'll make sure it isn't touched.'

'You're not hurt, are you, Luke?' I asked anxiously.

'Not a bit, just felt rather stupid being covered in cow sh --- dung.' Luke grinned. 'I'll show you the sack, Poppi, and put it somewhere out of the way. Could I have a bit of your wool to tie round it? That way it won't become confused with the others; then I ought to get back up to Fred and see if I can be of any help to him.'

Fred and Matt were still standing beside the pen when Luke arrived. 'I've sorted out the sack with Poppi. She knows which one it is and won't touch it.'

Fred nodded. 'I'm probably being over cautious. I'm pretty sure the cow is aborting.'

Luke frowned. 'According to the book I was reading the other day that happens if there is a malformed calf. Nature's way of getting rid of it.'

'Provided she is the only one it's no problem.'

'What will happen to her?' asked Luke

'Nothing; she'll deal with it and we'll watch to make sure that everything comes away as it should. Once that has happened she'll be fine again, but on the list for being sold. No point in trying to breed from her a second time as the same thing could happen again.'

'So she isn't ill?'

'Probably not, but can't be too careful. I certainly wouldn't want your mother to be ill at the moment.'

Luke mulled the information over. 'How would you know if Mum was ill when she's in the hospital having the baby?'

'I'll telephone your grandfather.'

'How?' asked Luke.

'We have a telephone for emergencies. I'd use that.'

Luke shook his head. 'Grandpa doesn't have a telephone. He'd have to go to one of the call boxes and telephone you.'

Fred frowned. 'That's not ideal. I could be anywhere out on the ranch and I'm not sure if Poppi knows how to use it. I'll have to arrange for a telephone to be installed for your grandparents. I can then call them and ask for any news. Once I know your Mum is in hospital I'll ride up to Derby and stay until the baby is born.'

'Can you show us how to use it? Then you can telephone to tell us if we have a brother or sister?'

'I'm sure that would be no problem. It's only sensible that you know how to use it in an emergency and it isn't difficult.'

Satisfied, Luke turned his attention back to the cow. 'How long will it take for the calf to be born?'

Fred shrugged. 'Difficult to tell as it's an early birth. Usually it's less than eight hours. Once the water sac has ruptured it takes anything from thirty to ninety minutes. Make sure you're not standing behind her when that happens.'

Luke grinned. 'I learnt a lesson the hard way today.'

'Don't feel bad about it. Every one of us has had that experience at one time or another.'

When Fred and Luke returned to the house later in the day they both looked relieved.

'The calf has been born and although she's small she's healthy,' announced Luke proudly. 'Matt's feeding her at the moment and he's going to show me how to do it tomorrow.'

'I thought the cow fed her calf,' I remarked.

'Of course,' Luke spoke knowledgeably, 'But when a calf is born prematurely the mother's milk doesn't always come in for a day or so. It's to do with the trauma of giving birth early. The calf has to learn to suck your fingers. She's a little beauty. You'll have to come and see her tomorrow.'

I smiled at his enthusiasm. I was sure that every calf was delightful when it was first born, but he must not form an attachment to her. Once fully grown it would be difficult to distinguish her from the rest of the herd and would be sold.

'I'm pleased all is well. Get washed up both of you and then we'll have some supper.'

'I'll tell Dimitris all about it whilst we eat.'

I shook my head. 'Not whilst we're eating. Afterwards you can tell him every grisly detail.'

I had never used a telephone and when Fred told me he was having one installed for my parents I insisted that he sat down with me and gave me explicit instructions. He raised his eyebrows when he saw I had written them in Greek.

'I can copy them for my parents and leave these instructions here for Poppi and the boys. When I stay with my parents I will telephone and show my father exactly how it is done. Then Poppi or one of the boys can telephone back so they become familiar with it and my father understands how to answer.'

My father was as nervous about using the telephone as I had been. I left the instructions with him and said that I would telephone when we arrived home and all he had to do was pick it up and speak to me.

'Don't worry if you have a problem at first. When I come to stay I'll show you exactly how to use it. We're showing Poppi and the boys so if they have any cause for concern they can contact you or even the hospital in a real emergency.'

I packed my clothes and some for the baby in a large bag. I was not sure what I should take to wear myself after the birth and finally settled on a skirt with an elasticated waist and a loose blouse with a jumper should it turn cold. I hoped I would soon lose the weight I had put on or I would have very few clothes that fitted me. I still felt well, although Poppi was insistent that I rested on my bed in the afternoon for at least two hours. I no longer rode Amber each day, but Fred would walk her up to the house for me to pet. Poppi would take one look and retreat inside the ranch house refusing to come out and meet my beautiful horse.

I had only been with my parents for four days when I realised that the baby was on the way. I telephoned the ranch and asked Poppi to tell Fred I was going to the hospital. I added that there was no need for him to gallop up and he must make sure all was well at the ranch before leaving. I also asked her to tell my boys.

My mother accompanied me to the hospital, but she was not allowed to stay with me. Once I had been examined she was told to go home and come back in about four or five hours to hear how I was progressing

'If any problem should arise we know your address and someone will come to fetch you. I understand that this is your daughter's third child and there's certainly nothing to worry about at present. She appears to be fit and healthy and the baby has a strong heartbeat. Everything is in the right place for a straight forward birth.'

I hoped that news would be as much of a comfort to her as it was to me.

For the next three hours I was visited intermittently by a nurse until finally the midwife appeared. She gave me a final examination and told me it would not be long now. From then on I began to push and within half an hour a small baby slipped between my legs. I gave a sigh of relief, it had certainly not been the ordeal I had been expecting now I was ten years older. I tried to raise myself up and a firm hand pushed me back down.

'All in good time. You have a perfect little girl. Once we have cleaned both of you up you can hold her.'

'A girl!' I felt disappointed for Fred. I knew he would have liked a boy. 'Can you let my mother know? She can ask my father to telephone my husband and tell him.'

'I believe your mother is waiting outside. There is a man with her. Would that be your husband or your father?'

'I don't know. If it's Fred, my husband, please can he come in, just for a few minutes.'

'It's not usual so soon after a birth.'

'If it is Fred he'll have ridden up here from the ranch and it takes at least two hours. It's not a convenient time for him to be away. The heifers are calving and he will be needed there.'

'I would have thought the birth of his daughter was more important than the birth of a calf,' the midwife replied.

'That's why he will have spent two hours riding up here. Once he has seen the baby and knows I am fine he can return with an easy mind.'

'We'll see,' was her response and she set about washing me and making me comfortable propped up on my pillows. My little baby was handed to me and I gazed at her in delight. I even dared to move her shawl to one side and check that she really was a little girl and no mistake had been made. I hoped Fred would not be too disappointed.

Just as I had given up any hope of seeing him and thought it must be my father who was waiting outside with my mother Fred pulled the curtain aside and came over to my bedside with a broad grin on his face.

He kissed me and stood looking down at the little bundle in my arms.

'I'm sorry, Fred.'

'Sorry? What are you sorry about?'

'It's a little girl and I know you would have liked a boy.'

'Am I complaining? She's beautiful, just like her mother. We can have a boy next time.'

'Next time! Fred, I only gave birth an hour ago and you're already talking about the next one.'

'No harm in making plans for the future. What are we going to call her?'

'I thought Maria, after my mother. If you think that sounds too Greek she could be called Mary.'

Fred nodded. 'I'm sure your mother will be pleased if she is named Maria. We can always call her Mary at home.'

The nurse pulled back the curtain. 'Mr Anstruther, I have to ask you to leave now. Your wife needs to rest.'

'How are the cows?' I managed to ask.

'Doing well. I'll come back tomorrow to see you again.' Fred kissed me quickly and left as I handed our little girl, Maria, to the nurse so she could be placed in a crib beside me and I could have some sleep.

True to his promise Fred rode up to Derby the following day and I felt guilty. He was not allowed to stay for longer than thirty minutes and he had ridden for two hours and then had to spend two more hours riding back to the ranch.

I assured him I was well and baby Maria was healthy. 'My mother will be allowed to visit me for a short while so you could telephone my parents in the evening. They will be able to reassure you that there is no problem. Besides, once the priest has been and Maria has been christened I will leave the hospital and stay with my parents for a few days. You can then telephone me and we can arrange when it will be convenient for you to come up with the truck so you can take us home.'

Fred frowned. 'I thought you had to stay in the house for forty days?'

'Strictly speaking I should to abide by my religious upbringing. It is an old custom that people adopted to protect the mother and child from picking up any infection. I will go to my parents as I did after having Dimitris but I do not need to stay with them for forty days. I will sit in the truck with you and once back at the ranch I'll not be going out and meeting people.'

'Are you sure?'

I nodded. 'I will be much happier back at the ranch and getting into a routine with Maria. Besides the boys need to have me back or they may think I no longer love them if there is a new baby.'

'I'm sure they are both old enough and intelligent enough to know that would never happen. I'm happy to take you home as soon as you feel ready.'

My mother fussed over my baby, although she disapproved of my plan to return to the ranch before my forty days seclusion had been completed. I reminded her that I had not been to church since going to the ranch. When the priest christened Maria I confessed my lack of attendance to him and he gave me a blessing. He assured me that if I said my prayers each day and brought my children up to do the same it made no difference if they were said in a church or in the privacy of a bedroom. I was relieved by this as I could not have expected Fred to drive us up to Derby for supplies on the Saturday and again to attend church on the Sunday.

The boys were delighted to see me and were immediately enamoured of Maria, remarking on her tiny hands and feet and both being allowed to hold her for a short while. Poppi was also entranced by her and I felt sorry that she had no child of her own.

The telephone was both a boon and a curse. My mother phoned me every day to ask after Maria and myself. It was not always convenient for me to answer and talk with her and I would ask Poppi to take the call and tell her that I was in the middle of feeding and I would telephone her later. At least she was not living so close to me that she could continually drop in unannounced.

It was beneficial to me that Poppi was there and willing to look after Mary, as we were now calling her, so that I could rest in the afternoon. When she woke during the night demanding a feed I would take her into her own bedroom and sit in there so that I did not disturb Fred too much. I was thankful that she appeared to be as placid and amenable as both the boys had been.

I had not been visiting my parents or the town of Derby since returning to the ranch and when Mary was three months old Fred suggested that we invited my parents to come for a visit. The room at the end of the passage had been cleaned and decorated whilst I had been away. The furniture that Fred's parents had used was polished by Poppi, but I insisted that they must have a new mattress and bedding. Fred would have to make a special visit to Derby to collect the mattress and I contacted the hospital and arranged to visit for a check up for myself and baby Mary on the same day. I could visit my parents and issue the invitation to them at the same time. The boys and Poppi had been going up each week when Fred drove up to buy supplies and I had written a letter to the library asking that they should be allowed to choose books for me. Poppi had also joined the library and said she would make sure that the books were suitable reading matter for both of them.

I told them that on this occasion they were not invited as there would be insufficient space in the back of the truck. This was not strictly true, but I was a bit concerned about my visit to the hospital. I was sure there was something not right inside of me. Once I had stopped bleeding after giving birth to Mary I had not bled again.

Mary was given a completely clean bill of health whilst I waited in trepidation whilst the doctor examined me.

He stood to one side and asked what I thought was wrong with me. I explained and he smiled.

'There's nothing wrong, you're pregnant.'

I gasped. 'I can't be. Mary is only three months old and I'm still feeding her.'

'Feeding her does not stop you from conceiving. You've obviously resumed a normal relationship with your husband and consequently you are expecting again.'

I bit my lip. This was entirely unexpected. 'Are you sure?'

'As sure as I can be at this early stage. Make another appointment for two months time. In the meantime should you begin to bleed it will probably mean you are having a miscarriage and your husband will need to bring you into the hospital.'

I nodded and wondered how Fred would take this news. The birth of this baby would coincide yet again with the calving season.

On the whole the visit by my parents was a success. My mother tried to monopolise Mary and I often had to bite my tongue when I found she had been cuddled to sleep in my mother's arms rather than being laid in her crib. I was already growing larger with the next baby and I could not keep the knowledge from them. My mother would look at me with pursed lips and shake her head in disapproval. She could not be persuaded to sit on a horse and was sure I should not be doing so and continually told me that 'in my condition' I should be careful. I reminded her that if I was still living in Fourni or Elounda I would be working up in the fields with Mary strapped to my back and no one would think anything was unusual about doing that.

My father was easier. He agreed to ride up with Fred to view the herd and Jim had lent him his own docile horse. Luke and Dimitris rode with them and Luke took pride in pointing out the cow that he had fed by hand.

'Did you know that their tongue is so rough it feels like sand paper? I was really surprised. I had expected it to be soft like ours. You see that one over there? She's the mother and Fred is going to sell her. She can't be trusted to carry a calf full term.'

My father had listened patiently to all the information that Luke imparted to him about the cows and later asked me when he would leave and go to school.

'The boy is fourteen. Shouldn't he be going off to a boarding school now so he can get some more advanced education? You've done a good job with him so far but he'll have no qualifications for a future career.'

I shook my head. 'There's no need for him to go away unless he wants to. We have a wireless and there are specific programmes each day to educate the children who live in the outback and cannot attend a conventional school. Fred has signed up so that both the boys can start to receive them. When Luke has completed those for his age group we can think about further education for him.'

My father said no more, but I think he was pleased that Fred was willing to take as much responsibility for my boys as he would for children of his own.

Once again I went up to Derby and stayed with my parents when my next child was due. I insisted that I took Mary with me as she was too small to understand where her mother had gone and why. I had weaned her so that I would have sufficient milk for the new baby, although I still allowed her to suckle for a short while each day. This would mean my milk was already available for the next baby.

I had George easily and I was delighted that he was a boy. My only concern was that Mary might become spoilt as she was a girl. Fred had visited me and admired his son before going to my parents and spending some time with Mary. Poppi came up to Derby when it was time for me to return to the ranch; that way she was able to hold Mary safely on her lap whilst George slept contentedly in my arms.

Each day then became a continual round of feeding and washing nappies. I was so thankful that Poppi was there to help me and most nights Mary would sleep through until after I had given George his early morning feed. Whilst George slept Mary would sit on a rug with some toys and she would watch Poppi and I whilst we worked in the kitchen. Mary was now finding her feet and we had to watch her constantly to ensure that she came to no harm. During the afternoon we would take both children out for a walk and either Fred or Luke would look after Mary whilst I visited Amber.

I took George to the hospital for his three monthly check up and also to have my own health confirmed. I was very relieved to be told that I was not pregnant again, but that did not last long. I began to feel very tired and often the thought of a particular food made me feel nauseous. I took little notice at first, thinking it was a reaction to having two children so quickly, but two months later I realised that despite Fred and I being 'careful' I had actually conceived again.

A visit to the hospital confirmed that I was indeed having another child. The little boy, Jake, when he arrived, was totally different from my other children. He demanded attention continually and would scream if he had to wait whilst Poppi and I attended to something else. We were both becoming exhausted although Poppi insisted that she saw to Mary and George if they woke in the night so I could get a little extra sleep. Either Fred or Luke would take care of Mary and George after our lunch so Poppi could get some much needed rest.

I was rarely able to have more than two hours sleep at a time as Jake would want a feed and would not settle afterwards unless I walked up and down the room cuddling and rocking him. I would often think he was asleep but as I went to lay him down he would open his eyes and let out a piercing scream and I would lift him and continue walking. Fred said I should leave him to scream, but I could not do that.

I mentioned the problems I had with him when I went to the hospital for the three month check up and they suggested that I gave him some extra milk from a bottle as I might not be producing enough to satisfy him. They could find nothing physically wrong with him to account for his behaviour and said I had to count my blessings that my previous children had been so placid. That was little comfort to me. Giving him an extra feed after I had fed him did seem to help, so I could only assume that he had been hungry and I felt guilty.

Jake did become more manageable, despite always being determined to have his own way, and I found I was expecting again. This time it was another little girl and we called her Eliza. To my utter relief she was not at all like Jake, but I could tell by the way he looked at her that he was not enamoured at having a small sibling who demanded my attention.

When I returned to the hospital for the usual check ups we left Mary and George for Luke and Dimitris to care for as we would only be away for the day. Fred left Jake with my mother whilst he collected some shopping and Poppi visited her relatives. My mother complained that Jake had been demanding and screamed when he was not given his own way and I realised I was asking a lot of my parents now they were older.

Eliza was almost too good. She would watch what was going on around her whilst I fed her. Mary or George would often come over and hold her hand and be rewarded by one of her beautiful smiles. Unfortunately Jake was more likely to throw one of his toy cars or bricks at her.

As Eliza became old enough to sit in the high chair she would watch the others playing and I would keep a strict eye on Jake who I kept in the play pen. I was so grateful for both these items. I had never seen them in Crete and babies were allowed to lay on the floor to crawl around as they pleased or carried everywhere on their mother's hip. I had done this with both Luke and Dimitris and knew how tiring it could be.

Eliza showed little inclination to walk, unlike the others who had hardly been able to wait to get on their feet. She was almost fourteen months old (and I was expecting again) when she finally pulled herself up and gave a smile of accomplishment. For another month she would walk around holding the furniture before she had the courage to finally let go and walk unaided. She fell continually, but undeterred she would pull herself up again.

I did become concerned when she still seemed to be falling over her feet when she was nearly two, but by then I also had Charlie. Eliza would stand next to me whilst I fed him and later I would see her mimicking my actions with a doll. She might have been slow in walking but she was certainly not slow in any other respects and could string her words together easily to express her needs or opinion. In many respects she was more mature than Jake, who still threw tantrums, often for no good reason, but just to get attention. I hoped he would grow out of the bad habit or he would not be a very nice teenager.

Eliza was clumsy and would fall frequently whilst outside playing and her knees were always scraped and her legs bruised. She never cried when it happened, just gave them a rub and declared it was nothing to worry about. I noticed that she was equally clumsy when she was eating, dropping her food or spilling her drink. I tried to help her co-ordination by giving her colouring books and pencils. However hard she tried she seemed unable to keep within the lines. I know now that she had a condition called Dyspraxia and was pleased that I had never scolded her. Jake had taken to calling her 'Tumble weed' and laughed at her when she fell or dropped things, but the other children were patient and always willing to help her if they saw she was struggling.

More than anything she liked it when Luke sat her in front of him on his horse. Both boys had outgrown their ponies and they had been passed down to Mary and George who were learning to ride. Dimitris had requested that Jake should never be allowed to ride Socks as he did not consider his brother was gentle enough and he was worried that he might whip him. Jake had shrugged and said he didn't like horses and had no desire to ride. I still visited Amber frequently and would sit on her whilst she walked around, even daring to trot for a short while. I knew I would never be a confident rider.

Fred had started to teach me how to drive the truck and each time, just as I began to become familiar with gears, clutches and accelerators, I would find I was pregnant again and it soon became uncomfortable for me to sit behind the steering wheel. He was now teaching both Luke and Dimitris, although neither of them was old enough to drive away from the ranch land. They were far better pupils than I had been.

Our daily routine had become difficult now there were so many of us having to share a bathroom and I spoke to Fred and asked if it would be possible to add another. He promised to speak to an architect to see whether it would be practical to add a small bathroom area to any of the bedrooms and with a little reorganisation if we could also have one in our bedroom.

Before the architect would give a firm answer he asked for the measurements of all the rooms and also wanted to know about the drain runs. Fred drew out a rough plan showing all the rooms and where the drains from the kitchen and current bathroom were situated. When the architect's plans arrived back I was amazed at his proposals. All but two of the bedrooms were large enough to incorporate a small shower cubicle, toilet and hand basin along with an extra bathroom next to the current one.

I wished I had suggested this before, but when I saw the astronomical price that was being quoted I thought it doubtful that Fred could afford the work and decided I would not ask for more than one extra bathroom. Fred told me not to worry and he would speak to the bank and was sure he would be able to get a loan to cover the cost of the work. Fred gave priority to the additional bathroom and once that was completed Luke and Dimitris shared a bedroom again whilst a bathroom cubicle was installed in both their rooms.

For the next few months we continually moved the children from their bedrooms whilst the work took place and finally we also had a bathroom cubicle in our bedroom. Poppi was delighted and said that more bathrooms would make life so much easier despite the extra cleaning that would be needed. The two smaller rooms where it had not been practical to install bathroom facilities would become bedrooms for the youngest children as they could not be expected to use a shower unsupervised. Jake had complained that it was unfair that he did not have his own bathroom, but Eliza accepted the arrangement without any protest.

No sooner had the work been completed than another baby arrived. I had become used to this happening at regular intervals and accepted the disruption to our routine, no sooner having one child out of nappies than having another to take their place. The washing machine seemed to be continually working and I was beginning to think we would run out of bedrooms for the children and need to have an extension built.

1958 - 1959
Children

We were having a rare peaceful evening when Dimitris said he wished to speak to both of us. My heart lurched. Was he ill? Had he picked up some infection from the cattle? He certainly did not look ill, just a little apprehensive.

'It isn't that I want to leave home,' Dimitris assured us, 'But I want to join the navy when I am old enough and to be accepted as more than a deck hand I need to have a knowledge of algebra, geometry and trigonometry. I've tried to study them on the radio service, but I need help to understand them fully and receive a qualification in mathematics. Once I have that I can apply to the navy cadet school and have further training in seamanship.'

'Are you saying you want to go away to school?' I asked.

'I'd like to go to the boarding school in Broome, the one where Fred attended. I could come home every weekend and during the holidays and I should only be there for about a year if I work hard.'

I was not surprised by Dimitris's choice of career, but I hated the thought of him going away from home. I was more surprised when Dimitris asked if he could change his name to Anstruther as he felt the Australian navy would find him more acceptable with a conventional Australian name. I felt hurt that he should want to discard his natural father's name, although I could not fault Fred and his attitude and dealings with my boys.

Fred assured Dimitris that he would be more than happy

239

to formally adopt him and he also asked Luke if he wanted to be adopted also. Luke hesitated and asked time to consider the proposal. Fred took me to one side and asked me to encourage him, explaining that he planned to leave the ranch to Luke and it could save any legal complications if Luke was his adopted son.

I was touched by Fred's proposed action and Luke was certainly the obvious choice to take over the ranch eventually. I did ask for one concession and that was for Luke to go to a farming school and actually gain qualifications in animal husbandry. That would mean both my boys leaving home, Luke to Perth and Dimitris to Sydney eventually. In some ways this solved a problem as now there were so many of us it was impossible for all of us to fit into the truck and Luke and Dimitris would ride their horses to Derby whilst the rest of us travelled in the truck and Fred had mentioned purchasing another once Luke was legally allowed to drive away from the ranch.

When I told my parents that both Luke and Dimitris were going away for extra schooling my father was delighted.

'You've done a good job with them and the radio lessons have helped, but now they need specialised knowledge they have to look further afield.'

I did not tell my parents that both boys were going to be formally adopted by Fred and take his name.

It seemed very strange to me when Dimitris went to Broome and only returned at weekends, riding his horse both ways being able to stable it at the school and care for it. Because Luke went to Perth he was only able to return to the ranch every three months when he was given a holiday from lectures. It would take him an hour to fly in an aeroplane from Perth to Broome and then he had the journey back to the ranch. On those occasions Fred would ride to Broome taking Luke's horse with him and they would ride back together.

The first time that Luke returned home he said he was

disappointed in his course. He reckoned he knew more than his tutor about breeding cows and problems that could be encountered with their health and during calving. Some of the other boys in his year sought him out and asked him to explain some things more fully as they did not like to keep asking for further explanations in the class. Fred asked if he wanted to leave the college, and go elsewhere to train as a teacher. Luke shook his head vehemently and said he would rather stay and hope that he would eventually learn something new. He certainly did not want to be cooped up inside every day telling boys about cows; he wanted to be out amongst the animals.

Dimitris declared he was very happy at Broome.

'Once I became used to sleeping in a room with three other boys it was no problem. One of them does snore unfortunately, but if he becomes too noisy I get up and poke him in the ribs to make him turn over. I'm not finding the lessons as difficult as I had anticipated. At least there is someone on hand that I can ask if I need help. With the radio I had to send in a question and wait until the following week for an answer. By then I'd either forgotten what my question was or found out the answer for myself.'

Both Mary and George enjoyed their radio lessons, unlike Jake who would make any excuse to avoid them. Mary was artistic and happily sat drawing items of clothing and later painting the model dresses she had created. I had no idea where she had inherited her talent as neither Fred nor I could draw. Fred said that his mother had sketched occasionally but he could not remember if her work had been particularly good.

George was an enigma. He was more studious and enjoyed reading. but most of all he seemed to enjoy organising the pantry storage so that all the tins, jars and bottles were arranged in order of size. He would then list them and when we went to Derby for supplies he always wanted to join Poppi in the general store. He would wander around the shelves and make lists of the items for sale and their prices.

241

Jake's behaviour did not improve and Fred gave him various punishments that seemed to mean nothing to the boy. He could be seen climbing on the water pipes or the roofs of the out buildings, throwing stones into the artesian well, opening the gate and swinging back and forth on it until one of us would go out and insist that he came back into the ranch. I even saw Hank swipe his hand across the boy's bottom on one occasion when he refused to get off the water pipes. Jake had come running to me to complain but I would not give him any sympathy and said that if he climbed on the pipes again I would ask Fred to smack him twice as hard. He had shrugged and walked away and I knew he would be disobedient again. He was the only one of the children who seemed to have been conceived under an evil star and he worried me.

Charlie was as contented as a baby as the others had been (except Jake, of course) and when Luke telephoned from Perth to ask if he could invite a friend to stay for two weeks in the holidays we were delighted. Until now Luke had only had Dimitris as a companion and we had never considered that he needed to mix with other youngsters of his own age. Fred agreed to drive the truck up to collect them and Poppi and I began to reorganise the bedrooms. Mary was agreeable to have Eliza share her room, but I did not dare to ask George to share his room with Jake. George's precious books would have been torn, scribbled on and damaged beyond repair.

The young man who arrived with Luke seemed quite bemused to have so many children around. 'I hope I'm not being a nuisance by coming to stay.'

'Not at all. We're delighted to have you. The only visitors we usually have are my parents. Don't let the children annoy you as you'll be a bit of a novelty to them.'

'They will be a novelty to me also. I've only got a sister,' Clyde explained. 'She's two years younger than me so I really have no experience of children.'

I assured him he would soon become used to them and I was sure Luke would be able to keep him occupied during the day and amused in the evenings.

Having shown Clyde his room Luke took him to meet the ranch hands, promising to show him the rest of the ranch the following day. 'I've asked Jim to arrange the hands' schedule so there is a horse free that you can ride.'

Clyde looked embarrassed. 'Actually I've never ridden a horse.'

Luke stared at him in amazement. 'You've never ridden? How do you get around your ranch?'

'We don't live on the ranch. I suppose you would call my father a gentleman rancher. He relies entirely on his employees. He raises the cattle for beef and sells them on when they are ready to be slaughtered and buys some more. He's not interested in the animals, only the profit.'

'Is that how you feel? That they are just a commodity to make a profit?'

Clyde shuffled his feet. 'Yes and no. You need to make a profit each year or you haven't got the income to keep paying your staff and buying more stock, but I think you would make more money by raising your own herd. I'd like to expand into breeding, but my father won't hear of it. He says there's no need to get your hands dirty.'

'So is that why you are at the farming college and asked if you could come here to visit?'

'I enjoy your company, better than being at home with just my sister and parents with nothing much to do. I also hoped I might be able to get some hands on experience. You seem to know exactly what the lecturer is talking about but I have no idea when he mentions retained placenta or milk fever.'

'That's not surprising if you are not breeding the animals but I'm not sure if being here or being at the college is going to be of any benefit to you if your father isn't interested.'

'He's not going to be around for much longer and then I will be expected to take over.'

Luke raised his eyebrows. 'Is he ill or just thinking of retiring?'

'He's ill and doesn't realise how serious the condition is. This is why I would appreciate learning how your ranch works, then if I think it is viable I can make changes eventually.'

'How does your mother feel about making changes? Have you spoken to her about your ideas?'

'She did approve and was going to try to talk my father into letting me have a small breeding programme to see how it worked out, but then when she found out how ill he was she refused to put the proposition before him. She said, quite naturally, that she did not want him upset or worried about anything.'

Luke nodded. 'The best thing you can do is talk to Fred, my stepfather. He's taught me all I know and could probably give you some practical advice. The first thing we need to do is get you on a horse.'

I found Clyde an easy guest. He and Luke would leave the ranch each morning and not return until late afternoon, eating with relish whatever meal was put in front of him and thanking me. Fred laughed at Clyde's lack of riding skill, but would spend time each evening answering any questions the young man had about a stock breeding programme.

The thing that seemed to worry Clyde most was employing suitable ranch hands who were capable of dealing with the heifers when they were calving. 'The current hands are efficient, they know what to look for regarding the health of the herd, but they won't have any experience of breeding. It's going to be a while before I am proficient, so I will need employees that I can trust.'

'You're serious about wanting to branch out?' asked Fred and Clyde nodded emphatically.

'If I give it a try for a year or two and find I'm not successful I can always return to rearing the animals just for meat. I'm not

244

too ambitious. I thought a dozen heifers to start off with and see how I get on, but I need someone experienced to look after them.'

'Let me know when you're ready and I'll speak to my hands and see if they can recommend anyone.'

By the time Clyde left, having thanked both Fred and I profusely for our hospitality it was time for my parents to pay their usual visit. They were delighted when they saw they had their own bathroom cubicle as I had not mentioned this to them previously, just said we were having an additional bathroom installed. I realised whilst they were staying with us that both of them were becoming older. I was not prepared to have them come to live with us eventually and made this quite clear to Fred.

'My father is reasonably easy to get along with, but I cannot live with my mother. She would criticise everything and want me to do exactly as she pleased. I know she loves the children dearly, but would disapprove of the freedom we allow them to have. Once the novelty of having their grandparents here had worn off they would become resentful of her interference and so would I.'

Fred had laughed at me, but said he understood. 'I have never forgotten the subterfuge you had to employ so we could get married. You don't need to worry, there are nursing homes here that will care for the elderly. It's not like it was in the old days when you were expected to look after your parents until the day they died. I think they will have a good many more years where they are capable of caring for themselves.'

I was relieved by Fred's words and then I told him I was expecting again. He looked surprised. 'Are you sure? I was beginning to think I was too old.'

'You are certainly not too old! We have to be much more careful in future or we will be asking the architect to return and design an extension to the ranch.'

Although I had not expected to have so many children I actually enjoyed being pregnant. I no longer made clothes for the children as they grew, but each time we visited Derby we bought whatever they needed, although their outgrown clothes were always passed down until they were no longer serviceable. Luke had grown and filled out before going to college and at last was able to have some Chaps which were his pride and joy.

Dimitris had applied to the navy and been accepted. Of course I was delighted on his behalf, but I also realised this would mean he had to go to Sydney and would only be able to visit occasionally. Before he left he packed up all his belongings and said that Jake could have his bedroom. That was when I cried. It seemed so final somehow, although he assured me he would return whenever possible and be willing to bunk down anywhere.

Charlie was moved into Jake's old room as soon as he was old enough to spend the night alone which freed up his room ready for the next baby. Maggie was born easily. I think my body was so used to giving birth by now that it had become automatic.

It was then that tragedy struck. Maggie was asleep and Charlie was building small towers of bricks and running a toy car into them to knock them down whilst Poppi was hanging out the washing. I heard her shout for me to come quickly. I thought she may have seen a snake around. She was kneeling beside Eliza who was lying on the ground. As I arrived she looked up at me, her face pale.

'Go and get Fred. Eliza has had a fall and is hurt.'

For a moment I did not move, then instructed her to watch the children. I ran as fast as I could to the stables and without waiting to saddle Amber I jumped on her back, curled my hands into her mane and began to ride to the area where I knew Fred was working. I had never ridden so quickly before, urging her on with my knees and heels and losing my shoes in the process. As soon as he saw me arriving Fred knew there was an emergency of some sort and rode to meet me.

'Eliza,' I gasped. 'She's had a fall. She's hurt.'

Fred nodded and without asking any more he turned Blaze's head towards the ranch and galloped away. I was shaking and grateful when Ted rode over to me. He slipped a rope around Amber's neck and proceeded to lead me back to the ranch.

Fred was kneeling beside Eliza, talking quietly to her and saying he would take her into the hospital and she would soon be well again. Her eyes had rolled up in her head giving her a grotesque appearance.

Ted steadied me as I jumped off Amber's back. Fred lifted Eliza and led the way to where the truck was kept. He waited until I was inside and then placed Eliza in my arms. I placed my hand on her chest and I could not feel her breathing. I had never known Fred drive so fast and we reached Derby in under an hour and a half. Fred stopped outside the main door and carried Eliza inside calling for a doctor. I followed him as he ignored a nurse and demanded a doctor attend Eliza immediately.

Fred and I held hands as we stood at the foot of the bed whilst the doctor examined Eliza. Eventually he drew the curtain around us and shook his head.

'There is nothing I can do. She has had a severe blow to her head. How did it happen?'

Fred looked at me and I shook my head. 'I don't know. She was outside playing. I heard the lady who works for us shout to me to come quickly as Eliza had fallen and was hurt. As soon as I saw her I went as quickly as possible to get my husband so we could bring her to the hospital.'

'Where had she fallen from?'

'I don't know. I didn't stop to ask. Eliza was always falling over, but this time she must have bumped her head.'

'To have caused the kind of injury that she has evidence of she must have fallen from a height. She did not just trip over whilst playing.'

'What do you mean?'

'You have to expect the authorities to visit you after a post mortem has been completed. They will want to know more details of her accident.'

Fred placed his arm around me. 'I drove here as fast as I could.'

The doctor shook his head. 'I regret to have to tell you that your little girl was already dead when you arrived. Had I seen her within five minutes of her fall I would not have been able to do anything to save her life.'

My lips were dry and a blackness seemed to be encompassing me. Fred's voice sounded faint and far away as he pushed me onto a chair. He placed his arms around me and kept repeating 'I'm sorry, Reen, so sorry.' I did not know what he was sorry about. It was not his fault. I just wanted my little girl, my little Eliza, with her sunny smile. As I recovered I stood by the bed and held her little hand in mine, willing her to open her eyes properly and look at me.

We drove back to the ranch in silence; I felt numb. Poppi threw open the door as she saw us pass the window. She hugged me and whispered in my ear 'Be brave, for the sake of the others.'

I had not considered how I would break the news to Eliza's brothers and sisters. Charlie and Maggie were far too young to understand, but Mary and George cried whilst Jake appeared unaffected. Fred went to telephone Luke and Dimitris, having to wait a considerable time before he was able to speak to either of them.

Poppi had given Maggie a bottle of milk whilst I was away but now she needed a feed from me. I sat there looking down at her as she sucked contentedly from me. I heard Jake raise his voice.

'You can't blame me.'

'I do blame you,' retorted Mary. 'I heard you dare Eliza to climb up on the roof of the barn and join you. You should not have been up there. If you did as you were told this would not have happened.'

I stiffened. I could not believe my ears. Jake, however inadvertently, was the cause of Eliza's death.

'Girls are just stupid,' replied Jake sullenly.

'Not as stupid as little brothers who don't do as they are told. I don't even want to talk to you.'

'You're not going to tell Dad, are you?' asked Jake anxiously. There was a silence, then Jake rose his voice again. 'I'll tell him that you've made it up and are telling lies about me.'

I did not know what to do. Had I heard correctly? Should I tell Fred about the conversation? If Mary had spoken the truth what would happen to Jake? Fred had never raised a hand to any of the children, but I could imagine him beating Jake to within an inch of his life. I winded Maggie automatically and made her comfortable for the night before I attended to Charlie who had been given his tea by Poppi, along with a meal for the older children, and now needed a bath to remove the jam that he had smeared across his face and into his hair.

Having dealt with the babies I went first to Mary's room and sat on her bed, holding her in my arms. She cried again and I saw that she was holding the small bear that Eliza had always taken to bed with her. I did not mention the conversation I had overheard. George was equally distressed and I asked if he would like his father to come and talk to him when he had managed to speak to Luke and Dimitris.

George had looked at me tearfully. 'Dad can't bring Eliza back, no one can.' I hugged him and my tears mingled with his.

I almost had to force myself to go to say goodnight to Jake. He was sitting on his bed tearing a comic book into shreds and looked surprised when he saw me. 'What do you want?' he asked.

I swallowed. 'I've come to say goodnight the same as I do every night. Do stop tearing up that comic, Jake. You'll regret it tomorrow.'

Jake shrugged. 'I can get another when we go to town next time.'

He did not approach me for a hug or word of comfort over his sister's death and as I placed my arms around him he pulled away.

'Goodnight, Mum.'

Feeling sad, hurt and worried I returned to the living room where Poppi was sitting. She held out her hands to me.

'Come and sit down. I'll bring you something to eat or do you want to wait until Fred comes? He said he was going down to speak to the ranch hands.'

'I can't eat. It would choke me. I still have to tell my parents.'

'Wait for Fred, then. I doubt he will be much longer.'

I saw there was a bottle of whisky sitting on the table and for the first time in my life I wanted to drink myself into oblivion and wake tomorrow to find today had been just a nightmare.

Fred arrived back and deposited my shoes on the floor. I had completely forgotten about them. He sat beside me and took my face in his hands.

'Reen, you must promise me never to do such a thing again, whatever the circumstances.'

'What do you mean?'

'I took little notice at the time, I was too concerned with Eliza, but Ted told me.'

'Told you what?'

'That you had ridden up to find me without saddling Amber. You had no reins and no way of controlling her. That was dangerous, even for an experienced rider.'

'I didn't think. I just wanted to reach you as soon as possible.' I felt embarrassed at his chastisement.

'I understand, but you should have taken just a few minutes to prepare Amber properly. Had you fallen you could have broken your neck.'

Unbidden his words from many years ago when he had encouraged me to ride confidently in case one of my boys had been injured and I needed to get to him urgently. How wise he had been, and I had ignored his advice. I vowed I would become a proficient and more courageous rider in future.

'Did you manage to speak to Luke and Dimitris?'

'I have, but I still want your promise, Reen. You will never ride Amber bareback and just holding her mane ever again.'

I felt my voice trembling. 'I promise, Fred.'

He kissed me and then gave me the news I had hoped for. Luke had said he would come home immediately and Dimitris was applying for compassionate leave.

'I haven't told my parents yet,' I finally confessed. 'I wanted you to be with me when I phoned them.'

'Do you want me to tell them?'

I shook my head. 'It will be better if I tell them in Greek. I just want you to be with me when my mother starts to wail and you can then tell them that I cannot talk any more tonight.'

Poppi rose and poured three glasses of whisky. 'I think we all need this. I can't tell you how awful I'm feeling and you must both be feeling ten times worse.'

'I shouldn't. I'm feeding Maggie.'

'It won't hurt her, just make her sleep a little longer.'

I shook my head. 'I can't have more than a mouthful.'

Fred filled my glass up with water. 'That amount wouldn't hurt a fly and you need to be able to sleep, Reen. Have a little now, then we'll phone your parents and have something to eat. You can finish the drink afterwards and then go to bed.'

Somehow I did manage to go to sleep quite quickly, probably due to the whisky, and did not hear Fred come to bed. When I rose in the morning he was asleep on the couch in the living room and the bottle of whisky was less than half full. I left him there, his grief was as great as mine and I could not blame him for drinking too much.

Mary and George were very subdued and I noticed that Mary was carrying Eliza's toy bear around with her and not speaking to Jake. They both did their radio lessons and then retired to their bedrooms. I did not stop them, they needed time to come to terms with their own shock and grief. I could see Jake wandering around outside and I dreaded to think of what mischief he would find to get up to.

Hank arrived, knocking on the kitchen door and standing there awkwardly as he said he spoke on behalf of all the ranch hands saying how sorry they were to hear our sad news.

I managed to phone my parents and had a sensible conversation with my father, explaining exactly what had happened the previous day promising to let them know when the funeral arrangements had been made. I knew Fred was not religious and I had not attended church since marrying him, but suddenly it became important to me that Eliza had a traditional Greek funeral. I said I would need to discuss the arrangements with Fred and that we needed to know how long Luke and Dimitris would be at home before we could set a date.

I tended to Maggie and Charlie as usual whilst Poppi made some lunch for the other three and began the preparation for an evening meal. I felt extraordinarily exhausted and was relieved when she said I should go and rest for a while and leave everything to her. Fred joined me on the bed and apologised for drinking too much the night before. I forgave him readily.

It was late in the afternoon when a police van drew up outside and a man and woman climbed out and looked around before coming to the door. Poppi spoke to them and then ushered them into the living room. She knocked on our door and both of us were awake immediately. Poppi said they wanted to speak to us and I could only think that some awful accident had happened to Luke or Dimitris.

I rushed into the room and looked at them wildly. 'What's wrong? What's happened?'

'Nothing to worry about, madam, we'd just like to have a few words with you and your husband about your little girl.'

I collapsed onto the couch in relief, Luke and Dimitris were safe. Fred sat beside me and took my hand whilst Poppi disappeared back into the kitchen.

The police showed their credentials and explained the reason for their visit. Although the cause of Eliza's death was obvious it was official procedure to carry out a post mortem. Whilst doing so a quantity of bruises had been found on her body and could we explain how she had received those. We told them that Eliza had always been clumsy, falling over and bumping into things hence the bruises. They had nodded sympathetically as we talked and then to my surprise asked if they could speak to our children.

Fred frowned. 'I'd like one of us to be present if you are going to talk to them.'

They agreed that was no problem, but we must not interrupt or answer on behalf of the child. Mary came in first and they asked her all the usual questions about her name and how old she was, did she enjoy her radio lessons and what did she enjoy doing most in her spare time.

Mary answered easily, saying she liked to draw and paint and thought she might like to design clothes when she was older or possibly become an art teacher.

The policewoman asked her to take off her blouse and Mary looked at me for permission. I nodded and I saw the woman looking at her arms and back. She then asked her to remove her jeans and I looked pointedly at the policeman and said that was not suitable before an unknown man. He agreed to turn his back and Mary complied, letting her jeans fall to her ankles. The policewoman nodded and said she could replace her clothing. The next questions began to frighten me.

If she was naughty how was she punished? Did either of her parents hit her? Had she seen them hit any of the other children.

Mary looked totally confused. 'I'm not naughty.'

The policewoman smiled. 'I'm sure you're not, but if you did something that your parents had told you not to do how would they punish you? Would they smack you?'

Mary shook her head and clutched Eliza's bear more tightly. 'If I do something really naughty Dad says he will take away my drawing paper and pencils for a week.'

'Does that happen often?'

'Only once. I'd rather do as I'm told and be able to draw.'

'What had you done that deserved a punishment? Do you remember?'

'I was swinging on one of the water pipes. We're forbidden to climb on them, but I thought swinging was different. Dad explained that I could still damage them and I was not to do it again. I disobeyed him and he saw me.'

'Where were you when your sister fell?'

'Outside with George. We were having a competition to see who could throw a ball through the hoop Dad had fitted up.'

'Where was your sister?'

I held my breath. How was Mary going to answer that question?

'I'm not sure.' Tears came in Mary's eyes. 'We had asked her if she wanted to play, but she said she wanted to get her bike and ride around on that.'

The policewoman persisted with her questions. 'I believe you have a younger brother. Where was he at that time?'

'I don't know. He didn't want to play with us and had wandered off.'

When George came in he was also asked to remove his clothing and then asked the same questions. He admitted that on three occasions Fred had refused to allow him to accompany Poppi when she was shopping as a punishment for disobedience.

Jake was surly and uncooperative and removed his clothes slowly when Fred insisted that he must do as he had been asked. No bruises were found on Jake's body, but there was a scrape on his shin.

'How did that happen?' asked the policeman.

Jake shrugged. 'Don't know.'

'Had you been climbing somewhere and slipped?'

Jake shrugged again. 'Maybe.'

'If you've been climbing again you know the punishment.' Fred spoke sternly.

'What's that?' asked the policeman.

'He is made to stay in his room and complete some outstanding lessons,' explained Fred. 'He hates being indoors and does everything he can to avoid doing his radio lessons.'

'You don't hit him?'

'What would be the point? We know he is difficult and unruly but hitting him would not change that.'

The police looked at each other and the man spoke. 'Thank you for being so co-operative. I understand how very difficult it must be for you at this time. We had to make this visit to check if your other children had any bruises on their body and I'm pleased to say that we have no reason to think that you might injure them, even accidentally, whilst chastising them.'

'We wouldn't hit our children,' I declared vehemently. I was relieved that Mary had not mentioned Jake's 'dare' to Eliza. He had probably scraped his shin when he scrambled down from the barn roof. He had teased Eliza about her clumsiness, but he should have known better than to encourage her to climb onto the roof of the barn and he should not have been up there either.

'We would like to have a word with the lady who lives here with you. I understand she saw your daughter on the ground and raised the alarm. We'd like her to show us exactly where she was at the time and where your daughter was laying.'

Poppi escorted the police to the area where she hung out the washing. 'I had just started to peg it up when I heard a scream and the next thing I knew Eliza was laying on the ground.'

The policeman looked up at the nearby barn and pointed. 'Do you think she fell from there?'

Poppi looked distressed. 'I think she must have done as I didn't see her around here when I brought the washing out.'

'How did she get up there?'

'The rubbish bins are round the other side. She must have climbed up on one of those.'

'And where were the other children at the time?'

'Mary and George were playing further down. I didn't see Jake.'

'Did she usually climb on the barn roof?' asked the police woman

'All the children are forbidden to climb on the roofs of the barns. It would have been the last thing I would expect Eliza to do.'

'The little girl said her sister was going to get her bike. Was her bike anywhere near her?'

Poppi shook her head. 'There was no sign of her tricycle so she couldn't have overbalanced whilst riding it.' She sighed sadly. 'She was always falling off.'

1959 - 1967
Growing Up

It was a comfort to me to have Luke home. He gathered Mary, George and Jake together and told them how sad everyone was to have lost Eliza, but that Fred and I were suffering even more as each child was precious to us. He asked them to be especially well behaved and obedient and to understand if Fred or I became impatient with them.

I knew I had to come to terms with my grief to ensure that life continued as normal as possible for my family, but my heart still ached for Eliza. I could not help but wonder how she would have grown up and her choice of occupation. Somehow I managed to get through each day and although Luke understood how I was struggling I do not think the younger children realised. Jake was still difficult and demanding and Poppi would attend to Mary and George whilst I tried my best to deal with Charlie and Maggie.

Dimitris arrived and he and Luke were willing to share a room rather than disturb Jake. They spent a good deal of time talking together and I was happy that my two young men were such good friends. Dimitris was only able to stay for a week before returning to Sydney but Luke remained with us until his new term started, even offering to stay longer if we needed him.

It was a tempting offer but he had his final examinations at the end of that term and he wanted to have a good result. Whilst he was with us Jake's behaviour seemed to improve somewhat and I hoped he might have grown out of his naughtiness.

'I need a good pass as a way of thanking Fred for paying for me to go to college,' explained Luke. 'I wouldn't want him to think I had wasted his money. Having a certificate could be useful to me in the future, although there is nothing like hands on experience. Clyde has made a suggestion to me that I will need to talk to Fred about.'

I raised my eyebrows. I could not imagine that Fred would be very happy to employ the young man on our ranch just to give him experience. 'Are you suggesting that he comes here to stay again?'

'No, particularly at the moment I wouldn't ask that of either of you. Clyde's father has had to be admitted to a nursing home. The family accept that he will end his days there and Clyde will take over the business, but he wants to experiment with stock breeding. He spoke to Fred about it last year. Clyde has asked if I would be willing to go with him to a cattle auction as I would know which heifers looked healthiest. He would then like me to spend a year working for him as a ranch hand who has experience of rearing cattle.'

'How do you feel about doing that?'

'It would be good work experience for me, but I don't want to agree to the arrangement and then find that Fred needs me here.'

'Just a year?'

'Well, I suppose if Fred didn't need me and I was happy there I could stay longer. I'd come and visit, of course.'

I tried to smile. I knew that once Dimitris was qualified to work on a ship he could be sent to sea for months on end, but I had been looking forward to having Luke back on the ranch permanently in a few months time.

'Talk to Fred and see what he says. If you're unhappy working with Clyde you can always come back home, you know that.'

Fred agreed to the arrangement providing Luke would not stay indefinitely with Clyde. 'I will need you here; not immediately, but definitely in two or three years time. Hank and Jim are both getting past the age of being out on a horse all day and I'll need you to take over as the head herdsman. The other hands are good and conscientious, but they haven't got the experience of the older men.'

'Nor have I,' protested Luke.

'You know as much about cattle rearing as Hank and Jim and you will have a certificate to say you are proficient in the knowledge. That's more than any of the others have, besides, you'll be the one to take over when I'm past it.'

'Me?'

'Of course. Who else? Are you suggesting your mother?'

Luke laughed. 'No, of course not, but I expected you to leave the ranch to all of us boys.'

'Dimitris only wants to be out at sea, George doesn't show any particular interest and Jake is totally unsuitable to work with animals I've had you in mind since you showed your aptitude right from the start.'

By the time the year was out our lives did seem to have returned to normality and I was expecting again. Mary still carried Eliza's bear around with her and could be heard talking to the toy.

'I feel as if I am talking to Eliza,' she explained and I did not try to break her of the habit.

Each time we visited Derby Fred and I would go to Eliza's small grave stone and lay some flowers and I know my parents went frequently. Mary and George often accompanied us, but Jake would wander off and could be seen climbing on the grave stones at the far end of the cemetery. When Fred took him to task about such disrespectful behaviour he had shrugged and replied that it didn't hurt them as the occupants were dead.

Luke returned to the ranch but he seemed restless. Finally he asked me if he could invite a friend to come to stay for a week or two. Of course, I said yes, and asked if it was Clyde. He blushed furiously and admitted that it was Clyde's sister.

'We seemed to get on pretty well when I was staying with them and I'd like her to see what a working ranch is like. Once we'd bought the heifers Clyde and I would go off onto their ranch for the day to keep an eye on them and talk to the ranch hands. Clyde has a two wheel buggy and although Ingrid asked to come there wasn't anywhere for her to sit and no facilities for ladies. Here I can ask Fred if I can drive part of the way in the truck and walk up to where the herd is grazing. I might even manage to get her to ride a horse.'

I smiled at Luke's excuses and felt sure there was more behind his request than just showing Clyde's sister the ranch. I was concerned for him as he had never had the opportunity to mix freely with girls. I hoped he would not rush into a relationship he might regret later.

'Does she work?'

'She's at college, training to become a teacher.'

'You'll have to ask her to talk to Mary. I think she's given up the idea of being a famous fashion designer and is seriously considering becoming an art teacher. Let me know when she will be arriving. I can put Charlie and Maggie in together for a week or so. I'm sure they won't mind sharing for a while.'

Fred allowed Luke to drive the truck to Broome to meet Ingrid. 'Good practice for you now you have your driving licence, but go carefully.'

I was anxious and continually looking out of the kitchen window until I finally saw the truck pull back in at the ranch. I had expected them to be here at least an hour earlier and worried that Luke may have had an accident as he was unused to driving. He opened the passenger door and helped Ingrid out and then collected her case from the back of the truck. I saw them exchange smiles and I hurried away from the window. I would not want them to think I had been spying on them.

Ingrid spent two weeks with us and I found her an easy guest to please. She admitted that she had never eaten Greek food before and her mother was an unadventurous cook.

'It was always good, wholesome food, but just the same meals each week. I love the chicken casserole that you cook with the lemon potatoes. I'd like to take some of your recipes back with me and try to cook them. Just because Dad always raised a beef herd there's no need to eat that meat all the time.'

Ingrid talked to Mary about college life and the subjects she would need to study along with art to become a successful teacher. She even sat with Jake and tried to help and encourage him with his homework, although he gave her scant thanks for her efforts.

'It's good practice for me,' she laughed. 'Before you can qualify as a teacher you have to go out to local schools for teaching practice. There's always a boy like him in every class and you have to find a way of engaging their interest. I have to admit that so far I've not found Jake interested in anything except his comic books.'

'Don't consider yourself a failure,' I said sympathetically. 'Jake seems to think he can go through life doing exactly as he pleases. I just hope that something happens one day that brings him to his senses and he realises that he has to grow up and develops a sense of responsibility.'

Luke had managed to get Ingrid to ride Bessie, explaining that as she was a pony she was nowhere near as big as a horse.

'Not so far for me to fall off,' she laughed.'

'Bessie is getting on a bit now, so let her take her time.'

Ingrid looked at Luke. 'I don't mind if she stands here munching grass. I realise now how far off the ground I am.'

'You're perfectly safe. If you were a larger lady I'd ask one of the hands to lend me their horse for you. There's a limit to how much weight you can expect a pony to carry.'

Ingrid suddenly realised that Luke was being serious. 'So tell me exactly what I need to do. You know I've never ridden before.'

Seeing them together over the two weeks I realised that they had a good relationship. Ingrid was happy to spend some time with Poppi and I at the ranch whilst Luke accompanied Fred up to where the herd were grazing. She did not cling to him and demand his company continually as some women did.

It was no surprise that the evening before Ingrid was due to fly back to Perth they both came to us, looking both pleased and embarrassed.

Luke cleared his throat. 'Ingrid and I have decided want to get married. Will you give us your permission?'

Fred laughed at him. 'You don't need our permission. You're both adults. Bring a bottle of wine and we'll drink a toast to you.'

'When do you plan to have your wedding?' I asked, thinking of my current condition.

'We haven't set a date yet. Ingrid needs to become a fully qualified teacher and the calving season needs to be over before we can make any firm plans.' Luke looked at me and grinned, 'You should be a little slimmer by then.'

We raised our glasses and then Luke announced that we must have a serious talk.

'When we're married I'd like Ingrid to come here to live. Provided you are willing for me to spend another season in Perth, Fred, and bearing in mind what you said about Hank and Jim getting near to retirement it's obviously practical that I return home then. How do you feel about that, Mum?'

What could I say except that I was sure that Ingrid would fit in very well with our life on the ranch and hope that would be so.

'There is another thing,' continued Luke. 'Ingrid would like a proper church wedding. We've discussed the practicalities and we think it would be best of we were married in Derby. There would only be Clyde and her mother then who needed to fly down to Broome and travel up to Derby to stay in a hotel, and Ingrid, of course. If we all went up to Perth it would cost an enormous amount and I'm not even sure if Grandma and Grandpa would be willing to fly.'

I think I may have sighed in relief. The thought of having to fly to Perth with a small baby, along with toddlers was daunting, even relying upon Poppi's help.

Fred nodded. 'That makes sense, provided they are willing to make the journey. Are you happy with that, Ingrid?'

'I think it is a good idea. That will mean that Clyde can give me away. It's a shame my father is no longer with us as he always wanted to walk down the aisle with me. At least I know he would approve of me marrying Luke as he considered him a very nice young man when they met.'

'How does your mother feel?' I asked.

Ingrid blushed. 'We haven't actually told her yet, but I don't think it will come as any big surprise.'

The only person who did not seem so happy about the news was Poppi.

'What's going to happen to me?' she asked. 'You won't need me around when Ingrid comes here to live.'

'Of course I will need you as much as ever. I'll have another baby to look after and Ingrid has no experience at all of small children or of running a ranch. I think the amount of work involved could come as rather a shock to her. All the time you are happy to live here we are more than happy to have you. I know I can rely on you. Ingrid appears to be very nice but until we actually live with her we won't know for sure. She might well expect to be treated as a guest rather than a family member.'

I could tell that Poppi was relieved by my answer, but I also knew that the day would come when the children were grown up and would probably choose to leave the ranch and live in the town. Then I would not need the help of Poppi, although I would miss her companionship. Maybe we should have left her living with her in-laws in Derby and she may have found a nice man to take Bill's place.

Luke returned to Perth with Ingrid and I received a letter from her thanking me for having her to stay so she could get to know the family. She went on to say that her mother had been delighted when she and Luke had told her of their intention to get married. They had still not decided on a date, but Luke had spoken to Dimitris to ask when he would be entitled to some leave. Dimitris had replied that it was too early to say yet and until he knew the sailing dates for the ship he was assigned to he could not make any plans to ask for leave.

Ingrid went on to say that she was planning to have her wedding dress made in Perth and she would like Mary to be a bridesmaid. She suggested that Mary designed a dress that she thought would be suitable for the occasion and provided it was approved by her and her mother she would arrange for it to be made in Derby so that Mary would be able to go for fittings.

Mary was excited by the idea and she said she had been considering all Ingrid had told her about teaching.

'I know the radio schooling is good, but Dimitris decided he needed to go to Broome for additional schooling so he could qualify for the navy. Could I also go to the school in Broome?'

Fred shook his head immediately. 'That is a boarding school for boys.'

'There must be one for girls,' protested Mary.

'We'll look into it,' he promised.

After Mary had gone to bed Fred asked me how I felt about Mary going away to a boarding school. I told him that I was not very happy about the idea but if she needed the schooling to enable her to go to a teacher training college then I would accept it.

'I've had a better idea,' said Fred. 'There's a good school in Derby now and if she went there she could stay with your parents during the term and come home during the holidays.'

I felt sure my parents would be delighted to have her to stay, but would not mention the idea to Mary until I had spoken to them. 'They may not want a young girl around. I don't want to get Mary's hopes up. I'll ask them the next time we go up to town.'

Although the wedding seemed a long way ahead there was a considerable amount that needed to be arranged, suits for Luke and Clyde, the church service, flowers, a reception catered for, accommodation for her mother and Clyde and also to decide where she and Luke would go for their honeymoon. I had an idea that Luke was leaving everything for Ingrid to arrange, but it did suddenly dawn on me that both Fred and my father would need a suit, along with suitable clothes for the rest of us.

I spoke to Poppi and we agreed that the next time we visited Derby we would look and see if there were any dresses that we liked. The children were not a problem, the boys could have grey or black trousers and a white shirt, Dimitris would have his naval uniform so I would only have to find a dress for Maggie. I could certainly not consider the forthcoming baby until it was born and I knew if it was a girl or a boy

Although I had not been ill during this pregnancy I had found it more difficult than the previous ones. I was often up in the night with heart burn and it was difficult to bend over as if the baby seemed to be lying straight up inside me.

I approached Fred tentatively, hoping he would understand.

'Fred, when I've had this baby I would like to be sterilised so I can have no more.'

Fred looked at me in surprise. 'I thought you enjoyed having babies.'

'I do and each one has been a joy to me, but I think my body is trying to tell me I have done sufficient. I read an article the other day and it said that once a woman had reached forty she should think carefully about adding to her family as her body was changing with age. There was a greater likelihood of having a child with a serious defect.'

'You mean like Eliza?'

'No,' I swallowed. I still found it difficult to talk about Eliza. 'She had a condition known as Dyspraxia, that just makes you clumsy. Depending upon her career choice she could have gone on to University, there was nothing wrong with her brain and in time she would probably have been able to control her clumsiness to a great extent. I'm talking seriously wrong, something that cannot be corrected with medicine or surgery.'

Fred frowned. 'You're serious?'

I nodded. 'But only if you are agreeable.'

Fred shook his head. 'I can't make a decision like that immediately. I need to think about it.'

I did not mention it again to Fred and the date of my confinement drew closer. I was surprised when he finally approached me and told me he had done some investigating of his own.

'I cannot agree with you being sterilised, Reen. I am the one to be sterilised.'

'You?'

'It is a far simpler operation for a man than for a woman. It takes about thirty minutes and then I just have to rest up for two or three days. I couldn't expect you to have an operation that is far more serious, particularly if you've just given birth. I feel guilty about not suggesting this some years ago.'

'I'm pleased you didn't. We would have missed having some of the children.'

'Your life would have been a good deal easier.'

'I'm not complaining, besides, I've had Poppi to help me. I certainly could not have coped without her. She's a bit concerned that she will no longer be wanted or needed when Ingrid comes to live here. I have assured her that she can always have a home with us.'

Four weeks before the baby was due Fred went to the hospital and was sterilised. 'This is the ideal time,' he assured me. 'It will only take me out of action for a short while and I won't be tempted to have a trial run until you have fully recovered. I know I can't ride back to the ranch so I'll arrange for someone to drive me up there and back again. Shame Luke is not here or he could have been my chauffeur.'

'If I could fit behind the wheel I could drive you. Maybe you should have made the appointment for earlier.'

'I wouldn't dream of letting you drive up there and then back on your own. You haven't the experience and suppose you had a tyre blow out. What would you do?'

'I'd have to limp back either to the ranch or to Derby.'

'I dread to think of the state of the truck if you did that. It would probably need a whole new suspension. No, it's much better that I arrange to be driven by someone.'

Fred telephoned me each day after his operation and assured me that he was feeling fit and well. 'A little sore where they put a needle in for the anaesthetic, but that will soon wear off. I've arranged to be collected tomorrow once I've had a final check up by the doctor so I should be home tomorrow afternoon. If there's any change to my plans I'll let you know.'

I had not told my parents about Fred's operation, but I did ask if they would be happy to have Mary live with them whilst she attended school in Derby. As I had expected, they were both delighted.

'She's a charming little girl,' said my mother, 'And George is a nice boy. I couldn't agree to looking after your Jake, though.'

I smiled. I could not imagine anyone except doting parents being willing to look after Jake.

Fred was certainly able to drive me up to Derby a week before the baby was due as he was back riding his horse, although he admitted that the first few times he had not felt very comfortable. I had persuaded George to join him on some occasions, saying that his horse needed the exercise, but really to make sure that if Fred did feel unwell George would be able to get some help. Once it had been decided that Mary was to attend school in Derby I expected George to ask if he could also go to school, but he did not mention it, but nor was he very interested in the cattle and I did wonder what work he planned to do when the time came.

Sally did not take long to make her appearance in the world and as Mary was in Derby she was allowed to visit me along with her grandmother. Mary looked at Sally and nodded.

'She looks a lot like Maggie,' she remarked and turned away.

I was sure she was thinking about Eliza and I noticed that she had the toy bear with her. I thought she might be going to give it to Sal, but she kept hold of it.

'Isn't she getting a bit old to be carrying a soft toy around with her?' asked my mother.

'That bear is very special to her. It belonged to Eliza. Please don't try to make her give it up.'

I left the hospital as soon as the priest had blessed Sal and myself and went to my parent's house where I stayed until Fred collected me that afternoon. Mary had asked if I could stay longer, but I explained that I needed to get home as I had only a few nightdresses and nappies with me for Sally.

'You'll be home for the holidays in a few weeks and be able to make a fuss of her.'

Mary showed me some preliminary sketches she had done of dresses that she thought would be suitable for her to wear at Ingrid and Luke's wedding. I was not so certain, they seemed rather fancy and frilly and I was not sure if that was the style Ingrid had in mind. I admired them and suggested that she did some more, leaving off the lace around the neckline and the flounces and frills on the skirt.

'You can send all of them to her so that you give Ingrid the choice. You need to complement her dress, not rival it.'

'I hope she won't choose orange or purple for my dress. I'd rather wear lilac or blue.'

'You'll just have to wait and see. It is her wedding so it has to be what she wants.'

Mary pulled a face and I thought I might have a quiet word with Luke and mention Mary's preference. I hoped Ingrid would choose a pastel colour and a simple design so I could make something similar for Maggie and Sally.

Having arranged for Mary to go to school Fred asked George if he would like to go to the boarding school in Broome. George shook his head.

'I don't see much point in me going off to school. I can learn all I need on the radio lessons.'

'Do you want to work on the ranch?'

George shook his head. 'Not really, I'd rather work in a shop.'

'A shop?'

'Yes, a general store, being in charge of ordering the stock and making sure it was well organised and attractive for the customers. I love going shopping with Poppi and looking around the shop, but they could do with someone to make sure the items are grouped together properly. They seem to place them around wherever there is a space. Poppi was looking for the flour last time and we finally found it next to some tinned fruit. Why would anyone look there for it?'

Fred had smiled and promised that if George still wanted to become a shopkeeper in a few years time he would see if he could get him an apprenticeship at the general store in Derby. It was only a problem if Mary was still staying with her grandparents as there would be no spare room to accommodate him.

'I could always go to Perth. I could stay with Clyde. I'd behave myself and not give him any trouble. He'll have a spare room as Ingrid will be living here.'

'We'll see. I would rather you were in Derby until you had completed an apprenticeship. You'll still be too young to live away from home and Clyde may not want to have you staying with him. It can be quite a responsibility looking after someone else's son.'

Of course, I was pleased that my children were growing up, but I was going to miss them. Once George left home I would only be left with Jake, Charlie, Maggie and Sally to look after.

Mary came home for the holiday from school and I was concerned at how pale she looked, but thought it could be because she had been inside for most days. She went to bed early and admitted the next day that she did not feel very well, but all she could really complain about was a headache. I left her in bed and she got up later in the day, saying she felt better. She played with Charlie and Maggie and sat and cuddled Sally before joining us for our evening meal. I noticed that she did not even say hello to Jake and that worried me.

I was worried about Mary as she had developed a rash, two days later George also had spots and both Charlie and Maggie were miserable. I telephoned the hospital in Derby and described the children's symptoms. I was told they were typical of measles and the childhood disease was going around Derby. I should keep them in a darkened room as any bright lights could affect their eyes and take their temperatures regularly. I was reassured when I was told that they should all be well again within about ten days.

Jake was difficult as usual and when I turned my back whilst taking his temperature he had placed the thermometer into my hot coffee. When he saw the horrified expression on my face when I read it he laughed. I tried to explain to him that it was not a joking matter but he had shrugged and declared there was nothing wrong with him. He did have measles but it was only mild in his case.

I was relieved that all the children had developed measles within a day or so of each other, rather than waiting until one recovered before the next one became ill. Although they all looked a little pale having been kept inside and none of them seemed to have much appetite although they were no longer ill.

George then became my next concern. He did not seem to have recovered as well as the others had and on a number of occasions after completing his daily jobs on the ranch he had retired to his room saying he was tired and going to have a sleep. This was unusual for George, but I thought that he may have had measles more severely than we realised. One evening he hardly touched his meal and said he was going to have an early night. He was not up and dressed as usual the next morning and I knocked on his door. He was lying in bed with his kneesdrawn up, complaining of having terrible stomach pains. He was feverish to my touch and when I placed my hand on his side where he said the pain was at its worst he groaned and bit his lip.

'Don't touch me there.'

'Can you try to get up and get dressed?' I asked. 'I'll find Fred and say we need to take you up to the hospital.'

George's eyes widened. 'I'm not really ill, am I?'

'I think you have an inflamed appendix. The hospital will know the best treatment to make you comfortable again.'

By the time I had explained to Fred and he had returned to the ranch George had dressed but asked me if I would put his socks and shoes on as it was so painful to bend down. I left Poppi and Mary looking after the children and collected some clean clothes for Sally whilst Fred helped George into the truck.

I felt most uncomfortable as Fred drove as quickly as possible to Derby. I had Sally in my arms and George leaning against me so I could hardly move. Sal was asleep and I did not want to disturb George who seemed to be feeling a little better.

We had to wait our turn at the hospital and Fred stood by George's bed whilst he was examined.

'Definitely appendicitis according to the doctor,' said Fred. 'Did he have anything to eat this morning?'

I shook my head. 'He didn't want anything at all.'

'That's good. I'll let the doctor know. He would like to operate this afternoon, but would have had to delay that if George had eaten breakfast.'

'Operate?'

Fred nodded. 'It's pretty routine. We can sit with him until he goes down to the theatre and we can telephone this evening to hear how he is recovering.'

The time dragged until two orderlies came and wheeled George away. He tried to smile bravely but I could tell he was rather frightened at the prospect of an operation. I refused Fred's offer of visiting my parents. There was no reason for us to worry them. We would drive up the following day to visit George and could tell them how he was feeling and let them know if they were able to visit him.

Sally was fretful on our drive home. I had fed her earlier but she had taken very little and then been sick. I could only think the motion of the truck as we drove upset her.

Once home I tried to feed her again but she refused and I laid her in her crib to sleep whilst I spent some time with Mary before bathing Charlie and Maggie and putting them to bed. Jake declared that he was quite old enough to shower himself when we had eaten and could put himself to bed. I checked on Sal throughout the evening and she appeared to be asleep and I hesitated to disturb her; she would let me know if she was hungry.

Fred telephoned the hospital and was told that George's operation to remove his appendix had gone according to plan and he was back on the ward sleeping off the anaesthetic. They suggested that we visited in the afternoon by which time he would be feeling much better.

By the time Fred and I were ready for our bed Sal woke up and began to make little mewling sounds. I took her in my arms and tried to feed her, but she refused, going alternately rigid and then limp in my arms. I had a horrible cold feeling in the pit of my stomach.

'Fred, we need to go back to the hospital.'

'I know. we're going up again tomorrow.'

'We need to go now. There's something wrong with Sal.' I placed her back in her crib and began to get dressed again.

Fred looked at Sally and felt her head and small body. She was hot to his touch. Without further ado Fred began to get dressed again and I went along to Poppi's room to tell her that we were leaving immediately.

I cuddled Sal to me and the journey seemed to take twice as long as usual in the darkness. Upon arriving Fred left me at the main entrance and went to park the truck. I hurried inside and searched frantically for a nurse or doctor, finally seeing a cleaner and asking where everyone was. He looked at me with the limp body in my arms and told me to follow him. He unlocked a door that led to the wards and signalled to the nurse who was sitting at a desk.

She took one look at Sally and said she would call the doctor. I was left standing there, holding my baby and wishing that Fred was there with me. The doctor took one look at Sally and asked me to follow him to where I was shown into a small room that held only a crib and a chair.

'This child has a high temperature.'

'Are you sure?' I asked. 'She didn't have one when we left here this afternoon.'

'Why did you come to the hospital? Were you concerned about her?'

'We brought our son up yesterday morning. He had his appendix out in the afternoon.'

The doctor turned his attention back to Sal, flexing her arms and legs and taking her temperature again and sounding her chest as she seemed to be having trouble breathing. 'When did you first become aware that there could be something wrong?'

'She was a little sick when I fed her in the afternoon but we had been travelling in the truck for two hours during the morning and I thought that had upset her. I tried to feed her again when we arrived home but she was not interested. I placed her in her crib whilst I saw to my other children. and she appeared to be asleep. I expected her to wake up hungry and checked on her continually but she didn't stir until we were just about to go to bed. She refused to feed and kept going stiff in my arms and her skin felt hot. My husband and I got dressed again and drove here as quickly as possible.'

The nurse had undressed Sally and was sponging her body with cool water to try to reduce her temperature when the doctor arrived.

'What's wrong with her?' I asked in alarm.

'I believe she has picked up a virus.'

'Where's my husband? He was parking the truck and is probably trying to find me.'

'I'll ask someone to look for him,' said the doctor. 'Whilst he is being found I'll take your temperature.'

The nurse continued to sponge Sal until she finally looked up and shook her head. 'I'll look for the husband,' she said and made a hurried exit from the room.

The doctor placed his stethoscope on Sal's tiny chest and frowned, finally turning back to me. 'I am terribly sorry, there is nothing more we can do for her.'

'There must be something.'

He shook his head. 'Tragically your little girl has died.'

'No!' It came out as a howl from me. 'It cannot be. You've made a mistake.'

I went to go over to the bed to pick Sally up, but the doctor stopped me and indicated that I should sit on the chair. 'Please do not touch her yet. You will be able to hold her later.'

Feeling stunned and helpless I sat there until Fred was shown into the room. I could tell by his face that the terrible news had been broken to him. He pulled me to my feet and held me close. I could feel his tears on my head as I sobbed on his chest. How long we stood there I do not know.

He did not say any of the usual things that people say in such circumstances, he did not remind me that we had other healthy children at home.

Finally regaining his composure he kissed my forehead and said, 'Sal will always have a special place in our hearts although she was with us such a short time'

I have no real recollection of events after that. I know Sally was taken to another part of the hospital as they said they needed to do tests on her. Both Fred and I had our temperatures taken and were then escorted to a small sitting room where we could sit together in private. The nurse reappeared after some time and asked if we would like some tea or coffee. Fred had looked at her gravely and said that whisky or brandy would be more appropriate. She had given him a thin smile and said the doctor would be along to talk with us shortly.

Later I had to ask Fred what the doctor had said as whatever words he spoke had held no meaning for me. Fred explained that Sally had contracted viral meningitis due to having measles at such a young age and even if she had been in the hospital earlier there was nothing anyone could have done to save her. We did not have temperatures or any other symptoms of the virus so now we could think about returning home to break the news to her siblings and making suitable arrangements for her funeral.

I asked if we could visit George before we left but were told we could only wave to him from the door. Although both Fred and I appeared to be healthy we were told that we must continue to take our temperatures each day to ensure that the virus did not develop. As a further precaution the hospital wanted to ensure George was free from the virus and that he had not caught it from Sal before any visiting was allowed. We did not visit my parents as we had planned and drove back to the ranch.

It was difficult, but we had to telephone my parents and break the news to them, then to Luke and Dimitris. Both of the boys offered to come home at once, but neither of them had seen Sally. To them she was no more than a name. We refused their offer explaining that until the tests had come back from the hospital showing we were all clear of infection it was in their own interest to stay away.

Somehow I managed to get through the next few days and although Mary understood how I was struggling I do not think the younger children realised. but we were still unable to visit George. My parents went to see him every day and I was grateful that my father took it upon himself to tell him about Sally and explain that we were unable to visit him until all the children had recovered from measles.

'Will I be able to go home then?' he asked his grandfather.

'Provided the doctor is happy with your progress. Wait until you've had your stitches out and see how you feel then. I've brought you some more books and your grandmother will be in this afternoon to keep you company.'

Secretly George wished it was going to be his grandfather visiting again. His grandmother shed tears and continually said how sad it was that Eliza had died only to be followed by Sal who was so young. No amount of tears would bring his baby sister back.

1968 - 1978
Young Adults

Fred hardly left the ranch for a few days and he confessed later that he had been worried that one or all of the children could develop meningitis as had happened to Sally. I did not mention this to Mary. She had obviously brought the measles infection back with her from school and would have been heartbroken if she believed she was the cause of her little sister's death.

To my relief the hospital finally declared that George was able to return home. He showed off his scar where his appendix had been removed with pride to Mary and Jake, but said he still had to be careful for the next few weeks until he had healed completely inside.

Despite Sally's death we insisted that Luke and Ingrid should go ahead with the plans for their wedding. Ingrid had sent back one of Mary's designs for a bridesmaid dress and asked for it to be made in a pale green taffeta. I was pleased at the one she had chosen. It had a scoop neckline, sat just off the shoulders and the bodice was fitted. The skirt was full and reached down to the ankles. Beneath the neckline and along the hemline was a row of white daisies with yellow centres and Ingrid had asked that a small green drawstring bag should be made in the same material.

I was puzzled by this and asked Mary. She had smiled and said she had asked Ingrid if she could have a little bag so she could carry Eliza's bear with her.

'It's only right,' she said firmly. 'Had Eliza been here she would have been a bridesmaid and we would have walked behind Ingrid together.'

I had no answer for her, but my heart warmed towards my future daughter in law. I made a green cotton dress for Maggie, and Poppi and I frequented the best dress shops in Derby until we both found dresses that we would be happy to wear without feeling conspicuously over or under dressed.

Mary was excited, and I accompanied her on her first visit to the dress maker where her measurements were taken and she was told to return in two weeks for a preliminary fitting. I was somewhat disappointed that I would not be the first to see her in her finery, but it was not practical for Fred to take me up to Derby when my mother was quite capable of ensuring that the dress was well made and would fit Mary perfectly.

George was relieved that he would only be expected to wear a pair of black trousers and a white shirt, but insisted that he felt strangled when he had to wear a tie. Jake had pulled his tie off roughly and thrown it onto his bed.

'I'm not wearing that.'

Patiently I tried to explain that all the men would wear a tie at the wedding and he would feel left out and different if he refused. I purchased a second identical tie that I planned to take with me should he deliberately ruin the one he had. I hoped he would not cause a scene on the day and spoil the event for Luke and Ingrid.

We drove up to Derby during the morning and Fred registered us at the hotel. Poppi had insisted that she would stay with her parents as it was only for two nights and Mary would be staying with my parents. We rented two rooms. Fred was going to share with George and Jake, whilst I had Charlie and Maggie with me. I hoped that with Fred to keep an eye on him Jake would behave himself.

Luke had said he would arrange to hire a car at Broome airport and drive them all up to the hotel in Derby. I felt quite nervous about meeting Ingrid's mother for the first time and thankful that I had not extended an invitation for her and Clyde to visit the ranch.

To my relief the small, dumpy woman, who only reached up to Clyde's shoulder, seemed to be very ordinary, but she was nosy. She wanted to know when and why we had left Crete to come to Australia; why hadn't my husband accompanied me; how had I met Fred? I answered as best I could but everything I said was followed by another question. I finally excused myself and said I needed to put Charlie and Maggie to bed, hoping that when I returned to the hotel lounge she would be talking to Luke or Clyde.

Fred had arranged for us to have a buffet meal and managed to place a chair for Ingrid's mother between Luke and my mother. Luke was obviously familiar with his future mother in law's ways and was asking her to tell his grandmother about her life in Australia.

'My grandmother understands English very well,' I heard him say, 'But she finds speaking the language somewhat difficult still. I can always translate if it is something of importance.' I saw Luke wink at me as I selected a vacant chair further away.

We all found the formality of the evening somewhat difficult and I was pleased when Ingrid said she wanted to have an early night and took her mother upstairs with her. My parents immediately said they must also go home and took Mary with them. I sat with Luke and Clyde whilst Fred insisted that George and Jake should also go to bed. Of course, Jake protested, but Fred said if the boy was tired and grumpy the following day he would be left in the hotel room whilst everyone else went to the wedding and enjoyed themselves. I was not sure if this was any threat to Jake.

I was just about to excuse myself when Luke persuaded me to stay downstairs for a few more minutes. He poured me another glass of wine, although I had not really wanted another, so I had to sit there. Fred returned to the lounge and poured a drink for himself.

'Jake appears to finally be asleep and I checked on Charlie and Maggie, they're fine. I thought you would have given me up by now and gone to bed yourself.'

'Luke poured me another glass of wine. It would have been rude to refuse.'

'Very unwise to have gone to bed.' Luke lifted his head and then threw open the door to the lounge. 'You made it, then.'

Dimitris stood there, a broad grin on his face. 'I told you I would. I wasn't going to miss my big brother's wedding.'

We walked the short distance to the church, although Jake looked sulky as he had finally agreed to wear a tie. I had to stifle a smile when I saw Ingrid's mother, Susan, her dress was cerise with frills all down the skirt that made her look shorter and fatter. I was polite and complimented her on the lovely dress she was wearing.

Dimitris looked very smart in his naval uniform and he informed me proudly they were his 'Number Ones' only worn on special occasions. Ingrid was wearing a cream satin dress, that fitted her perfectly and she looked so elegant. She had taken time over her makeup and piled her hair, usually worn in a pony tail, up on her head and fixed it with a small silver comb.

Mary looked equally as attractive. The pale green dress showed off her creamy skin and in her dark hair she had a circlet of daisies. My mother had allowed her to use some lipstick to colour her lips and she looked as beautiful as Ingrid. I saw Clyde give her a number of admiring looks and she was certainly going to be a beauty when she was older.

My mother surprised me. I had expected her to wear her customary black skirt with an embroidered blouse, but instead she had chosen a dark green skirt and jacket with the embroidered blouse beneath. When I told her how very smart she looked she said she would put the suit away ready for the next wedding. I expected that to be Dimitris, and hoped he would not want to get married in Sydney which would involve all of us in a long flight.

It was quite a relief to me when the wedding and subsequent celebrations were finally over and Luke and Ingrid had driven back to Broome with Clyde and Susan. Luke and Ingrid planned to take a flight from Perth to Sydney where they planned to spend two weeks in the city. Dimitris returned to the ranch with us as he had two day's leave before needing to report back to his ship and Fred would drive him up to Broome to the airport. The younger children, even Jake, had behaved themselves impeccably. Poppi said she had appreciated being able to spend some time with her parents, although there was no sign of any improvement in Andreas's condition, and she would be happy to return to the ranch. She had paid a quick courtesy call on her in-laws, but said she had not been made to feel welcome.

Once home, Fred decided that Luke's room needed to be decorated before Ingrid arrived and he ordered a new double bed and mattress to be delivered. I ordered some new sheets and Luke's old bed was moved into Maggie's room so she no longer slept in her cot. My only concern was how well Poppi and I would manage with a third woman in the house.

When Fred and I had married and the boys had come to live at the ranch Fred had given them pocket money. He said they had to earn this by doing jobs that needed to be completed each day. As Mary and George had grown older they had taken over Luke and Dimitris's duties and the boys had earned extra money working as ranch hands. Now Mary was at school Jake was expected to help George. I was not sure how much help Jake actually gave to his brother, but George did not complain and Fred gave Jake extra pocket money.

'When you are a little boy you receive pocket money. Now you are older you are expected to earn it,' Fred explained. 'It is good training for the time when you have to go out and work properly.'

Jake looked at the dollars in his hand. 'If I refuse to work do I still get extra pocket money?'

'No, you're too big now to be treated as a baby. You have to prove that you are reliable and trustworthy. No work, no extra money.'

Jake had scowled and turned away. Until now he had spent his pocket money on comics when we went in to Derby at the weekends, now he thumbed through the comic books and replaced them on the shelf. He always had a bar of chocolate to eat whilst travelling home in the truck so I could only assume that he had outgrown comics and preferred to spend his money on sweets.

George also spent very little of his pocket money and made no secret of the fact that he was saving up to buy a grocery shop. He kept a record of all his money in a cash book, adding his pocket money from Fred each week and deducting any small amount that he spent in town. Neither Fred nor I had the heart to tell him that however hard he saved he was unlikely to have sufficient to buy a shop of his own until he was at least in his mid twenties.

Ingrid asked if she could join us when we went up to Derby as she explained that she had not really seen the town and it would be useful to find out where she could buy whatever items she decided she needed. Having left Poppi (with George accompanying her) to place the grocery order that we would collect later, we walked up to my parents and asked if they would look after Charlie and Maggie for a short while.

'What about Jake?' asked my mother warily.

'He'll come with us and then I'll leave him with Poppi and George. We won't be very long. Ingrid just wants to know her way around and I want to be able to spend some time talking to Mary until Fred says he's ready to leave. I like to know how she is progressing at school.'

Ingrid did not seem particularly impressed by Derby. 'I thought it would be as big as Perth and Perth is tiny compared with Sydney.'

'When I first arrived I thought Derby was an enormous town.' I smiled. 'I had lived in a tiny Cretan village with conditions that you would find both unbelievable and unacceptable these days.

No proper toilets, a tin bath in the kitchen once a week and all the water had to be collected from a well.'

I was not sure if Ingrid believed me and I determined to ask my mother to describe how we had lived in Fourni. I expected modernisation to have taken place over there, but I had no way of knowing as we had never had a reply to any of the letters that we sent to my aunt and uncle. I had never heard a word from Lucas and did not know if he had ever received any of my letters. I accepted that Lucas had probably died by now and when I thought of him I still had a pain in my heart.

Ingrid fitted in well with us, she never intruded or tried to interfere in the routine that Poppi and I had worked out between us. Life was much easier as I had no small babies to deal with, but I did miss having one to cuddle and often thought I had made a mistake agreeing to Fred being sterilised.

I was overjoyed when Ingrid finally told me she and Luke were expecting their first child. It was no big surprise to me as she seemed suddenly to have blossomed out, an extra sparkle to her eyes, a bloom to her cheeks and added lustre to her hair, but I would not have dreamt of asking her or Luke the reason. This made me realise I was now more Australian than Greek; had I been in a Greek village I would have asked her as soon as I became suspicious and no one would have thought any the worse of me as I spread the gossip around.

I was concerned about arrangements for Ingrid to get to the hospital in time. I could hardly ask my parents to have her stay with them for a week or more and they had Mary occupying their spare room. Luke assured me I was worrying unnecessarily as he would drive Ingrid to Broome and they could fly to Perth a month before the baby was due and she could stay with her mother whilst he returned to the ranch. When the child was born he would fly up for a visit and then Ingrid would return to stay with her mother for a further month after she was discharged from the hospital. I could not complain that Ingrid's mother would have sight of her grandchild before I did.

Our life settled into a routine until Jake began to worry me. Mary's hobby had been her art work; George had his passion for shopping and everything in our pantry was stored just the way he liked it; Charlie was always happy with a toy car to push around and Maggie spent her day playing with her dolls, changing their clothes and arranging tea parties for them. Jake did not appear to have any interest in anything.

Fred asked him if he would like to go away to school and Jake had reacted angrily.

'You just want to get rid of me.'

'Not at all,' replied Fred. 'We just want to offer you the same opportunities as your siblings. You don't seem very happy living on the ranch and we thought you might like to go to school now rather than wait until you are a little older.'

'If you send me off to boarding school I'll run away,' replied Jake.

Fred sighed. 'We'll not send you away, but if you change your mind in a year or so let me know.'

'I'd rather live in the town. There's nothing to do here.'

'So what would you do in the town?'

'Plenty of things. There are the shops there.'

I tried to think of something that would interest Jake and finally suggested that when we made our visits to the town Jake should be allowed to wander around the shops unescorted by Poppi. This idea seemed to please him and we arranged that he should have time to himself whilst Poppi placed the grocery order, Fred visited the feed suppliers and the garage for petrol and I spent time with my parents.

For a number of months this seemed to work well, then Poppi called me to one side.

'The grocer has said that Jake is not allowed inside any more on his own. He has been hanging around the sweet counter and the assistant felt sure he was helping himself. She saw him put a chocolate bar in his pocket today and called the manager. He made Jake turn out his pockets and he had three chocolate bars.

He protested that he was going to pay for them and only put them there whilst he went to look at the comics.'

I looked at Poppi in horror. 'He can't have meant to steal them. It was very foolish of him to put them into his pocket. He should have paid for those and then gone to the comic stand. I'll not mention it to Fred or he won't be allowed to go around the town on his own any more. I'll speak to him when we get home.'

Jake repeated the story to me that he had given to the manager. 'The silly old man didn't believe me.'

'You should have thought what you were doing and how it could be misinterpreted. Please be more careful in future.'

'I will,' Jake assured me.

Fred had always been very generous, giving me more than enough spending money of my own whenever we visited Derby. Usually I spent most of this on the children as they seemed to grow so fast that they continually needed new clothes and there was little I needed for myself. I would often buy a bottle of wine for my parents or some little thing I had heard my mother mention that she needed or would like.

Now Mary was living with them Fred gave me some separate money to pass on to them to pay for her food and any school necessities. I always placed this in a separate compartment of my purse. I was most surprised when I went to hand the money to my father I saw that it was five dollars short. I could only think that Fred had made an error, although it was unlike him, and took the necessary dollars from my own money.

I thought no more about it until we visited Derby again. Once more the money for my parents was five dollars short. I decided that I must speak to Fred and tell him that he had made an error on two occasions.

Fred had looked at me in surprise. 'Are you sure? You didn't miscount it?'

'That would be possible once, but not two months running. I thought you had miscounted.'

'I'm sure I didn't, but next month I'll count it out in front of you rather than just handing it over.'

I felt sure this would solve the problem, but when I arrived at my parents and counted the dollars out once again it was short and this time it was ten dollars that was missing. I was now seriously worried. I had watched Fred count out the notes and then placed them in my purse. Someone must have helped themselves to my money.

I now had a dilemma. This had never happened in the past as far as I was aware and the only addition to our family was Ingrid. Surely she would not steal money from my purse? Should I speak to Luke about my suspicions? I thought about the problem all the way home in the truck. Ingrid and Luke were due to fly to Perth next week in readiness for her to have the baby. If I did not lose any money whilst she was away then I would know she was the culprit. I decided to say nothing of my suspicions to Luke, but confided in Fred that evening.

He found it as hard to believe as I did. 'Do you think it is something to do with her being pregnant?'

'It's possible,' I agreed, 'But she and Luke have bought everything that is needed for the baby. If Luke suddenly found himself short for going to Perth he would have asked you for a loan. Ten or twenty dollars would not have got him very far.'

'Have you spoken to Poppi?'

'It can't be Poppi.'

'I certainly don't think it is her, but she may have had some money taken.'

Poppi was embarrassed when I spoke to her. 'On a couple of occasions I thought I should have had a little more in my purse. I thought I had made a mistake when I was counting it or I had been short changed by one of the shop keepers.'

I did not voice my suspicions to her about Ingrid, but asked her to keep a careful check on her money and let me know at once if any appeared to be missing. There being no need for any money on the ranch I had always kept my purse in a drawer beside my bed, only carrying it with me if we were going up to town. I decided to leave it there; if some money was taken before Ingrid left and not touched during her absence it would indicate that she was the culprit.

Fred had a system whereby he drew sufficient money from the bank when we visited Derby to cover the wages for the ranch hands and Poppi, along with my allowance and the pocket money for the children. He had increased his withdrawal to cover the cost of Mary staying with my parents and paid the grocery bill by cheque. Payments for the sale of stock and the purchasing of more heifers were made by cheque directly through the bank and he had an account that he paid monthly for the animals' feed and any other essentials. He rarely had more than a hundred dollars in his pocket from one end of the month to the other.

Each night I counted the money in my purse and it was correct and Ingrid and Luke were leaving that day. I began to doubt myself and think the discrepancies had been my mistake. I was so pleased I had not mentioned my suspicions to Luke.

When we visited Derby that month the money for my parents was correct and I hoped I had made the mistakes previously. Poppi had not mentioned that she had lost any money and I hoped that after Ingrid had the baby and returned from Perth that there would be no more occurrences. I was upset when I saw Jake being spoken to sharply by a shopkeeper and he handed over the money for the comic he had in his hand.

'Why didn't you pay for the comic before you left the shop?' I asked sharply.

'I forgot,' he mumbled. 'I was reading it and just walked out.'

'Don't let it happen again. Forgetting to pay for something is not a good excuse. If the other ranchers forgot to pay your father for his stock we would soon be penniless. It's just the same for a shop keeper.'

Jake made no answer and I hoped he would heed my words.

Ingrid gave birth to a healthy boy and as soon as Luke heard the news he immediately drove to Broome and flew on to Perth. He telephoned that evening to say that all was well with both mother and child; he would stay in Perth the following day and then travel home in the early evening. I wished Ingrid was coming with him so I could see my new grandchild, but it was far too soon for either of them to travel.

Harry Frederick was a lovely little boy and his eyes were already following Ingrid as she moved around. He was happy to let me cuddle him and I had to impress upon Maggie that he was not a doll to be played with. George said he was pleased to be an uncle and Charlie wanted to know how long it would be before Harry was big enough to play with him; only Jake gave him a cursory glance and made no comment.

No more money had disappeared from either Poppi or myself and I could only think it was some strange effect that pregnancy had had on Ingrid. I hoped it would not occur again if she had another child in the future. I asked Ingrid if I should invite her mother to come to stay. I did not relish the thought, but no doubt she would want to see her grandson as he developed.

When Mary was due to have her school holiday I invited my parents to accompany her home so they could see their first great grandchild. After they returned to Derby Ingrid's mother came for two weeks and I have to admit the visit was easier than I had anticipated. All her attention was focused on Harry and telling Ingrid how she should manage him.

Jake seemed to spend a good deal of his time wandering around the ranch aimlessly.

Mary progressed well at school, passing her examinations with ease and asked if she could go to the same teacher training college in Perth as Ingrid had attended. We promised to look into the possibility but I confided in Fred that I did not want her living with Ingrid's mother and brother. Fred was surprised and I could only say that I had not liked the way that Clyde had looked at Mary during Luke's wedding.

I decided to approach Ingrid and began to ask her general questions about the college in Perth. It sounded eminently suitable for Mary but I was still concerned about where she would live. Ingrid immediately said she was sure her mother would be willing to have her stay with them, but I had my excuses ready.

'That would be very kind of your mother but I think it would be beneficial to Mary if she was able to live in rooms or accommodation provided by the college. She has either lived at home or with her grandparents. This is an ideal opportunity for her to have more freedom and be able to mix with the other students and go to social events.'

'I'm sure my mother would understand. I was allowed to go out with my friends.'

'I would not feel right about placing that responsibility on your mother's shoulders. Mary is a good girl but there are bound to be occasions when she did not return home at the agreed time and I am sure that would worry your mother. It would certainly worry me if the position was reversed. Another person's child is a great responsibility.'

Ingrid appeared to accept my excuses, maybe she was relieved not to have to ask her mother to have Mary live with them, and she said no more about the idea. She looked at me and smiled.

'I hope you will be willing to look after Harry for me when I go up to Perth for the next baby.'

For a moment I was speechless, then I hugged her. 'I'm so pleased for you and Luke and I would be honoured that you trusted me to look after Harry.'

'You have far more experience of small children than my mother and it would be foolish to take him away from the home he is accustomed to. I'll prepare him well so that it won't be a shock to him when I am not here. Luke will be here most of the time so there shouldn't be a problem.'

Fred discussed attending the college and where she would live with Mary and then spent some hours on the telephone. He was assured that Mary could live in the residential accommodation along with the other first year girls. Before he agreed to this he arranged to fly up to Perth with Mary and ensure that any accommodation was suitable and she was happy with it.

George was still adamant that he wanted to become a grocer and with Mary going to Perth this would mean that he could stay with my parents in the spare room. Fred spoke to the largest grocery store in Derby where we had shopped regularly over the years and the manager agreed that he could start there as an apprentice. George was delighted and counted out his savings to ensure they agreed with his account book.

He came to Fred with a problem, the cash and the book in his hand. 'I can't get my money to agree,' he said. 'I'm twenty dollars short and I've been up and down all the figures and can't find it.'

Fred sat with him and together they counted out the money. All George's addition and subtractions were correct but the final figure was twenty dollars short. Finally Fred admitted defeat.

'I can't find the difference. I can only think that at some time you made an error about the amount you entered.'

George frowned and shook his head. 'I'm always very careful.'

'I know, but errors can occur. Now you're old enough would you like me to open a bank account for you in Derby? You won't earn very much as an apprentice but a bit more than I've been paying you. Each week you can put some money into your bank book and will be able to watch the amount grow.'

George was delighted with the idea. His earlier concern about the discrepancy in his figures forgotten, but I was worried. Ingrid was expecting again and money seemed to be disappearing again. I warned Poppi and we both of us made a continual check on the amount in our purses, but apart from an odd dollar that could have been our mistake, nothing appeared to have been taken.

I did become very concerned when Hank confided in Fred

that he thought someone on the ranch was pilfering. He said that at various times over the previous three years all the ranch hands had noticed that a small amount of their money had disappeared. Fred questioned him closely and Hank appeared to become more and more embarrassed. He explained that he had not brought it to Fred's attention before as it happened irregularly and he had thought it was carelessness on the part of the men in spending more than they had realised.

All the hands had been working here for years, but the problem only seemed to have arisen during the last three. Whilst they were out working they took no money with them and the only people who would be anywhere near their quarters was Davy, the stable hand, along with Fred, Luke, George, Jake and occasionally Charlie. Ingrid, whom we had suspected and blamed originally when we had noticed shortages, went nowhere near their quarters or the stables unless she was with Luke. An awful thought occurred to me. I knew George was saving up with the idea of having a grocer's shop of his own one day - would he be stealing?

'Have you asked Hank if he has any idea who is stealing?' I asked.

'He said he had a fair idea, but no proof. He's told the men to either hide their wallets or carry them with them and if they see anyone around their quarters they are to let me know.'

Finally Jake appeared willing to ride properly and would listen to the instructions that Hank or Jim gave him. He was not interested in caring for his horse and would hand her over to Davy to rub down and care for whilst he wandered away. Fred took him to task and he replied that he was only learning how to handle a horse as the knowledge would be useful to him in the future.

After my foolhardy ride on Amber I now had more confidence in my ability. We treated both her and Blaze gently as they were coming towards the end of their riding lives. It was as we were returning home one afternoon that we saw someone down by the ranch hands' quarters. Fred took off at a gallop and I followed more sedately.

291

When I arrived he was speaking to Jake who looked sullen. 'I'm always the one in trouble with you,' he complained. 'I wasn't sure if George had filled up the mangers with hay so I came down to check.'

'Why didn't you ask George?'

'He said he had done that whilst I was checking the pipes and the fences. I didn't believe him. He had done it too quickly.'

'You could have checked with Davy.'

'That's why I'm down here. He doesn't appear to be around by the stables.'

There was nothing to disprove Jake's story and when Fred asked George later he said Jake had spoken to him about the hay.

'I think he is trying to prove how conscientious he is becoming now I'm going away.'

1979 - 1985
All Change

Hank and Jim retired and Fred did not look for replacement ranch hands as Luke was more than capable of taking their place. I was sorry to see them go as they had been nice men who had taken care of Luke and Dimitris whilst teaching them to ride.

George completed his apprenticeship and the manager was impressed by him. He offered to train him as a manager and George was delighted. At the end of a further year the manager recommended him for a vacancy in their Perth branch, and after discussing the move with Fred and I, he accepted.

Mary had graduated and was teaching art in a girls' school in Perth, renting a small apartment that she shared with a girl friend. George was the manager of a grocers, also in Perth and had an apartment above the shop and Ingrid and Luke had another little boy, Kevin Lucas. Charlie took his responsibilities on the ranch seriously and was also showing Maggie how to check the fences and the water pipes. They were as companionable as Mary and George had been at that age which delighted me. Although both were now proficient riders they were not allowed off the ranch unaccompanied and Jake sneered at them and called them babies when he rode off alone.

Jake was the one who worried me. Bert had returned unexpectedly early to his accommodation and discovered the boy going through the pockets of his jacket. Even Jake could not think up an excuse and Bert came up to the ranch to speak to Fred.

I had never seen Fred angry, annoyed sometimes, but never angry and he frightened me. His face had suffused with blood and he clenched his fists. He held Jake by his collar and demanded an explanation from him.

Jake had wriggled himself free and confronted his father. 'If you beat me I'll complain to the police and show them the bruises.'

'You are more likely to be arrested as a petty thief.'

Jake shook his head, 'I'm under age. They'd just give me a warning.'

'Only for two more weeks. Why are you taking money? What do you want it for?'

'None of your business. You'll find out.'

Fred flung the boy away from him and sat down in the chair, breathing heavily. 'I'd like to thrash him until his skin falls off.'

I sat on the arm of the chair with him. 'You've always said that beating children didn't do any good.'

'Jake is no longer a child. He is quite old enough to know better. How can we trust him in the future?'

I shook my head. I felt very guilty. We had thought it was Ingrid who had taken money and then I had suspected it could be George. I was so glad I had never voiced my suspicions to either of them. The atmosphere at the ranch was uneasy, Jake avoiding the house as much as possible, Fred and I avoided discussing the boy and his future and I did not mention the problem to Poppi. No more money went missing during the next fortnight and I hoped that now Jake had been found to be the culprit he would realise he had to give up the pilfering.

It was a shock when Bert arrived at the ranch to say that Jake's horse was missing from the stable. 'Davy insists that the door was securely locked when he did his rounds last night and we've had a quick look around to see if she is grazing anywhere. There's no sign of her and her tack is missing.'

It was unlike Jake to rise early and go for a ride. Fred left his breakfast and returned to the stable with Bert and saddled Blaze. The two men rode out, having told the other hands to look out for Jake and his horse, but they could see no sign of Jake although they rode to the furthest area of the ranch's land and all around the perimeter.

I looked in Jake's room and could see that his cupboards and drawers were empty of most of his clothes. Had he decided to run away to his grandparents in Derby? Had he done this I was sure my parents would have telephoned me upon his arrival.

Fred returned during the morning and I told him that Jake appeared to have taken most of his clothes with him.

'He'll no doubt be found soon enough if he has gone to Derby. He's known to many of the people who live there and if he hasn't gone to his grandparents he will have to find somewhere to eat and spend the night. I can't expect Blaze to take me that far again today so I'll drive up in the truck and see if I can find any sign of him.'

It was early evening before Fred returned and shook his head. 'I looked everywhere I could think of, asked the shop keepers and they hadn't seen him. I even called on your parents. I didn't tell them Jake was missing, just said I was in town, so I paid them a visit. I'm sure they would have told me if Jake had been there.'

I was worried. What had happened to the boy? He was only just sixteen, certainly not old enough to go somewhere alone without any friends or relatives.

'Do you suppose he may have gone to Perth?' I suggested.

'Why would he do that and how would he get there? It's too far to ride.'

'He may have cadged a lift from a delivery driver who was going through to Perth and might think he can stay with George.'

'I'll telephone George and let him know we are anxious and ask him to telephone us if Jake does turn up there. What about Mary? Shall I telephone her?'

I shook my head. 'I think that is the last place he would go.

He and Mary were not the best of friends. What about Clyde and his mother? Would he go there?'

'Most unlikely. I don't think he knows exactly where they live. I'll ask Luke to telephone Clyde, just in case.'

'Luke had been out all day looking for him. He thinks Jake may have decided to ride off into the uninhabited part of the area and his horse had an accident.'

'If such a thing has happened it could be weeks before he's located. I hope Luke had one of the hands with him for safety.'

'Do you think he may have gone to Broome?' I asked.

'Why would he go there? We've rarely been to the town and he knows no one there.'

'He may think that as he isn't known there he could get some work.'

'It's possible, I suppose. I'll drive over tomorrow and see if there's any sign of him.'

I could hardly sleep that night. I had visions of Jake being in the middle of the desert area with a lame horse and running out of water. If there happened to be a community of Aboriginals living near by they would care for him but it was a slim hope that gave me little consolation.

Fred set off early to drive to Broome and Luke said he and Pat would ride in a different direction from the previous day. He assured me that if they came across any Aboriginals in the area they would ask if Jake had been seen by them.

Fred returned in the middle of the afternoon and his news gave me mixed emotions. He had found Jake's horse tethered close to the airport at Broome. Despite enquiring around no one seemed to know who had left her there. She needed water and food, as well as a good rub down. He had walked her to some stabling and asked for her to be cared for. His dilemma had been when he wanted to pay them and found his wallet was empty. Jake had obviously helped himself before he left. He had drawn sufficient money from the bank in Broome, but it had taken time whilst they contacted his usual branch in Derby and released the money to him.

He had walked around, looking in the taverns for any sign of Jake and then gone to the airport and enquired about flights going to Perth. He was told he had missed the morning flight and tried hard to explain that he did not want to travel, but was looking for his son. Eventually he had spoken to the airport manager who had consulted his list of passengers for the previous two days and Jake's name was recorded as having bought a ticket for Perth.

At least I now knew he was not suffering in the middle of the desert area and took a deep breath of relief. Surely he would go to George now he was in Perth.

'That's not quite the end of it,' continued Fred. 'He'd taken all the money from my wallet before he left. Have you checked your purse?'

I shook my head. I had no reason to spend any money whilst at the ranch. My purse was empty and when I asked Poppi she confirmed that her money had also gone. Once Luke returned I told him we were certain that Jake had gone to Perth and then asked him to check his money and Ingrid's. He came back looking furious.

'He obviously helped himself to our money at some time. He knew we wouldn't need it until we visited Derby next. Had I known he had done that I wouldn't have bothered spending my time looking for him.'

'He is your brother.'

'Half brother - and half of him is rotten.'

Knowing that Jake was in Perth and had money with him alleviated some of my worry. Fred was adamant that he was not going to travel to Perth to see if he could find him.

'Once his money runs out he'll probably ask to come back home.'

'He might find a job there.'

'He might.' Fred sounded sceptical. 'He's not that fond of hard work.'

Fred had ridden to Broome and collected the horse that Jake had left there. She certainly looked far better than when he had last seen her and thanked the stable hand who had cared for her.

'Thanks to you she seems to have made a good recovery.'

'Had she been stolen from your stables?'

'In a manner of speaking. I'm glad I found her. She wouldn't have lasted more than another twenty four hours without attention.'

'A wicked thing to do. Steal her and then just leave her,' observed the stable hand. 'I don't understand how anyone can do that to a helpless animal.'

I had to break the news of Jake's absence to my parents. I didn't mention the missing money, just said that he had decided to go to Perth and look for work. I also telephoned George and he promised to let us know immediately if he did see Jake. I then telephoned Mary. She made no comment about Jake leaving home but agreed to let us know if she saw him and she would also ask a friend of hers, who happened to be a policeman, to look out for him.

I thanked her, but pointed out that he would not know what Jake looked like.

'I think I can describe Jake fairly accurately,' she replied. 'He's probably found somewhere to stay in the cheap part of the town. Tony can ask his colleagues to keep an eye out for him when they are patrolling that area.'

I tried to put Jake out of my mind, but it niggled away at me. He must have been planning this move for some considerable time and that was why he had taken the money. I wish I knew why the boy was so unhappy living with us. Although he had been punished for naughtiness we had still loved him just as much as our other children.

Mary returned home for visits during her school holidays and talked a good deal about her friend Tony. I sensed that he was more than a casual friend and waited to hear an announcement from them. Dimitris often arrived unexpectedly if his ship entered the port of Derby. He was loving the life and I knew he had made the right choice of career. George telephoned each week, he never seemed to have any news, but confirmed that he was happy in his work.

Ingrid and Luke were expecting their third child and hoping that this time it would be a girl. Luke made the same arrangements as before to take Ingrid up to Perth to stay with her mother and Poppi and I were happy to look after Harry and Kevin. Maggie was delighted to share in their care and willing to keep them amused. Charlie allowed them to play with his toy cars, but counted out how many he gave to them at any one time and insisted the same number should be returned.

Charlie appeared to have a new hobby. At one time he had spent most of his pocket money on toy cars, but now he scoured the second hand rubbish shops in Derby for any metal objects, particularly clocks or mechanical toys that were broken and in need of repair. He would take them apart and examine how they worked before he found some screws or brackets that fitted. Once completed and in working order he would take them back up to Derby and offer to sell them to the antique shops. He was beginning to be quite successful and Fred asked him if he wanted to be an antique dealer.

Charlie had laughed. 'I don't know anything about antiques. I just mess around with old bits and pieces. I enjoy putting parts together and making them work again.'

'Would you like to be an engineer?'

'Maybe. What would I have to do?'

'An apprenticeship in a garage or the ship yards. If you didn't enjoy the work you could always leave and do something else. Come back and work on the ranch if you wanted.'

'I thought you would expect me to stay here and help Luke.'

'I expect you to work at something that you enjoy. You're not obliged to stay on the ranch.'

'Where would I have to go?'

'I'm sure there's somewhere in Derby who would take an apprentice.'

When Fred told me this I was concerned, not about Charlie going to Derby, but where he would live. I felt my parents were too old now to be expected to look after a young man and mentioned this to Fred.

'It's not going to happen overnight. I think you should start suggesting to your parents that they would enjoy living in a Nursing Home.'

'They're not ill. They don't need a nurse,' I protested.

'They are called Nursing Homes,' Fred explained, 'But you don't have to be sick to live there. You can have a small apartment and look after yourselves until it becomes too much for you. Then you can arrange to have your shopping done, meals cooked and the apartment cleaned. If your health does deteriorate you can be transferred to the nursing wing.'

'How do you know so much about them?' I asked.

'I've looked into their details. I know you have always said you do not want to have to care for your parents so I thought that could be a practical solution. If they do agree, that would free up their apartment and Charlie could live there.'

I shook my head. 'It must cost a lot of money to live in one of these Nursing Homes. Their apartment would need to be sold to pay for it. It would be better to rent a small apartment for Charlie or arrange for him to have a room with a family.'

I was not at all sure that my parents would consider moving to a Nursing Home, despite being in their eighties.

When Luke escorted Ingrid to Perth he also arranged to meet George before he returned. 'You know how miserable it can be hanging around at an airport for your flight to be called. If you were able to meet me for a drink I'd be grateful.'

When George arrived he looked grim. 'I've had Mary on the phone. Her boyfriend has told her that Jake has been arrested.'

'What for?' Luke felt his heart sink.

'Breaking and entering. It's not the first time he's been in trouble with the law, but he's managed to get away with a caution before. This time he will have to appear in court and probably serve a jail sentence. He seems to be friends with a rather undesirable group of young people.'

'Do Mum and Dad know?' asked Luke.

'I don't see any need to tell them at the moment. There's nothing they can do. He's no longer under age so they cannot insist that he returns to the ranch. Let him take his punishment and let's hope he learns from it.'

'Why don't I tell them that you have seen him in Perth? I'm sure they would like to know where he is.'

After Luke had telephoned Ingrid to say he was safely back home he called Mary and asked her if the story George had told him about Jake being arrested was true.

Mary gave a deep sigh. 'I'm afraid so. I do wish he hadn't decided to come to Perth. It's embarrassing to have a brother who is a petty criminal. Tony says Jake appears to be hanging out with a crowd of undesirable locals and they have all been picked up at some time or another for being drunk and disorderly, but recently some of them have been found with drugs on them. That becomes a more serious matter.'

'Jake? Is he involved with drugs?'

'It would appear so. Tony doesn't say much, of course, but it doesn't look good on his record that he is going out with an offender's sister.'

'People won't know you are related unless you tell them.'

'Police records have a way of tracing relatives and Tony has been asked if Jake is my brother. He had to tell the truth. If it was found out that he had lied he would have lost his job.'

'Could Tony not ask for a transfer to a different area?'

'Probably, but he could be sent as far away as Sydney or Melbourne. We'd never be able to see each other then.'

'It's serious, then, between you and Tony?' asked Luke.

'Yes, we have our plans.'

'Do I hear wedding bells?'

'Possibly, but tell me about Ingrid. I imagine if you were in Perth you have brought her up to stay with her mother.'

'That's right. She's been keeping well, says she feels no different from the way she did when carrying the other two so I guess this one will be another boy.'

'Will you be disappointed?' asked Mary.

'No, the next one could be a girl.'

'Just because Mum and Dad had children one after the other you don't have to.'

'Another one or two won't be a problem provided Ingrid is willing. Mary, seriously, let me know what happens with Jake. I haven't told Mum or Fred. There's no need to upset them. I'm just going to say that George has seen him and he is quite safe.'

'Tony says Jake appears to be hanging out with a crowd of young criminals.'

Ingrid returned to the ranch with a beautiful little girl whom they had called Suzanna Irene. I was quite touched that they had given her my name and Ingrid explained.

'Harry was called after my father and Fred, We both just liked the name Kevin and it seemed to go well with Lucas as a second name. As Suzie is a girl we thought it appropriate that she was called after my mother and you.'

I smiled and wondered what they would call their next one.

'There won't be any more,' Ingrid continued. 'I know how much Luke wanted a girl and now he has her. It is quite a relief as we agreed that now I have produced a girl there will be no more.'

I was surprised. I had always enjoyed being pregnant, even when the next baby appeared before their sibling was out of nappies.

'You may change your mind in a few years time.'

Ingrid shook her head. 'I had quite a long labour with the boys and I was taking such a time with this one that they were talking about giving me a Caesarian. I wouldn't want to think I would need that in the future. The thought of having an anaesthetic makes my blood run cold. Suppose I don't wake up?'

I realised that Ingrid was truly frightened and I hoped Luke understood.

Before Suzie was a year old Mary telephoned to say that she had handed in her notice at the school. She and Tony had discussed him having a transfer to a different police department and it had been agreed that he could go to Adelaide. Mary was going with him and would apply for a teaching position once they were there.

'Adelaide! That's even further away. We'll never see you and we've not even met Tony.'

'That can be rectified as soon as the term finishes. Tony and I plan to get married, very quietly, just at the Magistrate's Office. We'll then fly down to Broome and travel up to the ranch. We'd like to have a church blessing in Derby so Grandma and Grandpa can come. It won't be a grand wedding like Ingrid and Luke had, so there's no need for a new wardrobe.'

'What about George? Will he come with you?'

'George and my friend, Felicity, are going to be witnesses. George can't get any holiday at the moment.'

'What about Dimitris?'

'He's at sea so he can't come to either venue. At least coming to the ranch and having a church blessing in Derby will give me the opportunity to see Grandma and Grandpa and meeting up with Charlie and Maggie before they go their separate ways.'

Mary confessed they had been living together for a year and seen no need previously to get married.

'It's a promotion for Tony, but the only way I can go with him is if I am his legal wife. That made the decision for us,' she explained. She did not add that she had urged Tony to ask for a transfer away from Perth, but she had not expected him to be sent to a different state. They had spent many hours discussing the

303

proposed move and deciding whether he should accept or decline the offer and stay in Perth.

'If Tony isn't happy working there he can ask for another transfer in a year or so or could request a return to Perth. You and Dad could always fly down to Adelaide and spend some time with us when we're settled.'

This was a new idea to me. I had never considered going to visit the children whilst they were away from home, they had always come back to see us. Once Charlie and Maggie were settled, and if my parents could be persuaded to move into a Nursing Home, I would see how Fred felt about the prospect. We could even visit George in Perth as we only saw him once a year when he had his annual holiday and Dimitris's visits were restricted by his naval duties.

'What about Tony's parents? Wouldn't they want to come?'

For a moment Mary hesitated. 'He has no contact with his parents. He did not have a happy childhood.'

I did not press Mary for details.

Tony was a little older than I had expected and apologised for taking our daughter so far away. He and Luke had bonded immediately, although he admitted that he would not want to be dealing with cows every day.

'Could be easier than dealing with people, but I'm a town person. I can't imagine what it must be like to live here without any neighbours and have to drive into town for all your supplies.'

Luke had smiled and shaken his head.' I wouldn't want to live in a town until I'm too old to live here any more. I lived in Perth for a while after I left college and it didn't attract me. I prefer the open space we have here and the only inconvenience has been when Ingrid was having the children and I had to take her backwards and forwards to Perth. Mum always went to the hospital in Derby but Ingrid wanted to be with her mother.' Tony had repeated Mary's invitation to visit them and Luke had said he would consider it when the children were older.

Ingrid, having qualified as a teacher before she and Luke married, was using her skills to educate their boys. Both boys were apt pupils, but preferred to be outside with their father. Harry had taken to riding at an early age and was a proficient horseman, although Luke would not allow him to ride out alone. Fred and I would still go for a ride most days and Harry delighted in accompanying us. Kevin was envious and although not yet able to match Harry's riding skills we would spend some time with him, walking around the paddock area before leaving him under the supervision of one of the ranch hands.

Maggie, although she could ride, preferred to spend her time with Ingrid and keeping Suzie amused. It was no surprise to me when she said she wanted to go to the hospital in Derby and train to be a qualified nurse.

'It will probably take me some years, but once I'm fully qualified I want to specialise in working with children.'

Although the population of Derby had increased dramatically from the time when I had first landed there so many years ago I did not think there were enough children living there that a specialist nurse was needed. I envisaged that Maggie would also move away to a larger town.

Fred had arranged that Charlie would become an apprentice at the airport in Broome. He lived with the family of another apprentice and I was pleased that he was not in a hostel or living in an apartment on his own. George had passed his driving test and bought himself a small car and he drove up to visit us at least once each month.

'I thought a car was a more practical investment than a grocer's shop,' he grinned as he showed it off to us. 'I can always sell it at a later date if I don't need it.'

This just left Luke and his family along with Fred, Poppi and myself living at the ranch. Harry, Kevin and Suzie all had a bedroom to themselves and we always made sure there was a room available for my parents or any of the family who paid us a visit.

The last time my parents were invited to visit they refused, saying that the upheaval of the journey would be too much for them. I realised that the time had come to persuade them gently to move into a Nursing Home.

My father seemed quite willing and I had an idea that my mother was no longer looking after him as well as she had in the past. I stressed to her how much easier it would be if her shopping was done for her along with housework. Finally she agreed and I think it was a relief to her to know that they would be taken care of properly during their last years. I did wonder what would become of Fred and myself when I was no longer capable of all I did at present. Poppi was a little older than me and I could not expect her to take on the responsibility of caring for us. Would Ingrid be willing?

1986 - 1996
Tragedies

I had not expected my life to be thrown into such turmoil during the next ten years.

Tony telephoned from Adelaide with the terrible news that Mary had been killed in a traffic accident. A driver had suffered a heart attack and his car swerved up onto the pavement where three pedestrians had been killed, one of them Mary. Tony was distraught and had been given compassionate leave. I immediately asked if he wished to visit us, but he refused.

'I have to come to terms with it. I'm having counselling, but that doesn't make up for losing Mary. I wish we had decided to have some children, but at the same time I'm pleased we didn't. Some poor child would have been left motherless.' Tony seemed to hesitate before he asked me a difficult question. 'Would you like me to send you the bear that Mary was so fond of?'

I swallowed hard before I was able to reply. 'No,' I managed to say. 'Please place it in Mary's coffin with her.' I could not bear the thought of Mary being separated from Eliza's bear even after death.

I cried for Mary and also for Tony when I came off the phone. She was the first child that Fred and I had together and he had doted on her from the start. He began to look his age now and was leaving more of the work on the ranch to Luke.

Then Poppi left me. She had been losing weight for some

time and complained of a pain in her side. She joked that she could have appendicitis the same as George had suffered so many years before, but I could see by the look in her eyes that she was frightened. We took her up to the hospital in Derby for an examination and the doctor returned to us with grave news.

'She does have a lump in her lower abdomen and we will have to investigate. It could be nothing to worry about, but we will need to do an exploratory examination to be certain. Does she have any relatives who should be informed?'

I did not like the sound of that request and asked if I could wait for the result of the exploratory operation before I told her sister.

When I told the doctor how long Poppi had been living and working with us the doctor said the decision could be mine, although she was not my relative. I talked to Fred and he said we should tell Poppi's sister now. If anything happened to Poppi whilst under the anaesthetic her sister would be hurt and annoyed that she had not had a final opportunity to see her. Reluctantly I agreed with Fred and we went to the apartment where Maria lived with her disabled husband.

Maria had listened to our concerns and agreed that she would arrange for a friend to stay with Andreas whilst she went to the hospital the following day.

'Does Poppi know how serious it could be?' she asked.

'She still believes it is her appendix. If she's correct then when they do the exploratory operation they'll take it out at the same time.'

'I hope she's correct and it will be as simple as that.'

Of course it was not. The lump was removed and sent for a biopsy where it was diagnosed as cancerous. Poppi would be given a course of radio therapy in the hope that any surrounding malignant cells would be destroyed and she could make a complete recovery.

Maria agreed that Poppi would go and stay with her in between her hospital visits for treatment. She had the room that their parents had originally occupied, but was concerned about any nursing attention that might be needed. Fred said that once a date had been set for Poppi to start to receive radio therapy and she was able to attend as a day patient he would finance a private nursing scheme that would make a nurse available throughout the day and also overnight if necessary.

I was grateful for his generosity. I had no idea how much of her wages Poppi had saved over the years she had worked for us, but it was unlikely to be sufficient to pay for private nursing.

Unfortunately all the care in the world could not prolong Poppi's life. The radio therapy left her feeling weak and ill and when the session was completed an examination showed that the malignant cells had multiplied. Each time we visited Poppi seemed to have become more shrunken and eventually the time came when she needed more care than a daily nurse could give and she was returned to the hospital. Three weeks later we helped Maria to arrange her funeral. I had lost my best friend.

The next event came out of the blue and I found it hard to believe that I would never see Dimitris again. A telephone call came from the Admiralty to say there had been a diving accident and Dimitris had drowned. I could not believe it. Dimitris had always been a good swimmer. Again and again I asked the naval officer on the end of the line if he was certain and he said that a letter was being sent to us with details that would explain the incident and ask us for funeral details.

I felt that my world was falling apart. First Mary, then Poppi and now Dimitris.

The letter from the Admiralty explained that Dimitris and some companions had been diving off the Great Barrier Reef. The air line of one of his companions had become entangled on some coral and been punctured. Dimitris shared his air with him as he tried to free him and another diver returned to the surface to alert dive control. Assistance was sent to them but by the time they arrived it was too late. Both men had asphyxiated by the time they were brought to the surface.

Part of me raged at Dimitris for staying to help his friend, but I also had to admire his compassion and bravery. He would have known the consequences of staying below and sharing his air supply until help arrived.

Luke was devastated. He and Dimitris had been so close as children and remained good friends over their adult years although being so far apart in distance. Fred was equally as distraught. He had brought Dimitris up with as much care and concern as if he had been his own son. I had to be grateful that Dimitris had not married and was not leaving a grieving widow behind. When we finally managed to discuss the tragedy rationally we decided that Dimitris should be cremated and his ashes scattered at sea.

No longer having Poppi to help me with the daily running of the ranch Ingrid took over many of her duties. Having spent the morning schooling her children she would turn her hand to cleaning in the afternoons whilst Fred and I went down to the paddock with the children and encouraged them to improve their riding skills. When I returned I would find the evening meal sitting in the oven and the kitchen spotless. She would often have tried a new recipe that she had found in a magazine and the only time we all had cause for complaint was when she had misread the quantity of chilli powder she needed to add. She had measured out a tablespoon in mistake for a teaspoon. It was quite uneatable, but we managed to laugh over the error and ate some fried chicken and chips. She had begged Luke to never tell her mother or she would never hear the end of her incompetence.

It was left to George to break the news of Jake's death to me. Much as he disapproved of Jake's life style he had offered to stand bail for him when Mary had told him that Jake had been arrested and likely to receive a prison sentence. George offered him a position as a stock filler in his grocery shop once he had served his time in jail. Jake had accepted, but within weeks stock was disappearing at an alarming rate as his friends arrived and he allowed them to help themselves. George had no option but to tell Jake he was no longer prepared to employ him. He had hoped that having a steady job would have made Jake realise that the life he was living and his companions unsuitable.

Since then he had seen his younger brother occasionally, wandering around looking undernourished and unkempt, appearing to be inebriated. It was no great surprise to him when he was asked by the police if he would go and identify the man who had been found lying dead in a back street.

There was no way I could grieve for Jake as I had for my other children. He had been given exactly the same opportunities as them, but turned his back on all of them, resorting to stealing to finance his life in Perth. Had we known how he was living and the prison sentences he had received I am sure Fred would have tried to find a remedy. I could only think that Jake had been born with a mental defect that he had been unable to control or he was subconsciously trying to punish himself if he had been responsible for Eliza's death as Mary had said. I had never asked her about the remark I had overheard her make and his reply.

It came as no great surprise to me when Maggie declared that she had applied for work as a children's nurse in the Philippines.

'There are so many little ones out there that need attention. I had thought of going to South Africa as I understand they also need qualified nurses, but that is so far away. I want to be able to fly back home reasonably quickly should you need me.'

I appreciated her concern, but hoped nothing more would happen to my family whereby I asked her to come home before she was due to have annual leave. I understood that neither of my parents would be alive very much longer as they were both now in their early nineties. I asked Maggie if she would want to come home when the inevitable happened to them.

Maggie shook her head. 'I'll visit them before I go away,

but there is little point in me returning. I can do nothing to help either of them then. I do hope that when one dies the other does not live on for years. That must be so lonely when you have been together for years.'

This reminded me that Fred was fifteen years older than me and sent a shudder up my spine. What would I do if anything happened to Fred? He seemed fit and well and although he left the day to day management of the ranch to Luke he still rode out regularly to inspect the cattle. Both Harry and Kevin would go with him and they appeared to be as interested in the ranch as Luke had always been.

I probably spoiled Suzie but I enjoyed having a small girl to fuss over. Neither George nor Charlie seemed to have any inclination to marry so I was unlikely now to have any more grandchildren. I could always pin my hopes on Maggie.

Despite the tragedies that had occurred over the years I refused to dwell upon the loss of my children, parents and friend, but then came the cruellest loss of all. Luke and the ranch hands were carrying a body back to the house on a hurdle. I rushed outside, thinking it must be Harry or Kevin only to find that it was Fred. For no obvious reason he had fallen from his horse. We made him as comfortable as possible in his bed and Luke immediately contacted the Flying Doctor Service. It seemed an age whilst Luke gave them details of Fred and the accident, but the doctor agreed to visit and arrived no more than an hour later.

After a full examination the doctor diagnosed that Fred had suffered a stroke whilst riding and the subsequent fall had not helped as it had rendered him unconscious. I asked how long it would be before Fred recovered and the doctor shook his head sadly at me.

'I think it unlikely that he will regain consciousness. If he does he could well be paralysed. I can transfer him to the hospital but I cannot hold out any hope for his recovery.'

I took Fred's hand in mine and kissed him gently. I don't know whether he knew I had done so, but I hoped he realised how much I cared for him.

Luke insisted on driving me to Derby and staying with me. We both sat beside Fred as he lay motionless in the bed, connected to monitors that recorded his vital signs. It was a long vigil and I remember placing my head down on the bed and closing my eyes. What would I do without Fred and if he was an invalid for the remainder of his life how would I manage to nurse him? He could not stay in the hospital indefinitely.

Fred lingered for three days and I spent each day and night at his bedside, holding his hand and sleeping whilst sitting in a chair with my head resting on his bed. Luke offered to take my place but I refused, although I was glad of his company and support. I could not eat, but drank the cups of coffee and tea that he brought to me gratefully.

Luke had contacted George, Charlie and Maggie and all three were making their way back to Derby as quickly as possible. George and Charlie arrived in time to say goodbye to their father, but Maggie was unable to obtain a flight until it was too late.

It was a sombre atmosphere back at the ranch. I felt helpless and did not know what to do. Luke took charge and insisted that I rested whilst he made the necessary arrangements. Fred was to be buried in the graveyard in Derby, next to Eliza and Sally.

Somehow I managed to stand beside the grave and listen to the priest as he conducted the burial service. I wanted to reach out and hold Fred's hand as I had in the past. I felt I was living in a dream and when I awoke the last ten days would never have happened.

Maggie had parted from me tearfully, having offered to give up working in the Philippines and return to the hospital in Derby. I would not hear of it as I knew how satisfying she found her current work. George had returned to Perth, assuring me that he could return at any time that I felt I needed him and Charlie proposed to visit me each weekend as he was in Broome. He said he could borrow or hire a car and drive up on the Friday evening and return on the Sunday.

I had no idea what the future held for me and once again Luke took charge. He visited the bank and registered Fred's death with them and asked about financial arrangements for the ranch. To his surprise the bank informed him that they had a copy of Fred's Will and once he and I had visited a solicitor to have Fred's wishes verified there should be no problem.

I did not know that Fred had made a Will as he had never discussed his financial affairs regarding the ranch with me. He had always appeared to have plenty of money to buy cattle and pay for the alterations he had made to the ranch.

Luke and I sat before the solicitor. I was feeling numb and Luke was nervous and anxious. He was worried that if there was insufficient money in the bank to finance the ranch it would have to be sold. That would mean that he, Ingrid and the children would be homeless along with me.

The solicitor handed us each a copy of the Will, but the legal wording meant very little to me and I asked him to explain in simple terms.

He looked at me and smiled gently. 'I know this will not make up for the loss of your husband, but you are now a very wealthy woman.'

I looked at him uncomprehendingly.

'Your husband has left the ranch in its entirety to your son, Luke, along with fifty thousand dollars and you are to have a home there for as long as you wish. To each of his other surviving children he has bequeathed the sum of a hundred thousand dollars.'

I gasped. Where was this kind of money going to come from?

'All your husband's stocks and shares, along with the area of land he owns at the Kimberley Diamond Mines are to be put into your name. Some of the stock may have to be sold to comply with the bequests to his children but that will still leave you well in excess of a million dollars.'

I looked at Luke. 'What does that mean?'

Luke squeezed my hand. 'You will have more than sufficient money to live on for the rest of your life and a home with Ingrid and myself for as long as you want.'

A million dollars! I did not even know how many noughts there would be if the sum was written down. I felt the tears coming into my eyes. No wonder Fred had never seemed short of money.

It did not take long for the solicitor to work out the legal expenses and bequests to the children. Even after they had been deducted I still had more money to my name than I could ever have dreamt of in the past. I was advised not to sell the land in Kimberley as it had not been explored fully for diamonds and could double or even triple in value if it was found to be productive.

I was so grateful that Fred had left the ranch to Luke. He loved the land, the cattle and the horses. I wished Dimitris and Mary had still been alive so they could have benefited from Fred's generosity, but I was pleased that Jake would not be able to have unlimited money to squander on drink and drugs.

George did not buy a grocery shop as I had expected, but bought shares in the Kimberley Diamond Mine saying they were an investment for his old age. Charlie was completely happy working as an engineer at the airport and the only thing he planned to do with his money was to buy an apartment and a small car to give him independence. Maggie asked for a quarter of her inheritance to be sent to UNICEF, specifically to help the children in the Philippines.

I gradually realised that my life would never be the same again. I had been heartbroken as a teenager when I was forcibly parted from Lucas, but without having Fred around it was like having a part of me missing permanently. I held conversations with him in my head and often woke in the night thinking I had heard him call my name.

Ingrid was solicitous and tried to involve me in the daily

running of the ranch and I did my best to appear interested. Provided everyone was well fed, particularly when Charlie or George visited, I did not mind what other events took place.

Suzie finally surprised everyone by saying she planned to stay at the University where she had been studying history. She now wanted to specialise and gain a Masters Degree in Aboriginal History and Culture. She said she hoped eventually to be able to write down their verbal history, customs and Dreamtime.I had to admit that when she spoke about their culture I did find it fascinating. It reminded me of the Greek myths my father had told me as a child. I had never taken any notice of the Aboriginals who lived in the region and occasionally visited Derby.

I wrote long letters to Maggie, although I am sure I often repeated myself. There was no real news from here. Harry and Kevin gradually took on more responsibility for the ranch and Luke made no secret of the fact that he would eventually hand the ranch over to them. They and the ranch hands no longer rode out on horses but had small buggies that they rode up to the area where the cattle grazed.

I was surprised when Charlie visited and said he was thinking of leaving the airport and spoke vaguely of doing other things. I knew he would have sufficient income to live comfortably, but I did wonder how he planned to occupy himself.

Luke eventually told me that Charlie had confided in him that he had prostate cancer. He would be undergoing treatment at the hospital in Broome, but thought it better to leave the airport now as he knew that once the chemotherapy started he would not always feel well enough to go to work. He expected the treatment to be successful and once he was fully fit again he would drive up to visit us.

Of course I was worried, but I had also been told by Luke that it was quite a common problem amongst men and usually successfully treated, I took consolation from that and at first Charlie seemed completely well and drove up and visited us.

A year later he had to return to the hospital for more treatment as the problem appeared to have returned. This time they used a different procedure that had been developed, but this did not seem to be effective. The doctors had told him that surgery was necessary. Charlie kept Luke advised of the operation but with strict instructions not to tell me. It came as a shock when Luke had to tell me that Charlie had died.

Charlie had never mentioned that he had a heart condition, possibly inherited from Fred, and whilst under the anaesthetic his heart had stopped beating. Despite all the expert attention he received there was no way he could be revived.

I was so depressed. I had born nine children in all and now I only had three left. Would they die and leave me completely alone in the world? These last few years had been the most miserable ones of my life.

Unbeknown to me Ingrid discussed my evident depression with Luke and a few months later Luke asked how I would feel about leaving the ranch and moving to live in Broome. I was most uncertain. I did not know Broome as we had only visited the town rarely. Luke had visited Derby on a number of occasions recently to deal with the sale of Charlie's apartment and car; the proceeds and his savings were to be shared equally between his brothers and sister.

Luke showed me on the internet how to look at properties for sale in the area and also the amenities on offer. I did not understand the internet and both Luke and Ingrid tried to explain to me that once I knew how to use it I would be able to contact both Maggie and George without the need to go to Derby to post a letter. I followed their instructions and was amazed that my letter arrived with both of them so quickly and I always received a reply within a few days. I wished I had known about the facility earlier.

Ingrid sat with me and we looked at the properties advertised on the internet site. She said the one they were interested in was reasonably priced, had four bedrooms and four bathrooms along with a swimming pool. It would be ideal for when their children visited and also large enough to accommodate Maggie and George whenever they wanted to stay.

I agreed that it did look attractive and very different from the ranch. Having voiced my approval I was told Luke had made an appointment for us to view it that weekend. I had an idea that whatever my objections might be they had both set their hearts on this house.

I was delightfully surprised when I saw how large the accommodation was. There were two rooms at the side, one was empty and the other had been used as an office.

'This is what made us think it would be perfect,' explained Ingrid. 'Those two rooms can be made into a bedroom and bathroom for you so you will have no need to climb stairs.'

I was not that old and incapable yet, but I knew the day could come.

'That will cost a good deal. I will only agree to coming here to live if you allow me to buy the property and pay for the conversion,' I said firmly.

We sat and argued for some time, but finally I had my way. I would transfer to the money to Luke's bank account and he would then pay for the purchase and have the property in his name. I was not sure if I had made the right decision, but it was too late to change my mind.

1996 - 2012
LIFE FIVE
Broome

It took a further six months before the house in Broome was renovated to Luke and Ingrid's satisfaction. When the rooms I was going to occupy were nearing completion they took me down to ask my opinion of the arrangement. I could not find fault with anything. They gave me the choice of purchasing new furniture or moving down some of the furniture I had lived with at the ranch for so many years. Much of it would have been too large and I decided the only item I wanted was the bed that Fred and I had shared. Everything else could stay at the ranch. I was sad to leave my home of so many years, but Harry and Kevin assured me that I could return whenever I wanted.

It was a novelty to me to go out and explore Broome. It was a far more interesting town than Derby, but we had been obliged to go there to visit my parents and even after they had died we continued to use that town for our supplies. We were well known by the shopkeepers and greeted as friends by most of them.

Of course, once we were settled in the new house we had visitors. George arrived from Perth and commented that we should have made the move years earlier rather than living in the middle of nowhere. Harry and Kevin both visited, but admitted that they did not appreciate living so close to other people and having to listen to the noise of traffic; they preferred to be able to see for miles without another building in sight and with only the sound of the cows to break the silence during the day.

Suzie came to stay when the University closed for the annual holiday and said how impressed she was, particularly with the swimming pool and she could be seen in there most days. I wished I was young enough to join her and sometimes I would sit on the side and dangle my feet in the water.

To my delight Maggie declared that she was leaving the Philippines and returning to Australia. I questioned her closely about her decision as I was concerned that this meant she was ill. She insisted that she was perfectly well, but had decided that having trained so many nurses over the years it was time she stepped away and allowed the locals to implement her ideas and improvements. I had to admit that when she arrived she did look well, although considerably thinner than in the past.

She lived at the house with us, helping Ingrid, whilst she decided whether to purchase an apartment and apply to the local hospital for some work. She then proposed that she stayed in the house with me whilst Ingrid and Luke had a holiday.

'You've not been away since your honeymoon in Sydney. Why don't you go back or visit somewhere else? This is an ideal time whilst I'm not working so I can stay here and look after Mum for as long as necessary.'

Ingrid shook her head. 'I don't want to go back to Sydney. I enjoyed my visit at the time, but it's really no different from any other large town. I've always dreamed of going to Italy and Greece. I'd love to visit Rome and Athens.'

I listened as Luke and Ingrid discussed the possibility and decided this was the time to tell Luke about his biological father. I explained how passionately Lucas and I had been in love and my heartbreak when he had disappeared and I was sent to live with my aunt and uncle in Elounda. How I had discovered that he was living on the island of Spinalonga as he had been diagnosed with leprosy.

Luke held up his hand. 'Wait a minute, Mum. Are you telling me my father was a leper?'

I nodded. 'His arm was infected. Lucas and I tried to keep our distance, but you have to remember I was only very young at the time and our passion for each other had not diminished. I then found I was expecting Dimitris and I was in a dilemma. If I became infected it would mean I could go to Spinalonga and live with Lucas, but if you were free from the disease I would have to leave you behind to be cared for by my parents. The decision was taken out of my hands as I had to eventually confess that I was expecting another child and Lucas was his father. Despite my tears and pleading my father decided that we should come to Australia and I would declare myself a widow.'

'So you had not contracted the disease, despite your intimacy with Lucas?'

I shook my head. 'We had to have medical tests to allow us to enter Australia and you and I were both declared free of all disease.'

'And Dimitris?'

'I did not tell the medical authorities that his father had leprosy. I just prayed that when he was born he would be as healthy as you.'

'Why didn't you tell me before?' asked Luke.

'I saw no necessity. I eventually married Fred and he was an excellent father to you and Dimitris. You never asked who your biological father was although I had told Fred.'

Over the following days Luke asked me more and more questions and I answered them as best I could. He searched for information on the internet, finding that the inhabitants of Spinalonga had suffered from starvation during the war and the island had finally been closed in 1957 and the surviving men and women transferred to the hospital in Athens. I wished I knew if Lucas had survived.

A month later Luke told me that he and Ingrid had decided to act upon Maggie's idea and take a holiday.

'We've decided to go to Europe so we'll be away for quite a while but Maggie will be here to look after you. We're visiting Italy as Ingrid wants to see Rome and we'll probably take in Venice and Florence before we go to Athens. From there we are going to Crete. After all, it is where I was born so I should visit the country.'

Luke asked me to describe all I could remember about Spinalonga and where Lucas had lived there, promising that they would certainly visit the island and bring me back photographs.

Receiving the paintings of Lucas's house on Spinalonga brought memories flooding back to me. I sat with them in my hands and thought back to the time that I had spent there with Lucas. When I was with him I was completely happy with no qualms about the future. It shows how very young and innocent I still was to believe that we would be together for ever.

When I received news from the artist lady in Crete that a man she knew had looked into the records of Spinalonga and found that Lucas Tsantakis had survived the war, been sent to the hospital in Athens and lived there for the remainder of his life. I hoped he had found some happiness as I had.

That time seems so far away now. Few people have experienced such a varied life as I have. Looking back it is as though I have lived five different lives - or maybe I have been five different people. Is this how people feel as they grow old?

Now I'm old and sitting here doing so little I thought I should re-examine my memories. I began to sort them away in my mind and mentally labelled them as 'Life One', 'Life Two', 'Life Three', 'Life Four' and 'Life Five'. I began to get confused and decided the best way would be to write them down. I could then add subsequent memories to the relevant 'Life'.

I asked Ingrid to buy me two large foolscap notebooks. She looked at me in surprise and asked why I would want two when I could only write in one at a time. I smiled and told her I wanted to use each one for something different.I thought it unlikely that

I would have so many memories to write down, but it was best to be prepared.

I can remember my childhood so well, carefree days, then falling in love and the sadness and utter despair that beset me. I suppose I should start there and entitle it 'Life One'.

I have only ever written letters to my children before but I have decided to write this as a record of my memories, rather than a list of facts and events. It could be more interesting to anyone who cares to read it in the future.

September 2016

Ronnie placed the last page of Eirini's writing on the pile that sat beside her. Now she realised why Luke had sent her paper copies, the writing was small and sometimes a word or whole sentence had been crossed out and re-written. She was not sure how she felt. Some parts of Eirini's life had been so sad, but she had obviously been a woman of strong character. During the winter months when she had more time she would read the life story again, sure she had missed some details having read only a few pages at a time as the opportunity arose. There were questions she would like to have answered.

She took a piece of plain paper of her own and began to make a list of her queries. When she and Kyriakos returned to Kastelli they would be able to make enquiries locally about the family. She would ask John for help in tracing Eirini's father and finding the family's surname. There was also the uncle who had worked as a manager at the salt pans, there should be a record of him. It was quite likely that the Tsantakis family still lived locally; and then there was the mysterious aunt who had lived in Elounda and Eirini knew nothing about.

The fact that Luke had played with her great grandmother on Spinalonga made her feel bonded to him and she was sure he would like to have the answers to her questions and any further information she could discover. She would not mention this to him in the e-mail she would send to him, telling him she had finished reading his mother's story and found it fascinating. She had to face the fact that she might not be able to find out anything and she would not want to raise his hopes.